Having studied psychology and criminology at King's College, Cambridge, Ruth Newman loved the city so much that she stayed, and now works as a Web editor for the University's business school. Her first book, *Twisted Wing*, won Long Barn Books' first novel competition and has now been translated into twelve languages.
Visit www.ruthnewman.net

Praise for Ruth Newman's debut novel *Twisted Wing*

'I absolutely loved it. It was so gripping, and I was both desperate and reluctant to get to the end. I found it scary, tantalisingly unpredictable and very, very hard to put down' Sophie Hannah

'A well-paced, rigorously researched and captivating crime novel' *Spectator*

'Intricate and gripping' *Woman & Home*

'If you're looking for a crime book that'll have you hooked after the first chapter and is riddled with mystery and brain-racing twists, this is it' *Now*

'A distinctive thriller that lets its clues slip out gradually and is liable to subvert readers' expectations by turning things upside-down at any moment. She's one to watch' *Glasgow Herald*

'Fantastically good' *Front Row*, BBC Radio 4

Also by Ruth Newman

Twisted Wing

The Company of Shadows

RUTH NEWMAN

SIMON &
SCHUSTER

London · New York · Sydney · Toronto

A CBS COMPANY

First published in Great Britain by Simon & Schuster UK Ltd, 2010
A CBS COMPANY

1 3 5 7 9 10 8 6 4 2

Simon & Schuster UK Ltd
1st Floor
222 Gray's Inn Road
London WC1X 8HB

Simon & Schuster Australia
Sydney

www.simonandschuster.co.uk

A CIP catalogue record for this book
is available from the British Library

Trade Paperback ISBN 978-1-84737-727-2
Hardback ISBN 978-1-84737-991-7

Typeset by M Rules
Printed in the UK by CPI Mackays, Chatham ME5 8TD

For Sylvia and Brett Van Toen

Two people made me a writer. One taught me to read; they both taught me to *read*. So thank you for the endless supply of books; for the typewriter, then the electric typewriter, then the electronic typewriter, then the Amstrad; and for teaching me that 'books give you someplace to go when you have to stay where you are'.

Mum, thanks too for the berry-crush handshakes, for letting my brother have *that* haircut, for Redgate and Bluegate, and for the Mandeer, for meeting me at the school gates with that letter in your hand and going backwards down the flume (I know you like to pretend it wasn't on purpose), for being a one woman PR unit and for your Machiavellian ways in bookshops up and down the country. Everyone says their mum is the best mum in the world, but mine would win any deathmatch.

Brett, thanks also for always being ready to teach and explain things to me – from chess to Manic Miner; from how to identify birds to how to identify what's under the bonnet of my car. For the rides on the Gold Wing, and the walks in Epping Forest. But not for the spinach on toast.

Acknowledgements

For their feedback, support and advice: Terry Daly, Grant Jerkins, Tim Loynes, Una McCormack, Philip Stiles, Paul Taylor, Brett Van Toen, Sylvia Van Toen and Steve Woolfries. Massive thanks too to Vivien Green, Gaia Banks, and the rest of the fantastic team at Sheil Land; to Libby Yevtushenko, Kate Lyall-Grant, Suzanne Baboneau, Florence Partridge, Joan Deitch and everyone at the lovely Simon & Schuster; and to Susan Hill, for opening an amazing door.

The Company
of Shadows

PART I

Miami

Chapter One

Last night I dreamt I went to Mandalay again. Not the beautiful old country house in Daphne du Maurier's *Rebecca*, but the rather more modern and ostentatious Mandalay Bay Hotel in Las Vegas. The hotel where Charlie and I spent our honeymoon.

I dream about Charlie nearly every night, it seems. Some nights it's a good dream, like this one. We're at the poker tables, losing money and laughing. The wedding ring on my finger gleams with newness. The hotel hears our news and moves us to one of their honeymoon suites. In the dream, I can smell his aftershave, can feel the heat of his skin under my fingertips.

Other nights I dream about the day he disappeared. In this nightmare, it's the smell of the lemons in the lemon grove that's still in my nostrils when I wake up, my heart thudding. Other nights still, it's the decomposing body with which my sleeping mind tortures me.

Even those dreams still give me a strange contentment that lasts most of the morning. It means I'm not forgetting him. It means he's still always, always on my mind.

I woke up from that morning's Las Vegas dream to the sound of the doorbell ringing. One minute I was in Charlie's arms, under the satin sheets of the golden honeymoon bed, sunlight spilling through the window, and the next I was on my own, in our one-bedroom flat in Islington. It took me a while to orientate myself, to realize why I was awake. The doorbell rang again and I flung myself out of the double bed and pulled on my dressing-gown, furious with whoever had snatched me from that dream, today of all days.

A small man holding a large bouquet of flowers peeked out from behind them as I yanked open the front door.

'Delivery for Kate Grey?'

White roses, and big red flowers I didn't recognize. 'Who are they from?'

'There's a card, miss. Could you sign here, please?'

Back in the solitude of the flat I pulled open the envelope. My hands were shaking like a nervous presenter at the Oscars. It was a year to the day since Charlie had died, and I was still looking for signs.

To Kate. I know this must be a difficult day for you. For me too. I just wanted you to know that I was thinking about you, and that I'm free tonight if you need some company. Love, Luke xxx.

For a brief moment I felt that crush of disappointment, then laughed. What was I expecting? Some cryptic message from Charlie – a message from a ghost? *Wait for me, my darling, I am just around the corner . . .*

It was sweet of Luke to be thinking of me. I knew I should have thought of him too. I'd only had Charlie with me for two years; Luke had grown up with him.

I didn't have to go to work. In fact, I hadn't worked since Charlie's death; my doctor had signed me off for a few months, and then the life insurance money had come through, and I'd realized it would be enough to live on for a few years. It meant I didn't have to face the world just yet; that I could

stay wrapped up in my memories of Charlie, and try to come
to terms with what I'd lost.

After lunch, I bought sunflowers from the florist's, and
drove to the cemetery in Highgate. Charlie's gravestone was
plain, the epitaph short and to the point, listing his date of
birth and his date of death, a mere thirty-four years later, and
the words *watching the slow door*. If anyone asked, I would
just tell them that it was from a poem. It was up to them if
they could be bothered to look it up.

The funeral had been almost too much to get through. It
came a month after Charlie's actual death, so that I didn't
have the advantage of that early stage of grief: numbness.
The majority of the people who came were our friends and
co-workers; Charlie's parents were dead, he had no siblings,
and the few distant relatives Luke did manage to contact
didn't seem willing to fork out hundreds of dollars in airfare
just to see a coffin laid in the ground. I'd fallen out with my
own parents when I was a teenager, and we still kept our distance. I knew they'd heard about his death, about the
funeral, but they didn't contact me, and they didn't send
flowers. I didn't care. I didn't care about anything much at
that point.

I replaced the dead flowers in the pot with my sunflowers.
The late-afternoon August sunshine made the yellow petals
glow. I sat down cross-legged by Charlie's grave, stroking the
granite headstone. A man walking his dog passed me, watching me out of the corner of his eye. When I met his gaze he
touched his finger to the brim of his flat-cap and nodded
hello.

'I dreamt about Mandalay Bay last night,' I said, my fingertips outlining his name, cut into the gravestone. I always
talk to Charlie, but it's usually just in my head. I'm pretty sure
that there's some special dispensation for being allowed to talk

out loud to your dead husband if you're by his graveside though. It doesn't score full marks on the loony test.

'I dreamt I was with you again. Do you remember going out to the desert, looking at the stars?' There seemed to be more stars in the desert sky, winking out of the darkness like a million distant lighthouses. 'Do you remember the woman in the chapel, the one who took our details?' Eighty years old if she was a day, and about the same number of pounds overweight, caked in foundation and powder, with eyes like spiders her mascara was so thick. *Well lookit you two lovebirds*, she'd drawled. *Are you here to make it official? Not had too many pina coladas, I hope.* We weren't even tipsy. That wasn't why we'd decided to get hitched after knowing each other only three days.

A few drops of rain threw up little puff clouds from the dry earth of Charlie's grave. I sat for a while longer.

Samantha yelled out, 'Coming!' through the thick front door, and I heard her clattering down her wooden staircase. She swung open the door, gold-blonde curls flying out, and hugged me hello.

'Wow, look at your tan,' I said.

She did a twirl for me. 'Not bad, eh? We only got back the day before yesterday though, so no doubt it'll fade soon.'

David appeared behind her, also looking enviably brown. 'Hey there, Kate. Sam, you going to let her in then, or does she need to admire you some more?'

Inspired by their visit to Miami, Samantha went spicy with the dinner. Over burritos, she told me about David's new partner at the law firm.

'He's very handsome, isn't he, Dave?'

David rolled his eyes. 'I don't know. You tell me.'

'Yes, he's handsome. And obviously he's doing well in his

career, to be made a partner before he's forty. He's quite funny, and he's into dangerous sports, so the two of you have got something in common.'

'Sam, he did a tandem parachute jump about four years ago,' protested David. 'He's not exactly Evel Knievel.' I looked at David in amusement, and he mouthed, 'Sorry,' at me.

'So how about it?' pressed Samantha.

I shook my head, twisting my wedding ring round and round on my finger. 'Not going to happen.'

'Kate, look . . . the thing is, it's been – what, over a year?'

'A year today, actually.'

'And you're still wearing your ring,' she said, the fact I'd just told her that it was the anniversary of Charlie's death not seeming to register, 'and you still haven't even looked at another guy.'

Across the table I saw David trying subtly to shake his head at her.

'Samantha, I'm married,' I said.

'But what are you going to do, live the rest of your life without ever having another relationship?'

I stared at her. 'I'm *married*.'

There was a silence, and then David started clearing away the dishes. 'There's chocolate tart for dessert,' he said. 'And Ben and Jerry's ice cream to go with it. Sam, why don't you get the photos and we can distract Kate with pudding while we force her to look at our boring holiday snaps.'

The photos were standard 7 x 5s, and varied in quality depending on whether David or Samantha had taken the photo. All of hers were in crisp, clear focus, nicely composed. His were hilariously bad, nearly all off-centre, or composed mainly of his thumb. My favourite showed Samantha posing next to a dolphin at Sea World. You could see all of the dolphin – in fact, you could see about five feet of space to the left of the dolphin – but of Samantha, to the right of the creature, you could see precisely half.

'I try not to take it personally,' said Samantha as she handed it to me. Biting my lip to keep from laughing, knowing David was sensitive about his inability to take a decent photo, I passed it onto him and he carefully inserted it in order with the others we'd already seen.

'Now here we are at this fantastic restaurant on South Beach that we went to on the last night of the trip,' Samantha said, handing me a photo of a turquoise-painted frontage covered in fairy lights. 'It's run by a family who came over from Cuba in the sixties; apparently it's been there years and is really popular with the locals. El Cangrejo Dorado, it's called – the Golden Crab.' There was another photo of a turquoise wall, this time with Samantha in front of it wearing a sarong and a white shirt, and pointing glee-fully at a sign that read *El Cangrejo Dorado*, although only the letters *El Cangrej* appeared in the photograph. I bit my lip again.

'It's really nice inside,' she said. 'They grow jasmine around the pillars and it smells divine. We had the most amazing seafood – and the best mojitos ever.'

She passed me another photo, perhaps taken by a waiter as it showed both Samantha and David at their table, heads together, grinning at the camera. I scanned the rest of the photo for the jasmine-covered pillars, and what I saw made everything stop.

'Our waiter took that photo,' Samantha was saying. I thought my heart had stopped beating. I wasn't breathing. They were talking, moving around me, as I sat locked in place, staring at the photograph.

'It's him,' I tried to say, but I had no breath to say it. Samantha was attempting to pass me the next photo. David had seen my face and was asking me if I was okay. I managed to suck in a breath, and felt my heart pound once, against my ribs, back to beating.

'It's him,' I said again, looking at the man in the background of the photo, familiar dark hair, familiar blue eyes, familiar smile.

'It's Charlie.'

Chapter Two

I stared at the image, not saying anything. The photograph shook so badly in my hands that I had to lay it down flat on the table to see it clearly. Rising to my feet and leaning over it for a closer look, I inadvertently knocked my dining chair backwards and made Samantha jump.

'Kate?' she said. She sounded scared.

It couldn't be Charlie. It couldn't be. He was buried under six feet of earth in a North London graveyard. I had his death certificate in a folder on the shelf where he used to rest his coffee cup. And yet when I looked at the photograph, I saw my husband.

'Kate, it can't be Charlie; we only took this photo a week ago,' David told me, a hand on my arm. He reached out to take the photograph from me, but it stayed stuck beneath the weight of my fingertips.

'I'll give it back,' he promised. Reluctantly I eased off, letting him pick up the photo and hold it close to his face. He frowned as he perused the image, then finally shrugged. 'I'll admit it does look a lot like Charlie. But it obviously *isn't* him.'

I snatched the photo off him. 'Look at the way he's smiling. *That's Charlie's smile!* Look at the way he's holding that beer! Jesus, David, he's the spit of him.'

'I imagine a lot of people in that part of the States look like

Charlie when they're slightly blurry and six feet away. Look, come on, let's look at it on the PC. You just need a bit more detail and you'll start to see the differences.'

'David,' interrupted Samantha, her voice loaded with warning.

'It's okay, Sam,' he said. 'Kate just needs to have her mind put at rest, and then we'll sit down and finish our dessert.'

He led the way to their spare room, where they'd set up a makeshift office. He fired up their PC and Windows began to load. Samantha, standing by my side, gazed at me with worried eyes. I half-smiled at her, trying to reassure her that she wasn't going to have to call in the men in white coats.

David double-clicked on the digital camera software icon. When it launched, he opened the folder labelled *Miami* and scrolled through to the photograph. It took up only a few inches on the monitor. He zoomed in so the image was displayed at 100 per cent, and clicked on the scroll bar to shift the focus to the man in the background. I waited, aware I was holding my breath.

Charlie's face filled the screen. He was smiling at something the man opposite him was saying, his fingers wrapped around the neck of a beer bottle as though he was just about to take another swig. I knew those fingers, I knew that smile. If the image had been moving rather than static, I could have predicted with absolute certainty the way the beer bottle would be raised to his lips, the way his Adam's apple would move as he swallowed, and the way he'd set the bottle back on the table.

We all stared at the screen, surprised into silence.

'Well, er . . .' said David, his plan backfiring in his face. 'His hair's too short. And I know Charlie was a regular at the gym, but this guy looks like he should be on the cover of *Men's Health*.'

I reached over his shoulder and clicked on the quick-print

button a few times. Their printer hummed into action. While the pages were scrolling out, I nudged David out of the way and navigated through the rest of the photos, but there were no more of the man who looked so much like my dead husband. In fact, it seemed as if he'd left his table shortly after that first photograph was taken. Just to be on the safe side, I attached the picture to an email and sent it to myself.

'Kate,' said Samantha. And then again, when I didn't turn round: '*Kate.*'

I looked round at her. She had obviously been thrown by the picture, but she wasn't going to admit it. 'You do know, don't you,' she said, 'that the man in that photo isn't him. It isn't Charlie.'

'I know,' I lied. 'I know it's not, don't worry.' I picked up the print-outs and folded them carefully before sliding them into my back pocket. I managed to fake a smile. 'Well, it's been a lovely evening, but I think I'd better hit the road. Thanks for dinner.'

'You can't leave like this,' said Samantha.

'Really?' I let out a laugh. 'Come on, Sam, you're overreacting.'

'Am I? You're in no fit state to go off home on your own.'

'Oh, don't be silly, I'm fine. Well, as fine as anyone would be, seeing their late husband's Doppelgänger in some photo. Look, don't worry, I know it's not him. It just wasn't what I needed when I'm feeling a bit raw. That's all it is.'

She searched my face, but I managed to hide the shock and confusion well enough that she decided it was safe to let me be.

'I'm sorry we didn't spot it ourselves,' she said. 'If I'd noticed there was someone who looked just like Charlie I obviously would have taken out that picture before we showed you the photos.'

'I know,' I said, squeezing her arm. 'Don't be silly, I know you didn't deliberately go round Miami taking photos of men who looked like him just to give me an adrenaline rush.'

It was a weak attempt at humour, but enough to relax them a little bit more.

'You're very welcome to stay the night,' Samantha said. 'I don't like the thought of you being alone when you're upset like this.'

I shrugged. 'To be honest, it wouldn't help. I just need to get through it.'

She gave me a big hug, and I tried to let myself feel it. But I wanted to be home, on my own, where I didn't have to wear this mask. 'At least take some pudding with you,' she said.

'Okay,' I said, reckoning it would be easier to let her switch roles from therapist back to hostess. I picked up my bag from the living room and my coat from the hook in the hallway, then accepted a Tupperware box containing a slice of tart and kissed my friends goodbye.

It was dark outside. When we opened the front door the bulb in the hallway cast a rectangle of yellow onto the path, my shadow stretching before me as I left their home and went out into the night. They watched me from the doorway. I walked away, waiting for the block of light to disappear, but instead felt their eyes on my back all the way down the street.

The further along the tunnels we went, the harder I found it to keep myself together, feeling exposed in the harsh fluorescence of the tube carriage. I was desperate to be alone, in the solitary place that was now my home. I wanted to close myself up in some dark corner of the apartment and let myself feel this pain that was waiting for me.

The flat was just a short walk from the Angel underground station. I held it all in as I hurried past the dark houses, curtains closed in every window, a faint drizzle making my hair and face damp, the rain fuzzy in the orange glow from the sodium streetlamps.

I kept my head down, and so didn't notice the tall man with the close-cropped, pale blond hair who was standing outside the front door to my building until I was halfway up the concrete steps. When I did belatedly see him, I nearly fell back down the steps.

'Jesus Christ, Luke!' I said, clutching at my heart. 'You scared the shit out of me.'

'Nice survival instincts you got there, Kate,' he said in his Louisiana drawl, his voice like a rattlesnake gliding through maple syrup. 'Really. Is it just night vision you have, or is there some kinda batlike sonar ability in there too?'

I got out my keys and let us both in. 'I could do without the sarcasm tonight,' I said as we went up the carpeted stairs to my first-floor flat.

'I know,' Luke said. 'Funnily enough, I don't make a habit of hanging around your front door on the off-chance you'll be home any minute. That's why God invented cellphones.'

'Samantha rang you,' I guessed, feeling some of the tension slide off my shoulders as we entered the flat, with its familiar smell of home and comforting reminders of Charlie in every room.

'Actually, it was David,' he said. 'He told me you freaked out at some vacation photo from their Miami trip – said you thought you saw Charlie.' Luke's tone was quite flippant, but he was watching me carefully.

I handed him one of the print-outs. He switched on the light in the living room and perched on the arm of the sofa, engrossed in the piece of printed A4 paper in his hands. He was so still, so focused, that for a moment I thought I could believe it, and blurted out: 'It's him, isn't it?'

Luke looked up at me, his ice-floe eyes about as sad as I've ever seen them.

'No, Kate. Charlie is dead.'

I felt like throwing up. If Luke didn't believe it was Charlie, then I knew I couldn't let myself believe it either. *It's not him, Kate. Don't fool yourself. It's too dangerous to let yourself think it might be him.*

'Maybe it's a cousin or something,' I said, once I was fairly sure I could say it without crying. 'A nephew, some kind of relative with a family resemblance.' Luke was nodding. 'It's just that there are a couple more photos from the same restaurant, and he's moved from the table he was at, almost as if he'd seen Samantha and David and didn't want them to spot him.'

Luke was sighing. 'Kate, c'mere.' I went closer to him, until our knees were touching, and he reached for my hands.

'He's been dead a year, Kate. Exactly a year. This guy looks like our Charlie, but so do lots of guys. I think maybe because it's the anniversary of when he died, you're especially sensitive to seeing what you want to see.'

'Oh, fuck off, Luke,' I said, wrenching my hands away. 'That guy could be his double, so don't tell me that he looks more like Charlie today than he would've done yesterday.'

'You know it's not him, right?' He stood up, leaning towards me. '*Right*?'

I couldn't hold it in any longer. 'I just . . .' I had to stop and wrestle back control of my voice. My larynx was making it all squeaky and uneven. 'For a minute I thought he was alive.' The muscles around my chin were constricting as I tried to speak. Tears were spilling down my cheeks.

Luke just grabbed me and wrapped me up in his arms and

I didn't have to explain any more, just sob and sob until finally I could breathe again.

Luke stayed over that night, but he got as little sleep as I did; I could hear him shift position on the sofa, get up and pace the living room, run himself a glass of water, flip through a magazine on the coffee-table. Eventually we both got up and I made him breakfast before he went to work. He kissed me on the forehead on his way out of the door, promising to phone me that night.

The minute he was gone I started up my laptop, downloading my email. I found the attachment and opened up the photo of the man in the restaurant. Ten minutes I sat there, not moving, just staring at the image. It was Charlie, it was Charlie, it was Charlie.

I got as far as firing off an online visa application and visiting the transatlantic flights website before slamming my laptop shut, knowing I couldn't trust my own judgement. After a few moments I made another cup of coffee and tried to distract myself with some TV.

I spent the next two days unable to concentrate on anything. Books, which had given me my only method of escape over the last year, were useless – I'd read for an hour only to find I'd stopped paying attention twenty pages back and had no idea what was going on. I went for a walk in the August sunshine and nearly got run over by a bus I hadn't heard coming. Samantha rang, but I ignored her calls. My mind went back again and again to the same thing – that bloody photo. I tried to stop myself looking at it, but it was like a hunger I couldn't satisfy.

'This is crazy,' I said out aloud, though there was no one else in the room. I was sitting on the sofa, my laptop on my knees, that picture on the screen. It couldn't be Charlie, I knew that. The problem was, I didn't actually *believe* it. I opened an internet connection and started searching for flights to Miami.

I was at Heathrow Airport waiting for my check-in desk to open when Luke phoned me.

'Just wanted to make sure you're doing okay,' he said. He'd rung me every day since the photo appeared, and every day I'd lied and told him it wasn't even on my mind.

'I'm good,' I said, just as an announcement was made over the airport's Tannoy system.

'What was that?' he asked, and I could imagine him sitting bolt upright in his office. 'Kate, where the hell are you?'

'Oh Jesus,' I said to myself, then put the phone back to my mouth. 'Okay, Luke, don't get mad, but I'm at the airport. I know it's crazy, but I just need to see for sure. Look, all that will happen is I'll get to Miami, it'll be a dead end, and I'll spend the rest of the week sunbathing and having a break. There's no need to worry.'

'Kate, you don't need to go all the way to the States to be sure that the man in that photo isn't Charlie!'

I perched on the edge of my suitcase. 'Look, I know it's not Charlie. At least, my brain does. The thing is, it *feels* like I've just seen a photo of Charlie, alive and well and eating seafood in Miami.'

'That doesn't make sense,' he complained.

'No, I know. Sorry, I'm not explaining it very well. Look, logically, we both know there's no way it can be Charlie. I keep telling myself this, but there's still this feeling of hope in me, and it's killing me. The only way I can think of to get rid of it is to find this man and have it made *so obvious* to me that it's a complete stranger that there'll be no way I can spend the rest of my life fooling myself that Charlie could still be out there somewhere. Because that's what will happen if I don't go.'

Americans always seemed to be talking about 'closure' – surely Luke would be able to see that the photo had opened a door that I needed to shut before I went crazy?

Luke's voice went hard. 'Charlie's dead, Kate. He's not coming back. We both saw his body on that mortuary table – or do you think some other poor bastard the same height and weight happened to wash up on the beach with the exact same tattoo? Jesus, I can understand better than anyone why you would want to believe the guy in that picture is Charlie, but to fly halfway around the world chasing a ghost—'

'Thanks for the sensitivity and understanding,' I said, and hung up on him.

There was a brief flare of 'my God, what am I doing?' in my stomach when the plane took off, but deep down I knew that I was right: if I stayed at home I'd spend the rest of my life wondering if maybe, just maybe, that really *had* been my husband in El Cangrejo Dorado, and I'd foolishly let my friends' disbelief and my own indecision stop me from finding him again.

The flight attendants handed out meals and free drinks, and because it was airline policy to pretend the plane was in the timezone of the place you were heading for rather than the place of departure, we barely had time to finish our desserts before they were handing out blankets and switching off the main lights.

The elderly woman next to me tried to catch my eye as I stared at the photograph from Miami that had been in my lap since take-off, my fingertip stroking the dark line of the face of the man who looked so much like my husband.

'Excuse me, dear,' she said finally. 'I just wanted to check with you that it wouldn't bother you if I keep my television on for a while.' The airline we were on had movies showing on monitors fixed into the back of the seats in front of each passenger. I looked up at the film playing on her screen. 'Johnny Depp,' she said with a wink. 'Wouldn't want to miss him.'

'Thanks for asking,' I told her. 'It's fine. It won't disturb me. I don't think I'm going to be able to sleep anyway.'

She nodded, and I waited for her to put her earphones back in. Instead, she indicated the man in the background of the photo and said: 'Is that your young man?'

I felt my lower lip start to vibrate, and bit down on it, hard. 'I don't think so,' I told her. 'But I wish it was.'

As the plane flew against the turn of the planet, gliding through blackness and wispy cloud, I thought about the day I'd met Charlie.

The Carnival Hotel is scheduled for demolition in November, which is why I don't want to miss trying out their roller coaster during my Vegas trip. Samantha's being a good girl and spending all day at the software convention – the whole reason we're here – so I'm hurtling round the rickety old track on my own while she networks and collects business cards. Sadly, the ride is a bit of a disappointment; the scariest thing about it is its age. The fear that the thirty-year-old rusty screws that hold it together might choose that moment to disintegrate, flinging me and my fellow passengers off the rooftop track hundreds of feet in the air, had been the only thing to speed up my heart-rate.

So now I'm waiting for the lift to arrive to take me back down to the ground floor. A blonde girl is also waiting, swapping her weight from one high-heeled foot to the other. She's wearing the shortest dress I've ever seen. Checking her watch, she sighs theatrically and presses the lift button yet again. Her fingernails are the same coral-pink as her dress.

The elevator arrives, and I let her get in first. I'm scanning my little guide book to the rides of Las Vegas, so barely register that there are two other people in the lift with us.

The doors close slowly behind us and we only descend a few feet before, without warning, everything goes black and the lift shudders to a halt. The girl I got in the lift with lets out a scream.

'Don't worry, it's okay,' says a man's voice. It's very calm and relaxed, the sort of voice you want to listen to late on a summer's night with your windows open and some ice in your rum. 'The power goes out in this building all the time. It's just old, that's all. The back-up generator will come on soon.' I've wondered once or twice if people who are blind can nevertheless be instantly attracted to someone they've just met. Now I know.

It really is completely pitch black. I wait for the emergency lights to come on, maybe some sort of red glow, but there's just darkness. That's when I hear the fourth person in the lift start to panic.

'Oh God oh God oh God oh God,' he's saying. He's trying not to, but he can't stop the words coming out. I can hear the sound of sliding material, and realize he's pulling his tie off. I take a step towards him, feeling for his shoulder so I can put my hand on it.

'It's okay,' I say, keeping my tone reassuring. 'These lifts are really quite big; there's loads of air in them. There's really nothing to worry about.'

'My mouth is so dry,' he tells me. 'I think my tongue is swelling up.'

I hear the sound of a water bottle then, liquid sloshing against the plastic. 'Here, I have some water,' says the warm voice, and fingers brush mine as the bottle is transferred to the panicking man's arm.

'Don't give it all to him!' complains the girl as the man throws off the cap to the bottle and takes a couple of long gulps. 'We might need that. What if we're stuck here for hours?'

I can hear the smile in the first man's voice when he says, 'Well, maybe we need to think about what we're going to do for food too, if it comes to that. Let's draw straws – pick who we're gonna eat first.'

I try to trap my laugh under my hand, but enough comes out that the others must be wondering if I'm amused or going into cardiac arrest.

'The air conditioning's stopped!' The drinking man's freaking out. 'It's too hot here, we're gonna suffocate, I swear.' He sounds like he's on the verge of hyperventilating, which might not be a bad thing. At least then he'd pass out, and not have to face what is obviously one of his worst fears.

The idea of being trapped in what amounts to a sauna in a lift shaft doesn't appeal to me either, but I try not to think about it. My guide book is pretty thin, thin enough to use as a fan. I start wafting the face of the claustrophobic guy, and he groans with relief. I don't know if he's even aware that it's not a breeze, it's just a flapping copy of a book about roller coasters that will probably end up whacking him in the chin if my night vision doesn't improve soon.

'Oh my God, he's right,' the girl starts saying. 'It's a hundred degrees out there – if it gets to a hundred in here . . .!' I'm about to tell her to shut the hell up – this guy really doesn't need her jacking up his phobia – but the other man is whispering to her, getting her to be quiet, calming her down. I feel a surprising surge of jealousy; of course he's keen to reassure her, he no doubt got a good look at her when she got in the lift and sees this as his big opportunity. Then I tell myself I'm being an idiot, that the lights are going to come on and I'm inevitably going to be disappointed when the face doesn't match that voice.

I focus on the claustrophobe. 'Close your eyes,' I say, though it's not like the lift is full of blinding light that would otherwise distract him. 'Imagine you're in an immense, snowy wasteland. It's night-time, and all around you there's nothing but the vast, dark sky and the ice under your feet.'

His breathing is starting to come under control. I keep going, throwing in lots of cold, spacious imagery.

'What about me?' the girl suddenly complains. 'Fuck the penguin guy, I'm just as scared as he is.'

'You want me to do a visualization for you?' says the man with the lovely voice. 'Okay, close your eyes. You're in a vast and empty shopping mall. All the stores are open, just for you.'

I choke on the word 'tundra', trying not to lose my concentration. I wish I could see this man.

And then, equally without warning, the lights flicker on and I don't even need to find him. We are already looking at each other; have been smiling at each other in the dark. Later, I could tell you he has black hair, tanned skin, a happy, handsome face; he's tall, with broad shoulders and long legs in dark blue jeans. But I see none of that in this moment – I just see his eyes. We are connected, locked together.

Somehow we both know that our lives as separate entities are now over. Our smiles fade and we just stare at each other for a while.

'Okay,' he says under his breath, obviously as thrown as I am by what's just happened to us. He holds out his hand to me. 'Charlie.'

'Kate,' I reply, and my smile comes back as I shake his hand.

Meeting Charlie was like coming home, not having realized till that moment that you were lost.

I woke up with a jolt, to find one of the flight attendants standing next to me with a jug in one hand and a cup in the other.

'Coffee?' he asked.

'Please.' I rubbed my face, trying to wake up, trying to remember what I was doing on a plane.

The photo. Charlie. Miami.

I drank the coffee in three long gulps. The elderly woman next to me patted my arm.

'Good morning, dear. You seemed to be having such a lovely dream that I didn't want to wake you, not when you thought you'd find it hard getting to sleep.'

What was I dreaming about? That first, shared look floated in my memory and I tried to hold onto it – but it slipped away.

'I think they're waking everyone up because we're nearly there,' my neighbour went on. 'You missed your friend, by the way.'

'My friend?'

She nodded, gnarled, veiny hands clamped around her cup of coffee. 'A very nice young blond chap. American, I think.'

Luke. 'He's on the plane?'

'He said to tell you he's nine rows back and that you snore. The latter's not true, by the way, but I did promise I'd give you the message correctly. Now would you mind letting me out? I'm afraid my bladder capacity's not what it used to be.'

I pushed myself out of my seat, limbs hot and heavy from sleep and the cabin pressure, and padded barefoot down the aisle towards the forty-seventh row. I stopped at a vacant toilet, and took the time to look balefully at my reflection. Mussed-up black hair, not exactly the sleek bob my hairdresser had been aiming for. Grey eyes bleared, eyeliner smudged. I smoothed my angular eyebrows back in place with my fingertips, and ran a hand through my hair.

It wasn't much of an improvement, but at least I was awake now. Time to hunt down Luke.

He was waiting for me in an aisle seat, and when he saw me he stood up and gave me a bear hug.

'This doesn't mean you're right,' he said. 'I just couldn't let you do this on your own.'

'I didn't see you in the departure lounge,' I said, full of relief that he'd be by my side.

'It was something of a last-minute decision,' he admitted. 'In fact, I didn't reach check-in till ten minutes after it'd closed.'

'Yeah? How did you persuade them to let you on the plane?'

'Are you kidding?' he said. 'The number of frequent-flyer miles I've racked up, I could charter my own jet if I wanted to.' Luke was in the import business, kept his passport in the breast-pocket of his jacket, and spent half his life on aeroplanes.

I smiled up at him. 'I'm glad you're here,' I said.

He brushed my hair back from my face, tucking it behind my ears. 'So am I. Miami's got some great crab shacks.'

We landed at Miami International Airport at midnight and Luke and I had to split up at security due to our differences in citizenship; I'd never applied for any of my rights as the wife of an American. Since Charlie and I had lived in London for the two years of our married life, I'd never anticipated the need.

'What is the purpose of your visit?' asked the immigration official.

A tricky one to answer honestly. 'Vacation,' I decided upon. 'Looking up some old friends.'

I wanted to get a cab straight to the restaurant, but Luke insisted on renting a car.

'You just want to drive an SUV,' I said at the rental desk.

'I've had enough of your little sedans and Smart cars,' he said. 'I want something with a driver's seat you need a ladder to get into.'

The heat hit me the minute we walked out of the automatic doors and into the Floridian night. Thankfully the behemoth of a hire car had air-con. 'Is it far to the city?' I asked as I climbed up into the passenger seat, which seemed to be about four feet off the ground.

'Nope, only a few miles.'

'I want to go to the Cangrejo Dorado,' I said.

'Kate, I understand that you're on pins and needles here, but it's half-one in the morning. The place is going to be completely locked up.'

'I thought the night-life was meant to be good in Miami?'

'You said it was a restaurant, not a club. The manager and the waiters are probably out dancing somewhere, drinking margaritas.'

I looked out of the window as we left dry land and drove above the ocean on the Julia Tuttle Causeway. We could see the lights of Miami Beach in the distant darkness.

'You seem to know your way around,' I commented.

Luke shrugged. 'I've been here a few times over the years.'

'Did you ever come here with Charlie?'

'Once or twice,' he said, concentrating on the road.

'Ever go to El Cangrejo Dorado?'

He glanced at me then. 'Of course not. I would have told you if we had.'

'Why did you guys come here? Holiday? Business?'

'We came here for spring break a couple of times in college.'

'Spring break,' I said. 'That's when all the horny college kids descend on the beach, drink too much, and shag anything that moves.'

'Pretty much,' he said.

'Nice.'

'Hey, we were just kids.'

'Charlie have any old girlfriends here?'

Luke shook his head. 'What, you think Charlie faked his own death so that he could run away to Miami Beach and hook up with some girl he met on spring break fifteen years ago?'

'I didn't say I thought Charlie faked his own death,' I pointed out.

'Yeah? What's your theory then?'

'I don't have one,' I said, trying not to get angry. I was grateful to Luke for coming with me, but I didn't want to spend all our time having the same argument. 'I don't need one. I'm not saying he's not dead.'

'Then what the hell are we doing here?'

I decided it was best not to answer. I wound down my car window, trying to escape the feeling of being trapped.

'The air-con won't do its job properly with that window open.'

'I don't care. Whatever happened to the joy of driving along with the wind in your hair?'

I watched him as he rolled his eyes. Luke resembles a young Paul Newman, but slightly off-kilter, so he's handsome from certain aspects, but too sharp from others. He's got the nose of a Roman statue, but thin, quite cruel lips. His eyes are his best feature – they're blue, but a very, very pale blue. If it wasn't for the ring of indigo around them, he might look as though he didn't have any irises at all. He knows how to work them, as well. It's quite entertaining watching him in the summer, approaching a girl with his sunglasses on, then casually raising them. The increase in the target's interest can be quite dramatic. Especially when he smiles to break up the intensity of the look.

He and Charlie made quite a tag team. I could imagine them in their teens, stripped to their trunks on the beach, seducing the co-eds.

'You think me and Charlie would have hit it off if we'd met when we were at college?' I asked Luke.

'Who knows? He would still have fallen for you, but I'm not sure that he would have behaved himself.'

'So you're only soulmates if you find each other at the right time in your lives?'

'I don't believe in soulmates.'

'Charlie did.'

'Charlie wasn't a romantic until you two met.'

'No,' I said. 'Neither was I.'

We reached the island of Miami Beach, and were welcomed by palm trees lit up with neon. It was time to look for a hotel.

South Beach, the area in which the restaurant was located, was famous for its Art Deco buildings, constructed in the 1920s and 1930s following a hurricane that flattened what had been built before. At night their pastel hues were largely swamped by the shocking pink and lightsabre-blue neon signs that seemed to glow from the walls of every hotel and bar on Ocean Drive.

'Let's try the Moonlite,' suggested Luke, and veered over the road to a valet parking sign. The valet, a young guy with a half-assed moustache that he'd probably spent six months trying to grow, swapped our keys for a card and clambered into the driver's seat. The porter was surprised that we only had one suitcase.

'I can't believe you don't have any clean clothes,' I said to

Luke for about the third time since he'd told me at the baggage claim that his last-minute decision to come with me
meant he hadn't had time to go home and pack.

He shrugged. 'It'll give me an excuse to buy some white
suits and loafers. I won't need any socks, and if I roll my
sleeves up right, I'll get the Don Johnson look down pat.'

I looked around us at the mixture of tourists in shorts and
trainers, and beautiful locals in skin-tight black dresses and
sharp designer suits.

'I don't see anyone kitted out like Crockett and Tubbs,' I
pointed out.

'Now that's because you have to have my looks to pull it
off,' Luke explained.

The lobby of the Moonlite was all brushed chrome and blue
walls the colour of duck eggs.

'Are you after a double or two twins?' asked the desk clerk.
Luke raised an eyebrow at me.

'Two twins, please,' I said emphatically. 'Preferably at opposite ends of the hotel.'

The clerk frowned. 'I'm afraid we're still quite full, so the
furthest away I can put you is about a floor apart.'

'She's just kidding,' Luke told him. The clerk nodded and
pretended to chuckle. 'She's English,' Luke added under his
breath.

My room was spacious and clean, with a widescreen TV
mounted on the wall and a gleaming marble bathroom.

'We should be slumming it,' I told Luke. 'That plane ticket
cost more than my car.'

'You wanna check into a flea-ridden dive miles from the
restaurant, be my guest,' Luke said. 'Personally, I don't find
cockroaches to be ideal bed companions. Not unless there's a
cockroach out there that looks like Marilyn Monroe.'

I picked up my mobile phone and set the alarm clock

function to go off in a few hours' time. Luke swiped it from me, cancelling the alarm and setting it back down on my nightstand.

'Sweetheart, the restaurant's not going to be open at nine in the morning. Trust me. Get some sleep, and I'll come wake you up when I've had a chance to buy some clothes that don't smell of aeroplanes and manly sweat.'

He kissed me on the forehead. 'Sleep tight.'

Easier said than done. I lay in the dark, watching the head-light beams from the cars outside as they slipped through the gap in the curtains and travelled across the ceiling. Twisting my wedding ring around my finger, my thoughts turned to Charlie.

The four of us are standing on the street, just outside of the Carnival. The sun is low in the sky, bouncing orange light off the mirrors that border the entrance. We're each holding a credit note – apparently being stuck in one of the casino's lifts for ten minutes entitles you to a hundred bucks of free gambling.

The claustrophobe – a guy in his forties with a goatee and Ferragamo loafers – shakes my hand.

'Thank you,' he says. 'I think I woulda lost it in there if it hadn't been for you.' He pulls a business card out of his wallet and hands it to me. 'In case you ever need a good deal on some insurance. I'll knock off my fee.' And then, hailing a cab, he heads off back to his hotel, 'where I'm gonna take the *stairs* to my room and order a large cigar and some Chivas Regal'. I raise my hand in farewell as his taxi disappears off down the Strip.

The girl in the mini-dress is twirling her hair around her index finger, looking up at Charlie. Her back is turned to me.

'Hey, Charlie,' she says, making her voice all sugar-and-spice. 'You wanna come back to my hotel for cocktails? They make the best Appletinis in town.'

He just smiles at her and says thanks, but he has other plans. Then he looks at me, the late-afternoon sunlight turning his face golden, illuminating his twilight-blue eyes.

And so half an hour later I'm standing on a platform a couple of hundred feet above what looks like a tiny swimming pool, towels wrapped around my ankles to protect them from the eventual tightening of the bungee cord. The sun has nearly set, night-time blackness rising in the sky like spilt ink.

'Ready? Jump on the count of five,' the instructor tells me. Charlie's a distant figure down by the pool, looking up and waving at me. *So Kate*, he'd said on the street outside the Carnival, *if you're still hankering after an adrenaline rush, I know just the place*. Even from this height I can tell he's laughing, and reel off a string of expletives in his direction.

'One,' says the instructor, and I think, Why wait? Four more seconds on this platform aren't going to put off the inevitable. So I bend my knees and launch myself forwards as though I'm actually planning on diving into that pool.

For a moment I'm flying free in the air, then the pool gets larger and larger and the water hits me, the bungee cord gently pulling me back up into the sky. Thousands of Vegas lights twinkle around me as I twist in the Nevada wind. Bouncing in ever smaller rebounds, I see Charlie beaming with pride, as though I was his kid and not some girl he met less than an hour ago. As soon as they unclip me, laughing at the fact that I'm whooping and dripping, I run over to him and he doesn't care that I'm soaked but wraps me up in a hug of joy and exhilaration.

*

The room was saturated with light as Luke whisked back my curtains.

'Morning, sunshine,' he said, throwing my mobile on the bedsheets.

'Ever heard of knocking?' I asked, squinting against the brightness and pushing myself up on my elbow. Good job I was still wearing my long-sleeved T-shirt from the night before. Luke was kitted out in a new cream-coloured suit and a white shirt, and there was a pair of Ray-Bans perched on the top of his head.

'I did. You apparently slept through it.'

'What time is it?'

'Half-eleven.'

That late already? I stumbled out of bed and started pulling my jeans on.

'Whoa, Nelly,' said Luke. 'Not that I don't enjoy seeing you in your panties, but don't you think a shower and some fresh clothes are in order? The restaurant's still going to be there in a half-hour's time. Plus their doors don't open till noon.'

'Fine,' I said, grabbing a clean set of clothes and disappearing into the bathroom. Twenty minutes later I emerged washed, dressed and ready to go. Luke was sitting on the bed, a strange expression on his face. He walked past me into the bathroom, searching the shelves and even my washbag.

'What the hell are you doing?' I asked.

'You forgot your meds,' he said.

I frowned, preparing for a fight. 'I didn't forget them. My prescription ran out.'

'So why didn't you ask Dr McCormack for more?'

'Haven't seen her in a while.'

'Oh yeah?' he said. 'Define "a while".'

'Luke, I'm really not in the mood for this,' I said. 'Please, just drop it.'

'You were meant to see her every week,' he pushed. 'So how long's it been?'

'Long enough to have weaned myself off those painkillers she had me on,' I said. Human beings are meant to feel pain when we're grieving; it's not natural to numb yourself to it. I'd hated feeling that I was trying to escape from my grief, as though by doing so I was betraying Charlie in some way.

Luke shook his head at me and disappeared out of the door. After a second or two, I followed him.

The sky outside was cobalt blue, a vibrant contrast to the white sand of the beach. We walked down Ocean Drive, admiring the Art Deco buildings with their curved corners and eyebrowed windows. The candyfloss pink walls of one abutted the mint green of another. In a building of baby-blue stripes, a section of glass bricks reflected the bright Miami sun.

Ocean Drive was chock-a-block with traffic: sleek BMWs, sparkling Harleys and retro, tail-finned convertibles. On the pink pavements, old ladies carrying umbrellas to shield them-selves from the UV rays hustled past surfers in baggy shorts and teenagers playing tinny tunes on their mobiles. A dog ran past us on a lead, shortly followed by a rollerblading girl in a bikini.

'Christ,' I said as the girl skated by us. 'Are they in the middle of filming a tampon advert or something?'

If I was trying to make Luke laugh, it wasn't working.

'There it is,' he said. He gestured from the photo of El Cangrejo Dorado, in his hand, to the real thing.

The large glass doors in the restaurant's turquoise façade were open, white drapes billowing out in the breeze. The smell of jasmine wafted across to us as we walked through the doors and into the restaurant.

It was larger than it had appeared in the photos, and the

sunshine coming in through the open doors meant there was no need for candles or fairy lights, but at the same time it was strange actually standing there, as if I'd stepped into the pages of a picturebook.

A man in a white shirt and black trousers came up to us, nodding to Luke but addressing me: 'Table for two?'

'Actually we're here to ask you if you could help us with something,' I told him. 'We're trying to find a friend of ours, and we know he was here on the tenth of this month.' I handed him a print-out of the photo.

He took the print-out from me and then handed it back. 'I'm sorry,' he said. 'He doesn't ring a bell.'

I opened up one of the photo albums and showed him a picture of Charlie, a close-up of him that I'd taken in a bar in Islington two Christmases ago. The man glanced at it, and scanned the other photographs, but did so whilst shaking his head. 'Sorry.'

'Could we look at your reservations book?' I asked. 'We know that he must have been eating between eight and nine in the evening, and there were four other people at his table, so the reservation must have been for at least five people.'

Luke was standing behind me, and the maître d' looked up at him with his eyebrows raised, then back down to me. 'Is the man in the photograph your husband?'

'Yes,' I said.

'Does he owe you money for child support?'

'No. It's more complicated than that.'

'Look, if he's skipped out on you and owes you money, maybe you can get a court order or something, but if not, I'm going to have to say no. We have to respect the privacy of our patrons; I can't open up my reservations book to people that have just walked in off the street.'

'I understand, but if you just heard us out . . .'

'I'm sorry, I—' He looked surprised as a man in an identical shirt and trousers walked in. 'I thought you'd called in sick.'

The man came over, removing his baseball cap and sunglasses. 'Yeah, boss, but I started feeling better and I need the cash.' The maître d' exchanged glances with Luke, and just as it seemed as though the new arrival was about to be shooed into the kitchens, he spotted the photo of Charlie's table.

'Hey,' he said with a grin, taking the photo from me. 'That's Alejandro.'

Chapter Three

'That guy?' I asked quickly, pointing at Charlie.

'No, I don't know that guy's name. But the guy at the end of the table, that's Alejandro, one of our regulars.'

Ignoring the stare of doom that the maître d' was channelling in his direction, I asked the waiter where I could find Alejandro.

'He's got a furniture shop in Little Havana,' he told me, and wrote the address down on the back of one of the print-outs. 'Gotta go,' he said then. 'Customers are gonna start rolling in now. Are you guys eating?'

'Afraid not,' I said, smiling sweetly at the maître d'.

'Shame on you,' said the waiter, heading to the back of the restaurant and to the kitchens. 'We do the best stone crabs in Miami. *Hasta luego*!'

We were left with the maître d', who shrugged when I looked at him.

'One of your regulars, apparently,' I said.

'You didn't ask me if I recognized Alejandro,' he pointed out.

'Semantics.'

'I think you should leave now.'

Back on Ocean Drive, I turned on Luke. 'So what happened?' I said.

He frowned at me, kept on walking. 'What do you mean?'

'You didn't say an entire word the whole time we were in there. Some intimidating testosterone stuff might have helped.'

'I thought it would be best to see if the sweet'n'soft feminine touch worked before I stepped in. I didn't realize you were going for the direct approach.'

'Lucky that waiter arrived when he did, or we would have got *nada*.'

Luke nodded. 'Yeah. We were lucky. If we hadn't bumped into him, you wouldn't have picked up so much Spanish.'

'*Hablo mucho español*, thank you very much,' I assured him. 'You don't seem very excited.'

He jammed his sunglasses over his eyes. 'What's there to be excited about? We're going on a wild-goose chase that's gonna end up with you having your heart broken all over again.'

Little Havana was back on the mainland, near downtown Miami. It was where a huge number of Cuban exiles ended up in the sixties after Castro seized power, and they'd tried to create their own little Cuba on the streets of Miami. The area was a quiet one, with neat houses and sherbet-coloured shopfronts, all with Spanish names. Of the few inhabitants we saw, a large percentage were elderly men playing dominos outside coffee houses. We passed shopping centres, florists, car dealerships and hotels that looked like they were stuck in a fifties time-warp.

'What's that smell?' I said, enjoying the rich scent.

'Tobacco,' Luke told me. 'They have a lot of factories here where they roll cigars. Now how many times do I have to tell you, the air-con won't work if you've got that window open?'

We drove through the Latin Quarter, the roads lined with olive trees. The buildings here seemed to be in much better condition, with white stucco walls and red-tiled roofs.

Alejandro's furniture shop – *Muebles d'Alejandro* – was in one of these buildings, his leather sofas and pine tables on display in the windows.

We pulled up outside.

'Do you want me to do that macho thing you were talking about earlier, or do you want to try the flirty female approach first?' said Luke.

'I'm not sure I do "flirty female",' I retorted. 'Though you can give it a go if you want.'

Alejandro himself – I recognized him from the photograph – came out from the back of the shop to welcome us.

'*Buenos tardes! Cómo está?*' he asked.

'*Bien, gracias. Y usted?*'

'*Muy bien. Inglésa?*'

'*Sí.*'

'What can I do for you?' he asked, switching to heavily accented English.

'I'm afraid we're not here as customers,' I said. 'We need to get hold of a friend of ours, and one of the waiters at El Cangrejo Dorado told us that you were having dinner with him a week or so ago.'

'Really?' said Alejandro, smoothing down his moustache, which seemed to have been groomed to look as if two leeches had attached themselves to his upper lip. 'Can you tell me more about this friend? I eat at El Cangrejo all the time, and rarely on my own.'

I handed him the photograph of Charlie. He looked at it and nodded decisively.

'Yes, I ate with him last Thursday. He's a friend of Bruno's. What was his name . . .'

'Charlie,' I prompted him.

He looked at me strangely. 'No, no, I'm certain it wasn't Charlie.'

My heart sank. 'Something similar?'

He thought a bit more, stroking his leeches. 'Joe. I'm pretty sure this guy was called Joe.'

I felt like sitting down very heavily on one of Alejandro's plump leather sofas. 'Did you talk to him much during the meal?'

'Not really – we were at other ends of the table. Seemed like a nice guy though. I hope nothing's wrong?'

'No, nothing major. We've just got some news he needs to hear.'

'Well, he and Bruno seemed very friendly. If I recall correctly, Bruno said Joe was a friend from way back when. There was a lot of reminiscing, a lot of nostalgia.'

'As though they hadn't seen each other for a while?' I suggested.

'Perhaps. I'm sure Bruno could tell you more.'

'Can you let us know where to find this Bruno?'

Alejandro looked Luke and me up and down. The way Luke was dressed, and the manner in which he was casually leaning against the doorframe, he could almost have passed for a plainclothes police officer. It was a shame I was blowing that illusion with my make-up-free face and crumpled jeans.

'If you're friends of this gentleman,' Alejandro said, 'why didn't you know his name?'

I wasn't sure how to answer that, and just gazed at Alejandro plaintively. Luke stepped forward.

'To be honest with you, he's a bit of a player. A nice guy, but he uses a few aliases when he needs to, if you know what I mean.'

Alejandro nodded slowly. 'He sounds like a lovely man. I can see why you'd be friends with him.' I didn't like maligning my husband, even if it was a lie necessitated by my jumping in too fast with Charlie's name.

'We grew up with him,' explained Luke. 'We're trying to get him on the straight and narrow, and that's kinda hard to do when we can't find him.'

The furniture store owner seemed to take pity on us then. 'I'm sorry, I'll find you Bruno's address. It'll be in my BlackBerry. Please wait here.'

We waited silently in the showroom, admiring the exquisitely carved mirror frames and hand-tooled leather armchairs. I bit my thumbnail, not wanting to think about the fact that the man we were searching for didn't bear my husband's name.

I, of course, wanted to head straight to Bruno's place in Coral Gables, but Luke insisted on lunch. 'It's gone two, and I'm starving,' he said. 'Plus I'm guessing you've never experienced the joy of Cuban cooking.'

We found a restaurant on Calle Ocho with a spare table, and between us ordered roast pork, palomilla steaks, sweet plantains and paella. It was a bizarre combination of foods, but Luke insisted I try all of his favourites.

'Are you okay?' he asked me after a while. 'You've been very quiet.'

I pushed rice around on my plate with my fork. 'Mmm,' I said.

'Is it the fact Mr Muebles said that guy's name was Joe? Now you're starting to wonder if you spent the best part of a fortnight's salary coming over here to chase down Joe Shmoe from Boca Raton?'

I pushed my chair back and stood up. 'I'm going to the bathroom.'

I went to the toilet, though I didn't really need to, and washed my hands in the tepid water. The tiles around the mirror were faded and cracked, and the mirror itself had become filmy over the years, and rusted in the corners where the iron screws held it in place.

I stared at myself. My eyes are normally quite a clear grey, but today they seemed murky and unfocused. I leaned, weary, closer and closer to the glass until my forehead was resting against its cool surface. The underside of my arms felt itchy beneath my shirt-sleeves, and I found myself scratching them gently with my fingernails. I closed my eyes and thought about Charlie.

Down by that pool after the bungee jump, hugging me, enjoying my excitement.

'Come out to dinner with me,' he says. I step back from the hug, out of his arms, and look down at my sopping T-shirt.

'Where?' I say. 'Is there a restaurant that hosts wet T-shirt competitions in the evenings?'

'Not as far as I know, but that's a great business idea,' he replies, smiling. 'Come on, trust me.'

'Can I go back to my room and get changed first?' I ask.

'Nope. Don't worry, you'll make the dress code.'

We manage to hail a cab with a driver who doesn't seem to notice that the back seat of his car is getting dripped on, and Charlie gives him an address I don't recognize. I reflect on the fact that there's no way I would let any other guy do this. Already all my defences are down.

We drive for quite a while, leaving the city of Las Vegas behind us as we venture farther into the desert. Finally the driver slows down and pulls off the road. There's a little diner here, next to a petrol station. The only decoration this eatery boasts is a neon sign of a plate of spaghetti, with an animated fork lifting a few strands up into the air.

Charlie pays the driver, who zooms off back in the direction we came from.

'So why are we here?' I ask gently. Charlie takes me by the shoulders and turns me around. There, on the edge of the horizon, a haze of colour and light glows in the darkness. I can make out the green sheen of the MGM Grand, the shimmering golden windows of the Mandalay Bay, and the concentrated beam of light that shoots out of the apex of the Luxor's obsidian pyramid and into space. In between are the million lights of suburban Las Vegas, echoed by the stars in the clear black sky.

'It's beautiful, isn't it?' I say. Charlie wraps his arms around me from behind and rests his chin on my shoulder. We stand together looking out over the desert with the oasis of colour in the distance. I can feel his breath against my ear, and the contact of our bodies is turning me on.

'Are you cold?' he asks me. In Vegas the damp T-shirt was quite pleasant in that heat; out in the desert, I'm starting to shiver a bit. He straightens up and takes off his shirt, which he hands to me. I wish he was bare-chested underneath, but he's wearing a tight white T-shirt that shows off the curves of the muscles in his arms and shoulders.

There's little point putting the dry shirt on over my wet T-shirt, so I pull the latter off over my head, looking him in the eye. I stand before him in just my bra and jeans, but he simply carries on smiling at me without breaking eye-contact. It's as if he's saying that my body is irrelevant; it's not what matters. But it doesn't seem asexual, or gentlemanly, because he's looking at me as though in his head he's throwing me down on the sand and ripping the rest of my clothes off me. There's static electricity crackling through the Mojave Desert air.

I pull his shirt on and slowly button it up. I can smell him on the collar. He puts out a hand to me.

'C'mon,' he says. 'Let's eat.'

*

The door to the women's bathroom swung open, the handle banging against the near wall, and I snapped out of my reverie, pulling my forehead back from the mirror and leaving a patch of condensation.

'*Está mareada?*' asked a little old Cuban lady who only seemed to be about four feet tall.

'No,' I said. '*Soy bien, gracias.*'

Back at our table, Luke was talking into his cellphone. He saw me coming and hung up.

'Anything important?' I asked.

He shook his head. 'Just checking my voicemail.'

'Oh. I thought I saw you saying something.'

He looked at me sideways, with a crooked smile. 'I was changing my outgoing message. Is everything okay?'

I looked from one pale-blue eye to the other. 'Everything's fine.'

'You were in there a long time. Got food poisoning already?'

'No, cheeky sod. Just shooting the breeze with the locals.' I noticed the tiny cup of coffee sitting on my placemat. 'Espresso?' I asked.

'Sort of,' Luke said. 'Try it.'

I took a wary sip. The coffee seemed to be half-caffeine and half-sugar, and delivered a jolt right to my cerebral cortex.

'Wow,' I said.

'No need for coke or speed when you've got café Cubano on tap,' Luke told me with a wink.

'Apparently not.' I downed the rest of the thimbleful and picked up the bill, put a couple of twenty-dollar notes on top of it, anchored it with a pepperpot and said, 'My turn to pay.'

'Ready to go?'

*

The district of Coral Gables was just a few blocks from Little Havana. Magnificent gateways opened up onto quiet streets that were almost Mediterranean in the way they curved and meandered. The area was very lush and verdant, with beautifully manicured lawns in front of each colonial-style house.

We passed a gardener who was clipping a piece of shrubbery into the shape of a chess piece.

'Pretty swanky,' I commented.

'You should see the gardens on the other side of the houses. There's a fancy yacht moored at the bottom of half of 'em.'

I consulted the map again as we crawled along at five miles an hour. 'Where the hell are we? I can't read any of these bloody street signs.' Whether out of a misplaced emphasis on the aesthetic, or more likely a desire to make the area more confusing for lowly non-residents, the name of each street appeared on tiny white rocks down by the ground. 'Your choice of rental car is proving to be something of a disadvantage.'

Almost half of Luke's body was leaning out of his car window. 'Savona,' he read out from the nearest rock.

'Then you need to turn left at the end of the street.'

Bruno's terracotta-roofed house was huge, and towered over the wide lawn and sweeping driveway. In the terrace to the side of the entrance gushed an ornate fountain that wouldn't have looked out of place in the Plaza España in Seville.

'Nice,' I said, getting out of the car.

'Very nice,' agreed Luke.

'You get the impression Bruno's loaded?'

A black woman in a grey shift dress appeared at the door, her hair smoothed back into a neat bun.

'You here to see Mister Luna?' she asked in an accent that sounded half-French, half-East African. 'He expecting you.'

We swung the car doors shut and followed her through a house with dark wood furniture, tiled floors and shuttered windows. Bruno Luna was sitting in his expansive back garden, a sea of closely clipped green grass around him, and hibiscus flowers dipping down from the lattice beside him. He was around forty-five, tanned and plump, and was smoking a big fat cigar.

Rising to his feet, he assessed us with eyes shaded by the brim of his Panama hat, then smiled broadly. 'Alejandro called to tell me you'd be coming by.'

Luke stretched out a hand. 'Luke Broussard,' he said. 'And this is Kate Grey.'

I shook Bruno Luna's hand. The wet stub of his cigar poked against the palm of my hand.

'We're sorry to disturb you,' I said. 'We wouldn't be bothering you if it wasn't important.'

'Please,' he said. 'Have a seat. Would you like something to drink? Coffee, perhaps?'

'That's very kind,' I said, 'but I think I've just had enough caffeine to keep me awake for a good few years.'

He laughed wheezily. 'Ah, you've tried the Cuban stuff, I take it? Would you like something cold then? Lemonade?'

'That would be lovely, thank you.'

'And you, Mr Broussard?' he asked Luke.

'Sounds good.'

Bruno sent the maid back to the house with an order for three lemonades, and settled back in his seat. We joined him on the somewhat uncomfortable wrought-iron garden chairs. He surveyed us, puffing on his cigar.

'So, my good friend Alejandro tells me you're looking for Joe,' he said.

'If Joe's the man in this picture,' I said, laying the print-out of the photo from El Cangrejo Dorado on the garden table. He slid it closer and nodded.

'That's Joe. Can I ask why you're looking for him – and

why you told Alejandro that the name Joe was just an alias? I don't appreciate you casting aspersions on my friends.'

He wasn't happy, and I began to realize that his solicitous welcome might have just been a way to take us off our guard.

'The man in the photo is a dead ringer for my husband,' I told Bruno. 'I was just hoping you could tell us more about him.'

'What, you're wondering if Joe's leading a double life?' Bruno laughed, coughing up balls of cigar smoke. 'Trust me, it is unlikely.'

'Why?' I asked.

'Joe's wife and kids would probably notice if he went missing for long periods of time. It's not like he works on an oil rig or anything – he's in construction, works from eight in the morning till it gets dark. I think the few days he spent here were the first vacation days he's taken for about three years – other than Christmas, of course.'

Luke took over. 'Is Joe still here?'

'No. He went back to Phoenix the day before yesterday. His wife is heavily pregnant and he didn't want to risk being away for too long.'

Luke took one of my cherished photo albums from my lap and passed it over to Bruno Luna.

'Is this Joe?' he asked.

The maid came out with the drinks and set them down in front of us, moving the print-out aside so there was enough room for the chilled glasses. I watched her boss as he peered closely at the photos of Charlie, his gullet puffing up under his bristly chin. He chuckled.

'There's a very strong resemblance,' he admitted. 'Very strong. They could be brothers. But no, that's not Joe.'

He looked across at me and noticed I was shaking. 'Forgive me for saying so, Kate, but you don't seem very relieved that your husband isn't leading a double life after all.'

'My husband died a year ago,' I said, gripping hold of the arms of my chair to try and stop my hands from shaking. 'He drowned.'

Bruno just looked more confused. 'I don't understand. Was his body not recovered?'

'Yes, they found him,' I said. 'They identified him. I just . . . had to be sure.'

He nodded, though he was frowning as though he couldn't understand why I'd come. 'I'm very sorry for your loss.'

'Thank you very much for your hospitality,' Luke said, having glanced across at me and seen the state I was in. 'I think we'll have to take a raincheck on the lemonades though.'

'What's Joe's surname?' I asked Bruno, my voice croaky as I tried not to cry.

'Cantelli,' he told me gravely.

'Not Benson?'

'No, Kate. Not Benson.'

'Does he have relatives?'

'Of course. But Joe is from an Italian-American family: none of them have surnames like "Benson". Why? Would it make a difference if he was a relative of your husband's? He resembles him, certainly, but he wouldn't make a good substitute. He already has a wife, children.'

'That's not why I was asking,' I said quietly. 'I just . . . I don't have much left of him. His parents are dead and he had no brothers or sisters. Sometimes it feels like he's slipping away from me, and maybe if there was a relative, someone who looked like him, who had his mannerisms . . . it might help to bring him back for a while.'

There was no more sympathy from Bruno Luna. He stubbed out his cigar, not looking at me. 'I'm sure that the resemblance is coincidental rather than genetic. I've known Joe a long time, and have met his family on many occasions.

I'm certain that if *you* met Joe in person you'd discover the similarity is strong on the two dimensions of a photograph, but that his manner is very different. Put Joe Cantelli out of your head and focus on moving on with your life.'

I swiped tears from the edges of my eyes before they could escape, and took back my photo album.

'Thank you for your time,' I said bitterly, getting to my feet and heading for the house. Luke didn't follow me, no doubt smoothing the waters after my not-very-sincere farewell.

There were framed family portraits in the dark hallway and their smiles seemed unbearably smug as I walked by them with my dreams shredded at my feet.

'Miz Grey?' said a woman's voice from behind me. It was the maid, hovering on the staircase. She looked nervously in the direction from which I'd come, and indicated that I step closer. 'Are you looking for the man in the picture?'

I opened up the album, pointing to a photo of Charlie. 'Yes, this man.'

She tapped the flat image, her black eyes narrowing. 'Yes, I seen this man.'

I shook my head. 'Not according to your boss. You just had a house-guest who looks like him, apparently.'

She blew air through her nose. 'He tell lies. The man is a liar through and through. Meet me tonight, I tell you the truth.' She had a piece of paper in her hand that she slid into my shirt pocket. 'Don't say nothin' to your friend.'

We heard Luke's footsteps in the hallway, and the maid pretended she had just been coming down the stairs.

'Thank you for coming,' she told us, bustling us out of the front door. '*Passez une bonne journée.*'

Chapter Four

I couldn't wait to be back in my room, alone. My head was spinning. What did the maid mean, 'he tells lies'? Did she believe he was lying about Charlie?

Luke wanted to come into the hotel room with me.

'Luke, I'm sorry, I just really want to be on my own,' I told him, rubbing my forehead.

'You sure you're not going to do anything stupid?' he asked. I reflexively pulled my sleeves down around my thumbs, folded my arms.

'I'm fine,' I insisted. 'I just need some time.'

'Okay, don't get mad. I'm going to go tell the hotel that we'll be leaving tomorrow, and sort out our return tickets.' He sighed. 'Look, Kate, I'm sorry.'

'Sorry for what?'

'Sorry it didn't work out the way you wanted. Sorry that I didn't manage to talk you out of coming all the way here just to find out this guy's nothing to do with Charlie. It wasn't very responsible of me.'

There wasn't much I could say to that, not when as far as I was concerned I wasn't done yet.

'I'll come and check on you around dinner-time,' he promised.

After he left I waited a few minutes for him to reach his own room, then double-locked the door and pulled the maid's note from my pocket. It was written in black ink on a scrap of lined yellow paper.

8 p.m., Botánica Laurent, 54th Street. Ask for Claudette.

The hotel included gratis street maps in their welcome packs. I looked up 54th Street and found it was in the neighbourhood of Little Haiti, back on the mainland. If I was going to follow Claudette's instructions and not tell Luke about our meeting, then I'd need to find some alternative transport.

Why didn't Claudette want me to say anything to Luke? Did she know something I didn't? Had Luke really been changing his outgoing voicemail message? Why had he stayed behind to talk to Bruno on his own, no matter how briefly?

'Kate, you're being paranoid,' I told myself. If Joe Cantelli had something to do with Charlie, Luke would want to know almost as much as I did.

I went into the marble bathroom and turned on the shower. The showerhead was one of those huge chrome ones that cover you in a square foot of water. I left my clothes on the bathroom floor, and stepped into the steaming water.

I shut my eyes and there in my head was a mental picture of Joe. Not Charlie; Joe. He was in a hard hat and lumberjack shirt, swinging a sledgehammer against a wall. Then he was walking through a front lawn – at first the lawn was green and fresh, but then I thought, No, he lives in Phoenix, and the lawn was replaced in my head with a stone path, gravel and a cactus plant. He opened his front door, and a kid yelled, 'Daddy!' and ran into his shins. He picked the kid up and went into the house, kissing his pregnant wife as she cooked at her stove. The wife was a beautiful brunette, willowy despite the huge bump at her belly.

I groaned and opened my eyes, vigorously shampooing my hair. There was no way Charlie was carrying out a double life, with another family tucked away somewhere in Arizona. He and I had spent only two nights apart since he'd emigrated to England to be with me – once when he and Luke went out on a stag night, and once when I had to visit a sick friend in Scotland.

And what if Joe Cantelli did look like him? What if he even sounded like him, smelt like him? It still wouldn't be Charlie. Even if someone offered me a clone of Charlie, that wouldn't be enough. What made him Charlie, what made me love him, wouldn't be there.

I remembered Samantha, who'd been with me in Vegas, asking me, 'But how can you love him? You've only known him for one day – you can't possibly have got to know him that quickly.' And I remembered that even then I was thinking that I might not have known all his history, or even all his personality, but I knew his soul.

In the little spaghetti house in the desert, which only has three tables, the owner-cum-waiter-cum-chef knows Charlie by name.

'Charlie boy!' he says. 'You here for dinner?'

'We are, Gino.' Charlie's still holding my hand. I don't think he wants to let go. I don't want him to let go. He smiles at me. 'Gino, this is Kate.'

Gino, who's somewhat portly – probably eats too much of his own pasta – and who has a comb-over attempting to disguise his shiny bald head, wipes his hands on a tea towel and holds out one for me to shake.

'Nice to meet you, Katie,' he says. 'Take a seat, take a seat.'

We order *spaghetti ai frutti di mare*, which comes with mussels still in their shells – though Lord knows how fresh they are, considering Gino's desert location – and lamb in red wine sauce. Gino suggests a bottle of Médoc to go with the roast lamb, and it's like drinking an alcoholic mixture of blackberries and vanilla ice cream. Gino is discreet, out of sight and out of earshot, as though he knows we want to be alone. There's no one else in the restaurant.

Sucking up strands of spaghetti that leave olive oil on your chin should be embarrassing on a date, but Charlie and I tuck in with our forks and throw caution to the wind.

'There's a clam on your face,' he tells me at one point.

'Really?' I say. 'What does he want?'

'It's hard to say,' he shrugs. 'I don't speak shellfish.'

'Perhaps he wants to rejoin his little friends on my plate.'

'I don't know, he seems pretty attached to your face.' Charlie reaches towards me with a napkin and wipes my chin. A piece of clam about the size of a match head comes off on the napkin.

'That was my clam?' I ask, pointing at the napkin with my fork. 'How did you see him? He's practically invisible to the naked eye.'

'Kate, your face was starting to look like the set of *Finding Nemo*,' Charlie tells me very seriously. I kick him under the table. He catches my foot between his legs and holds it there. I let him.

'So what are you doing in Las Vegas?' I ask. He's an expert at rolling spaghetti onto his fork. No fish on the chin for him.

'Gambling,' he tells me. 'I'm a professional. None of the casinos will let me in any more though, since I started beating the house every time, so now I'm reduced to hanging out in old casino elevators, hoping they'll break down so I can seduce any hysterical women.'

I kick him with my other foot, and this time manage to connect with his shin.

'Ow!' he says. 'Okay, truth?'

'Truth.'

'I'm visiting a friend who lives here.'

'Male or female?' I want to know.

He smiles at the implied jealousy. 'Male. His name's Luke – no doubt you'll have the pleasure of meeting him at some point soon. And you? Truthfully.'

'I'm here for a convention,' I say. 'Right at this moment, I should probably be trying to schmooze people at some evening event. I was bunking off when you met me, to be honest.'

'Bunking off?' he repeats.

'Skipping school, cutting class. I just couldn't bear to waste my time here going to software demos and sales pitches. I mean, I've wanted to come here since I was a kid.'

'And does it live up to your expectations?'

'I love it. I've never been anywhere so . . . outlandish. I can't believe they've actually got gondolas in the Venetian, it's just insane. Do you like it?'

His smile falters somewhat. 'Yeah,' he says hesitantly. 'I do, as long as I don't think about it too much.'

'What do you mean?'

'There's just a sadness to it sometimes. Behind the scenes, or first thing in the morning when the only ones playing are the gambling addicts and the people with nowhere else to go.' He puts down his fork on his plate to signal that we've finished our starters, and pours me more wine. 'So what do you do back in the UK? How do you make a living?'

'Well,' I say, 'I've had many brief and unsatisfactory jobs. Sales girl in a shoe shop. Behind the counter at a bagel bakery. Tried working as a taxidermist's assistant, but discovered his collection of bestiality porn, and had to quit. Went out for a week or two with a boy from the funfair, and helped him on the dodgem cars. Worked on the phones at a psychic hotline – that was fun, conning people out of money by pretending you could predict their life, loves and travel plans. Oh, and I worked in a pet shop, but they sacked me.'

'What for?' says Charlie, who's trying not to laugh.

'I got in an argument with my manager about the way they treated the animals.'

'Hmm . . . anger management issues?' he asks, amused.

'No, not really. I just wasn't going to keep my mouth shut for the sake of hanging on to a shitty job. I'm afraid I find it hard not to act on my impulses.'

'Really?' he says. 'I'll have to remember that.' I see the heat in his eyes, and have to stop myself climbing over the table and kissing him hard on the mouth.

'How about you?' I ask him, as Gino reappears and sets our main courses down in front of us. 'What do you do? Other than the professional gambling, of course.'

'Charlie's an architect,' says Gino, slapping Charlie on the back. 'Designed my house. Did it all from scratch, wouldn't accept a penny in payment.'

'Apart from the free *osso bucco* for life that you promised me,' Charlie says. Gino laughs and melts away again.

'I'm impressed,' I say.

'What, that I designed Gino's house? Don't be, it's just a little two-bed place that takes up pretty much every inch of the plot he bought. He's trying to help me win you over.'

I look at him over my wine glass as I take a sip. 'You don't need any help,' I tell him.

Charlie grins at this, sitting back in his seat. Then: 'You know, Kate, you described all your previous jobs and never told me about your current one.'

'Nothing too interesting,' I shrug. 'I work for a software company in London. It pays the bills. Life gets a bit crazy when we've got a product launch, but the perks are good.'

'Business trips to Vegas?' he says.

'Exactly.'

'Sounds like you've moved up from bagel stores and fair-grounds.'

'The benefits of a good education. The bagels and the for-tune-telling were how I paid my way through university.'

'Your parents didn't help you?'

I look out of the window at the dark desert, the thought of them making me frown. 'No. I left home at sixteen and never went back. We don't get on.'

Charlie takes my hand, strokes the skin between my thumb and forefinger. 'I'm sorry, Kate.'

I smile at him, though I can't help feeling sad that I don't have the kind of parents that I can't wait to introduce him to. 'It's okay. It's been that way for a long time. It's just best for us if we don't see each other.'

'Do you have any brothers or sisters?'

That makes me smile for real. 'Three older brothers. Two of them are idiots, but I'm pretty close to my half-brother, Kytell.'

'You still see him?'

'Every once in a while. And always on my birthday.' Kytell comes by with presents of alcohol and ostentatious jewellery. I try to send the jewellery back with him.

'What about you, Charlie? Are you close to your family?'

Now it's his turn to look sad. The dark blue of the night sky seems to be reflected in his eyes.

'Very close, growing up. Then I went to college in another part of the country, met a girl there, stuck around after I grad-uated . . . I think they were hoping that when we split up I'd go back to Chicago, but instead I ended up in San Francisco. They're real proud that I'm an architect – or that I "build fancy places", as my mom likes to put it – but it separates them from me, because it's something so far removed from their world.'

'But every parent wants that for their children, don't they? For them to take a step further up the ladder – to achieve what they didn't?' Even as I was saying it, I was thinking that it wasn't true for me. My mother and father *wanted* me to follow in the family footsteps. It was my deviation from this that had estranged us.

'You're right. It just seems to be a shame that once you do that, take that next step, it just removes you further from the people you love.'

The food's practically forgotten as we sit there, legs entwined, hands touching. He's gazing at me, perplexed.

'This is so strange,' he murmurs.

'I know.'

'It feels like I've known you for years and years . . . that I've always known you.'

I lean forward over the food, candles flickering on either side of me, and kiss him softly on the mouth. His lips are smooth and warm, and they taste of wine.

I was slumped on the floor of the shower, curled up as if I was being attacked by dogs. Lord knows how long I'd been there – all I knew was that my joints hurt when I straightened myself up, and that my fingertips had puckered up. The bathroom was full of steam.

I stepped out of the shower and wrapped myself in one of the hotel's huge, fluffy white towels. The other room felt chilly in comparison, the air-conditioning having been on high. My watch told me it was six in the evening, and I knew I'd have to get out of the room soon if I wanted to avoid Luke.

My packing had been haphazard at best, and seemed in retrospect to have mainly involved jeans and socks. I managed to locate a pair of black linen trousers and a black shirt. I looked rather as if I was going to a fancy dress party in Little Haiti as a ninja, but if the alternative was the thick material of denim, I was going to wholeheartedly embrace the ninja look.

My stomach growled, which was unsurprising considering it was eleven o'clock at night back home, and I'd been thinking about Gino's roast lamb. I left the hotel and wandered down Ocean Drive till I found a café that served burgers. I wolfed one down with fries and a banana-flavoured *batido* shake, then went on the hunt for a taxi that would take me to Botánica Laurent.

'You sure you wanna go to Little Haiti?' checked the cab driver as we drove across the causeway to the mainland. The bay was sprinkled with yachts, and colossal cruise ships cast shadows over the waves. Electric lights were beginning to come on in the distant skyscrapers.

'I'm sure. I'm meeting someone.'

'It's not too safe at night, especially for tourists.'

I looked out the window grimly, thinking what a long drop it was to the water. 'I'll be okay.'

He shrugged. 'It's your funeral.'

Little Haiti was a poor neighbourhood and, like Little Havana, it was largely populated by people who were escaping the dictatorial regime of their home country. Most of the woodframe houses were shabby; many were dilapidated. I saw chickens running around in some of the front yards, making friends with the local pigeons.

Alongside one street, a tree with veined green leaves and aubergine-shaped pods had various things nailed to it: cloth bags, jewellery, even a pack of cigarettes.

'It's a *ceiba* tree,' said my driver, noticing my interest. 'The Haitians think it's holy. Those things on it are offerings.'

'To what – the tree?'

'No. You heard of *santería*?' He went on to give me a brief history lesson. Turns out that many of the slaves brought over to the Caribbean from Africa belonged to a polytheist religion but, banned from worshipping their own gods, they cleverly translated them into Catholic saints to whom they could pray without fear of reprisal.

'Sounds like voodoo,' I said.

'It's similar. There's plenty of voodoo around here too. This place you want me to take you to – you know it's a shop for this kinda stuff?'

'No,' I said. 'I thought it was a florist's or something.'

He laughed. 'Yeah. "Or something" is right.'

We turned onto bustling 54th Street, Caribbean music blasting out of the many record stores so loudly it seemed as if the street itself was vibrating with the bassline. Shopfronts were far more brightly coloured than the pale tones of Miami Beach: raspberry, lemon, lime. I wondered if the vivid colours reminded the inhabitants of home.

The driver pulled up next to a store with the words *Botánica Laurent* painted on it in patterns of flowers and bones.

'Good luck,' he said. I paid him off and got out of the cab. It was already dark, and the largely black pedestrians seemed to notice a white, non-Hispanic woman on their street. I wasn't nervous. Just because these people were poor, didn't make them criminals. At the same time, I was aware that there might be someone who had seen me and marked me out as a fish out of water. I wasn't wearing a camera around my neck, the baseball cap of a sports team from out of state, or the American vacation uniform of shorts and trainers with white socks, so if I was lucky they'd peg me as a Miamian, not a tourist. Still, I stepped quickly through the door of the Botánica Laurent.

A bell jingled as I entered the shop. The place was dimly lit, and smelt of exotic incense. I passed rows of gaudy statuettes – saints with black faces and white robes – and shelves stacked with candles and glass jars full of herbs.

A woman with braided hair and too much eyeliner was waiting for me at the counter.

'Hi,' I said. 'I'm here to see Claudette.'

She nodded, not taking her eyes off me, and turned to a door on her right.

'Claudette!' she shouted up the staircase, then something else in what sounded like French. 'You're early,' she told me.

As I waited, arms folded defensively over my chest, I looked over the products she was selling. There seemed to be potions for everything: love, money, luck, health, virility. Many of the thicker candles had brightly-coloured pictures of the saints/gods on their sleeves. There were stacks of tarot cards and spell kits, and voodoo dolls in packets with a quiver of pins attached. On perhaps the strangest shelf, what looked like stuffed monkey heads sat next to dried alligator flesh and bottles of something that claimed to be black cat repellent.

A curtain of pink and gold beads was swept to one side and Claudette appeared as though stepping through a waterfall. She was wearing a white vest and baggy blue trousers, and her hair was out of its neat bun and in a halo around her head.

'Come with me,' she said, and held the strings of beads aside.

I moved past her into the room at the back of the shop. There were numerous framed pictures on the walls of what looked like the same two saints; little tea-light candles were underneath each picture, their flames reflected in the glass. A TV in the corner looked old and battered, and the sofa was still covered in its plastic. A cat – tabby, not black – looked up at me with half-closed eyes from its spot on the sofa cushion, and then relaxed its head back onto its paws.

Claudette sat me down opposite her at the little wooden table next to the TV set.

'What can you tell me about this man?' I asked her, taking the photo out of my pocket. She took it in both hands and placed it down on the table so that its borders were precisely aligned with the edges of the table.

'His name is Joe. At least, that is what Mister Luna call him,' she told me.

'Do you know what his surname is?'

She shrugged.

'Luna told me he was called Joe Cantelli.'

She shrugged again. 'I call him Mister Joe. I ain't heard the name Cantelli.'

'What about the name Charlie? Did either of them ever speak about someone called Charlie?' Claudette shook her head, and I felt my energy beginning to drain away. 'How long did he stay with you for?'

'Just a few days. Mister Luna was very happy to see him.'

'Did he get a lot of phone calls at the house? From his wife?'

'I don't know. He have a cellphone. People call him on that.'

'Did he ever talk about her, or his kids?'

'No. He was polite to me, but he weren't friendly. Mister Luna don't like me to chat to his guests.'

I was learning nothing new here. 'Claudette, why did you ask me to meet you? What did you want to tell me?'

'That you cannot trust Mister Luna. He is not a good man. He makes money from bad things.'

'What bad things? Are you saying he's a criminal?'

'I seen drugs in the house. He have many guns. The men he associate with, they all carry guns, under their jackets.'

'Have you told the police any of this?'

She laughed, displaying a set of large and brilliant white teeth. 'No, Miz Grey. I need my job. I have a family back home in Haiti that need the money.'

·'So why are you telling me?'

Claudette's forearms were already on the table, forming a triangle around the photograph of Charlie. She stretched forward and took my hands.

'Mister Luna is not the person you should be asking for help finding your husband. *I* can help you.'

'How?' I asked, uncomfortable. She turned my hands over so the palms were upward, and looked down at them, then her eyes travelled up the inside of my forearms until the point where they were hidden by my shirt-sleeves.

She released my left hand, and stroked the lines of my right with her fingertip. Her skin was rough from too many hours spent scrubbing with bleach on stone floors.

'You have been through much hurt,' she told me. 'Your heart line is very strong here, but then the line is broken by all these knots. My poor girl, you are in the darkness now. You suffer the company of shadows. Deception is all around you.' She squeezed the skin on the edge of my hand, under my little finger. 'Do you have children already? The lines say you will have two, a boy and a girl.'

I snatched my hand away. 'I'm not planning on having children.'

'We can do a spell for you,' Claudette assured me. 'A charm to find your husband. And, if he truly is dead, a spell to find you a new one. A spell to banish your shadows.'

'Are you fucking kidding me?' I said. 'You brought me here just to sell me one of your *spells*?'

'We can help you!' she pleaded, and it took all my self-control not to lash out at her. The other girl appeared in the doorway and looked down at my twitching hands.

I snatched the photograph from the table and stormed out of the room, Claudette's friend jumping out of my way. The beaded curtain swished back down behind me in a cascade of clacks and clicks.

Claudette didn't have any information for me. To her, I was just a punter and she'd simply been trying to con a few dollars out of me. That was why she'd told me not to bring Luke – I was more vulnerable on my own.

'Fuck!' I swore, back on the street, thumping the wall as I walked.

A few feet in front of me, a man was leaning with his back against the window of a liquor store, one leg bent, foot against the glass. As I passed him he pushed off from the window and began to follow me.

I think he thought I was so riled up that I hadn't noticed him. As we crossed the entrance to an alleyway he grabbed me with one hand around my mouth and one arm pinning my arms to my waist, and pulled me into the alley. So this was why I wasn't meant to visit Little Haiti at night. This guy was giving the neighbourhood a bad name.

'I'm not gonna rape you,' he said. 'I just want your cash and your credit cards.'

For most white tourists who found themselves in a rough part of town, in an alley, with a big scary black guy asking them for money, just the fact of him asking would be enough to make them give him everything they had. But I'd been brought up in the East End of London, where half my mates had been big scary black guys, and as a teenager, I'd done my own share of naughty stuff. In addition to which, I was already very, very angry.

I kicked back hard with my booted right foot, aiming for his kneecap. The joint bent in the wrong direction.

He let go of me immediately and fell to the ground, clutching at his knee. I hadn't heard the kneecap go, so he had probably got away with a snapped tendon. He didn't make a sound – he was still too shocked.

I was panting hard, more due to adrenaline than to exertion. 'I grew up with three older brothers, mate. You want to pick your targets a little more carefully.'

At that he tried to get up, but his injured knee wouldn't bear his weight and he collapsed back on the ground. He glared up at me and I walked quickly back to the main street, keeping an eye on him as he sat there between the bins and the sacks of rubbish.

'*Salope!*' he shouted. '*Putain!*'

Chapter Five

I caught a cab straight back to the hotel and ran up the stairs
to my room. Luke was waiting there, pacing the floor.

'How the fuck do you keep getting into my room?' I
snapped at him.

'They set the key card so it opens both our rooms,' he said,
surprised. 'Since they're both in my name an' all. Do you have
a problem with me being in your room?'

'Is a little bloody privacy too much to ask?'

'No,' he said through closed teeth. 'I won't do it again.
Now, do you want to tell me just where the hell you've been?'

'I went to Little Haiti,' I told him.

'Jesus, what did you want to go there for? Is that where you
got the bruises on your face?'

I went to the mirror and checked the side of my face. There
were very faint marks on my jawline from my would-be mugger's
fingers when he had his hand over my mouth. 'It's nothing,' I said.

'What the hell were you doing there?'

'I went to meet Bruno Luna's maid. She has a *botánica*
there. She said she had information for me.'

'And did she?' There was an odd expression on his face; I
couldn't tell if it was fear or hope.

'No. She just wanted to sell me some hocus-pocus.' I sat
down heavily on the bed and began to cry. 'Oh Luke, can we
just go home?'

He sat down next to me and pulled me to him. I burrowed my head into his chest and sobbed.

'Ssh, Kate,' he said softly, stroking my hair. 'Don't cry. It's okay. It's okay.'

'It's not okay. Charlie's dead. He's always been dead.' I could see him floating face down in the ocean, bobbing on the waves. 'There's just some bastard called Joe Cantelli who's walking around with his bloody face. Luke, what am I doing here? I've been so stupid.'

He rocked me in his arms. 'Sshhhh. You're not stupid. You needed to know, to be sure, Charlie was dead.'

'But, Christ, Luke!' I said, raising my face to his. 'I saw the body, I saw the tattoo. I knew it matched his DNA. Why did I have to do this to myself to be sure it was Charlie's body?'

'I don't know,' he said, and he too had tears in his eyes. 'I'm sorry.'

Back on the Strip, Charlie and I have hit the casinos. We keep winning hands on the $30 blackjack table, and the dealer loves us because we tip him every time. Charlie tries to teach me how to play craps, but it's so complicated I end up throwing the dice while he just shouts out which number we need to get.

'Seven!' he yells at the dice, and the gamblers around the table whoop as the dice land with seven spots showing.

From one of the clubs I can hear my current favourite dance track, and drag him onto the dancefloor. We move together, the crowd in rhythm around us, heating up with the movements, our clothes hot and damp with sweat, swaying in a slow-motion grind.

I'm so close to Charlie that all my senses are inhaling him, and it just makes me crave him more. I want him inside me.

His hands are on my hips, my waist, and I can't stop touching him, loving the feel of his skin, loving the feel of the hard muscles of his back as I slip my hand under his T-shirt. When we kiss it's like being in a haven of warmth and darkness. I'm not aware of anything but him, his sweet mouth – the softness of his kiss, the urgency of his kiss. It's as if he's drawing me into him, that we're fusing together.

We're up in my room. The curtains are open on the lights of Vegas below us. He's peeling off my black bra. I'm unbuttoning his jeans. I love the feel of his chest against my bare breasts. We're on top of the covers, under the covers, in the shower, leaning against the dressing-table. As soon as we're finished, I want him again. I've never felt passion like it: the overwhelming need to feel completely physically connected.

When we finally can't work up the energy any more to act on our desire, we curl up together, legs and arms entwined, my hair in a black fan on his chest, my foot caught up in the bend of his knee. We talk and talk and talk. About favourite films, favourite books, favourite food; and then move onto the serious stuff, like politics, religion, previous partners, and whether either of us want children. We certainly don't agree on everything, but even the beliefs he expresses that are different to mine just make me love him more.

We both know one of us will have to at some point address the Big Question, and finally he takes the leap of faith.

'So how about you come and stay with me in San Francisco for a while?' he asks me.

I snuggle even closer. 'I'd love to. Unfortunately I can't take any more holiday until December.'

'December!' he protests. 'How the hell am I gonna wait that long?'

'Well, you could come back to London with me,' I say, and he smiles.

'I'll have to see about work. Maybe I can talk them into a few weeks off.'

Two days later, and we're getting married in the Little Chapel of the West. The chapel's sign is hanging from a log outside, and I laugh at the idea that I'm getting married in a place that uses timber for décor. Samantha is my maid of honour, and she thinks I'm crazy, but she loves Charlie to bits and is getting swept up in the whole romance of it. Luke is Charlie's best man, beaming away like a Great White Shark.

The four of us go to the Bellagio for cocktails and toast one another.

'To my darling wife, the lovely Mrs Benson,' says Charlie.

'I told you, Charlie, I'm keeping my maiden name,' I say, swatting him with my bouquet.

He just grins at me. 'Can I call you Mrs Benson if I let you call me Mr Grey?'

I stand up in my white evening gown, bought from one of the hotel boutiques that afternoon, and raise my champagne glass.

'To my darling husband, the lovely Mr Grey!' I say with a laugh, and we all clink our glasses.

The radio alarm clock beside my bed told me it was gone 2 a.m. I lay there for a while, trying to hypnotize myself to sleep by watching the car headlights again, but couldn't stop the waves of hopelessness that threatened to sink me.

Charlie was dead. The man in the photo was called Joe Cantelli. He was a construction worker from Phoenix with a wife and kids. Charlie was dead.

Despite all my self-warnings, I'd let myself believe that

maybe it *was* Charlie in the photo. How could I have been so stupid? Those people who thought hope was a virtue were just fooling themselves – hope was nothing but a curse.

I had butterflies in my stomach, a sick feeling of dread. What point was there for me on this planet without Charlie, without even the hope of Charlie . . .

Whichever part of my brain contained my survival instincts took over then, kickstarting my motor functions and propelling me out of my bed. I slipped on a pair of jeans and a hooded top, ran my fingers through my knotted hair, and went down to the hotel bar.

The bar was nice and quiet, just a cuddling couple on the comfy chairs talking to each other in murmurs, and an elderly man sitting on one of the stools by the counter. The music was subtle, merely background noise; some kind of lounge jazz.

I took a stool, five to the right of the old man's. The barman came over, wiped the counter, and laid a coaster down in front of me.

'What can I get you?' he asked.

I surveyed the rows of colourful glass bottles behind him.

'JD on the rocks, please.'

I nursed one drink after another, watching the ice cubes melt and thinking about the phone call I'd got from Charlie just a couple of weeks after returning to London. He'd told me his parents had been killed in a car accident, and he needed to be with me. I told him I'd be on the next plane, but he wanted to get away, he said. Just a few days later he'd arrived at Heathrow, his life turned upside down. He ended up reassessing everything. There were long nights when, woken up by his nightmares, all I could do was hold him and try to transfer some warmth to his cold and tired bones. Eventually he began to thaw, to smile at me again, to be

flirtatious and affectionate. We began to go out more, especially when Luke relocated to London. The nightmares
became more and more infrequent. Charlie was given official
approval to work in the country, and quickly got a job at an
architectural firm in the City. Life settled down. I was sad that
I'd never get to meet his mother and father, but we were
together. We were happy.

Did I have a future, without Charlie? What was next for
me, now this crazy little episode had come to nothing? Tomorrow Luke would take me back to England, back to my empty
flat. I'd make another appointment with Dr McCormack, and
let her prescribe more anti-depressants. I'd survive without
living. Years and years stretched before me, empty years alone
on a dark path.

'So are you here for business or pleasure?' said a voice from
far away. I refocused, followed the direction the sound was
coming from.

The elderly man had left, perhaps some time ago, and now
a man in a dark suit and glasses was sitting in his seat. He was
drinking some brown liquid – maybe Jack Daniel's, like me.

I had to clear my throat to speak. 'Neither, really.'

'I'm here on business,' he told me. I checked his left hand
for a wedding ring and saw one. I hoped that meant he wasn't
about to try and chat me up. I drank some more, making sure
my own wedding ring caught the light. 'So what do you think
of Miami?' he asked.

I blew a laugh through my nose. 'To use one of your
American phrases, it sucks.'

He sipped his drink. 'I wouldn't say that.'

'Don't take offence,' I told him. 'I'm on my fourth glass of
whiskey, and I've had a really crap day.'

'That's okay,' he said, and to my dismay he seemed to take
my half-apology as an invitation to move to the stool next to

me. 'You do look like you've had a rough day. Perhaps you'd let me buy you a fifth drink?'

He saw my expression and said, 'Don't worry, I'm not coming on to you. I'm a happily married man. It's just that it's the middle of the night, I'm in a strange city, and I'd like someone to talk to.'

I hunched my shoulder up, blocking him off. Perhaps he'd respond to body language. 'I'm not the person you should be speaking to if you want cheering up,' I said, turning back to the bar.

The man took off his glasses, the frames an old-fashioned style from the fifties, and rubbed them with his tie. The female half of the couple on the sofa came up to the other end of the bar to request a drink, and the bartender went to serve her.

The demeanour of the man next to me seemed to shift as soon as the bartender was out of earshot. The easy smile dropped from his face, and his body straightened and stiffened.

'Ms Grey,' he said, all the while looking down at his glasses, 'I think it's time you and your friend left Miami and returned home.'

'What?' I said in surprise.

He lifted the glasses to his face and inspected the cleanliness of the lenses. 'You need to forget about Charles Benson' – his mouth twisted as he said my husband's name – 'and stop asking questions. If you keep turning over stones, eventually you're going to come across a scorpion.'

He slid the glasses back onto his nose and smiled at me. 'Perhaps you should avoid that fifth drink, and go upstairs to pack.' His eyes were cold.

Luke answered his door in just his boxer shorts, rubbing his short blond crop as though trying to wake himself up.

'What's up?' he said, squinting his eyes against the hallway light. 'Kate, why have you got your suitcase?'

'We've got to go,' I said urgently, pushing him into the room and closing the door behind me. 'Something's going on, something to do with Charlie. Get dressed and let's get out of here.'

'Are we going back to London?' he asked, pulling on his jeans.

'Only to throw them off,' I said, determination firing up my body. 'Then we're going to Sicily.'

PART II

Sicily

Chapter Six

Charlie had only managed to get a two-week stretch off work by calling in favours and working till all hours to get the current part of his project finished, and he was exhausted. I sat next to him on the plane, entertained by the sweet sound of his snoring.

Just before the pilot announced we were about to begin our descent, something made Charlie start awake. He looked around bleary-eyed, and narrowed his eyes at me when he caught me sniggering.

'It's like sitting next to a warthog,' I told him. 'Seriously. I didn't realize you were allowed to take livestock on board a plane. I thought they had to be kept in the hold.'

He poked me in the ribs. 'Hey, talk about the pot calling the kettle black. At least I don't sound like an oil tanker. The seismologists don't call *me* up when they pick up a point nine on the Richter scale, just to make sure I'm awake and not affecting their readings.'

We picked up a hire car and I let Charlie drive, since he'd had many years' experience of driving on the wrong side of the road. Sicily was hot, even though it was towards the tail end of summer, but there were also heavy white clouds over the hills.

'It's a lot greener than I thought it would be,' Charlie said.

'Me too. I thought it would be more arid, more like southern Spain.' The hills were covered in thick grass and poplar
trees. 'Maybe we've just both seen *The Godfather* too many
times.' When Michael Corleone goes to Sicily, it looks very
dusty and dry.

Charlie did a great Al Pacino impression. 'Don't think of it
as losing a daughter,' he said. 'Think of it as gaining a son.'

The only Al Pacino impression I could do was a bad one
from *Scarface*. 'Say hello to my leetle friend,' I leered at
Charlie.

'When we get to the hotel, you can say hello to my little
friend,' he assured me, patting me on the knee. I was wearing
shorts, and the palm of his hand was hot on my bare skin.

The hotel was on the outskirts of Cefalu, in its own complex. You had to buzz reception to open the gates and let you
in. The grounds were landscaped, covered in pathways and
hibiscus flowers, and the infinity pool next to the outdoor bar
looked out over the slope of apartments down to the sea. It
was beautiful, and I hugged Charlie's arm in joy.

We checked in and the receptionist gave us the keys to our
apartment, along with a map of the complex.

'Hey, there's a crazy golf course,' Charlie told me happily,
pointing at the map.

'You get excited at the weirdest things,' I said, but I was
smiling.

The apartment was clean and comfortable, with a terrace
that had a pretty view of the lemon grove that bordered the
hotel's own beach. We unpacked quickly, wanting to get an
hour or two by the pool before evening settled in. Charlie was
ready first, standing impatiently by the door in a pair of swimming shorts and a towel as I shoved things into a tote bag.

'Kate, we're not going to the North Pole. Just get changed
into a bikini and grab a towel, and let's go.'

'We might want some water,' I pointed out. 'And should we take something to read?'

He pulled me towards him and started undoing my blouse, then unhooking my bra.

'Are you going to want a snack?' I checked. 'I'm feeling hungry already.'

My shorts and knickers came off next, and Charlie stepped back and looked over my naked body with a wry smile on his face.

'Don't even think about it,' I said. 'You were giving me grief just thirty seconds ago for not being on my way out the door.'

'I know, I know.' He rifled through my drawer of swimming costumes and threw a blue and white striped bikini at me. 'Undressing you, I'm good at. Dressing you isn't something I've had much practice in.'

I pulled on the bikini. 'You know you should apply suntan lotion at least twenty minutes before you go in the sun?'

He bent down and threw me over his shoulder in a fireman's lift, patting my arse with his free hand as he walked out of the door.

'Don't forget the key!' I shouted in vain as the door locked automatically behind us.

The hotel had a second restaurant on the terrace where we had a late dinner, surrounded by heavy white drapes and thick candles. We listened to the waves of the Mediterranean, breaking up on the sand far below us. Charlie was wearing a black shirt like the one he'd worn the day I'd met him in Las Vegas.

'Can you believe it's been two years?' I said softly.

He smiled, holding my hand under the table. 'In some ways it feels like we've only been together two weeks. In other ways it feels like a lifetime.' He laughed at my expression. 'I don't mean that in a bad way. It just feels like we've always been together. Looking back on those years when I didn't know you, it seems strange that you weren't with me. I keep expecting to find you in my memories.'

'That's possibly the corniest thing I've ever heard you say,' I teased him.

Our waiter came over with our food and asked us something in Italian. We both looked blank and he gave up and just said: 'Risotto?'

Charlie raised his hand. The waiter gave him his plate of risotto with prosciutto and parmesan shavings and laid my quattro formaggi pizza down in front of me. The wine came in a glass carafe.

'This is my kind of joint,' said Charlie. 'Vino in a jug.' He poured me out a glass of wine. 'So, what do you think of the place so far?'

'It's great. Sicily's beautiful, and I'm looking forward to exploring the town.'

He nodded. 'You like Italy?'

'Of course!' I thought of the places I'd been to, saying, 'Venice is incredible. I love Florence too, and Rome's fantastic. Why, don't you?'

He shrugged. 'This is my first trip. Actually, I think my parents took me to Italy when I was a baby, but I don't remember it.'

'So why did you choose it?' Charlie had found the resort and booked the trip.

'Have you heard of Sicilian maggot cheese?'

'*What?*'

'One of my great-uncles who was stationed in Europe during the Second World War told me about it. They leave the cheese out so the flies lay eggs in it, then when the maggots hatch they eat the cheese. It's a delicacy. Nice combination of meat and cheese.'

'Are you sure this isn't one of your great-uncle's urban legends? Like the time he told you about the woman who found a finger in her fried chicken?'

'That was a well-documented case,' Charlie told me.

'So you booked this holiday with the express plan of finding and eating some maggot cheese?'

'Hell no,' he said. 'Well, the finding part would be okay. You can do the eating part and I'll debrief you afterwards.'

I looked at him. 'I love you,' I said.

He grinned. 'I love you too, Katie.'

Later the waiter came over to take away our empty plates. 'Dessert?' he asked me.

'*Sono piena*,' I said, trying to make an effort by telling him in Italian that I was full up. I patted my stomach. Charlie snorted, and the waiter grinned at me.

'Si?' he said. '*Congratulazioni.*'

'I think you just told him you were pregnant,' said Charlie.

The waiter turned to the maître d' and repeated my highly amusing language mix-up. Chuckling, the maître d' came over and made a show of hiding the carafe of wine from me. He spoke pretty good English; Charlie started chatting to him, and before I knew it, the restaurant was closed and we were sat at another table with the waiting staff and a couple of guys from the kitchen, still in their chefs' whites. I called it 'the Charlie effect'. He made instant friends everywhere we went.

At midnight the receptionist came off shift, and brought a half-finished bottle of Amaretto over to the table. She waved it at me with a smile on her face.

'Yes, please,' I said, and she sat down in a neighbouring chair.

'What are your names?' she asked.

'She's called Katerina,' interrupted the maître d', Gian-Luca. 'And this is Carlo.'

'Charlie,' he corrected, almost sharply.

'And you?' I asked, frowning at him.

She pointed at her name badge. 'Sofia.'

'Sofia's from Milan,' said Gian-Luca. 'That's why her accent is so strange.'

She said something rude to him in Italian and turned her chair so it was angled more towards me and less towards him. He grinned at me and went back to his conversation with Charlie and our waiter, providing some useful translating skills.

Sofia and I got progressively more drunk, discussing the major differences between Italian men and English men (I didn't want to claim any expertise on American men, Charlie being my only experience of the species). She looked blank when I asked her about maggot cheese (which Charlie later put down to her not being a local), but waxed lyrical on some nearby towns and churches that we should visit. She also wrote down on a napkin the name of a seafood restaurant in the town.

'What's wrong with you?' Gian-Luca chided her. 'Why are you sending her away from our restaurant?'

'You know they do the best fish in Sicily,' Sofia told him, tapping him with one of her acrylic nails.

By one in the morning we were playing cards and had moved on to whisky and brandy. By two, our waiter had cleaned us out of all the cash we had on us, and we went back to our apartment. Charlie and I found it hard to navigate our way down the sloping paths of the complex, which were far too steep for people as drunk as we were. Charlie gave up on walking – he bent down and started doing a forward roll, and I had to slap a hand over my mouth so my laughter didn't wake up the poor people who had gone to bed at a reasonable hour.

Back in the apartment, which a kind porter had had to open for us earlier after we'd locked ourselves out, I drank half a litre of water from the bottle in the fridge and lay on the bed groaning. Charlie flicked on the TV and channel-hopped. There were no English programmes, but we did find an episode of *Walker, Texas Ranger*, dubbed into Italian, that was far more enthralling than anything a UK cable channel would have been showing. One of Walker's Native American buddies was hiding in the woods, on the run from a murder beef, and Walker seemed to be trying to find him by tying a strip of cloth round his head, taking his shirt off and smoking something hallucinatory.

'Funny thing about Italians,' I said, only slurring slightly. 'They always want to translate your name.'

'What do you mean?' Charlie asked.

'I tell them I'm called Kate, and instantly I'm Katerina. You tell them you're Charlie, and instantly you're Carlo. But if we met someone Italian in England, we wouldn't say "your name's Giovanni, but we're going to call you Johnny". Gian-Luca wouldn't get called John-Luke.'

Charlie, not taking his eyes off the screen as Chuck Norris kick-boxed some bloke who was getting off a helicopter, leaned over and squeezed my big toe.

'We've just hooked up with this new contractor at work,' he told me. 'He's from Japan, name of Takeshi. Know what his team calls him? Tom.'

'Fine,' I said, yawning. 'But you call me Katerina, and I'll deck you.'

The next morning I woke up before Charlie. I turned onto my side and watched him sleep. He looked so sweet and sexy with his hair mussed up. After a few minutes he scratched his side and then rolled over himself so that his back was towards me.

I moved over to his side of the bed and wrapped myself down the length of his body. With my forefinger I stroked the short hairs at the nape of his neck. They grew diagonally rather than straight down, and I loved that about him.

He stirred and reached his hand behind him, clasping my leg. I hooked it over his hip, pulling him towards me, and kissed the back of his neck.

'I take it your hangover's manageable, then?' Charlie said into his pillow.

'Yep. Yours?'

He rolled onto his back and looked at me with one eye. The other was still scrunched up against the morning light. I rubbed his chest and ran my fingernails over his ribcage. 'I'll live,' he said eventually.

'You feeling up to an early-morning workout?'

He yawned. 'I'll just lie here. You do what you want with me.'

'Sorry, sacks of potatoes have never turned me on,' I said drily, and got out of bed. I sauntered naked over to the shower, knowing he was watching me.

The water was hot, and soon the whole bathroom was soaked in a humid cloud of steam. I heard him walk in and pause for a while, and then he pulled back the shower curtain and joined me.

Later, when we were towelled dry and ready for the beach, I went back in the bathroom and found he'd written 'Carlo ♥ Katerina' in the steamed-up mirror.

The night seemed to be hotter than the daytime. Charlie stood on the edge of the walkway that bordered the sea, leaning against the railings and looking out at the last smears of red and pink on the horizon. The warm colours tinged his tanned face; the warm breeze lifted the curl of hair that fell onto his forehead. It was hard to read his expression, but to me it seemed sad, regretful.

I rubbed my hand up and down his back and kissed his shoulder, wanting to bring him back to me. After a moment he looked down at me and smiled, pulling me around him. I nestled my head against his white shirt, inhaling his smell as though I needed to steal such an intimacy. Sometimes I felt as if I needed to record as much about him as possible; maybe there was some kind of premonition as to what was about to happen, a warning that soon all I would have would be memories, so I needed to remember *everything*.

'Could you see us living somewhere like this?' he asked in my ear.

I was surprised by the question. 'Maybe when we retire,' I said evasively.

'You wouldn't want to spend every evening out here by the sea, sipping prosecco and eating fish caught just a mile away?'

The thought of being away from London almost panicked me. 'No cinemas? No clubs? No theatres? What happens when you get your late-night bagel cravings, or I get a sudden urge to rent all the Tarantino movies? Do you really want to be stuck watching *Walker, Texas Ranger* every night?'

He shook his head at me. 'But you love travelling, seeing different countries. I didn't think you were so attached to England.'

'It's not necessarily England,' I conceded. 'Although I do like having seasons. I could live in New York, San Francisco, somewhere like that. Any city where it's as easy to get a curry as it is to get a steak.'

'That's your main criteria?' he laughed. 'The ability to procure curry?'

'It's important! If you think I'm eating fresh fish for the rest of my life, you're very much mistaken.'

'So small towns are out of the question.' He was half-smiling, but I could tell he was getting narked.

'For now, at least. I'm sorry, I just need the variety. Maybe when we're older, or when we've had kids, my priorities will change and all I'll care about will be the crime statistics and the quality of the local school.'

'So you'd consider moving somewhere smaller, more private, if we had children?'

I frowned at him. 'Why, are you thinking of getting me knocked up just so we can move out of London? I thought you liked London.'

His blue eyes always looked darker in the night-time. 'I do like London. But I could be anywhere, as long as I was with you.'

I pushed him away and walked along the path. 'Don't try and turn it around like that.'

'Like what?'

'You make it sound as though I wouldn't put up a struggle if I loved you as much as you love me.'

'I didn't mean it like that,' he objected.

'Where the hell did this conversation even come from? One minute we're eating ice cream and admiring the sunset, the next minute we're talking about emigrating and becoming sodding fishermen!'

Charlie burst out laughing. 'I didn't suggest we become fishermen.'

'Well, good, because I've heard it's a very smelly occupation. Don't think you'd get lucky every night if you came home stinking of fish guts.'

He put his arm around me and kissed the top of my head.

We found a cellar bar with a band playing live music, and danced into the early hours of the morning. Walking back to the car through the narrow streets, we passed little shrines built into the walls, small electric lights illuminating icons of the saints. Tea glasses held one or two wild flowers, and often the names of ships appeared under the shrine; prayers for men away at sea.

Walking in heels on the cobbled streets with feet sore from dancing was not fun, and Charlie picked me up in a piggyback and carried me back to the car, heels swinging from my hand by their straps.

The hotel was deserted when we got back – no waiters, no barmen, no Italian delegates playing cards after their company conference. We waved at the sleepy receptionist as we walked past the desk and he stood up.

'Mr Benson?' he said. 'There's a message for you.'

'For me?' Charlie asked. We looked at each other. 'It's probably just Luke,' he said.

Getting a message from home when you're on holiday usually means bad news, so I was apprehensive as I waited for Charlie to read the message, relaxing only as he started to smile.

'It's from the Crestenzas,' he said. 'Some old friends of my parents. They're here on vacation too, and found out from Luke that we were staying here. Do you mind if we go see them tomorrow? I haven't seen them since my parents' funeral.'

'Of course we can,' I said, happy to see him excited, curious about the Crestenzas – since other than Luke, I rarely got an insight into Charlie's previous life in the States – but also very, very tired. 'I'd leave it till the morning to ring them though, babe. Unless they've got really bad jetlag, they're going to be away with the fairies for a good few hours.'

'Good night, Mr and Mrs Benson,' said the receptionist. 'Sleep well.'

Chapter Seven

I woke up at 9 a.m. with aching feet and ears ringing from the loud music the night before. Rolling over, I stretched out an arm and reached for Charlie. Finding his side of the bed empty, I opened my eyes.

The cord from the apartment's telephone was stretched out across the floor to the patio doors. Through the open curtains I could see Charlie out on the terrace, speaking to someone on the phone. Wrapping the sheet around me, I got out of bed and walked over to the patio doors. For a moment, through the thick glass, I thought I could hear him speaking Italian, but when I pulled back the door I only heard English.

'That's great,' he was saying. 'Yeah. Of course. See you then.'

He put the phone down and looked round at me. 'Sorry sweetheart, I was trying not to wake you up.'

I yawned. 'Don't worry, it's late enough. Who were you talking to?'

'The Crestenzas. I hope you're feeling sociable, 'cos we're meeting them for lunch.'

'In town?'

'No, they're a couple of hours' away. I offered to drive there – didn't want to put them out. Is that okay?'

'Yeah, of course. I'd better jump in the shower then.'

Picking out which clothes to wear was strange: in the absence of Charlie's parents, it almost felt as though this was my opportunity to impress Charlie's family. Shorts seemed too informal, and it was too hot for trousers, so I dug out one of my summer dresses and a pair of pretty sandals.

In the car we switched off the air-con and enjoyed the feel of the hot Sicilian wind in our hair. I navigated along a couple of motorways, and then we came off the main roads and went through the countryside, taking dusty roads through green hills. Sunlight winked off the tips of the waves in the distant ocean. We were high up in the Sicilian mountains, the panorama of the island beneath us, hot blue sky above us, brilliant sunshine all around us.

'According to the map, there should be a turn-off in the next half a mile,' I said. A few minutes later, a road sign appeared directing us to the town of San Giordano. Arriving there though, it seemed less of a town than a village. There was a small square, a bar, some chickens, and a stall selling vegetables and fruit. An old woman in black sat on a doorstep and pursed her wrinkled face at us.

'Scorsese should give her a call,' I said. 'She could do with an agent.'

'Straight out of central casting,' Charlie agreed, sounding somewhat preoccupied.

'Where's their pensione meant to be?'

He peered through the car window up at the nearest building that could potentially be a hotel. 'Not sure. They said to meet them in the bar. Looks like there's only one candidate.'

The bar didn't have a hoarding, but the old metal signs for Coke and Peroni tacked to the wall gave away its location. We went inside, our eyes taking a while to adjust to the relative darkness. Two locals were inside, and turned around to gaze at us suspiciously. Both of the men looked first at my face, then up and down my legs, even though both were seventy if they were a day.

'*Buon giorno*,' said Charlie to the man behind the bar, having quickly scanned the place for signs of his friends. '*Due acqua minerali, per favore.*'

One of the old locals snorted in apparent disdain at the choice of beverage. I was tempted to do a Bob Hope and add, '– in a dirty glass,' but I didn't know the right Italian.

We sat near the door and sipped our water. A large dog, a Lurcher, wandered out from behind the bar, sniffed Charlie's shoe, then went off through the door. Five minutes later he sauntered back in, turned around in one spot for a bit, then settled down in a patch of shade under one of the tables. The place was so quiet in between the mumbled scraps of Italian from the old men that we could hear the cicadas grating in the long grasses of the countryside surrounding the village.

I tried making conversation, but Charlie would just answer monosyllabically and look down at his water.

'So how long did they know your parents for?' I asked.

'Years,' Charlie said.

'Were they close?'

'About as close as friends can get.'

'And you haven't heard from them at all since you came over to England?'

'A couple of letters, a couple of calls.'

Then we heard voices outside, and Charlie straightened up. The Lurcher's ears swivelled like satellite dishes. A man's silhouette appeared in the bright doorway.

'Carlito!' I heard the man say, and he moved forwards and enveloped Charlie in a massive bear hug. He kissed him on both cheeks, twice, and then hugged him again.

A woman stepped into the bar behind him, holding a bag in front of her with both hands. When she saw Charlie she smiled, but there were tears in her eyes and I knew then how fond they must both have been of him, and how hard it was to lose him to another country so soon after losing their friends.

Charlie turned to the woman and they too kissed each other on both cheeks and then he gave her a hug. She held her hand to his face and looked from eye to eye, as though searching his face for something.

'It's so good to see you both,' he said, taking her hands and squeezing them. Still holding her hands, he turned round to me, and all three were looking at me.

'This is my wife, Kate,' he said. 'Kate, this is Angelo and Francesca Crestenza.'

Mr Crestenza, a portly man of around seventy with a neat white beard and a jaunty cream hat, threw his hands up as he came towards me.

'Mr Crestenza,' I said, smiling and offering my hand.

He ignored my hand. 'Angelo, please, Angelo,' he said, and held my shoulders as he kissed my cheeks. His wife stepped past Charlie and nodded at me shyly, taking my hands as she too kissed me.

'It is very good to meet you, Kate,' she said.

'You too, Mrs Crestenza.'

She smiled. 'Kate, listen to my husband. None of this "Mr and Mrs Crestenza". Please, call me Francesca. Or I shall be forced to call you Mrs Benson!' She was a very handsome woman, younger than her husband by ten years or so, with cheekbones that were obviously going to keep her attractive well into old age. Yet there was a weariness to her that made her seem older than her years, as did the veins of grey in her flint-coloured hair.

'Are you hungry, Kate?' asked Angelo Crestenza.

'Starving,' I said, grinning at him.

'Can your appetite cope with a short walk?'

'I should think so.'

Charlie paid for the mineral waters, and we stepped out into the warm sunshine.

There were two men with the Crestenzas that Angelo introduced as nephews of his cousin, who lived in San Giordano. Neither of them spoke any English, and they walked in front of us chatting in Italian.

Angelo's cousin had a farmhouse on the crest of the hill overlooking the village. We walked through a field of wildflowers, Francesca Crestenza and I falling behind Charlie and Angelo. Charlie strode through the long grass, Angelo puffing next to him, using his cane.

'This is the most exercise he's had in years,' Francesca said, smiling.

'Do you come to Sicily often?' I asked her.

'No. Neither of us likes to fly. We go sailing, sometimes, or visit the Caribbean.'

'Is your family from Sicily too?'

She shook her head. 'Bologna. Not that I know Bologna well either – I was born and raised in America.'

'How did you and Angelo meet?'

I saw her glancing at me sideways, then her gaze returned to where she was stepping. She was wearing heels, and was finding the terrain tough going. 'Our families have been friends for many years.' She looked at me properly then, her brown eyes lit up by the sunlight. 'And you and Charlie – we've all heard how you two met.' She was laughing. 'I've heard of whirlwind romances, but that takes the prize.'

I shrugged. 'It worked though. We're still here.'

'And you still love him?'

'More than ever.'

She nodded, taking my arm to help balance herself as we came to the edge of an olive grove. I could see the farmhouse through the spindly trees. 'Can I ask – what made you choose him?'

'Charlie? I just knew he was the one.'

I didn't tell her that I hadn't realized half of me was missing until I found him.

'But what was it about him that appealed to you?'

On American TV shows it always seemed that women were very interested in dating professional men – lawyers, bankers, architects. Was this what she was trying to find out? Was Charlie's main appeal to me his status? I was tempted to tell her that one of the things that appealed to me was Charlie's butt, and another was the curve of his biceps, but I knew that Charlie would want me to play nicely. So I was honest.

'Truthfully, I don't think love works that way,' I said. 'If you ask a person why they love someone, they'll reel off a list of their qualities – but I don't think you fall in love because of those qualities.'

'No?' She raised her eyebrows.

'No. You fall in love with someone *despite* their qualities. If Charlie stopped being generous, I'd still love him. If he stopped making me laugh, I'd still love him. I mean, I love those things about him, but only because they're his. Does that make sense?'

She chuckled. 'No, not really. By that token, you would love someone's bad points as much as you loved their good ones.'

I beamed. 'Exactly.'

'And what are Charlie's bad points,' she went on, 'that you love so much?'

I looked ahead of us, at my husband walking in his white shirt and blue jeans through the shade of the olive trees.

'He loses his temper very easily, though never with me. He has no patience. He never takes no for an answer.' Almost as if he could hear me, Charlie turned around and smiled at me.

His eyes seemed to glow blue in the soft shadows of the leaves. I smiled back, and said under my breath, 'And he always cheats at Scrabble.'

We ate fresh fish and then huge bowls of pasta in tomato and olive sauce, with torn loaves of crusty white bread on the side. Angelo's cousin Cesare sat at the head of the large wooden table, pouring the red wine and regaling us with village gossip and stories of the olive oil business. Charlie sat next to me, and between courses would affectionately squeeze my knee under the table.

I was too full for pudding, but drank coffee and soaked up stories of what Charlie was like as a child. Francesca was especially good at remembering all the various misdeeds and embarrassing incidents, to the extent that Charlie, hiding his head in his hands, pleaded with her to stop.

Angelo asked me about meeting Charlie, and though they had obviously heard the story before, they all listened as I told them about the broken lift and the bungee jump.

'I don't know how you can stand those heights,' Angelo said, wafting his face with the brim of his hat.

'I suppose it wouldn't be so much fun if it wasn't scary.'

'And now Charlie tells me the two of you are into scary sports,' he said.

'Extreme sports,' Charlie corrected him.

'Oh, I'm sorry, *extreme* sports,' Angelo said sarcastically. 'Do you swim with sharks?'

Charlie chuckled. 'Not Great Whites, no. We swam with some Tiger Sharks though, when we were scuba diving last year.'

Charlie would probably quite happily swim with Great Whites, but I'd seen *Jaws* and didn't want my head to end up bobbing around in some bloke's sunken boat.

'You don't do that thing in the ground, do you?' asked Cesare.

We looked at him blankly.

'You know, the worm thing. In the rocks.'

'You mean potholing?' asked Charlie. I shuddered involuntarily, and he rubbed my arm. 'Yeah, we tried it once, but Kate didn't enjoy it. Squeezing through little tunnels underground turned out to be more of an ordeal than a thrill.'

Cesare seemed disappointed in me.

'Come on, who needs to go potholing when you can go skydiving, or rock climbing?' I told him. 'In the autumn, we're going white-water rafting for the first time.'

'So why aren't you doing anything scary this vacation?' asked Angelo, lighting up a cigar.

I looked at Charlie. 'I don't know. Charlie's choice. We take it in turns to choose what we do for our breaks.'

Charlie blew out his lips. 'Just fancied some R'n'R, I guess. Though I'm sure we can find some really old elevators to get stuck in if you like, sweetheart.'

After lunch – which, being in Sicily, only took around three hours – we sat in the back garden under the trees. Cesare had two small boys, and when they got home from school they changed into shorts and kicked around a football in the olive grove, two trees acting as goalposts. They got their dad to play, which meant they were down a team member. The older one came over and launched a stream of Italian at Charlie, who looked at me with an expression of self-sacrifice.

'Go get 'em, Pele,' I told him, sending him off with a kiss.

Charlie's football skills were, it has to be said, rubbish. He was an athletic guy, strong, a fast runner, but he aimed at the dead centre of the goal and managed to land the ball in Cesare's stomach. Cesare sank, winded, to the dusty ground, and I had to take his place. I wasn't much good either, at least not compared to two football-obsessed kids. Compared to Charlie, however, I was World Cup material.

I feinted right and went left, skimming the ball around him and dribbling towards the olive-tree goalposts of our opposition. The smaller kid bounced from foot to foot, trying to anticipate where I'd aim. Then I felt an arm around my waist and was suddenly whisked in the air. Charlie whacked the ball away with his foot and set me down again, running off in the other direction.

'Foul!' I yelled. 'Referee!'

Angelo and Francesca were laughing as I ran indignantly after my husband, who had my teammate in a headlock and was kicking the ball past him into the goal.

'Oh my God, you are such a cheat!' I protested. Cesare's other son came pelting through the trees, high-fiving Charlie and sliding to his knees triumphantly in front of an invisible yet apparently deliriously applauding crowd. 'Don't encourage him, Benito.'

Cesare had got up from his lawn chair and was ambling over. 'Referee,' I said, 'those were two blatant fouls. This man should be red-carded.'

Cesare held his hand up. 'Charlie, I'm giving you a warning. No more fouls or you're out.'

A bit aggrieved that Charlie was still in the game, I redoubled my efforts and we went three-one up. Charlie tried for a penalty by diving in the box, but since there was no demarcation I successfully argued that even if he wasn't a diver, he was at least three feet from the penalty box. He tried to get me back by tickling me during a tricky bit of footwork, but I nutmegged the ball between his legs and went on to score goal number four.

The shadows lengthened and dusk came. When we couldn't

see the ball any more, the game packed up and the others went inside. I went to get my cardigan from the tree on which it was hanging.

The skinny limbs of the olive trees were silhouetted against the mauve-tinged sky. I stood for a moment in the grove, inhaling an air that smelt of a mixture of salt, tree bark, and of the food from our meal earlier. The earth was soft and powdery under my bare feet. I spread my toes, digging them into the soil.

Charlie came to find me, his white shirt glowing in the dimness. He was shoeless too. He pressed me against the tree, the bark rough on my bare shoulders, and kissed me with both his hands in my hair. I ran my hands under his shirt, felt the dry warmth of his skin run down through me and out into the earth from my bare soles. The silver-green leaves of the olive tree whispered over our heads.

When we left, there were lots of big hugs, held for too long. Francesca, on the verge of tears again, cupped my face with her hand, her wedding ring cool on my cheek.

'Charlie's parents would have liked you very much,' she told me.

I felt tears prick my own eyes. 'Really?' I said. 'That means a lot to me.'

She nodded, and kissed me abruptly on both cheeks. We drove back to the hotel, Charlie's eyes fixed on the road ahead.

Chapter Eight

A little winding trail meandered through the hotel complex to
the beach, bordered with bright pink flowers and broken up
with stone steps to other destinations. A gecko zipped across
our path and disappeared into a cluster of trees. Charlie was
holding my hand and I squeezed his, a little skip of happiness
in my step.

The path took us through a lemon grove, soil flattening
under the soles of our flip-flops, the leaves of the trees dark
green and waxy, the branches laden with heavy, glowing
yellow fruit.

On the other side of the grove, a gateway proclaiming *Hotel
Guests Only* opened out onto the narrow beach, enclosed on
both sides by spiky rock. The sand was fine and white, and the
sea stretched out under a sky only slightly marred by drifts of
cloud.

A lifeguard in a pair of red shorts and some trendy sunglasses grinned at us. 'You want sunbeds?' he asked in English.
People who have been in the tourist trade a while can always
tell your nationality at a glance, just as Londoners can recognize Italians by their backpacks and Germans by their
spectacles and interesting denim choices.

'That's okay, we'll find them,' said Charlie, never happy at
getting other people to do things for him that he was perfectly
capable of doing for himself.

A dog was tied up by the stack of sunbeds, his long fur covered in grains of sand. He was already panting in the morning heat.

'Hello, fella,' said Charlie, making a beeline straight for him.

'Watch out for him,' said the lifeguard dismissively. 'He's a little crazy.'

Charlie rarely listened when people told him what to do. He crouched down near the dog and stretched out his hand to it.

'Careful, Charlie,' I said. My parents had owned one or two crazy dogs in their time, and they could look adorable even as they were making plans to gnaw your leg off.

'You're not crazy, are you, dog?' he said in a low voice. The dog looked up at him with brown doggy eyes and whined a bit. He sniffed Charlie's hand and seemed happy with what he smelt. Soon Charlie had his hands buried in the dog's fur, giving him a damn good pet. The dog woofed, and lay on the ground, rubbing its back into the sand.

'His water bowl's empty,' Charlie told the lifeguard. The man looked over at the dry, stainless-steel bowl and looked away again.

'Can't leave the beach till the other lifeguard comes,' he said curtly.

Charlie caught my eye and gestured at our bag. I took out our two-litre bottle of mineral water and handed it to my husband. He filled the bowl, and the dog immediately slurped it all up. Charlie filled it again, and again the dog drank it all. The third time, the dog just took some experimental licks and then sat down on his haunches. He woofed at Charlie, who rubbed him behind the ears and gave the bottle back to me.

'Save the rest for him,' he said. 'We can always get a drink from the bar down the beach.' He then pulled two sunbeds off of the stack and took them down the beach, glaring at the life-guard as we passed him.

Other than that, our morning was uneventful. Charlie wasn't in a chatty mood, and after a couple of aborted attempts to get him to tell me what was bothering him, I left him to his reflections. I got halfway through my novel; Charlie read one chapter of his, got restless and went for a swim.

After ten minutes I propped myself up on my elbow and scanned the water for him. He was about fifteen metres out to sea, throwing himself up on the waves. I loved his joy at being in the ocean, his pleasure in the elemental.

He came back, read another chapter, took his snorkel and went back into the sea. Once again I watched him, enjoying the seawater streaming down the tanned muscles of his back as he broke the water's surface and stood up. The Sicilian sunlight was glinting off of his wet skin.

'You want to get some lunch?' he called to me.

We went to one of the little ristorantes on the harbour with outdoor tables. It was still early, and most of the other patrons were tourists, the Sicilians themselves preferring to have a late lunch. As it was a Sunday the main beach was chocka with people, all the locals enjoying the weekend sun alongside the holidaymakers.

I picked out the pizza I wanted straightaway, but Charlie spent ages perusing the menu. I people-watched while he decided between dishes, especially entertained by the English guy I could hear at the table behind us, who was asking his wife if she thought the restaurant did stuffed-crust pizzas.

A man in a short-sleeved shirt and baseball cap came in and sat at the table behind Charlie. The waiter brought him a menu and he ordered a bottle of San Pellegrino to drink. Every so often he scribbled on his newspaper, presumably doing a crossword puzzle. He didn't take off his sunglasses. I wondered if he was here on his own, or whether he'd left his wife at the hotel while he did some sightseeing.

'That guy's a Yank too,' I told Charlie, *sotto voce*. 'I heard his accent when he ordered the water.'

Charlie half-glanced over his shoulder. 'Hey,' he said brightly. 'Maybe we know each other! America's only a small country, after all.'

I pulled a face at him and then turned it into a smile for the waiter who had appeared unexpectedly at my elbow. I asked for a *quattro formaggi* pizza, and Charlie went for a *tagliatelle alla napoletana*.

'Adventurous,' I said, eyebrows raised, looking out to sea.

'You're the one that always orders four-cheese pizza,' he countered.

We sat in silence for at least quarter of an hour, sipping our red wine.

'Are you going to tell me what's up?' I asked finally.

He shrugged. 'Just thinking about my parents.'

'Did seeing Angelo and Francesca yesterday stir things up?'

Charlie laughed. Well, it was a sort of laugh. We could talk about pretty much anything, but when it came to his parents the drawbridge went up, and I was left on the other side of the moat, calling out 'Hello? Charlie?' at the castle walls.

'People fade away, don't they?' he said. 'When they die. You try to remember what they look like, what they sound like, but gradually the details disappear. You can't hear them any more. You can look at photos all you want, but you close your eyes and still all your imagination can conjure up is just a blank-faced person.' He looked up at me. 'And then you see something that refreshes everything. It's like the colour comes back, and the memories have their own life again.'

I reached out and took Charlie's hands, just as the waiter

repeated his David Copperfield routine, appearing apparently out of nowhere. His timing sucked, but at least he was bringing food. We went through the whole, 'Black pepper? Parmesan?' thing, and then were on our own again.

'It's good though, isn't it?' I resumed. 'That it gets – you know – freshened up?'

'I don't know,' he said. 'It's sorta painful.'

At the next table, the American sneezed three times as the waiter ground pepper onto his food, making a sound like laser beams shooting out of his nose. If my conversation with Charlie hadn't been so serious, I would have found it funny. The American held a tissue to his nose and got up to visit the gents, glancing at us from behind his sunglasses as he passed by.

'You think it's better to let them fade away?' I asked Charlie.

'Maybe it is. It's not like it's supposed to remain raw for ever.'

'But it's not as if you can cut yourself off from things that might remind you of them.'

'I know. I'm not saying that. It was great seeing, y'know, their friends yesterday. Almost like the old times. To be honest, I should make more of an effort.'

'We can go and see them again if you like,' I suggested. 'I'm sure they'd love to see as much of you as they can before they go home.'

Charlie speared a few strands of his pasta. 'Unfortunately they're flying home today.' He looked at his watch. 'In fact, their plane should have left already.' He put down his fork and raised his wine glass to the sky. 'Safe journey, guys.'

He changed the subject after that, and we talked about Luke – which girl he was currently dating, and whether Miss X had ever found out about Mrs Y; about Charlie's job – there was a promotion on the cards if he wanted to take on more responsibility; about my colleague at the software company who was dating a much younger man – he was twenty-three and she was forty – old enough to be his mother; and about whether Martin Scorsese or Francis Ford Coppola would win in a wrestling match – Charlie backed Coppola, but I thought Scorsese had a canny wiriness that might put him at an advantage.

We ordered chocolate ice cream and cassata for pudding. The American sat behind Charlie put down his pen and got to his feet again.

'Looks like someone has a urinary tract infection,' I observed with a wink at Charlie.

'Pardon me?' he said, perturbed, spoon half-raised to his mouth.

'That's the second time in half an hour that guy's gone to the loo,' I said, nodding my head at the American guy as he disappeared inside.

'It's a wonder to me that you never joined the police force,' Charlie told me. 'Seriously. You were designed for stakeouts.'

'Mmm,' I agreed. 'They tend to have doughnuts and coffee, don't they?'

We left payment and a tip on the table and headed out of the restaurant. As we walked past Cystitis Guy's table, I glanced down at his newspaper. He hadn't been doing a crossword after all, but making notes. The words he'd written in the margin made me frown, but at the time they didn't mean much to me.

It was over a year before I worked out just exactly what those words meant.

Chapter Nine

Charlie and I went back to our beach, buying another two-litre bottle of mineral water on the way for Charlie's new friend, Beach-Dog. Our prime position sunbeds were still, surprisingly, free, and we dumped our stuff and stripped down to our swimming costumes. Charlie went to give the dog his water and I pulled my novel out of my bag.

A few pages in, Charlie came back and picked up his snorkel. 'I'm going for a swim,' he said.

'Okay, sweetheart,' I told him, engrossed in the book.

'I think there's a beach over in that direction that's meant to have some caves,' he said. 'I was thinking I'd go take a look.'

'If you find any treasure, let me know.'

He kissed me as he left. Not properly, just a 'see you later' peck really, half on my lips and half on my cheek. I didn't watch him go. I read that stupid book. It was the last time I ever saw him, and I paid more attention to my book than to him.

I read a couple more chapters, my eyelids slowly growing heavier and heavier. Drinking a glass of wine at lunchtime is always lethal for me – I feel a strong urge to doze shortly afterwards. The sun wasn't helping either. I chucked the book down on the sand, rolled over onto my stomach and closed my eyes.

When I opened them again, the sky had clouded over and it was noticeably chillier. I rubbed my eyes and turned on my side towards Charlie's sunbed. It was empty. I sat up, looking up and down the beach and at the café behind us. I couldn't see him. Perhaps he was still swimming? I squinted at the people in the sea, but he wasn't one of them.

I pulled my watch out of my bag and was surprised when I saw I'd been asleep for nearly two hours. Surely Charlie couldn't have been gone that long? He'd probably come back, seen that I was sleeping, resisted the urge to find a pen and draw a moustache on my face, and gone for a walkabout round the hotel complex on a search for the mini-golf area. In which case, he'd be back soon enough, even if just to make sure I didn't go lobster-red in the sun.

I picked up my book and tried to get back into it, but found it hard to stop checking my watch every few minutes. Growing more and more annoyed with Charlie for buggering off and leaving me on my own for so long, I beat out a tense rhythm on the end of the sunbed with my foot.

After another twenty minutes I dumped the book, pages splayed, on the taut indigo material of the sunbed and pulled my T-shirt and shorts on over my bikini. The lifeguard smiled as I approached – a smile that faltered when I was unable to smile back.

'Have you seen my husband?' I asked him, hoping he recognized me.

'No,' he said. 'Is he on the beach?'

'I don't know, that's why I'm asking if you've seen him. Did he pass by here? Did you see him go up to the hotel?'

He shrugged. 'I haven't seen him, but I don't always sit here, you know? I have to go up and down the beach. He could have gone to the hotel when I was – how you say it – bat-rolling?'

Normally that would have made me laugh. 'Patrolling,' I
said. 'Look, if you see him, could you tell him I've gone to
look for him and to stay put, to stay where he is. I don't want
him trying to find me when I'm trying to find him.'

'Okay.'

'You understand?'

'Yes, I speak English. I see him, I tell him to stay here.'

I went back to the sunbed and stuck everything in my bag,
including Charlie's towel. God forbid that someone might nick
our stuff just because I was in too much of a flap to bother to
take it with me. For a moment I wondered what would
happen if Charlie came back, saw our stuff was gone, and
missed the lifeguard. Surely he'd assume I'd gone back to the
room?

Hefting my bag over my shoulder, I went back to the guard.
'Forget what I said earlier. If you see my husband – his name's
Charlie, by the way, my name's Kate – can you tell him I said
to go back to the room?' Our apartment had a table and
chairs outside it on the patio, so he'd have somewhere to sit
and wait for me if he got back before me. I had the key, so he
wouldn't be able to get inside the actual apartment without
me.

Did I have the key? I checked in the bag, thinking if I
couldn't find the key that would probably mean Charlie had
got it and was in the room.

But the key was still in the bag.

Before leaving the beach I scanned it one last time. There
were only a few people still in the water, and they were
together, a group. I sighed sharply, turned on my heel, and
went to look for Charlie in the hotel complex.

The path back up to the hotel reception was steep. Some of
the more elderly guests overtook me in their little silver golf
buggies as I trudged up the hill. I went to the reception first.

'I'm looking for my husband,' I explained. 'He went swimming and hasn't come back yet. I don't suppose he left a message?'

The receptionist looked blank. 'I'm afraid not, madam. Have you tried the pool area? Or maybe he's in our shop?'

'Thanks,' I said, pushing my bag strap up more securely on my shoulder. 'I'll try there.'

The pool area was practically empty; just a skinny Italian woman and her two kids. I went round the corner to the two-aisle shop, but that too was quiet. Looking for the signs to the sports area, I bumped into Sofia, the other receptionist that we'd been drinking with a couple of nights before.

'Are you okay?' she said, when she saw my expression. Her concerned hand on my arm made me want to cry.

'It's Charlie,' I said. 'I can't find him.'

'Where did you last see him?' she asked.

'On the beach, a couple of hours ago. He went swimming, and I fell asleep. Surely he should have been back by now?'

'I'm sure he's fine,' Sofia said, although she looked worried. 'He probably just didn't want to wake you up. Have you tried your apartment?'

'No. I've got the key, so he can't have gone back to the room.'

'It's worth looking though, no?'

I nodded. 'I was going to try the mini-golf place,' I told her. 'He said it sounded like fun.'

She pulled a face. 'But he wouldn't play on his own, would he? Look, you try the room, I'll try the golf. If he's not there, I'll come and find you. If he is, I'll tell him off for you.'

'Okay, thank you,' I said gratefully. 'We're in 217.'

Walking back to the apartment, my fingers were tightly crossed. 'Please be there, please be there, please be there,' I chanted under my breath with each step. I rounded the corner, visualizing him sitting in one of the patio chairs, willing it to be real. When he wasn't there, I hurried up the steps and turned the key in the lock, bursting into the room.

No Charlie in the living room. No Charlie in the bedroom. The bathroom door was shut. I couldn't hear the fan that started up when the light was on, but still I prayed as I opened the door. No Charlie in the bathroom either.

I dumped the stuff from the beach on the floor and clenched my fists.

'Charlie, where the fuck are you?' I hissed to myself. Without much hope, I checked for a note, but the room had obviously been undisturbed since the maid had cleaned it in our absence.

I went back out to the patio and stood on tiptoes, looking out for Sofia. I wanted to go out to meet her, but didn't know what route she might take from the mini-golf to our apartment. Finally I saw her in her uniform, walking head down along the path. She's going to say, "He'll be down shortly, he's just finishing his round,' I thought. She'll tell me he's sorry, he didn't mean to worry me. But the girl looked up as she got closer, saw me waiting, and shook her head.

My fingernails were digging into the palms of my hands as she reached the patio. 'He's not there,' she told me. 'Come on, let's go to the beach and speak to the lifeguard.'

Not trusting myself to say anything, I let her lock up the apartment and lead me back down to the beach.

The lifeguard looked nervous when he saw us approaching. He and Sofia talked quickly, in Italian, their voices low.

'Sofia,' I said, too quietly for her to hear me. I reached out and tugged on the sleeves of her blue polyester jacket. 'Sofia.

He said he'd heard there was a beach nearby with some caves. That's where he went.'

She nodded, and turned back to the lifeguard. He pointed over in the direction further up the coastline, and repeated something to me in Italian. I could only shrug. I hadn't seen which direction Charlie had gone in.

The lifeguard picked up his two-way radio and spoke to someone.

'It's okay,' Sofia told me. 'They're sending a boat over to the beach where we think Charlie went. Is he good at swimming?'

I nodded.

'Well it takes about thirty minutes to swim there from here. He probably swam over, explored, got tired, and now he wants to rest before he swims back.'

She saw I was trying not to cry, and took me over to sit on one of the empty sunbeds. We watched the sea. I scanned every wave, looking for Charlie. The lifeguard's boat zipped past on its way to the beach with the caves. I sent a silent prayer along with it.

Sitting there, waiting for the boat to return, my belly sick with barely restrained panic, I thought about how quickly we can forget how scared we were. Someone sees your lost dog poster and calls; your child turns up in the playpit, distracted away by some other kids; your lover comes back out of the ocean. There's a smile on his face, a snorkel mask in his hand. 'Did I scare you?' he says, and then everything's okay again, and you forget that you were once teetering on the thin line between your normal life and awful, unthinkable tragedy.

When the boat came back without him, my mind seemed to go numb. I could only act on auto-pilot, my body going through the motions without anything to guide it.

The lifeguards called the coastguards. When the chief

coastguard arrived, the sky had completely clouded over and most of the other sunbathers had left the beach. Those who stayed knew something was wrong, and stared at me. I looked back at them with hollow eyes, and they glanced downwards and away.

Sofia introduced me to the chief coastguard.

'I'm Kate Grey,' I told him, and he shook my hand. 'My husband is called Charlie. Charlie Benson.' Sofia translated for me – the chief didn't seem to speak much English – and I repeated the little I knew: Charlie was a good swimmer; he'd been gone over three hours now; he'd told me he was going to the beach with the caves. The chief asked me what Charlie looked like.

'Six feet tall,' I told him. 'Dark hair, blue eyes. He was wearing blue trunks.'

The coastguard asked something else. 'Does he have any distinguishing features?' Sofia translated. I frowned, blinked, pointed to my left shoulder.

'He has a tattoo, on the top of his arm. A black sun, with rays coming off it.'

The chief thanked me, and told me, via Sofia, to go back to the apartment and wait there. He'd let me know if there was any news.

'I don't want to leave,' I told Sofia.

'Come on,' she said, steering me gently away from the sea. The sun appeared then, dipping out from underneath a raincloud. The slate-coloured sky was suddenly lit up, the clouds reflecting back the golden light like burnished steel. The dark grey glowed, like a sunny day in a world in which the sky wasn't even meant to be blue.

As we walked through the lemon grove, fresh with the smell of the smooth yellow citrus, I wondered how knowing about Charlie's tattoo could help the coastguard to find him, and,

suddenly realizing that the question was more about identi-
fying a body than locating a lost swimmer, my stomach
clenched. I clutched at the nearest lemon tree, and threw up
violently.

I spent two hours pacing, frantic, in the apartment. Sofia sat
on the sofa, leaning forward, elbows on her knees, and
watched me.

'I'm sorry,' I said eventually, coming to an abrupt standstill
in front of her. 'I'm very grateful for all your help, but if you
don't stop looking at me, I'm going to scream.'

She stood up and went into the kitchenette area. 'I'll get you
a glass of water,' she said.

'I don't need water,' I told her, trying not to raise my voice.
'Can I just be by myself for now? *Please*.'

'What if the coastguard needs to speak to you?' she said,
reasonably enough.

'Then I'll call up to reception.'

Sofia set the empty glass back down on the kitchen counter.
As she walked past me on her way out, she paused and kissed
me on the cheek. She closed the door behind her.

I waited till she was far down the path, then let out this
short, controlled yell of fear and frustration, my hands tensed
into little balled fists. I wanted to release my panic, to smash
up the apartment, but knew that it wouldn't help. Nothing
would help but getting Charlie back.

I sat down on the floor, leaning against the side of the bed,
and called Luke on my mobile.

'It's Kate,' I said, and that was the first time I cried.
'Charlie's missing. I don't know what to do.'

It got dark. Sofia came with the coastguard to tell me that they
were going to resume the search in the morning.

'What if he's out there?' I said. 'You can't just leave him.'

'It's impossible to find someone in the dark,' Sofia translated for me.

'No, they can't! What if he's only just holding on? What if he drowns during the night?'

She rubbed my arm. 'This way his men will be fresh when they look again in the morning. Don't worry, it will be light again very early.'

The chief left and Sofia tried to persuade me to eat something. I told her I'd cook some pasta, and when she went away I pulled on a jumper and walked down to the beach in the darkness. The gate was locked, so I climbed over it. The sand was silver in the moonlight, and apart from a few sparkles where the crest of the waves caught the light, you could hardly tell the sea from the sky, both were so black.

I huddled under a tree and waited. I didn't feel hungry, or sleepy. I felt frozen in that time, as though all that existed was the sand, the water and the air, and the waiting. Time stretched out and it was as if my whole life was suspended in that moment.

When dawn came it was a cracked egg of yolk-yellow in the grey edge of the sky. I rose to my feet, stiff with not moving all night, and walked in the half-light back through the lemon grove.

As I reached the path I looked over at the apartment, a few hundred yards away, and saw a light on through the curtains.

I sprinted along the path, hope putting wings on my feet, and took the stairs to the apartment door three at a time. My hands were shaking as I turned the key in the lock and opened the door.

'Katie,' said Luke, getting up from the sofa. 'I got in two hours ago. Where have you been? Is there any news?'

Without even thinking about what I was doing, I slapped

him across the face with all my strength. He just stood there, looking shocked, and then grabbed my wrists. Rigid with anger that he wasn't Charlie, I only let him restrain me for a minute, then shook him off.

'What happened?' he asked.

'Charlie went swimming yesterday, after lunch, and he didn't come back.' I snatched up Luke's jacket and hunted through the pockets for his pack of Marlboros. There was a lighter in with the cigarettes, and I lit one. 'The coastguard searched for him until it got dark, then the fuckers stopped. They told me they'd start again when it got light, but I'm not sure I trust them. How do I know they're not enjoying a bloody lie-in?'

'Is anyone from the hotel helping you out?' asked Luke.

'A girl called Sofia. She speaks English.'

'I suspect the manager will be involved by today,' said Luke. 'We can use him to exert pressure on people if we have to.' He used the apartment phone and dialled reception, speaking rapid Italian to whoever answered. Whatever he said, within the hour we had the regional manager of the hotel chain in the apartment, shaking my hand and telling me he was doing everything he could. He hadn't shaved, and obviously who-ever had called him had got him out of bed.

The chief coastguard arrived, the manager yelled at him in Italian, he yelled back, then walked off jabbing his cap in the air. Luke followed after him, asking him what we could do. But there was nothing we could do; we didn't have a boat, and they wouldn't let us on one of their boats. So we waited and chainsmoked in the apartment and on the patio, on the path as we walked in circles around the complex, and at reception – ignoring the No Smoking signs – as we waited to speak to the manager or Sofia or the chief.

*

The search was called off after seventy-two hours. Sofia wouldn't translate exactly what the chief told her, but I could tell from his gestures and the tone of his voice that he'd said it was pointless to keep looking. The next morning – my third morning of waking up without Charlie – I went into the bathroom and stared flatly at my blank reflection, my void eyes. I brushed my teeth, rinsed off my toothbrush and slid it back into the cup next to Charlie's. The next part of my morning routine was taking my contraceptive pill. I popped it out of its blister pack and placed the little white pill in my mouth. Why am I still doing this? I thought. Who am I kidding? Don't I know by now that I'm not going to need this protection? I still swallowed it; not doing so would have meant giving up.

Although the coastguard had stopped looking for Charlie, I couldn't leave. The room was only paid for until the end of the next week, but I was going to stay until he came back to me. Luke didn't try to convince me to return to London; he didn't want to go either.

I ate very little during those days of waiting. The only things I could stomach were raw things like apples and tomatoes, nothing like bread or pasta that would just sit on my tongue feeling dry and stale and dead. I could drink though, and on the seventh night of waiting, Luke and I bought two bottles of Jack Daniel's from the overpriced hotel shop and took them down to the beach with us. We climbed over the gate and perched on some black rocks on the edge of the sand.

'This is a very nice place,' said Luke in his Southern drawl. 'Very pretty.'

'Yeah, a real paradise,' I said bitterly, taking a deep swig of the whiskey. We were sat side by side, his elbow brushing my knee as he raised his JD bottle to his lips.

'You explore the island much?'

'Luke, you're talking as though nothing's happened, like at any moment he's going to come back.'

'How do you *wanna* play it?' he said. 'Let's not go there unless we have to. For now, we're just sitting here shooting the breeze, and you're telling me what my two pals have been up to in sunny Sicily while I've been working my ass off back home in the big smoke.'

I played along. 'We chilled out, mainly. There were some family friends of Charlie's in town, so we met up with them for the day.'

'Oh yeah?' said Luke. 'Anyone I know?'

'Dunno. Angelo and Francesca Crestenza?' He pulled a face and shook his head. 'I feel bad. I should let them know Charlie's in trouble, but I don't have their contact details, and their friend who lives near here doesn't seem to be answering his phone. Maybe tomorrow we should head out there in person.'

'What would you tell them?' Luke pointed out. 'No need to worry them when they can't do anything.' He took another swig of JD, looking out to sea. 'You meet anyone else? Bump into any other Yanks?'

I didn't even think about the guy in the restaurant. 'Nope.'

'Charlie fall out with anyone? Get into any arguments?'

'Only the lifeguard, when he was letting his dog go without water.'

Luke chuckled. 'Sounds like Charlie.'

'It was nothing that would cause the guy to go out after him though. Not unless he's a complete psychopath.' I was already a good third of the way through the Jack Daniel's, and was feeling distinctly drunk. 'Why are you asking this anyway? Who would murder Charlie?'

Luke pushed a finger over my lips. 'Don't say that word, Katie. Remember, we're not going there unless we have to.'

There were sudden tears in my eyes. 'I don't feel him any more, Luke. I think he's gone.'

He turned away. 'Don't say that,' but he was welling up too. 'Keep it together,' he told me.

'He wouldn't just leave. If he could come back, he would.'

Luke's shoulders hitched, and he pulled me close so I couldn't see him cry.

I only let him hold me for a minute, then drew away. I was so tense with waiting that I couldn't stand feeling restricted, even by someone trying to comfort me.

'Let's go back to the apartment,' I said, as Luke wiped his eyes with his shirt-sleeve. 'The smell of the sea is making me feel sick.'

He laughed shakily. 'You can blame it on the sea, Kate, but you never could hold your liquor.'

We gingerly climbed down from the rough-surfaced rocks which scraped at our skin. Grains of sand crept into my trainers with every step along the beach. On the way back up the path to the apartment, we saw some other hotel guests in the distance, laughing loudly and having fun. When they spotted us, recognized us, it was as if God had pressed mute on His remote control. We passed them in silence, and they wouldn't make eye-contact.

'*Buona notte!*' Luke said pointedly to their backs.

'Fuck 'em,' I grunted, keeping walking. That was when the apartment patio came into view, and I noticed a figure sitting on one of the chairs, in semi-darkness. Even from that distance I could tell it was Sofia, and something about the way she was holding herself made me start to shake. I stopped walking so abruptly it was like I'd bounced off some invisible wall between me and her. My feet seemed to sink into the tarmac of the path.

Sofia saw us and stood up. She came down the steps and walked towards me.

'No,' I said under my breath. 'No, no, no, no.' Light from the lamps that bordered the path revealed a silver line on each of her cheeks: two tracks made by tears. I backed away from her, but she clutched at my hands.

'I'm so sorry, Kate,' she said. 'They think they have found his body.'

Chapter Ten

'It's not him,' I kept telling Luke. 'Trust me, they've found someone else. Charlie's a strong swimmer; it can't be him.' Luke did not reply, but I saw the despair on his face, and the edge of his jaw working.

All Sofia had been able to tell us was that a man's body had washed up on the main beach, the one in town. A couple taking a midnight stroll along the shore had found it. At some point a doctor, someone hired by the hotel, turned up and gave me a sedative. The regional manager was in the room, but I don't remember much of what he said. It was an hour or two before the police arrived, and they seemed somehow surprised that I'd already heard. 'Was there a tattoo on the body?' I kept asking them, but they were just uniformed officers who didn't really know anything, and could only shrug.

The sun had been up for at least an hour by the time some other, different officers, still in pale blue uniforms, came to drive us to the station. We hung around in the reception area while they made casual chit-chat in Italian with the police guy on the front desk. Even under sedation, I found it hard not to start kicking and screaming until someone just fucking *did* something.

Only when the inner door opened and a plainclothes officer came out did I realize the uniforms were waiting for him to take custody of us. They nodded goodbye to Luke and me, calling out, '*Ciao*,' to the desk officer as they left the station.

The plainclothes officer was around fifty, with crewcut white hair and nut-brown eyes. There were deep smile lines around his mouth and creases at his eyes. Like nearly all Sicilians, he was very tanned, especially in constrast to the pale lavender cotton of the shirt he was wearing.

'Mrs Benson?' he said, and I didn't bother to explain I used my maiden name. 'And Mr . . .?'

'Broussard,' said Luke. He didn't give his first name.

'My name is Eduardo Graziani. I am a detective here. Would you like to come through?'

He took us down a corridor, up a flight of steps, and down another corridor. The police station was practically empty. We ended up in a room with three office desks. On one desk a computer was switched on, a screensaver drifting across the screen. Graziani sat at this desk, indicating that we should sit down on two other castor-wheeled office chairs opposite him.

'As you know, the body of a man was found on the beach last night,' he said. 'You have been brought here so we can ask you to identify the body.'

'It's not him,' I said, arms wrapped around myself.

'I'm afraid it's very likely that it *is* him,' said Graziani, not unkindly. 'Your husband is the only man reported missing at sea over the last few weeks. And the body does match his description.'

I whispered something.

'Pardon me?' said Graziani, leaning towards me to hear better.

Very quietly, I repeated: 'Is there a tattoo on the body?'

He gazed at me gravely. 'I'm afraid so. A tattoo of a black sun, which I believe matches up to what you told our coast-guard.'

I covered my mouth with my hands.

'Mrs Benson? Are you all right? Would you like a glass of water?'

I shook my head. 'I just want to see the body,' I said, the words muffled by my fingers and palms.

'The Coroner is conducting the autopsy at the moment, but as soon as she is finished—'

'An autopsy?' I closed my eyes. Of course they would be doing an autopsy. Even though I hadn't yet accepted that Charlie and the dead body were one and the same, the idea of someone cutting him up was abominable, criminal.

'We need to find out what happened,' said Graziani.

'Are there any signs of foul play?' asked Luke, frowning.

'It's hard to say until the doctor has finished examining the body. There has been some damage done, but that's very common with victims of drowning who get washed up, as their bodies tend to have come into contact with the rocks that are close to the shore.'

'Did you see the body?' I asked.

'Yes.'

'Was it bad?' It came out as little more than a murmur.

Graziani's eyes flicked away, and I followed his gaze to a framed photograph on his desk, taken in a photographer's studio, of himself with his wife and two sons. He blinked.

'You have to understand that when bodies have been in the water for a number of days, there is some bloating, some skin and tissue loss. The top layer of the skin will have come off. There will be no colour. It might be hard to recognize your husband. You may have to judge using his height, build, and so on – and of course the tattoo – rather than going purely by his face.'

'Jesus, do you have to be so brutal?' Luke snapped. 'Can't you see you're upsetting her?'

Graziani smoothed down the front of his shirt. 'I'm sorry, Mr Broussard, but it's best that she is prepared. The body has been in the water long enough to have endured damage not only from the rocks, but also from the fish and other animals in the sea. I don't want this to be a shock to her. Now I'm afraid I need to ask you some questions, Mrs Benson.'

I just looked at him.

'Firstly,' he said, 'can you tell me what occurred on the morning of your husband's disappearance?'

'We were on the beach.' I told him about Charlie's shortness with the lifeguard, but emphasized that it was minor. 'We went to a restaurant there for lunch.'

'Did you talk to anyone there? Did anyone talk to you?'

'No. Just the waiter.'

'And then afterwards?'

'We went straight back to the beach. And Charlie went swimming.'

'What about the lifeguard?'

'What about him?'

'Was he around?'

I nodded. 'I fell asleep for a couple of hours. When I woke up, he was on duty on the beach. It didn't look as though he swam after my husband and killed him, if that's why you're asking.'

Graziani made a note on the pad on his desk.

'What kind of mood was Mr Benson in?'

'Christ, I don't know. He was fine, normal.'

Luke raised his hands in exasperation. 'Look, the guy wasn't suicidal, if that's what you're trying to suggest.'

'He wasn't depressed,' I agreed. 'Charlie was a happy guy. *Is* a happy guy. Look, if there's nothing to indicate that this wasn't an accident, why do you need to ask me these questions?'

'What about you, Mrs Benson?' Graziani asked. 'Are *you* happy?'

'Oh, I'm just fucking ecstatic,' I said.

'You and your husband didn't argue on the day he went missing?'

'No,' I said, glaring at him.

'Fine.' He put down his pen, laying it across the notepad. 'I'm afraid we're going to have to ask you to wait a while before we can take you to view the body. In the meantime, do we have your permission to try and retrieve DNA samples from your husband's possessions? Even if you do manage to positively identify his body, I'd assume you would want to be sure?'

I nodded, and dug the apartment key out of my pocket. 'Take whatever you need.'

He held up a hand. 'You keep that. I'm sure the hotel can let us into your room.'

I had thought that waiting all those days for news of Charlie was bad, but waiting those two hours before we could see the body they had found was far, far worse. There was a thick band of dread constricting my ribcage. Around us, the police station seemed to be waking up as office hours began and people arrived for work. And Luke and I sat and waited. The Italians were more relaxed than either the British or the Americans about smoking, and gave us an ashtray for our growing pile of fag ends. The room we were put in fogged up with cigarette smoke, even with a window open. Luke and I barely talked.

The Coroner's office was a few streets from the police station. A purpose-built, single-storey concrete block with square windows and a metal door, it seemed to squat on the edge of the park square.

The autopsy room itself was in the basement. Graziani took us through a door and down a grey staircase lined with bare concrete walls, and it was like descending into a cold, grim hell. Along an anonymous corridor we stopped in front of a door with a sign on it in Italian and Graziani looked at us as if to say, 'This is it.'

'You don't have to come in with me, Luke,' I said. 'If it is him, it's bad enough that one of us has to see him like this.'

He nodded, his face almost as grey as the wall behind him. 'Let me do it then,' he offered.

'I'm sorry,' interrupted Graziani. 'It has to be next-of-kin.'

I shrugged at Luke, feeling my lower lip and chin trembling. I went to walk into the room and he grabbed my hand and held it tight. He wasn't about to let me do this on my own. Holding hands, we nodded in unison at Graziani.

He knocked on the door and we went in. The room was small and spartan, and I took in its contents in just a few seconds. A small sink in the corner. A few of those stand-up air fresheners, not so discreetly dotted around the room. A gurney with a body on it, covered with a sheet. The smell was awful. Over the body, a fluorescent strip-light buzzed blue-white, casting an artificial glow on a woman with dyed blonde hair and dark roots who stood next to the gurney. She was wearing a white coat with an ID card attached to it that read *Dr Sabrina Bianchi*.

'This is our pathologist,' said Graziani. Bianchi inclined her head but didn't offer her hand to shake; I wondered if she generally found that people didn't want to take it.

'Are you ready?' she asked us.

I wasn't ready. I was terrified. How could I bear to see this? And yet I swallowed hard, gripping Luke's hand, and nodded at her. She reached over and pulled back the sheet to show us his face.

I gasped and it suddenly seemed ridiculous that my legs were meant to hold up my body as they became nothing more than polythene bags holding slippery water. The man's face – I couldn't think of him as Charlie then – was almost impossible to recognize as a face, let alone a particular person's. It was covered in red-raw abrasions, the nose was squashed flat against a cheek and the lips were almost entirely missing. Strips of skin were torn away from the man's neck and scalp, and I could see the stitches along his head from where the pathologist had cut him open to pull the skin away to look at the skull. On the side where I was standing, there was no ear, just a ragged piece of flesh where it should have been.

'Jesus Christ,' said Luke, turning away.

I let go of his hand, and took hold of the top of the sheet. It was crisp, starchy, against my fingers. Graziani made as if to stop me, but Bianchi shook her head at him. 'It's okay,' she said. I pulled back the sheet farther, exposing neat sutures along the massive Y incision that crossed the corpse's chest, and uncovering the top of its arm.

In my head, I was running through a frenetic slideshow of all the variants of black suns that must be displayed on tattoo parlour walls across the world. Small spiky ones; larger, more elaborate ones. Angular, geometric ones. Freehand, delicate ones. But it was Charlie's. It was Charlie's tattoo. The same size, same design. Being in the water and losing so many layers of skin had made the body a ghost-white, and the tattoo seemed blacker in contrast, but there was no doubt in my mind that it was the same design. I ran my fingers over it, over the skin slightly raised where the tattoo ink had been embedded.

'Why is he cold?' I said, my voice sounding as if it was coming from somewhere very far away.

Sabrina Bianchi said something to Graziani in Italian. 'The

goosebumps are from him being in the sea,' he told me. 'Something to do with the hair follicles becoming stiff.'

'Can't you turn down the air conditioning?' I said.

Luke stepped up behind me and wrapped his arms around me. I didn't know why he was holding me like that. I felt him kiss the top of my head.

'Come on, Katie,' he said. 'Let's get out of here.'

Chapter Eleven

'What do you mean, "throw them off"?' Luke said, pausing with his T-shirt only half-tugged on.

'Luke, this conversation will have to wait. If we hurry, they said we can get to Miami Airport in time for the six-fifteen flight to Heathrow.' I looked at my watch. 'I'll see you down in the lobby.'

'Honey, I've got nothing to pack but one suit and one shirt. You can't wait for me?'

'I'll check out. You pack your *Miami Vice* outfit and meet me downstairs.'

My suitcase in one hand, I looked in the bar, but the man in the suit with the fifties spectacles had gone. I glanced around, sure that someone, somewhere, was watching me.

I went up to the front desk and told the girl we'd be checking out.

'No problem,' she said with a plasticky smile, tapping away on the keyboard with her nail extensions. 'That's now been charged to Mr Broussard's credit card. We hope you enjoyed your stay at the Moonlite, and look forward to seeing you again next time you're in Miami.'

Luke appeared, still looking somewhat befuddled, but carrying his holdall. He ran his fingers in a jagged path through his blond crop, trying to wake himself up.

Going from the cool, air-conditioned Moonlite lobby into the Florida heat was like stepping from a fridge into an oven. The poor valet parking attendant had tiny globes of sweat on his upper lip and perspiration patches under each arm. As we waited for him to bring around our rental car I saw the man who'd spoken to me in the bar, sitting in a car on the other side of the road, the lenses of his glasses reflecting the blue neon of the Moonlite's sign.

'Over there,' I said, nudging Luke and indicating with my head. 'That guy. Look at that guy.' Luke followed my gaze. The man saw us looking, and nodded with a smug, closed-mouth smile that made me want to go over and kick seven shades of shit out of him. 'You recognize him?'

'No,' said Luke, frowning. 'Who is he?'

'I don't know. But he knows us.'

Our car arrived, and we eased into the traffic. Luke checked his rearview mirror, watching as the man followed us in his car. After a while Luke concentrated on the road ahead, his face set.

'So do you want to tell me now what the hell's going on?'

'I went down to the hotel bar for a drink, and that guy back there came over. He called me by my name, and told me to forget about Charlie and go home.'

Luke looked up at the sky, apparently exasperated. 'For Christ's sake,' he said under his breath.

'What?' I demanded.

'I'm just wondering how this translates into us making a beeline for Sicily.'

'Well, obviously someone's got something to hide,' I said indignantly, turning in my seat to better read his expression.

'And you don't think it's just Bruno Luna making sure you don't turn up at his pal Joe Cantelli's house claiming he's the reincarnation of your long-lost husband?'

'No, I don't. I didn't get warned off Joe Cantelli. "You need to forget about Charles Benson" – that's what he said. Not "forget about Joe Cantelli". He was talking about Charlie.'

'What else did he say?' Luke eventually asked.

'He said, "If you keep turning over stones, eventually you're going to come across a scorpion". What do you think that means?'

'I think it probably means that if we do find something out, we're not going to like it.' He glanced across at me, and finally his ice blue eyes were concerned. 'Katie, are you sure you want to follow this through?'

I folded my arms. 'Of course I'm sure. Look, if you're not up for it I'll do it on my own.'

'I'm not saying that. But sweetheart, I'm just curious as to what you think you're gonna find.'

I looked out of the window, the streetlights zipping past the car as we cruised along. The dark sky over the city was tinged red from all the artificial lights, even at this hour of the morning.

'I don't know,' I said quietly. 'I suppose I won't know until I find it.'

'You know, these guys sound pretty scary. Are you sure you want to mess with them?'

'They're not that scary,' I said.

'No? You're not scared by men who have apparently been following you, men who you seem to have made a little bit nervous? You know, sometimes when people warn you off, you need to pay attention.' He sighed then. 'Though they obviously haven't been tailing you that long, or they'd know the worst thing they could have done was let you in on the fact that there was more to find out.'

'So are you in?' I asked.

'I don't know. Maybe we should be hiring people who

know what they're doing,' he said. 'We're not private detectives.'

'While we just – what? Kick back in England, watching TV and going on with our lives, getting phone calls every week from our hired staff, keeping us informed about any new developments? Fuck that.'

'So what's *your* plan?'

'Go back to London, let them think we're doing as we're told. Then fly to Sicily and work out what really happened there.'

Luke had to brake sharply to avoid running a red light. 'How do you know that what they're trying to cover up had anything to do with Sicily? Maybe it's something in Charlie's past that they want kept hidden.'

'Well, Luke,' I said, staring at him hard, 'I'm assuming that you, as his best friend since childhood, would have had some idea if there was some major secret in his past. Am I wrong?'

He wouldn't meet my eyes, although granted that could have been because he was driving. 'No.'

'So it must have been something to do with what happened in Sicily.'

'Fine. So what do we do when we get to Sicily?'

'Visit Graziani. Visit that pathologist, what was her name? Bianchi.'

'Not exactly flying in under the radar.'

'We don't have much choice. I want to go to San Giordano too, to look for the Crestenzas' cousin, Cesare.'

'What can he tell you?'

'I don't know, that's why I need to speak to him.'

The flight back to London seemed to take for ever. I sat through film after film on the in-flight TV embedded in the back of the seat in front of me, letting the dialogue wash over me unheard, drumming my fingers on the chair rest, thinking of all the questions I had to ask the Sicilians.

The man in the suit and spectacles didn't follow us onto the plane, but as we'd taken off from Miami Airport I'd imagined him in the departures lounge, watching us leave.

The plane landed mid-evening local time, and I adjusted my watch. I'd hardly been in America long enough to have jetlag, and 9 p.m. seemed to fit more with my body clock. Compared to Florida, the 26 degrees Centigrade temperature of London Heathrow felt a little chilly and I put on my hoody. We picked up my suitcase at baggage reclaim and went through customs. In the arrivals hall were the usual batch of relatives and drivers waiting for the travellers to come through. Luke and I weren't looking out for anyone, knowing we weren't expected, but as we walked past the expectant crowd I caught the eye of a tanned guy in a nondescript suit and neat haircut. His eyes slid off me as though he was trying to make me think we'd never actually made eye-contact, and I saw him mutter something into the mobile phone he was holding to his ear, turning slightly away from us.

'He's one of them,' I whispered to Luke.

'One of who?' he asked.

'I bet he's got an American accent like the bar guy.' I turned on my heel and walked past to the man in the suit, tapping him on the shoulder across the strap that acted as a barrier separating fliers from greeters. 'Excuse me,' I said loudly.

The guy clacked his mobile shut and swivelled his eyes around the people on either side of us before acknowledging me.

'Could you please tell me the time?' I asked with a sweet smile.

He assessed me for a moment, then snapped out his arm so his shirt-cuff rode up and exposed his wrist. He smoothly rotated his arm and looked at his gold watch. 'Nine-thirty,' he said. Definitely an American accent.

'Thank you so much,' I told him.

He just nodded, fake-smiling back at me, but wasn't going to venture a 'You're welcome'. I turned back to Luke, who was looking at me as though I'd gone insane at some point down the Nothing to Declare passage. He took my elbow and steered me towards the exit.

'Look behind us,' I said as we waited for a bus to take us to the car park where I'd left my Fiat. 'He's there, isn't he?'

Luke glanced over my shoulder. 'Yeah, he's there. He probably thinks you were trying to pick him up. I 'spect he'll come over in a minute and slip you his number.'

I looked back myself, and saw Watch Guy hovering a few bus stops down from us. 'Funny how he's not with anyone, despite the fact he was ostensibly waiting for an arrival.'

'I haven't heard "ostensibly" used in conversation since the last time I watched *Newsnight*,' said Luke.

Our bus arrived, and watch guy didn't follow us onto it. During the short drive to the car park I scanned the other passengers that had got on with us. A blonde woman in a smart grey suit with no briefcase or handbag was my number one suspect.

'I bet you fifty quid she gets off at zone L,' I leaned over and said in Luke's ear.

He leaned back and murmured into my ear: 'You are driving me crazy. Seriously. You have gone completely paranoid android.'

'Shake on it then,' I said at normal volume.

He gave me a look of pity from under furrowed brow, then shook my hand. 'Fifty bucks.'

'Fifty quid, actually.'

'Fine, fifty pounds.'

We passed through four other zones and the woman sat motionless, waiting. When we arrived at zone L she stood up, brushing some imaginary lint off of her skirt, and followed us off the bus.

'Holy shit,' said Luke under his breath.

'Just keep walking, monkey boy,' I said, and we made our way over to my car almost huddled shoulder to shoulder. As we drove out of the zone we saw her standing between two locked cars, watching us go and talking on a mobile.

'You're buying dinner,' I told Luke, shifting gears and speeding back to North London.

We sat in my front room on opposite sofas, eating pizza that had been delivered by the takeaway joint around the corner. Luke had a Hawaiian. I had a Cheese Feast. It was dark now, but not so dark we couldn't see two people sitting in the front seats of a car that was parked outside the flat. They'd been there over an hour now, waiting in the shadows.

'How the hell are we going to make it to Sicily if we can't even leave the flat without being followed?' Luke asked.

I swallowed some pizza crust. 'We need an escape route. Maybe out the back? We'd have to go through Hannah and Agnetha's though.' Only the ground-floor flat had access to the garden.

'What about the fire escape?' asked Luke, head inclined towards the pile of rusty iron outside the living-room window.

'It's a death trap. Let's hope the guys don't mind us invading.'

Luke hesitated. 'Are you sure about this?'

'I'm sure, yeah. If you're not, Luke, you don't have to come.'

He rolled his eyes, wiping his fingers clean on a paper towel. We left the flat with just my set of house keys. If the coast was clear, we could then come back for some stuff to take with us.

Hannah and Agnetha had lived downstairs for years, but I'd only really got to know them after Charlie died. They'd been a lifeline for me then – once almost literally – doing things like bringing me food from the local supermarket and popping by to check that I was okay. I'd recently had the honour of being a witness at their civil partnership, and though it had of course reminded me of my own wedding ceremony, I'd been happy that day.

It took Hannah a while to answer our knock on the door as she was in her wheelchair, but she seemed glad to see us.

'Kate, my darling, how are you? And Luke, you handsome boy, you're a sight for sore eyes. Do you want to come in? Aggie's having her Friday night soak in the tub, but don't let that stop you.'

'Actually, this is going to sound a bit odd, but we were hoping we could nip out into the garden,' I said.

Hannah tilted her head and looked at me. 'Bat-watching again?'

'Something like that.'

'Fine. Come on in.'

She went ahead of us, spinning her wheels. Hannah's arms were in great shape, with lovely, well-defined tricep and bicep muscles. Watching her in action was sometimes like watching athletics. The back door key was hung on a hook at waist height, and she flipped the lock and opened the door for us.

Luke and I looked at each other, both of us finding it hard not to laugh about what we were doing despite the seriousness of the bigger picture, and tiptoed out into the darkness.

'You want the patio light on?' asked Hannah.

'No!' we both hissed back at her.

We skulked along the pathway till we reached the fence at

the back of the garden. We unlatched the gate and stuck our heads through. The gate opened onto a small passageway that backed along the gardens of the next three houses on the street. There was only one direction we could go in if we didn't want to climb through other people's gardens, and that was onto the street that ran at right angles to the one our guards were parked on.

We crept down the passageway and peered around the corner.

A silver saloon was parked right where the passageway opened onto the street. There were two people in suits in it. They saw us, and one of them waved. It looked like the guy who'd told me the time earlier in the airport.

We waved back sheepishly and retreated into the passageway.

'Well, that's that,' said Luke.

I shook my head. 'We just need a Plan B.'

Back in the girls' kitchen, we found Aggie in a bath towel, dripping on the lino and looking at us in bemusement.

'Hannah said you were watching for bats?' she said in her Dutch accent.

'No, I said they *were* bats,' said Hannah drily. 'What on earth is going on?'

'There are two cars – one parked on Stiles Street, the other on Kennerley Place – and they're watching the flat,' I explained. 'We need to leave without them seeing us.'

'Do you have a spade?' drawled Luke.

'I think there might be one in the shed,' said Agnetha. 'Why?'

'Maybe we can do a Steve McQueen and tunnel our way out,' he said.

Chapter Twelve

'I've got an idea,' I said. 'We need to call Samantha.'

'You want to run it by me first?' Luke suggested.

'Why, are you in charge?'

He lifted his eyes heavenward. 'Guys, is it okay if we use your phone?' he asked.

'Of course,' said Hannah. 'Might I ask what's wrong with your own phone?'

'Yeah,' I echoed. 'What's wrong with our phone?'

'Might be tapped,' he said, handing me the handset.

'I thought the police needed to have the permission of at least one participant in the conversation in order to tap a phone,' I said.

He gave me an odd look. 'What makes you think the people out there are following any kind of legal process?'

I wasn't sure. 'The suits?'

Luke gave a short laugh. 'You ever heard of Enron, sweetie?'

I used my middle finger to deliver a universally recognized symbol of abuse and then dialled Samantha's number. She answered on the third ring.

'Sam, it's Kate.'

'Kate? Kate, what's going on? Did you go to Miami? Is Luke with you?'

'Sam, please, calm down a minute. Look, do you and David have any plans for the Bank Holiday weekend?'

'No,' she said, sounding wary. I couldn't blame her. She thought the mad widow was about to invite her over for a barbecue or something.

'We need your help. Me and Luke. There are people following us, and we need to get away.'

There was a lengthy silence on the other end of the phone. 'Kate, I'm worried about you,' said Samantha finally. 'I think maybe you need to see somebody.'

'She thinks I'm mental,' I said to Luke, handing him the phone.

'Samantha, she's not going crazy. There are two cars outside the house, each with two men inside them. They're watching us.' He listened for a moment. 'No, I have not heard of the contagion of paranoia.' I heard her voice say something else, but couldn't make out the words. Luke lowered his head. 'No, Charlie's not alive. But *something's* up.'

I took the phone back from him. 'Why are we being followed if we're not onto something? Please, Sam, we need your help.' I waited, nothing but silence on the other end of the line. 'Thank you,' I said in the end, taking the silence for acquiescence. 'Here's what we need.'

That night I slept like a log, waking up in the same position in which I'd dropped off. I had a quick shower and made some coffee. Luke was asleep on the sofa in his boxer shorts and T-shirt. He reminded me of some Greek statue when he slept – something about dreaming made his face softer, more serene, and took away the cynicism and hardness that usually seemed to shape his bones.

I curled up in the armchair opposite him, sipping my coffee and watching him. He'd often slept over on the sofa after a long night when he couldn't face the drive home to his place by the river. Charlie and I would have friends round for poker

games and beer, and Luke always seemed to win the pot. Too
many years in Las Vegas to be beaten by a bunch of
Londoners, I suppose. The others would drift away one by
one until it was just Charlie and Luke left, drinking beers in
the kitchen and talking into the night.

I glanced over at the kitchen and half-closing my eyes could
almost see Charlie there, sitting on one of the kitchen chairs
in a dark blue T-shirt and pair of tracksuit bottoms, rumpled
socks on his feet, one foot resting on a strut of the chair.
Swigging from a bottle of beer and laughing at some wisecrack
from Luke.

There were hundreds of memories here. After Charlie's
death they had overwhelmed me; I was surrounded by so very
many things that sparked off a memory of him. Sometimes it
was too much, and I had to leave the flat and drive until I
found somewhere that we'd never been together. For a while
it would calm me, but then I'd panic at the lack of his presence
and need to return to the things that reminded me of him. I
always remembered what he'd said about forgetting his parents, and was terrified of losing his face, his laugh, his voice.
I put photos of him all around the flat, on every wall space. I
asked our friends if they had any pictures of Charlie that they
had taken themselves. Each one was like seeing him for the
first time. I'd play the answerphone message he'd made again
and again, and it became like a mantra to me. I'd lie awake at
night with his voice repeating the banal words *'This is Katie
and Charlie's phone, leave a message and we'll get back to
you,'* over and over until they had their own rhythm, like the
chug-a-chug of a train on the tracks. They became as familiar
as a comedian's catchphrase or the lyrics of a song, and eventually lost their resonance, so it might as well have been a
robot reciting the words. Hearing his voice saying those words
didn't remind me of Charlie any more, and when I lay in bed

trying to replay the sentence in my head I seemed to hear every voice other than Charlie's – until I nearly threw my bedroom lamp across the room.

When Luke and I had returned from Sicily with Charlie's body I was numb for a long time, feeling mainly disbelief. Each morning I'd wake up and be sure I had dreamt it all, expecting Charlie to be beside me. There was a constant feeling of dread in my stomach, knowing that I was nowhere near facing up to what had happened, but that the time would come when I would have to. I knew I wouldn't be strong enough, and I was right.

Luke was the one who spoke to people and told them what had happened. The first person I called was my brother Kytell, and telling him was one of the hardest things I've ever done. Because saying the words 'Charlie is dead' meant that it was true. That's why I made Luke tell everyone else while I hid in the bedroom with my headphones on, playing Charlie's favourite albums on a continuous loop.

At first our friends were great. They came round and sat with me, and it was only after the funeral that they began to drop away. I couldn't blame them – I hated them for not knowing what to say. When they avoided speaking about Charlie, I hated them for being cowards and for thinking I cared about anything else they might have to say. When they had the courage to talk about Charlie, I hated them for being able to speak of him without losing it, without feeling the crushing pain I felt. Luke was the only one I credited with having any idea about what I was going through.

I joined a support group for young widows and widowers, desperate to be around people who could understand. For a while I felt I could be myself, that I didn't have to watch what I said to avoid making other people uncomfortable. There were two women there who had lost their husbands about the same time as me. Six months later, one had taken off her wedding ring. 'I wear it around my neck, on a chain,' she showed me. 'If people have any nous, they see it and realize I'm not married any more, but that I still love my husband. One or two think I'm divorced, but most seem to realize I must be widowed.' I just looked at her. How had she managed to take off her ring? It was when the other woman who'd joined at the same time as me got engaged that I left the group. 'Just because I've fallen in love again doesn't mean that I loved Jim any less than you loved Charlie,' she told me. 'You're so judgmental. You think your pain is worse than anyone else's.' She was right.

My friends had been happy when I'd joined the group. They thought that it meant the group could handle the difficult conversations and it took the pressure off them. They wanted me to move on so they didn't have to worry about me any more. I inwardly shrugged and let them go. The ones who still came round, who still called, who still asked me how I was and actually wanted to hear the answer, those were the ones I took with me.

Luke stirred on the sofa, wrinkling the throw. Charlie and I had bought the sofa in Ikea, tossing a coin because he'd preferred the larger version. I remembered us grunting manfully and straining our biceps as we manoeuvred it through the door to the house; then getting the giggles when Hannah and Agnetha's cat had jumped up on it and sat regally in the centre cushion as we hefted it up the narrow staircase to our first-floor flat. I remembered coming back from a shopping trip and modelling my new scarlet underwear for Charlie, and the christening of the sofa that occurred soon after. I remembered Samantha and David sat on it, dressed in black, as we waited for the funeral cars to arrive. I remembered sitting on it with Agnetha, her clothes wet, a bloodsoaked beach towel in her hands.

'A penny for them.' Luke was awake and gazing at me.

'You don't want to know,' I said. 'Coffee?'

As we'd arranged, Samantha rang at half-ten.

'Hi, Kate, this is Samantha,' she said, sounding as if she was reading from a script. 'How are you? David and I were wondering if you'd had a good time in Miami?'

Resisting the temptation to respond as if I too was reciting the English translation in a 'learn a foreign language' tape, I told her we'd had fun. 'Nice weather too. Come over for brunch and you can look at some holiday snaps.'

I popped down the road to the local Tesco's to pick up some groceries so Sam and David would have something to eat. One of the occupants in the car waited till I was halfway up the road then got out and followed me. I had fun in Tesco's weaving an erratic path through the aisles so he had a hard time keeping me in sight.

Sam and David's Renault arrived shortly after I got back at the flat. Samantha had her blonde curls tied up in a clip and was wearing her old reading glasses with their thick tortoiseshell frames. David had on a black baseball cap with the peak low over his face. We watched them out of the window and I noticed Samantha making a great effort to look casual and not peer up and down the road on the hunt for two men in a stationary car.

We buzzed them in through the front door and Samantha gave me a massive hug the minute I opened the door to the flat. I looked over her shoulder at David, who was regarding me with a narked expression.

'Did you manage to get everything?' I asked.

He thrust out a carrier bag. 'What are you getting us into, Kate?'

I took the bag from him. 'Come in and we'll explain.'

Luke cooked us a full English breakfast and we told them about the events in Miami; about tracking down the man in the photo, about Bruno Luna and his friend Joe Cantelli. Samantha looked a bit upset at that point, which made me wonder how much she was hoping I'd been right that it was actually Charlie. I told them about the maid, Claudette, and going to her *botánica* only to discover she was trying to rip me off with her voodoo crap. I didn't tell them about my attacker and my attempt to crack his kneecap. Finally I relayed my story of going down to the hotel bar, all hope taken from me, and of the man who'd warned me off my search for information about Charlie.

'And you think the man who you spoke to in the bar has something to do with the men who have followed you here?' asked Samantha, her food left untouched.

'Yeah,' said David, who'd already eaten two hash browns and a sausage and was tucking into his pile of scrambled egg. 'Who do you think they are? MI6? Do you think Charlie was a spy?'

Luke practically spat out his mouthful of coffee. 'Man, that's a good one. No, Dave, I think it's pretty safe to say Charlie was not a secret agent.'

'Well what then?' asked David. 'I mean, you've known him longest. What do you think these people have to do with him?'

Luke shrugged. 'I don't have a clue.' He wiped his hands on a tea-towel and pulled a cigarette out of his pack. 'Kate, you mind?'

'Yeah,' I said. 'Wait for Sam and David to finish their meal, you cheeky bastard.'

'So all this cloak and dagger stuff, this is to convince them that you're following orders and staying at home,' asked Samantha, who'd finally picked up her fork and started eating her brunch, no doubt worried if she left it too late she'd be inhaling fag smoke as she chewed her sausages.

'That's right. We need to have at least a couple of days in Sicily without them on our backs,' I said. 'Are you sure this is okay with you? You can stick the whole Bank Holiday week-end out here, without leaving the flat?'

'We'll be all right as long as we've got Charlie's film col-lection and plenty of Pinot Grigio,' said David. 'At least it got me out of putting those shelves up in the spare room.'

Samantha elbowed him in the ribs. 'You can stop pretend-ing to be Mr DIY right now, Dave. Was it you who retiled the bathroom? No. Was it you who put together that flatpack wardrobe from Ikea? No, didn't think so.'

When we'd all finished eating I shook the contents of their carrier bag onto the coffee-table. A long blonde wig. A black bobbed wig. Two pay-as-you-go mobile phones, since if we were going to worry about the landline being tapped it made sense to worry that our mobiles were also being monitored, and worse, that we could be tracked using their signals. I didn't wonder at that point if our paranoia was justified, and if it was, who had the technology and money to be able to surveil us at this kind of level. I just knew we had to assume the worst and act accordingly; that way we couldn't be caught out.

'Sam and I will get changed in the bedroom,' I told the guys. 'You take the bathroom.'

The curtains were already pulled in my bedroom. I saw Samantha glance at the bed. You could see only one side had been slept in; even though Charlie had been gone for a year now, it didn't feel natural to take up more than my half of the bed.

Sam and I had always been the same size and when we'd been in our twenties we'd often borrowed each other's clothes.

'This brings back memories,' she said, turning away from me and undoing her black blouse. I stripped off my shirt. 'Do you remember when you loaned me your Karen Millen dress for that wedding and I got red wine on the sleeve?'

'Yeah,' I said, swapping tops with her and putting on the black blouse over the long-sleeved white T-shirt I was already wearing. 'In fact, the cost of the contents of that bag should cover it.' I smiled to show I didn't mean it.

Her jeans were low-slung hipsters, and needed a belt if I wanted to avoid displaying my knickers to all and sundry. 'Sorry,' she said. 'You told me you'd prefer a pair of jeans and that I wasn't likely to see them again, so I brought you the pair that I never wear because my belly fat squeezes over the top. Good job you've got a flatter stomach than me.'

She scanned the clothes in my wardrobe. 'I'm going to look forward to trying some of these on.'

'Well, just remember Dave's the only one who's going to get the benefit.'

'Good point.' She went down the end where my sexy dresses and skirts were kept.

'Please God, if you have sex in any of my clothes please make sure you dry clean them before you give them back,' I warned, reading her mind.

'Course I will,' she said. 'Who do you think I am, Monica Lewinsky?'

Not wanting to take any chances, I unhooked the coat hanger bearing my favourite red dress from the clothes rail and laid it on the bed to be packed.

We brushed our hair into tight little buns and then tried on the wigs. Sam actually looked damn good as a brunette; a little like an older version of Natalie Portman in *Léon*. I looked like Dolly Parton having a bad hair day. Giggling, we set about combing through the tangled curls and tying them back in a clip. We regarded my reflection in the mirror. I had Barbie-blonde hair and black eyebrows.

'Well you don't look like Dolly any more,' said Samantha. 'More Madonna circa "Who's That Girl".'

'I look like a cross between a librarian and a hooker,' I said. 'Why did you have to wear red lipstick today?'

'Hey, you said to try and have things people will notice.'

'You're right, I'm sorry.' I'd said that if you wear things people can easily remember, like thick-framed glasses and bright red lippy, then they're not likely to focus on the aspects of your appearance that are more permanent and harder to disguise, like your nose or the shape of your chin.

Just then I heard a pattering on the window, and got up to look at the skylight. 'Thank Christ for that, it's raining.'

'That's a good thing?' asked Samantha.

'Means I can use an umbrella.'

I picked up Samantha's handbag and emptied its contents onto the dresser. 'Now you're sure this isn't one of your favourites?'

She pulled the edges of her mouth down. 'It's mock croc. What do you think?' She caught a pen that was rolling off the edge of the dresser and placed it back on the pile of crap from her bag.

I stuffed the bag with my passport, underwear, toothbrush, hairbrush, my jewellery box and a few tops. Samantha watched me.

'You seem different,' she said eventually. 'As if a light's been switched on in you.'

I gazed at her, pausing with my hand in the bag. 'Maybe it's having a purpose again.'

Her turquoise eyes cut through me. 'You still think he's alive,' she said. 'Don't you.'

I turned away from her, zipping the bag shut. 'I did. I tried not to, but I couldn't really help it. But the DNA they took from the body in Sicily matched Charlie's. How could he still be alive?'

'He couldn't,' she said. 'I'm just worried that you're still hoping you'll find him alive somewhere.'

'No. It's not Charlie I'm looking for any more. It's whatever these guys are trying to hide. I don't know, maybe Charlie was murdered. Maybe that's what they're trying to stop us from finding out.'

'Murdered? But who would want to murder Charlie?'

'I don't know. But if he was murdered, whoever did it is going to be in trouble.'

'From you or from Luke?'

It was a fair question. A group of us had been out drinking once, and there were a bunch of lairy lads who'd wanted to pick a fight. One of them went after Luke with a beer bottle. Luke broke two of his fingers and left him crumpled in a shop doorway.

'Come on,' I said. 'Let's show the boys our makeovers.'

Samantha got off the bed as I opened the bedroom door. 'Are you sure this is a good idea?' she asked me quietly.

I cleared my throat. 'No, probably not. I have to do it though. If it was David, you'd do the same.'

She looked sad. 'Maybe. Maybe not. I'm not as brave as you.'

'It's not bravery. Just bloody-mindedness.'

Luke and David had very different reactions to our new looks.

'Helllooo, baby,' David said, looking Samantha up and down. Two people who had just discovered role play for the bedroom.

'You look like a drag queen doing Jayne Mansfield,' Luke told me.

'Thank you so much. Nice cap.' Luke was wearing David's baseball cap.

'I want you to know I'm ditching this thing the second I can,' he told me. 'Christ, David, the LA Raiders?'

David had obviously been listening to this same rant for the last ten minutes, and said patiently, 'For crying out loud, I'm not a baseball cap kind of guy! I only bought it because it was raining and I popped into Oxfam for a hat. Would you prefer it if I'd brought my cricket hat?'

'Nooo,' said Luke, making me laugh.

'Are we all set?' I asked. 'Luke, you got your passport and David's keys?'

'Yes, Mom.'

'Then let's go.' We exchanged hugs, and I slipped on Samantha's glasses. 'Christ, Luke, you'd better drive. I'm going to do some damage if I get behind the wheel with these babies on.' I grabbed an umbrella and the bag, and we left the flat.

Downstairs we found Hannah and Aggie in the hallway. 'Good luck,' they said, nothing more, and then went back into their own flat and closed the door.

Luke and I looked at each other. 'Yeah,' he said. 'Good luck, Kate. If this doesn't work, we're back to the tunnel-digging plan.'

He pulled his cap low and I got the umbrella ready to go. We opened the front door. Large drops of rain were turning the stone path wet. I pushed the umbrella open and held it at an angle that hid most of my face from where I knew the watching car was parked. They would hopefully only get a glimpse of dark-framed specs and red lipstick. We walked briskly to Sam and David's car, Luke using the keyfob remote to switch off the car alarm and unlock the doors. Luke had to adjust the driver's seat as obviously Samantha had been the one who'd driven to my flat. Each moment we were in view of the surveillance team made me nervous.

'C'mon, c'mon, c'mon,' I said under my breath. Luke adjusted his seat and started the car, and we pulled onto the road.

'Don't look behind us,' said Luke. 'Act normal.'

I stared in the rearview mirror, where I could see the corner of their car. It didn't move. We turned a corner and got onto the high street. For five minutes I checked the mirrors, and couldn't see anything following us.

'I think it worked,' I said, giddy with relief.

'Good,' said Luke. 'But let's stick to the plan, just to be sure.'

The plan, which we followed through, was to drive to Samantha and David's house in Belsize Park and let ourselves in as if we owned the place. Samantha had packed us a suit-case with enough clothes for both of us for at least a few days. I'd warned them that they might never get the clothes back, and so they were the kind of items you usually found at the back of your closet – things that had been trendy once but now you'd wear for painting or gardening. Luke's pile of tops from David were mainly size L – promotional items that he'd apparently won at his local pub's quiz night, ranging from a blue Labatt's sweater to a V-necked black Jack Daniel's T-shirt.

'I'm going to look like an alcoholic,' he said.

'I'm going to look like I've travelled in time from 1999,' I said, picking up a lime green shirt. 'Does it matter?'

'And only a short while ago I was *Miami Vice*,' said Luke sadly. 'It was nice having style.'

Still in our disguises, we left via the back door just in case 'Samantha and David' had been followed to their house as a

precaution. The people following us would hopefully not have
the resources to cover both their exits too. And just to be 100
per cent sure, as we sauntered down the high street we made
a sudden right angle at the entrance to the tube station, jogging down to the barriers and scanning our Oyster travel
cards. As we clattered down the escalator I looked behind me,
and couldn't see anyone who seemed to be after us.

The tube train was stifling; it was a hot day despite the rain-
storm. With a great deal of relief I put the spectacles in the
handbag and removed my blonde wig. A few of the people
around me stared as I pulled off the hairband and shook out
my real hair, and I smiled at them. The other occupants of the
tube train, probably Londoners, were completely unfazed and
continued to sit and look nonchalantly at their free news-
papers.

At Liverpool Street Station we caught the Stansted train,
reasoning that our pursuers couldn't cover every major
London airport, and hoping that they weren't in cahoots with
the UK police as there was no way we had time to sort out
fake passports.

At the airline's front desk I got out my stack of banknotes.
'Two tickets for your next flight to Sicily, please.'

Chapter Thirteen

It was an uncomfortable feeling, arriving at the airport in Palermo. Last time I'd been there had been on my way back from our ill-fated holiday, just a day after the inquest. 'Accidental Drowning' was the verdict. I had a folder at home with important documents in it like our marriage certificate. One day I'd thought I'd be adding birth certificates for our children. Instead it was joined by Charlie's death certificate.

I remembered waiting in the lounge for our flight home to be called, feeling as if I was surrounded by a thick glass wall that muffled all noise and sensation. Around me, life was going on as normal. Business people and holidaymakers watched the clocks, bought duty free, ate snacks from the food court. I looked at them from inside my bubble and wondered how come the whole world hadn't shuddered to a halt.

As Luke and I queued to go through security, he saw I was remembering and put an arm around me reassuringly. 'It's okay,' he said. 'We'll be out of here soon.'

'You don't understand,' I said. 'Everything's going to be like this. Everything.'

We rented a car from the same place Charlie and I had hired ours, and sat in the car park.

'I think we should try this Cesare guy first,' said Luke.

'Yeah?' I said. 'Not the cops?'

'If you're right and there *was* something suspicious about

Charlie's death, the cops *had* to have been involved. Maybe we can get some local intel from this guy.'

'Okay then,' I agreed, with more decisiveness than I felt. 'San Giordano it is.'

The sky was a beautiful cerulean blue, only a few hazy clouds high overhead. It was warm but not oppressive, a soft breeze shaking the fronds of the palm trees that lined the road. It was a long drive along the centre of the island to get to the small town where Charlie and I had spent the day with Cesare and the Crestenzas. Luke pushed the radio buttons, trying to find a station that wasn't playing Italian songs or Euro pop. Finally he found one playing Puccini, and the plaintive sound of 'Un bel dì, vedremo' filled the car, making my heart hurt.

'You might as well try and get some sleep,' he said. 'It'll be a couple of hours.'

'No,' I said. 'I want to be awake for this.'

Driving along a dusty road through the dark green hills was bringing back Charlie to me. After an hour and a half I started to recognize the surrounding area.

'We passed that church before,' I told Luke, twisting in my seat to watch it go past. There was, I must admit, some dis-combobulation involved in being in Miami less than twenty-four hours ago, then London five hours ago, to Sicily here and now – and I started to wonder if I was having some feverish dream that had begun with me answering the door to the flowery delivery guy on the first anniversary of Charlie's death. Perhaps any moment now I'd wake up and find there'd been no photo, no warning from the stranger in the hotel bar, no chance of anything other than Charlie having died an unfortunate but unremarkable death.

I reached under my shirt-sleeve and scratched my arm, hard, and found the pain was sharp and real.

'What are you doing?' asked Luke, pulling my arm away from my other hand.

'Just making sure I'm really here,' I told him. 'There! There's the turning.'

I remembered the dress I was wearing that day, and how Charlie had looked in his white shirt, the wind from the car's velocity playing in his hair, making his shirt-sleeves billow. It was almost as if he was in the car with us, a ghostly shape with half-opacity overlying Luke's image. One eye shut and Luke's there. Blink it shut and open the other and it's Charlie.

There was the sign bearing the tiny town's name: *San Giordano*. We pulled up into the square, getting out of the car, and nothing had changed. I spun on my feet and yes, she was there, the same old lady who, Charlie had joked, should be available to every film that needed to cast a wrinkly Italian widow.

'There aren't any other roads,' said Luke. 'So unless we have to go back the way we came, we've gone the wrong way to get to this Cesare guy's place.'

'I don't know how to get there from here by car,' I admitted. 'We walked before.'

Luke reached through his open driver's door and got his sunglasses out of the space in the dashboard. He closed up the car and grinned at me mirthlessly from behind his dark shades.

'Lead on, Macduff,' he said.

I set off in the same direction we had taken a year before, and as we walked past the shadowy bar I glanced in through the windows, as though if I looked hard enough I might see Charlie, still sitting at that table sipping his water and waiting.

The field of tall, dry grass looked exactly the same as it had a year before; green and gold with violent splashes of red where the poppies bobbed among the grass stalks. Charlie's ghost, in his jeans and white shirt, drifted ahead of us, leading the way. Tears welled up in my eyes and I wished I'd thought to bring my sunglasses so Luke couldn't see that I was upset. But without even seeming to look me in the face, he slipped my hand into his and held it as we walked up to the olive grove.

We were halfway down the grove's centre avenue of trees when the back door to the farmhouse opened and a man came out. Despite the heat he was wearing a dark blue suit, and his hand was reaching into his inner pocket as he looked over at us. Behind him, Cesare came out of the house, looking far more relaxed in a shirt with rolled-up sleeves. He squinted at us, then put a hand on the other guy's arm, before coming over to me with a smile and his hands wide.

'Katerina!' he said as he reached me. He grasped my arms above the elbows and pulled me in for a three-cheeked Italian kiss. 'What are you doing here?'

'It's a long story,' I said. 'Can we come in?'

The farmhouse was cool after the heat of the Sicilian afternoon. Cesare sat us in the kitchen, made us coffee and told me how sorry he was about Charlie. I explained that Luke and I had tried to see him after Charlie's body had turned up, but that the farmhouse had been locked up, empty.

'We were on vacation,' he said. 'I didn't even hear about what happened until we returned a few weeks later. I'm so sorry I was not here for you, Katerina. But why are you in Sicily now? I cannot understand why you would want to come back here.'

I left out the way our journey had started and only told Cesare that men had been following me, and one in particular had warned me not to dig my nose into the details of what had happened to Charlie.

'I'm not sure that I understand,' said Cesare. 'I read that Charlie had drowned. That they ruled out – what do you call it – bad play.'

'Foul play,' corrected Luke. 'That's what the pathologist said. Your typical drowning case.'

I glared at Luke. How was this helping? Cesare just looked at me with a frown.

'Pathologists' reports can be doctored,' I said. 'I think the police are covering something up.'

'The police?' he said.

'I'm sorry if this offends you,' I said, 'but Sicily's got something of a reputation for corruption.'

Cesare put down his coffee cup on the table hard enough for it to rap on the wood.

'Twenty years ago now, there was a war over territory in my country,' he said. 'Many Sicilians died. Not all of them were *cosa nostra*. There were many assassinations of investigators, men who had the job to put these criminals behind bars. They weren't corrupt, Katerina. They were honest men, and they died doing their jobs.'

'I'm sorry,' I said.

'Just down that road,' he told me, gesturing with an angry hand, 'buried by my church, is the grave of Armando Graziani, Eduardo Graziani's older brother. He died aged just forty-two – killed because he could not be bought. Eduardo is the same. Trust me, Katerina, there is not enough money in the world to persuade him to cover up a murder. If he says it was an accident, then it was an accident.'

Luke and I got into our rental car and stared blankly out of the windscreen.

'If it wasn't Graziani, then it must have been the pathologist,' I said.

Luke closed his eyes in frustration. 'Bianchi?' he said, incredulity dripping from every syllable.

'We need to see the case file. Let's go to Graziani. From what Cesare told us, he'll want to help expose any cover-up.'

Luke sighed heavily and started up the car. We left San Giordano.

'I'm sorry, it's completely out of the question,' said Graziani. We were sat at his desk in the police station. He looked exactly the same as he had a year before – white hair and moustache, walnut-brown skin, short-sleeved pale pink shirt. He didn't look corrupt, I admitted to myself. He looked like a kind man, a family man. Though I'd known at least one 'family man' who would happily kneecap anyone who stiffed him on a deal.

I shifted in my seat, uncomfortable at remembering the time I'd sat there previously, listening to Graziani tell me my husband's body would probably be unrecognizable. Being back in Sicily was making me feel as though the last twelve months of grieving and healing had never even happened.

'But it's my husband's file,' I insisted. 'I have a right to see it.'

'No you don't. It's confidential. The file is the property of the police.'

'What are you trying to hide?' I said, raising up towards him like a snake about to strike.

Next to me, Luke put a warning hand on my arm. After a moment, the pressure of it made me relent, and I sat back down.

'She has a point,' Luke said to Graziani. 'Surely everything in the file was covered during the inquest. What's the harm in her seeing it?'

Graziani leaned back in his office chair, tapping a pen against his bottom lip.

'So why do you want the file?' he asked. 'Since, as you say, everything in it was brought up in the inquest?'

'He might believe that,' I said. 'I don't.'

Graziani set the pen down on his desk. 'I've been working in this job for thirty years, Signora Benson. I've never taken a bribe, never even accepted a free coffee in a café. And you think it is acceptable to accuse me of lying on a police report? When you come from a country where men and women were beaten into confessing to murders they didn't commit just because they were Irish and they made good suspects? Or your country, Signor Broussard, where they move trials to white counties so policemen can be declared innocent of beating unarmed black men even when caught on tape?'

'Whoa, if you're talking about human rights, how about—'

This time it was me that cut Luke off.

'Okay, so maybe none of our countries has got a perfect record when it comes to honest cops,' I said. 'But all I know is that something isn't right here. I've got men following me, wanting me to go back home and pretend that nothing's happened. Well, *fuck that*. They wouldn't warn me off if there was nothing for me to dig up. Maybe it wasn't you, Signor Graziani, maybe it wasn't your force, but something happened to my husband, something more than came out at that inquest, and I'm damned if I'm going to forget it all just because you've got a chip on your shoulder about missing out on some free lattes. Now *give me that fucking file*.' I smiled at him sweetly. 'Please.'

Muttering some Sicilian curses under his breath, Graziani pushed his seat back and walked out of the office.

'You think that little tirade worked?' whispered Luke.

'Either that or he's gone to get some Mace and a truncheon,' I whispered back, crossing my fingers.

A few minutes later Graziani returned with a manila folder in his right hand. He laid it down in front of me on his desk.

'That's the original,' he said. 'It doesn't leave this office. There's a photocopier in that corner if you want to make a copy, and you can use that computer over there. It has an internet connection if there are any Italian words Signor Broussard is unable to translate.'

'Thank you,' I said, resisting the urge to pinch his cheeks and kiss him. 'I'm sorry I was rude to you – it was uncalled-for. Thank you so much for letting us have this.'

He shrugged. 'There's nothing new there, Signora Benson. I don't think you have anything to thank me for.'

Two hours later, seated at a spare desk in the open-plan office, I had to agree with him as I closed the file with a sigh. The cover of the folder was blank apart from BENSON, *Charles* written along the tab in blue marker pen. Luke, sitting next to me, rubbed my shoulders.

'You know, it was worth a shot,' he said.

'Was it?' I laughed without humour. 'What did I expect to find – an autopsy report with *Cause of Death: Gunshot Wound* crossed out and *Death by Drowning* written in? Christ Almighty, Luke, what are we doing here?'

'We're here for Charlie,' he said. 'We owed it to him to check this out. So it's come to nothing; maybe that's for the best. You don't really want to find out that he was murdered, do you? Wouldn't that be worse than it being an accident?'

'I don't know,' I said dejectedly. 'At least then I'd have someone to blame.'

'Someone to take revenge on, you mean,' he said. 'Come on, let's get out of here. We need to find a hotel.'

'We're staying at the Hotel Ricci,' I said.

'We are?' he said, surprised. 'Kate, why on earth would you want to go back *there*?'

'That's where it happened. Where he went missing, at least.

I don't want to go home without checking out everything. Look, it's only a matter of time before those bozos back home realize it's Samantha and David they're watching, but with any luck we'll be gone by then. I want to see Sofia, maybe ask the people who work there some questions, things we wouldn't have asked them back then because we didn't know to ask.'

'Like what?' asked Luke. '"Did you see someone hit Signor Benson on the head with a brick and drag him out to sea?" "Oh yeah, I did. Sorry I didn't tell you before, but if you'd just asked . . ."'

'That's not funny,' I said. 'You're being very obstructive.'

'Obstructive?' he repeated. 'You're kidding, right? I've followed you from London to Miami, Miami to London, London to Sicily, just because you saw a guy who looked like Charlie in a photograph.'

'That's not why we're here,' I said, angry now. 'We're here because a complete stranger came up to me in a hotel bar and told me to stop digging into what happened to Charlie.'

'So you say,' Luke said, looking away.

'What does that mean?' I grabbed his arm.

'Nothing, forget it.' He raised his hands, warding me off.

'No, I won't forget it. Are you saying I'm lying about the man in the bar?'

'I didn't see him, Kate. I'm sorry. For all I know, you made him up so I'd come with you to Sicily. Now *please*, can we just drop this? Charlie's file matches exactly what they told us at the inquest. There's no big secret, no big conspiracy. How long are we gonna look before we accept there's nothing for us to find?'

'But what about the men that were following us in London?' I asked disbelievingly. 'You saw them yourself.'

'Maybe they're private investigators,' said Luke. 'Maybe you're fooling around with some married guy I don't know about, and his wife's hired them. Maybe you hired them your-self, to try and convince me to go along with you.'

I looked at him for a moment then slapped him, hard, across the face. He let me do it, didn't try and ward off the blow or restrain me. I didn't make a habit of hitting my friends, and the feel of my hand stinging reminded me of walking into our apartment the year before, desperate to find Charlie there and finding Luke instead.

'I'm sorry,' I started to say, but he just shook his head and then he was gone.

I bought an Italian-English dictionary in the local bookshop, and then caught a taxi to the hotel. The cab driver tried to talk to me but soon gave up, probably more due to my demeanour than the language barrier. I didn't recognize the man on recep-tion who welcomed me to the Hotel Ricci, but the barman going through the lobby saw me and immediately went off to tell the other employees that the Englishwoman whose hus-band had died here was back.

I requested Apartment 217, though I wasn't quite sure what I expected to find after a year – maybe a secret passageway or a message hidden under a loose floorboard. When the recep-tionist told me that Apartment 217 wasn't free, some part of me was relieved. It wasn't a place I ever really wanted to go back to.

He gave me a key to number 225 instead. 'It's just as nice, same décor and same size,' he told me.

'Fine,' I said. 'Does Sofia still work here?'

'No, I believe she left last summer.'

I wondered if having to deal with the death of a guest had anything to do with her decision to leave, but knew he wasn't likely to tell me if it had. I suddenly felt a pang of missing her. She'd been a friend when I'd needed one. I could have done with her understanding and practical support right now.

Apartment 225 was on the opposite side of the pathway to number 217, but other than that it was identical. The curtains were the same striped blue, white and cream, the TV set was the same make – and I soon discovered that the bathroom shower leaked in the same way. The only differences between this and the apartment I'd had with Charlie were that it was painted white and not magnolia, and that the design was flipped over, so the door to the terrace was on the left side of the room not the right, and the bathroom was in the north-west corner, not the north-east. After my shower I stood in front of the steamed-up bathroom mirror and wondered if I could climb through, back to my old life and away from this reflected world, this parallel universe where I'd lost half of myself.

I sat on the bed, wrapped in a towel, and didn't know what to do next. I was still furious with Luke, and it was distracting me from working out my next step. Would he follow me to the hotel, or was he on a plane back to London? How could he think I was making any of this up? I'd never lied to him before. That's not true, my conscience reminded me, flashing up a memory of calling him from hospital and telling him I was going to visit some friends for a week. Fine, I clarified to myself. I've never lied to him about anything that actually involved him. He certainly didn't have the right to suggest I might be involved with someone else, let alone a married man. As if I'd ever cheat on Charlie. Luke was a complete bastard, and I was better off without him. At least now I could do what I needed to do without having to try to convince him at every turn.

So what *did* I need to do? All I had was the conviction that there was more to Charlie's death than an accidental drowning, and that was due to the man with the fifties-style spectacles in the bar of the Moonlite Hotel. What had he said to me again? 'You need to forget about Charles Benson and stop asking questions. If you keep turning over stones, eventually you're going to come across a scorpion.' He was implying that I would place myself in danger if I kept digging, and I'd assumed he meant that someone had something to hide; something they would commit violence to protect. Had Charlie stumbled across a piece of information that someone had killed him to cover up? And if so, what was it? A murder? An infidelity? Some kind of political scandal?

What I couldn't understand was why, if Charlie had witnessed or discovered something so shocking, he hadn't told me. The pieces just didn't seem to fit together. The answer had to be that he hadn't understood the significance of whatever information he'd received – that someone had assumed he was a risk to them when actually he'd had no clue that he'd seen or known something he shouldn't.

This train of thought was getting me nowhere. I focused on the mystery man himself. What did I know about him? He had looked around fifty-five years old. He was smartly dressed, in a plain suit. I was no expert on designer clothing, but it hadn't looked expensive. Not cheap either. So he was on a decent salary, but not the budget to splurge on bespoke tailoring. The accent was American, but not one of the distinctive ones; there was no Bostonian drawl, Southern twang or Brooklyn staccato. Mid-West maybe? West Coast? Luke would probably have recognized it, but then Luke hadn't been there, as he himself had so clearly pointed out.

What else? He had a wedding ring, so he was either married or pretending to be. Maybe one of those guys who keep the ring on although their wife left them years before. I tried to imagine Mrs Fifties Specs Guy, and saw a woman in a pink twin-set, enthusing about a new labour-saving device called a dishwasher.

Back to the suit. The men following us had worn suits too. So not private investigators then, who tended to blend into the background. I made a two-fingered gesture to Luke, wherever he might be. What an arsehole! American guys in suits, and he tells me they're PIs. Yeah, right. But who else wore suits on a regular basis? Jehovah's Witnesses. Businessmen. Lawyers. Politicians. Secret Service guys (but I hadn't spotted the President). Police detectives. None of whom would be likely to descend en masse to London to tail us with a view to making sure we knew we were being tailed.

I was getting nowhere. From my bag, I pulled out the copy of the file I'd made back at the police station after Luke had left. Not knowing what might be useful, I'd photocopied every single page. It had taken over an hour.

I sat back down on the bed, crosslegged on the pillows, with the sheets of paper spread out in front of me. I resolved to go through each page in order, thoroughly, making sure I was completely satisfied with its authenticity before I moved on to the next, but my eyes kept getting drawn to the pile of autopsy photos. The copy quality was fine for text, but the colour photographs were rendered flat and indistinct in black and white. I picked up one A4 sheet and stared hard at the picture of my husband's face. When Luke and I had identified his body his eyes had been closed, but the photos were not so merciful. Charlie's right eye was frosted over like a beachcomber's chard of coloured glass turned opaque by the sea. Where his left eye should have been was just an empty socket. Turning the photo face down, away from me, I had to bite down hard to stop the tears coming. My husband had had such beautiful eyes, like glowing pieces of sapphire, like the Indian Ocean.

Losing him had seemed so unfair. Why him, why us? Why

couldn't it have happened to someone less loved, someone more deserving of such cruelty? But if it was no accident, his death at least made sense. If someone had made a conscious decision that he was to be removed from the earth, then all I had to do now was find that person and make the same decision for them that they'd made for Charlie.

Newly determined, I went through each and every page of the report over and over again, ingesting the text and committing it to memory. It took hours. When I'd finally finished, my hair had dried on its own and my eyes were refusing to focus. I had learned nothing that could help. Demoralized and suddenly exhausted, I checked my watch and saw it was nearly midnight. I didn't even have the energy to brush my teeth, take off my towel and get under the covers. I slept, dreaming about men in suits with clouded eyes.

When I woke up seven hours later, cold and huddled up on top of the bedsheets, I was completely disorientated. My half-awake brain saw the light coming through the striped curtains and smelt the familiar scent of the washing powder they used on their linen here, and for a moment I was back in the Sicily of a year past, waiting for Charlie to come back from the sea. There was still time, there was still hope. And then in flooded the additional memories of the morgue, the funeral, the empty life.

I moaned and turned away from the sunlit window, closing my eyes in the hope it would block out the last twelve months and I could pretend for another few moments that Charlie might be about to walk back in.

The first thing I saw when I opened my eyes again were two sheets of photocopied paper from the autopsy report. Along the bottom of each sheet the laser printer had automatically added the time it had been printed. *10:15, 22 agosto*, I read on one. *13:10, 25 agosto*, I read on the other.

I sat bolt upright and grabbed the sheets of paper, doublechecking. There was definitely a different time and date on page 9 of the report than there was on pages 8 and 10.

Placing the three pages in a row, my eyes flicked across the footers of each. 'Holy shit,' I said to myself.

The autopsy report had been changed two days after it was first printed. But what had been on that ninth page? And who had changed it?

Chapter Fourteen

Dr Sabrina Bianchi arrived at the morgue at 8.16 a.m. I was sitting across the square from the squat, ugly building, in a café which had been serving me lattes since half-past seven that morning. To say I was experiencing a caffeine rush would be putting it mildly, and when I saw the pathologist arrive in her smart silver car I was nearly out of the café before I remembered I hadn't paid yet.

Throwing down some Euros on my table, I ran across the road and intercepted Bianchi before she had the chance to unlock the doors to the Coroner's office, which didn't open officially until nine.

Not having yet changed into her doctor's garb, she was wearing a stylish trouser suit and lots of gold jewellery. She no longer had dark roots; a more professional dye job made her appear to be a natural blonde despite her brunette eyebrows and deep brown eyes.

'Doctor Bianchi?' I said as I caught up with her.

'*Si?*' she replied, turning to look at me. I saw recognition on her face, yet she made the mistake of pretending not to know who I was, when drowning accidents involving tourists must be rare enough that she'd be unlikely to have forgotten me just twelve months later.

'I'm Charlie Benson's widow,' I reminded her, though with one of those smiles that very effectively lets the person you're smiling at know that you think they're full of shit. 'You performed his autopsy last August.'

She cocked her head as though trying to recall.

'He drowned,' I said.

'Oh, of course, Signora Benson. I'm sorry, how can I help you?'

'May I come in?' I indicated the glass door of the office's reception area.

'Oh.' She looked around her, perhaps hoping a colleague would appear and rescue her, but we were alone on the street. 'Very well, come in.'

Inside, the ground floor of the Coroner's office was designed to soothe, the way I remembered it – soft carpet, light wood furnishings, gentle colours. Abstract prints in aluminium frames. Bianchi typed a code into the security alarm and then locked the door back up after us.

'My office is down here,' she said. I followed her down a beige-walled corridor to a similarly bland office. Bright morning sunshine bounced off the walls, and she twisted the blinds to block it out. Slats of shadows segregated her face.

'What can I do for you, Mrs Benson?' She avoided meeting my eye by shuffling through her post and the other papers on her desk. Back when I was a kid my dad had taught me everything he knew about reading people, and I was watching for micro-expressions – facial expressions that flash for a tiny moment before being suppressed. Only a small percentage of the population notice them with any kind of consistency, but the very fact that I was looking for them increased my chances.

'Graziani gave me a copy of my husband's autopsy report yesterday,' I said. I could tell she didn't like the fact I was calling him just plain Graziani, not Detective or Signor. She was wondering why the lack of respect. I didn't carry on, but let her stew.

Her legs were crossed, and she was grinding the stiletto heel of the lower foot into the carpet. 'Yes?' she said eventually.

'I was hoping you could tell me why you changed it.'

We sized each other up across her desk.

'I don't remember making any changes,' she said cautiously.

I laid my copy of the report down in front of her, on the top of her polished desk. I tapped page 9 with my finger.

'You made a change to this page.'

She scanned it as though attempting to remember what she might have altered.

'I'm sorry, I think you're mistaken. This all looks accurate to me.'

I just pointed to the printer-annotated date on page 8, then where it changed on page 9, before reverting back to the original date on page 10.

Bianchi seemed relieved, even smiled for a brief second. 'This could be anything. Pages trapped in the printer. Or I may have noticed a typing error which I corrected.'

'What does this page cover?'

'I don't understand.'

'What does it say about the body?'

'Of course, you don't speak Italian.' She looked even happier at that news, and I didn't tell her I'd already translated the page. I was hoping she would deliberately miss something out as she read it to me, because then I would know whatever she omitted had some significance.

She picked up the ninth sheet. 'Stomach contents . . .' she translated, scanning the page. 'Red wine. Partially digested pasta. Tomato sauce. No toxins or narcotics present. Suggests the subject died a couple of hours after his meal. Contents of the small intestine . . . fully digested food. No toxins present.'

Bianchi looked back up at me. She'd translated it just as I

had. 'Did you have lunch with your husband on the day he went missing?' she asked me.

I nodded.

'And did he have pasta with pomodoro sauce and red wine?'

I nodded again.

'So I don't understand what is the problem. I found nothing suspicious in his system.'

Her mahogany-brown eyes met mine and refused to look away. She was no longer on the defensive, secure now in the knowledge that I didn't know what part she had played in concealing whatever it was that had happened to Charlie. I would have to push her further.

'My husband was murdered,' I said bluntly.

Bianchi laughed, the sound a little too high. 'Mrs Benson, you are wrong. I did the post-mortem. All the evidence leads to drowning.' Her well-manicured hands remained rested on the arms of her chair. It's said that when people lie they unconsciously cover their mouth or obscure their face in some way, but my Dad had taught me that the opposite was true. People who are trying to convince you of a lie will strive to appear open and honest, and will actually make a conscious effort not to betray their lie with their body language. They will be more still, less expressive, than someone telling the truth.

'You're lying,' I said, with more certainty than I felt. 'Whatever you originally wrote on page nine of the autopsy report, it proved that it was murder. What did you find, Doctor Bianchi?'

She stood up. 'I want you to leave now, Mrs Benson.' When I made no move to go, she picked up the phone. 'The police station is just down the street,' she reminded me.

'Fine.' I rose to my feet, collecting the pages of the autopsy report from her desk and walking out of her office and to the front door. She hung up the phone and followed me, unlocking the glass door so I could leave. 'You're meant to be a doctor,' I said as I walked back into the hot Sicilian morning. 'How could you do this?'

There it was, the micro-expression – guilt flared across her face, just for an instant, and I knew I was right; whatever had happened to Charlie, she'd been involved in some way.

She swung the door shut and locked me out, staring at me through the glass. I walked back across the piazza to the little café, glancing behind me to see if she was still watching me, but she'd gone back to her office. I would have given anything at that moment to see what she'd done next. Had she called anyone? Warned someone that I was on their trail?

Back in the café I ordered an orange juice – I'd had enough coffee to last me a week – and sat down at the same table. I didn't know how long I had before whoever she was protecting came after me. Bianchi knew something, I was sure of it, and if she wasn't going to play nicely then I would have to resort to more extreme measures.

I had one of the pay-as-you-go mobiles that we'd bought in England in my bag. I switched it on, received a 'welcome to Italy' text from the local service provider, and dialled a number from memory.

'Yeah?' answered a deep, masculine voice.

'It's me,' I said. 'I need your help.'

My half-brother Kytell tends to make quite an entrance. He's six foot five and as wide as an entire row of brick shithouses. He wears sleeveless tops, even in the cold, in order to show off his massive biceps and chunky shoulders. His skin in the winter is the colour of milk chocolate, and in the summer tans to a dark brown, though his greeny-hazel eyes betray that there's at least some Caucasian heritage mixed in there.

Kytell came to live with us when he was about ten and I was seven. His mum had died, and Dad had taken him in. I didn't realize at that age that he was my half-brother, but my mum worked out straight away that this little mixed-race kid was the result of one of my dad's 'work perks' and threw a complete shitfit. It didn't make any difference – what Dad said went. Now I look back and realize it was an incredibly huge thing to ask of her – to raise the offspring of her cheating partner – but she still didn't have the right to take it out on Kytell. She didn't beat him or anything, but he always got the smallest portion of food, the last choice of cereal in the variety packs, the hand-me-down clothes when the rest of us were in the latest gear, and the stingiest, most unsuitable present at Christmas. Constant, tiny digs to let him know he wasn't as deserving as the rest of us.

Even back then I'd loved to piss her off, and that was why – at least to start with – I made Kytell my favourite. She hated that he was the first person I said hello to in the morning, and that my crayoned drawings were always of just the two of us. I'd swap my piece of pizza with him so he had the larger slice. My overt affection towards him made him grow, his true personality unfurling out of that closed bud of withdrawal. He started to laugh, to crack jokes, to tell me secrets. When my other brothers picked on me he fought my corner, even though back then he was smaller than they were. As we got older, he'd give me a lift home from clubs when I'd stayed out late and was too drunk or stoned to get home safely. When I was threatened with expulsion from the posh school Dad had sent me to, Kytell visited the Headmistress with a bouquet of flowers and tried to sweet-talk her into reducing my punishment to suspension. When that hadn't worked – the woman wasn't someone who could see past either the intimidating bulk or the dark skin – he'd taken a spanner to her car windscreen.

Kytell was the only member of my family that I had let Charlie meet. Kytell was suspicious of him at first, unhappy that I'd married someone he hadn't even met. He practically gave Charlie the third degree, the older brother equivalent of a 'what are your intentions towards my daughter' chat, but the more they got to know each other, the more Kytell could see what I saw: a good man. Once he knew that Charlie was taking care of me, that he would protect me the same way that Kytell already did, he relaxed and they became genuine friends.

The café doorway seemed to shrink as Kytell walked through it, having almost to manoeuvre his bulk through the gap. The waitress took in the melon-sized biceps and thick gold neckchain, and looked nervous. Kytell ignored her, making a beeline for me. I stood up and he grabbed me in a massive hug, lifting me clear off the ground.

'Easy, tiger,' I said. He put me back down and sat opposite me, squeezed into the space between our table and the one next to it.

'Are you okay?' he asked in his London-accented bass voice. Sometimes when Kytell talked, you seemed to feel vibrations rather than hear any sounds.

'I'm fine, apart from the fact that my bladder might explode at any moment. I've been needing a pee for the last five hours.' I pointed to the Coroner's office across the square. 'Yell for me if you see a blonde woman in a dark grey trouser suit leave that building. Her car's the silver Lexus on the corner.'

Kytell nodded, immediately focusing all his attention out of the café window.

Finally getting to pee was like sinking into a feather-stuffed bed, having not slept for three days. I let out a deep sigh of satisfaction. It seemed to take forever for my bladder to finish emptying, yet when I went back to my table I could tell that Kytell hadn't shifted a millimetre since I'd left him on watch.

'Did you hire a car at the airport like I said?' I asked.

'Yeah – it's just outside. Are you gonna tell me what the hell's going on now?'

I looked round at the waitress, who was still absorbed in Kytell's musculature. 'Not here,' I said, looking at my watch. 'Let's go and sit in the car. She could be leaving soon.'

Kytell's eyes widened when he saw the bill. 'Three Dr Peppers, two juices, two iced teas and three slices of pizza?' he read out.

'Ky, I've been here over eight hours,' I said. 'What did you expect – that I'd get one coffee and take only a sip every thirty minutes?'

'Next time you're staking someone out, I'd recommend you go a bit lighter on the liquids, that's all I'm saying.' He shrugged, his shoulders rising like two boulders pushing their way out of the ground.

Kytell's hire car was a decent-sized black Audi with tinted windows. We shifted it around the square so it was two cars down from Bianchi's Lexus and settled back into the comfortable front seats. While we waited I told my brother everything that had happened in the last few days.

He absorbed it all without asking a single question, but when I finished speaking he asked me how I could be so sure that Bianchi had lied to me.

'The most obvious explanation is that there *was* a typo,' he said. 'What makes you think it was something sinister?'

'She's scared and she's guilty,' I told him. 'You know me, Ky. I'm not paranoid. You'll just have to trust me when I say I know she's lying.'

'I trust you,' he said with a sigh. 'But Luke obviously doesn't. Where is he, anyways?'

'I don't know,' I said, focusing out of the window. In the

gap between the buildings you could just make out the shore, and a strip of the dark green sea that I hated so much. 'I haven't seen him since yesterday afternoon. He must have gone back home.'

If my brother disapproved of Luke for abandoning me he kept it to himself. 'What's your plan?' he wanted to know, but before I had a chance to lay it out for him, Sabrina Bianchi emerged from the Coroner's office.

Despite the tinted windows we slid down low in our seats and watched her come towards us. Although her expression was pensive, her stride was long and confident, like a catwalk model sashaying down the runway. A leather handbag with a gold G for Gucci buckle swung on her arm. She reached inside it for her car keys, and bleeped the Lexus's doors unlocked with her remote.

Kytell fired up the Audi, and as she drove off we eased away from the pavement and followed her.

'Keep at least three cars between you,' I told him.

'You're telling me this?' he said with a chuckle.

'But don't lose the bitch.'

'Do you wanna drive?' he asked.

Bianchi took us to the edge of town and then out into the countryside. After half an hour I was beginning to wonder whether she was actually going home, but then she took a left and the roads became dotted with houses and we entered another town, with more modern buildings and wider streets.

She accelerated up a hill, then pulled to a stop outside a two-storey white building surrounded by a high fence. She buzzed another remote in the direction of the gates, which parted to let her into the driveway and then clanged shut behind her. We watched from a distance, the motor running, then Kytell drove past the house and carried on till we were on the edge of some fields and out of sight. He parked the car on a dusty patch of ground under some trees.

'You got anything useful in that bag?' he asked me.

'Like what, a skeleton key? No.'

'There's a baseball cap, gloves and some clothes in the back.'

I shifted in my seat and grabbed the blue Yankees cap, pulling it down low over my face. The navy-coloured shirt I tucked under my arm. Kytell had his own plain black baseball cap.

'You think that's going to help you keep a low profile out here?' I asked him, amused. 'Exactly how many six foot five black men do you think they have in this neighbourhood? We're not in London now, Ky.'

Kytell ignored my sarcasm and got out of the car without saying another word. We walked back up to Bianchi's street, trying to look inconspicuous. We were in an area on the out-skirts of town, obviously recently acquired by developers who were building spacious detached houses, with a decent amount of land between them. There were only a few other properties nearby, and two of them looked brand new and empty, no doubt only just on the market.

We made our way round the back of Bianchi's shiny new house, with its pristine white walls and clean lines, and found we were in luck – the property backed onto a building site, where the workers had now left for the day. If we got up close to the fence, we could see through gaps and knotholes into Bianchi's back garden, past her swimming pool and through her patio doors to her living room.

'Nice pool,' I said.

'Nice house,' Kytell agreed.

'How many public-sector workers do you know with a posh new house, a swimming pool and a Lexus?' I asked him.

We sat and watched Bianchi through her garden fence. She went upstairs for ten minutes and came back down in a pair of silk pyjamas, her blonde hair tied back in a ponytail. She poured herself a large glass of white wine and curled up on her large cream-coloured sofa, appearing to be watching TV.

'To be honest,' said Kytell eventually, 'she don't look like someone with worries on their mind.'

'She's just a cocky cow,' I said. 'She knows I don't have anything on her. How long are we going to wait?'

'Till it gets dark,' Kytell said. 'Just relax.'

Time passed. We watched as Bianchi made herself some salad for dinner, accompanied by another two large glasses of wine. The thin clouds over the corner of the horizon where the sun had set were now a brilliant pink, the sky beneath them darkening to indigo in the east. As that blot of indigo soaked into the rest of the atmosphere, Kytell stood up and stretched, rotating his shoulders and shaking out his limbs. My own legs creaked as I straightened up, pins and needles lancing through my calves and feet.

The evening wasn't feeling much cooler than the day, but I wanted to be ready so I pulled on the black shirt, doing it up over Samantha's long-sleeved lime green shirt. Kytell was already wearing black – a black sleeveless T-shirt and jogging bottoms. Even his trainers were black. He liked to coordinate.

'When I say "let's go", I need you to be ready,' he said.

I nodded, tugging on my gloves. 'I'm as ready as I'll ever be.' I felt light on my feet, springheeled. The adrenaline was pumping, trying to boost me into action. When Kytell hunkered down again to look through the fence, I was reluctant to return to our previous positions. I was ready to move, *now*.

'Here we go,' he hissed suddenly.

Kytell was surprisingly agile for such a big guy. After giving me a leg up over the fence, he swung himself over and landed in a crouch, before edging along the perimeter of the fence until we reached the bushes at the side of the patio.

'Anyone would think you'd done this before,' I said to him, and he smiled back, his diamond-capped tooth winking in the light from the poolside lamps.

We peered through the bushes' leaves into the window of the large kitchen area and I realized what had prompted Kytell into action. Bianchi was chucking an empty can in the bin and putting a bowl of cat food down on the floor. We hadn't seen a cat in the house, which probably meant . . .

I ducked down as I heard the patio doors being unlocked and slid back.

'Porcellino!' I heard Bianchi call out. From somewhere nearby a cat miaowed and I saw a ball of white fluff with legs and a tail skip across the lawn towards the house, closely followed by my brother.

Bianchi saw the cat first, and smiled at her pet, bending down to welcome it back into the house. Then she saw the large black guy behind it, charging towards her. She gasped, eyes wide, and instinctively slammed the door closed again, twisting the key in the lock. Most people's momentum would have carried them straight on into the door, but Kytell was spooky and could stop dead in his tracks. He stared at her through the door, his breath fogging up the glass, though he was breathing as slowly as if he'd sauntered up to the door.

Bianchi looked back at him through the glass, horrified. The cat, poised at his feet, lifted a paw and tapped on the door, mewing. Seeing Bianchi's expression at this, Kytell scooped the cat up in one hand and placed his other gloved hand around its neck as if he was about to wring out a wet towel.

'*No!*' cried out Bianchi, her voice muffled by the glass.

'Then open the door,' rumbled Kytell.

I couldn't believe it when she actually did so. For all Bianchi knew, Kytell was a serial rapist who beat his victims to death, and yet her love for her cat made her throw all common sense out of the window.

She stood in front of him, hands shaking, already starting to cry. I could feel no sympathy for her. She had colluded in the cover-up of Charlie's murder.

Kytell dumped the cat in her arms and pushed her backwards into the living room. At that point I came out of the shadows and jogged across the patio and through the doors, sliding them shut and locking them behind me.

Bianchi's expression changed from fear to defiance when she recognized me.

'*You*!' she said. 'What do you want? Do you want me to lie to you? Would that make you leave me alone?'

Righteous anger flamed through me and I stormed towards her. She dropped the cat, who ran under the glass coffee-table, and held up her arms in defence.

I grabbed her face, squeezing my fingernails into her cheeks. 'All I want,' I whispered, right up close, 'is the truth.' Then I pushed her back down onto the sofa.

Kytell took hold of the back of the matching armchair and dragged it across to the edge of the sofa. He sat down so he was knee-to-knee with Bianchi, who was fighting back tears, then scooped up the cat and sat there stroking it like a Bond villain.

'My husband, Charles Benson,' I said. 'Was there anything about his death that was suspicious?'

'No!' she cried.

'Something in his stomach contents,' I insisted. 'Did you find any toxins?'

'No.'

'Sedatives, tranquillizers, painkillers?'

'*Non, non, non, mi dispiace*!'

Kytell looked at me sideways. We were both good at telling a lie from a truth, and we could see that Bianchi wasn't lying.

Something else then, if there was nothing toxic in his stomach contents. I'd read a lot about drowning in the months since Charlie's death, torturing myself with details of how he must have suffered. I knew what she had to find to conclude he had drowned.

'Did you find diatoms in his blood?' I asked.

'Yes,' she nodded, not looking at me.

'Seawater in his lungs?'

'Of course. The middle bones in each inner ear were crushed, there were weeds and small stones clutched in his hands, indicating cadaveric spasm due to drowning. All this is in the report. There's nothing more for me to tell you!'

I went through everything I had memorized about the report, and nothing I asked her made her change her story. Running out of ideas, I got some dishcloths from the kitchen, tore them into strips, and tied her hands behind her back and her feet to the legs of the sofa we'd sat her in. Kytell cut the phone lines with his pocket-knife, and we left her trussed up while we searched the house for anything that might mean something.

The décor was minimalist, all glass, neutral colours and metal. She didn't clutter the place up with photos or decorations. Her papers were all filed neatly away in a cabinet in the upstairs study, but as I hadn't brought the dictionary I couldn't have translated them from Italian into English even if they'd looked promising. There was no safe, no wads of cash with signed 'thank you' notes pinned to them. Bianchi didn't appear to have any family, or even many friends. The only person she seemed to spend money on was herself, judging by the flatscreen plasma TV and the surround-sound Bose stereo equipment.

The more we interrogated her, the more places we searched, the higher my stress levels became. I couldn't concentrate properly on what we were doing, because the question I'd managed to keep at the back of my mind was now pushing its way to the front. And that question concerned how far I was prepared to go to force answers out of Bianchi. The longer she resisted, the more I had to face the fact that we were headed down a very unpleasant road.

Finally I took Kytell to one side.

'This isn't working,' I said, quietly so she couldn't hear. 'We can't stay here for ever, playing nice with her.'

'She's not gonna change her tune,' he agreed. 'We should go.'

I shook my head violently. 'No. I'm not leaving. If I don't get her to tell me the truth, then I'll never find out what happened to Charlie. We can make her talk, Kytell, you know we can.'

He tilted his head and fixed me with his hazel eyes. I could see I'd made him angry. 'Is that what you brung me here for?' he whispered. 'To do the things you can't stomach, so you can keep your conscience clean and still get what you want?'

'Oh, don't play the innocent,' I snapped. 'We both know what you're capable of!'

He snorted. 'You don't know me as well as you think you do, princess. I ain't never hurt a woman, and I'm not starting now, not even for you. If you're prepared to take that step, you're on your own.'

We stared each other out, both knowing the other wouldn't back down.

'Fine,' he said, unlocked the patio door and left.

Trying not to panic, I slid the door shut behind him and relocked it. Bianchi was still sat huddled on the sofa, though Kytell's departure seemed to have given her some hope that her ordeal wouldn't, at least, get any worse.

She was wrong.

I slowly took off my gloves and tucked them into the pocket of my jeans. Then I strode back across the room and punched her as hard as I could in the face. Blood began to stream from her nose, and I felt sick. She looked shocked, obviously only just beginning to realize that I was capable of hurting her.

Too scared to take her eyes off me, and crying almost silently, Bianchi tried to get out of the bindings that tied her wrists together behind her back.

'I don't want to do this, Sabrina,' I said, bile in my mouth. 'Please, just tell me the truth. You owe it to me. You're a doctor, for Christ's sake! You're meant to help people! When did money become more important to you than that?'

'I needed it!' she suddenly screamed at me. 'I owed people money, and I didn't want to lose the house!'

I took a step back in surprise and realized I hadn't actually expected her to admit to lying. Did that mean I had thought she was telling the truth, but was prepared to torture her, just to be sure?

I crushed my conscience away inside me. 'What did you do?'

'It was nothing,' she sobbed. 'Really, just a small change. I thought it had no significance. It wasn't a lie – it wasn't.'

'Tell me!' I shouted, desperate now to hear the truth.

She wiped her nose on the shoulder of her pyjama top, leaving a smear of blood and mucus.

'His last meal,' she said, sounding exhausted, but still not taking her eyes from my face. 'I changed the word "spaghetti" to the word "pasta".'

'What?' I said, almost laughing. Was this the big secret I'd broken the law and hurt someone to uncover? 'Someone paid you for that? Gave you money to change "spaghetti" to "pasta"?'

'Oh God, you don't believe me,' she said, starting to cry again. 'Please, I'm telling you the truth. That was all I changed. I'm so sorry, but I would not take money to hide a murder. The body was in exactly the state I described. All I did was make a description of something more general, that's all.'

I dropped down into the armchair, my head in my hands. Why would anyone pay money for such a small detail?

Because it's significant, said a little voice in my head. But why would it be significant? What was it about spaghetti, of all things, that revealed Charlie's death to be murder?

I tried to remember our last meal in the smallest detail. The waiter. The sneezing American who kept visiting the bathroom. The English guy who wanted a stuffed-crust pizza. Could any of them put something in Charlie's food? I conjured up a picture in my mind, playing the events, the conversation, like a movie on the back of my eyelids. Sipping the wine. Charlie's sadness. The American doing his crossword. Charlie shaking black pepper onto his tagliatelle.

My eyes flew open and I grabbed Bianchi's shoulders, making her gasp in shock. 'The pasta – was it definitely spaghetti?' I asked her.

She nodded. 'Yes, spaghetti.'

'You're sure? Definitely not tagliatelle?'

Her eyes half-closed and I could swear she smiled. 'I am Italian, Signora Benson. I know the difference between tagliatelle and spaghetti.'

'Even in someone's stomach?'

'The noodles were only slightly digested. It was easy to tell.'

Suddenly I was fired up again, full of energy and determination. 'Who paid you?' I demanded. But her face closed down, like a trapdoor shutting on a cellar full of treasures.

'He's a good man,' she said. 'He doesn't deserve what you might do to him.'

'A good man!' I laughed. 'He paid you to hide evidence of a murder. How does that make him a good man?'

'I know him,' she insisted. 'He must have had his reasons. Your husband must have deserved what happened to him.'

'He didn't deserve it!' I shouted. 'Don't you dare fucking say that!'

I had to fight to get control of my hands; my fury at her blasé assumption that Charlie somehow deserved to die was like molten metal in my gut, flying through my body and into my arms, wanting to pummel her ignorant face into oblivion. I forced myself to take a step back from her.

'He found out something,' I said, my voice shaking. 'Something he shouldn't have, and someone killed him because of it. Now maybe the man who you're protecting isn't the same man that killed Charlie, but he's sure as hell involved. I need to know who he is!'

Bianchi slowly raised up her head, spitting out a trail of saliva onto her lap, the clear liquid pink with blood. She stared at me and shook her head.

Once, someone had tried to teach me that often things had to get physical before a person would take you seriously. The same person had also told me that even breaking bones wasn't enough sometimes – people know that bones knit together again, that bruises fade over time. But the threat of losing something for good, like a finger, or an ear: that could work like magic.

Desperate now, I spun on my heel and strode into the kitchen. There was a block of stainless-steel knives on the brushed metal countertop, and I snatched up the nearest one and went back into the living room. Bianchi's eyes widened to the size of saucers when she saw the knife, her pupils huge and black as though trying to absorb as many clues as possible about the limits of my capacity for violence.

I grabbed for her hands, still tied behind her back, and she leapt up, trying to run. But her feet were bound to the metal legs of the sofa, so only her upper body had any impetus. The ankle bindings snapped tight and she dropped face-first onto the floor, only missing the hard edge of my chair by millimetres.

She twisted over to face me, pushing against the sofa with her bare feet, trying to get away. I hated myself for the fear I saw in her eyes. How could I do this to another human being?

But I told myself I didn't have a choice. I closed my eyes and thought about Charlie's corpse. I thought about waiting in that hotel room for news of my missing husband. I thought about coming back to London without him; stepping into our home and knowing it would never be the same again. I remembered sitting in a bath full of pink water turning cold and knowing that there was nothing in the emptiness inside me except an infinite longing to be with him again.

I gripped the knife handle hard and opened my eyes. She saw the resolve there, that my decision had been made, and said a name as though her mouth was acting independently, in pure self-preservation.

'Graziani,' she said. 'Graziani asked me to do it.'

I left her locked up in the house with her hands still bound, throwing her mobile phone into the bushes by the front door on my way out. Making for Kytell's car, not knowing if he was still there, I had to stop abruptly by the side of the road and throw up into the gutter.

I'd spent years trying to stop myself becoming the person I'd been back in that room. I thought I'd changed, evolved, become someone far too civilized to ever contemplate treating another human being that way. But all it took was for me to lose my temper and there she was: the woman I could have been. Hiding round the corner. Waiting for me.

The car was where we'd left it, the engine off and the lights dead. Kytell was waiting for me in the driver's seat. I climbed in, crying, wiping my mouth. 'I'm sorry,' I said to him. He looked me over and nodded.

'Are you done now?' he asked.

I cleared my throat, shook the tears from my eyes and composed myself. My hands curled into determined fists in my lap.

'Not yet,' I said.

Chapter Fifteen

We found a bar back in Cefalu, and Kytell ordered whiskies while I checked the bar's phone book. There were three Grazianis in it, but only one E. Graziani – at 42, Via Condotti. We downed our whiskies and got back in the car. I checked the map; Via Condotti was reached by taking the coastal road out of town, then making a left at the third set of crossroads.

The house was easy to find, a farmhouse standing alone on a hillside, with stone walls and no lights on.

'You don't have to come with me,' I told Kytell. 'It's not your fight.'

'I don't think you should do it on your own,' he said. 'A policeman is a different prospect from a civilian, Kate. He's probably armed.'

'He has kids, Ky. Doesn't that bother you?'

'What bothers me is that it don't seem to bother you.'

'I won't hurt them.'

'I know *that*! You won't mind hurting their dad in front of them, though.'

I shrugged. 'He's brought it on himself.'

Ky pulled his baseball cap on. 'I'm coming with you, sis.'

We left the car halfway down the hillside, and walked up the track to the farmhouse. Kytell's knife was tucked into the waistband at the back of his jogging bottoms. I still had the knife from Bianchi's kitchen, which I was keeping in my hand for now, though I knew I'd have to lose it before too long.

Nothing illuminated the path ahead except moonlight. I marched through the long grass, thinking about what I'd say to Graziani when I got him alone. My first priority was to find out if he was involved in Charlie's murder, and if not, why he was involved in the cover-up. Mainly, I just wanted to know why.

As we got closer to the farmhouse we walked more quietly. Reaching the stone walls, we crept around the building, looking in each window. The curtains were closed in all the upstairs rooms and one downstairs room, but none of them were lit up with electric light, suggesting either the rooms were empty or their occupants were asleep.

The other, curtainless rooms on the ground floor were quiet too. Items of furniture made bulky shadows in the grey darkness. The family must have gone to bed.

'The top part of the kitchen window is unlocked,' whispered Kytell in my ear. 'Do you think you can fit through it?'

I followed him round to the back of the house, where some trees and a small outbuilding provided some cover. I peered into the kitchen. It was only small, with an old stove and some tiles that looked like they'd been put up in the seventies. An old-fashioned broomstick, with twigs instead of man-made fibres, was propped up in the corner, and a pile of neatly chopped logs lay stacked by the stove. There was no evidence of the kind of wealth that Bianchi seemed to enjoy and I wondered what Graziani spent his hard-earned bribes on.

Kytell reached up a gloved hand, fingers spread, to one of the smaller windows, and pushed gently with his fingertips. It began to open. We nodded at each other, and he let it close again.

'Go and keep watch round by Graziani's room,' I whispered

to my brother. We'd scouted out the rooms on the upper floor from the outside, and knew that the parents in a house always have the biggest bedroom. In this house that meant the only room with curtains that spanned two large windows, which was on the opposite side of the house from the kitchen.

'As soon as you get in, unlock the front door and let me in,' Kytell whispered. 'Don't think you can do this solo.'

'Okay,' I breathed back.

'Promise.'

'I promise,' I mouthed, and impulsively gave him a hug. Hugging Kytell is a bit like hugging a wall, all solid, flat surfaces. He smelt of some fancy aftershave.

'What do you want me to do if I see the light go on in the bedroom?' he asked. My head was resting on his chest, and the rumble from his diaphragm made my ear vibrate.

I pulled away. 'It sounds silly, but ringing the doorbell and hiding might be your best bet.'

'What – Knock Down Ginger? Haven't played that since I was a kid. You don't want me to ask him if he's discovered the Lord?'

I tried to laugh, but wasn't in the mood for joking. My head was still full of the smells of Bianchi's house – the cat food, her perfume. Her blood.

Kytell kissed the top of my head and scooted around to the front door while I stood working up the nerve to break into the house. The unlocked window was about six feet from the ground. Taking a deep breath, I pulled myself up on the kitchen windowsill and reached up, pushing at the unlocked piece of glass.

I felt a hand on my ankle and immediately assumed it was Kytell, wanting to warn me of something, but then realized I could feel warm skin touching mine, and my brother was wearing gloves.

I simultaneously kicked my ankle free and twisted my upper body round to look at the person who had grabbed me. Blue eyes, cool in the moonlight, were frowning up at me.

'Get down, Kate,' Luke said. 'Now.'

'What the hell are *you* doing here!' I hissed.

Luke caught my hand and lifted me down off the windowledge. I struggled to get free, furious with him for interfering. 'Leave me alone,' I growled, but he started to drag me away from the house, away from Kytell.

'Get off me!' I said, my voice rising, and I dug my heels in.

It turned out it didn't need Kytell to warn me of any lights going on in the farmhouse. Someone switched on a light in the main bedroom, and the rectangle of yellow light that was cast on the grass was easily visible from our side of the house. Kytell came running round the corner and in the darkness could only really see that a tall guy was manhandling me. He charged towards us, lowering his centre of gravity so that he dove into Luke's stomach like a linebacker taking out a quarterback. Luke ended up on the ground, my brother kneeling across him, punching him hard in the ribs.

'Don't, it's Luke!' I said, clutching at Kytell's arms. He stopped immediately, looking down at my husband's best friend as though he needed to make sure for himself. He grunted, then pushed backwards on his heels and straightened up. Kytell's weight now off him, Luke curled up in the fetal position, clutching at his ribs.

'Kytell, you motherfucker,' he wheezed.

'Come on,' my brother said, tugging me in the direction of the car. We could hear the back door being unbolted.

'We can't just leave him here,' I said, looking at Luke.

'Why not? He left you.'

The back door flew open and a figure was silhouetted in the block of light. We heard the ratcheting sound of a shotgun being cocked. Graziani, wearing just a T-shirt and a pair of boxer shorts, came down onto the kitchen step, his gun aimed in our direction. With the light behind him, and our eyes adjusted to the night time darkness, I could hardly make out his face.

'How dare you?' he said in English, his voice like nails. 'How dare you come near my family, you pieces of shit!'

Pure fury burned white-hot in my chest. 'How dare *you*,' I cried, spitting the words. 'How dare *you* talk about family, when you covered up the murder of my husband?' I went for him.

Graziani raised the shotgun, and from behind me I heard the sound of a pistol being primed.

The next thing I knew, I was spun round in the air and thrown flat on the ground, my face pressed into the rough stalks of grass. I struggled against the weight on my back, trying to look at what was holding me down. I was facing away from the house now, my head in the direction of the trees at the back of the property.

I managed to raise my head an inch off the ground and saw the smart shoes and lower legs of a man standing just a foot in front of me. The part of my brain that was still rational, still trying to work out what the hell was going on, reminded the animal part of my brain that I'd heard a gun being cocked a few seconds before; the chances were this man might be the gun's owner, in which case it would be wise to stop struggling.

The second I stopped wriggling, the pressure relaxed, and I was pulled to my feet with such ease that I knew it had to have been my brother who had restrained me, knowing it was the only way to avoid my being shot by Graziani.

I gazed at the man in front of me, familiar even in the shadows. He was holding the handgun casually, as familiar with it as most people would be with holding a pen or a telephone.

As he was facing all four of us – me, Kytell, Luke and Graziani, I couldn't know for sure which of us the gun was meant to scare.

'I admire your passion,' Cesare told me. 'Really I do. But you must stop now. You don't want to die, do you, Katerina?'

I looked at him, at the shiny silver gun glinting in the light from the farmhouse, and then at Luke. Luke was sitting up now, a few feet from me, to the left of Cesare. He was cradling the left side of his ribcage with his arm. He showed no surprise at Cesare's appearance; in fact, he wasn't even watching him, but me. I realized then that the two men had come here together, to lie in wait for me, watching over Graziani.

I backed away from them, away from Graziani too.

'Take her back to London, Kytell,' said Luke tiredly.

I could feel Kytell's eyes on me, feel his worry. Graziani's face was impassive, unreadable, as Kytell put an arm around my shoulders and steered me away from the farmhouse.

As we walked through the long grass back to our car, I could hear Graziani's voice, in the distance now, addressing Luke and Cesare: 'What are you doing here?' I wanted to stop and listen to their response, but Kytell pushed me ahead of him, kept me walking.

'We need to pick up your stuff and get out of here,' said Kytell, starting the car. He put it in gear and we zoomed off down the hill.

'The hotel's on the other side of town,' I said. 'Follow the signs for Patrezzi – it's on the way there.'

My head was spinning. I looked out at the thick, black clouds, their undersides lit up by the moon. 'It's gonna rain.'

'You got a second passport?' asked Kytell.

'No,' I said. 'Not everyone makes a habit of taking fake IDs with them everywhere they go.'

'Shame,' he said. 'Might've come in handy.'

'Bianchi was tied up pretty well,' I said. 'And none of the phones in her house are working. It's gonna be a while before anyone finds her.'

'Fine,' he said. 'But what's to stop Graziani from putting out a warrant for you?'

'Self-preservation,' I told him. 'He wouldn't risk it.'

'Let's hope you're right.' Kytell kept his eyes on the dark tarmac road in front of him. In the distance I heard the faint sound of thunder.

'Kytell, what was going on back there?'

'You're asking *me*?'

'Why was Luke there – with Cesare? They only met each other this morning. Or at least I thought they did.'

'And why were they protecting the man who helped cover up Charlie's murder?' added Kytell.

'Maybe Luke wasn't there to protect him,' I said, wanting what I was saying to be true. 'Maybe he was worried I'd go after him, and was there to stop me doing something dangerous.'

'Maybe,' my brother agreed. 'But from what you said earlier, Luke wouldn't have known you were after Graziani. Why would he go there, of all places, if he was just keeping an eye on you?'

'You're right,' I admitted unhappily. 'The last Luke knew, I was heading to the hotel to grill the people there. If he thought I'd end up at Graziani's, he must have known there was dirt on Graziani for me to dig up.'

'Either that,' said Kytell, 'or they hadn't got a clue you were gonna make an appearance and were there under their own steam.'

Fat drops of rain splattered across our windscreen, and Kytell got the wipers going.

'As we were leaving, Graziani did ask them what they were

doing there,' I pointed out. 'So they weren't invited. He seemed as surprised to see them as I was.'

'Maybe,' said Kytell, executing a smooth right turn onto the road to Patrezzi, 'they were there to kill him.'

I thought about that. 'But why? I mean, anyone who loved Charlie would have a motive, but Cesare hardly knew him. He only met him that one time, last year.'

'As far as you know, anyway,' said Kytell.

Had Cesare known Charlie better than I'd realized? I thought back to that afternoon at his farmhouse, eating lunch there, playing football in among the olive trees. I was sure that they hadn't known each other before that day. So why was he in the grounds of Graziani's house, with a handgun? And why was Luke with him?

'None of this makes sense!' I groaned, rubbing my face with the heels of my hands. My fingers were starting to swell up from the punch I'd given Bianchi.

'What did the pathologist tell you?' Kytell asked. I hadn't wanted to talk much after leaving her house, and had only told my brother that she'd grassed up Graziani.

'It doesn't make much sense unless you know all the facts,' I said. 'She changed the report so the stomach contents referred to "pasta" instead of "spaghetti".'

'What the fuck?' laughed my brother.

'It's here, on the right,' I said, pointing out the road that led down to the hotel. 'It sounds crazy, but I think I know why they wanted her to change it.'

'Why?' The hotel lights, a blur of yellow-white through the rain smearing the windscreen, were growing larger.

'Because Charlie had tagliatelle for lunch that day.'

'You're sure?' Kytell asked, frowning.

'I'm sure. And Bianchi's equally sure it was spaghetti she found in Charlie's stomach.'

'So what difference does it make?'

'I don't know,' I said. 'Just that the lunch we ate together wasn't the last meal Charlie had before he died. But they wanted us to think it was, otherwise the whole accidental drowning verdict would go out the window.'

Kytell veered into a parking spot in the hotel car park and yanked on the handbrake. 'How specific was the time of death?' he asked.

'Not that specific – just to within a few days.'

'So the only thing that "proves" he died on the day he left you on the beach was the stomach contents matching the last meal you had?'

I froze in my seat. My memory had dredged up a mental image of some words written in the margin of a newspaper. At the time I'd thought it was just a forgetful man's way of remembering what he wanted to order: *spaghetti – tomato sauce – red wine*.

'The guy with the paper, the Yank!' I said, grabbing Kytell's arm. 'There was a man at the next table when we ate our last meal together. He wrote down what Charlie was eating!'

'So you were being followed,' said Kytell. 'If they knew what Charlie had ordered, they could've held him for a day or two, then fed him the same food they thought he'd eaten that last day with you so it looked like he died the same day you saw him last.'

'It's the only thing that makes sense. I mean, it's completely crazy, but it does make sense.'

We sat there for a moment. I'm not sure what Kytell was thinking about, but I was imagining Charlie being given this meal of spaghetti to eat, and wondering whether he knew the significance of what he was eating. Did he know he was helping them cover up his own murder?

'You know, Kate,' said Kytell, his voice as low as the rumble of the engine, 'I thought you were gonna say she faked the DNA match.'

Tears stung my eyes. 'I wish, Ky. I wish. She didn't do the DNA testing though. It went off to a lab in Rome. Plus, you know, the tattoo and everything . . .'

'Yeah,' he said, not looking at me. 'Yeah, I know.' He reached out a huge hand and squeezed one of mine. 'Go and get your things,' he said. 'I'll pay your hotel bill while you're packing.'

I got my room key from reception and jogged through the rain to the apartment. The hotel complex seemed almost empty; only a few lights were on around the place. Raindrops drummed on the leaves of the plants in the beds that lined the pavements, assaulting the delicate petals of the pink bougainvillaea.

I rocked to a halt as I rounded the corner. There was someone sitting in the shadows of the covered terrace in front of the apartment. I saw the end of a lit cigarette glow orange, then a misty string of smoke drifted past me and was absorbed by the rain-soaked air.

I knew it couldn't be Luke or any of the others – there was no way they could have overtaken us on our way here. And it seemed unlikely that the American man who had warned me off digging into Charlie's death would allow his people to keep watch on someone by taking a seat on their patio and smoking a fag. I took a cautious step forward, trying to make out the person's face. Whoever it was heard me, and stood up into the light from the apartment next door.

'Kate?' the figure said, peering out into the darkness.

I walked up the stairs to the terrace. 'Hello, Sofia,' I said, and tried to smile at the woman who had guided me through those anguished days of waiting.

She kissed me on each cheek. 'But you're soaked,' she said. 'Come inside and let's get you dry.'

I let us both into the apartment, and she found a towel for me in the bathroom. I started to rub my hair dry.

'What are you doing here?' I asked. 'I was told you quit after . . . what happened last summer.'

Sofia nodded, stubbing out her cigarette in the ashtray. 'Well, not exactly. After a couple of months I requested a transfer, and the hotel moved me to another branch in Sardinia. But I heard you were in town, and I wanted to see you.'

'You came all the way from Sardinia?'

She shrugged. 'It's not that far. How are you, Katerina? Why have you come back here?'

I frowned at her, too suspicious now of anyone and anything to trust her when she said it was only concern that had made her come here from her new home. 'I'm fine,' I said. 'I just came back for a couple of days. I'm leaving again now. Do you know when the next flight is back to the UK?'

She looked at her watch. 'If the schedules haven't changed in the last year, there should be a flight in a few hours.'

'Perfect.' I grabbed my suitcase, which I'd never properly unpacked, and went round the apartment stuffing it full of the few things I had taken out.

'Are you sure everything is okay?' Sofia asked. She rested a hand on my arm, making me stop what I was doing. She reached out and pulled my hand over to her, looking at my red knuckles. 'Something's wrong,' she said. 'Isn't it.'

I put down the case and looked her dead in the eye, hoping I could trust her, that she wasn't part of this conspiracy. It seemed unlikely that whoever had killed Charlie had managed to install a plant in a hotel that we'd only picked out at the last minute, but my paranoia was running rampant.

'Yes,' I said finally. 'Something's wrong. I think Charlie was murdered.'

'What?' she gasped.

I sat her down at the table, and over a quick cigarette I told her a condensed version of everything that had happened over the last week, leaving out my interrogation of her country-woman and the attempted break-in of a police officer's house. To give her her due, she didn't ask many questions, just listened and took it in.

'I have to know,' I said at the end. 'Is there anything you remember, anything at all, that didn't mean much at the time, but that might mean something now? Anyone strange hanging around the week Charlie went missing? Anyone asking about us?'

Sofia was already nodding. 'Yes, yes. But we thought what happened to Charlie was an accident – we didn't realize or I would have told you back then – a master key went missing – one of the maid's. She was sure it was taken, but there were no thefts reported, so we thought maybe it was just lost somewhere. The cost of the replacement came out of her pay.'

'When? When was this?'

Sofia closed her eyes, trying to remember. 'The day you went out, I think. I'm not sure, but I think I remember wanting to warn you to put anything valuable in your safe, just in case, but you were out for the day . . . and after Charlie went missing, it didn't really seem important. Do you think it's part of it?'

I didn't have a clue. 'Maybe. I keep thinking maybe Charlie had something, some piece of evidence that they needed to find.'

'And he hid it in your apartment?'

'Possibly, although I don't know where he could have hidden it without my coming across it. He couldn't have left it in the safe, for example. Could it still be in the room, concealed behind one of the paintings or something?'

Sofia was shaking her head. 'No. The rooms are all repainted each November; the decorators would have found something. But where else could he have put it? Could it be hidden in your flat in London?'

I laughed at the extent of my lack of knowledge; my ignorance was like a vast plain as far as the eye could see. A few enigmatic shapes on the horizon were my only clues to the truth of Charlie's death.

'If it was, I'm sure my flat would have been ransacked a long time ago.'

'Maybe they searched it without you noticing,' pointed out Sofia. I hoped not. The idea of those evil parasites searching through our things, invading the shrine of our life together, made me want to throw up again.

I looked at my watch. 'I have to go. Thank you for coming – I'm sorry we couldn't talk properly. It was sweet of you to come and see how I was.'

Sofia smiled, her eyes suddenly brimming with tears. 'I lost my husband,' she said.

'What?'

'He died in a car accident when I was twenty-three.'

'Oh.' It all seemed to make sense then, the care and compassion she'd shown to me during that awful week, and why she was here now. I hugged her then, hard. 'Thank you,' I whispered. 'And I'm sorry.'

Sofia waved me and Kytell off. I turned in my car seat and watched her through the back window until she was just a faint dab of paleness in the distance.

'It might be a coincidence,' Kytell said, when I told him about the master key.

'Do you really think so?'

'No,' he grinned, all big white teeth in the darkness of the car.

'So do we assume they have whatever they were looking for?' I said. 'Or do we go through our place back home with a fine-tooth comb?'

Kytell looked at his watch. 'I've got to be back in London tomorrow for a meet,' he said. 'Can't miss it. But I'll keep it short and sweet, and then I'll be yours to command.'

At the airport we returned the hire car and went to buy tickets for the flight back to London.

'Let's split up,' I said. 'If anything's been reported, they'll know my name but they won't know yours.'

'Good luck,' Kytell said.

I tried to look relaxed and casual as I handed over my credit card and passport. The girl at the check-in desk only looked at me once, when she was matching my face to my passport photo. It didn't seem that I had anything to worry about, but there was still over an hour to go before the flight actually took off.

I went through security and took a seat at a coffee bar in the lounge. There were plasma TVs at each end of the seating area, one showing CNN, the other showing an Italian channel. I ordered a coffee and watched CNN, only vaguely taking in the news stories.

Kytell came through and sat a few tables away from me, facing in my direction. We pretended not to know each other. Five minutes after his mineral water arrived, I caught his eye and he flicked his gaze over to the other TV, the one showing the Italian channel. Shifting in my seat to get a better view, I nearly jumped out of my skin when I saw the Grazianis' farmhouse on the screen. The picture then changed to show Bianchi's house, the front yard full of police cars, lights flashing. The words *doppio omicidio* were stamped in a banner under the images. I felt sudden colour flare in my cheeks.

The Italian to English dictionary had been checked in with my suitcase, but I didn't really need it to translate the words. *Double homicide.*

'Oh fuck,' I said under my breath. 'Luke . . . what in God's name have you done?'

Chapter Sixteen

Kytell and I sat as far apart as possible on the plane, and he kept his distance as we went through passport control. As the machine scanned my passport I felt sure that an alarm was about to go off that would send every UK Border agent in the airport swarming in my direction, but once the facial recognition software had considered me for what seemed like half an hour, the gate opened and I was free to go.

I followed Kytell to his car in silence, neither of us speaking until we were inside with the doors shut.

'Bloody hell, I felt sure they were going to have an alert out for me,' I said, my hands shaking as I pulled a cigarette out from the packet in Kytell's glove compartment. Kytell doesn't smoke, but my other brothers are always leaving half-empty packets there.

'After I left you alone, with that pathologist,' he said, 'did you . . . is there anything you didn't tell me?'

I paused in the middle of lighting my cigarette to glare at him. 'Are you asking me if I killed her?'

'Did you?'

'Christ, Ky, I thought you knew me better than that.'

'The Kate I know wouldn't have hurt someone for information either.'

'Yeah, I know.' I let out a hard breath. 'But don't forget, that bitch covered up Charlie's murder.'

'So she got what was coming to her?'

'I didn't say that. But am I sad she's dead? No. She and Graziani can rot in hell for all I care.'

'You're assuming the second dead guy is Graziani,' said Kytell.

Shit, he was right! I hadn't even considered that it might have been Cesare – or, God forbid, Luke.

'What next?' asked my brother.

'Home.'

'Not a good idea. Even if your name hasn't come up yet, it soon will. You sure you wanna be sitting in your flat waiting for the police to arrive?'

'No, but I don't have much choice. My friend back at the hotel says a master key was stolen, which means someone was searching through our room. I don't think they found what they were looking for though, as I can't imagine anywhere Charlie could've hidden something without my coming across it – which means it might still be back at the flat.'

Kytell tried to point out that the missing master key could have been a coincidence; that Charlie might have successfully hidden something in the hotel room that the bad guys might successfully have found; and that if they hadn't found what they were looking for, there was a very good chance that they would already have searched our London flat at some point in the last year.

'You weren't burgled, were you – soon after you got back?'

'No, I would have told you.'

'Still. They could've been very tidy burglars.'

'Trust me – I would have noticed.'

In the end, he abandoned his attempts to talk me out of my search. He knew me too well; knew that I can't give up once I've started something. That's why when we were kids and he first lent me his GameBoy, he didn't get it back until I'd beaten all my brothers' Tetris high scores.

When we got to Islington Kytell cruised up and down my street a few times before we were happy that nobody was lying in wait for me.

'You sure you don't want me to come in with you, check everything's all right?' he said.

'No, I'll be fine. Look, if you see the old man, promise me you won't tell him about this, yeah?'

Kytell chuckled, a sound that came from low down in his chest. 'You're being dumb, Kate. He could help.'

'Like he'd give a shit. He made that pretty clear when he couldn't even be bothered to get in touch when Charlie died.'

'He misses you, you know. Asks after you.'

I didn't want to hear that. 'I can't ask him for help,' I said. 'I'm not that much of a hypocrite. Can you imagine what he'd say? "Funny how quick you come running back around when you're in a spot of bother. Decided my skills aren't quite so distasteful to you after all, have you?"' My lip curled. 'I wouldn't give him the satisfaction.'

'You're heading down a path that's gonna take you all the way back home,' said Kytell. 'You know that, don't you?'

'Things have gone too far now. I can't help it.' I bit at my lip, not wanting to get emotional. 'Fuck, maybe Dad was right all along. Maybe I'm not cut out for the life I want.'

Kytell covered my forehead with his palm. I looked at him, nonplussed.

'Just checking you've not got a fever,' he said.

'Yeah yeah, very funny.'

'Look, have it your own way – I swear I won't say a word. But I want you to promise me something too. If Luke turns up, don't answer the door, yeah? I don't know exactly what game he's playing at with this thing in Sicily, but this world is made up of goats and tigers, Kate, and he ain't no goat.'

I saw guilt in Kytell's amber eyes. 'What aren't you telling me?'

He looked away. 'I know I probably should have told you this at the time, but a few months back he hooked us up in the States. And I'm talking major players.'

'What the fuck?' I said. 'How could you do that?'

'Keep your knickers on. All Luke knows is that some friends of his are doing business with some friends of mine. He seemed keen to know exactly how well I knew the people I was recommending, and I made out like they were just some guys I'd run into in the past that I knew to be reliable. So you don't have to worry; he's got no idea that I happen to be related to them – and trust me, we're keeping it that way. Your secret's still safe.'

I got out of the car, slamming the door shut behind me. Kytell, looking chastened, put the engine in gear. He stopped when I turned on my heel and knocked on his window.

'What about Charlie?' I said, when he wound the window down.

'What about him?'

'Did you reckon him for a tiger, too?'

My brother thought for a moment. 'I've never seen Luke uncomfortable round violence. Charlie, though – he seemed used to it, but never comfortable with it.' He leaned towards me then. 'A bit like you.'

Kytell buzzed the window back up and headed out on the high street.

As I walked up the steps to the front door, I noticed the curtains were pulled shut, and felt a bite of anxiety for Samantha and David. The hallway was quiet, and I put my ear to the door to our apartment. Silence.

The key turned smoothly in the lock, but the door creaked as it opened. The lounge was empty, in half-darkness.

'Samantha?' I called out, too nervous to go into the bedroom for fear of what I might find.

David suddenly stepped into the bedroom doorway, holding my bedside lamp in his hand.

'Oh thank fuck,' he said. 'I thought I was going to have a
heart attack.'

Samantha appeared from behind him, wielding my heavy-
duty frying pan. 'Jesus, couldn't you have called ahead first?
I might have brained you with this pan.'

'A pan?' I said. 'I think you guys have been watching too
many cartoons. There's a whole array of knives in the kitchen
that might be more use in a fight.'

'I didn't want to kill anyone,' explained Samantha.

'No, just give them a really bad headache,' agreed David.

Ten minutes later they were seated on the sofa having a cup
of coffee, while I perched on the edge of the armchair and listened to the events of the past couple of days.

'I think we fooled them for quite a while,' Samantha told
me. 'I'm not sure what gave us away, but suddenly there's a
pounding on the door, like these guys are trying to break in.
I knew we couldn't open the door, so I called out "What the
hell do you want?" – you know, trying to sound like you.'

'What did they say?'

'"Open the goddamn door!"' Samantha did a pretty good
American accent. 'We didn't, of course, and luckily no one else
in the house was inclined to buzz them in. After about five
minutes the banging stopped, and we thought they'd given
up.' She shuddered. 'Then one of them appeared outside the
window. Christ, Kate, it was like something out of *Salem's
Lot*.'

I looked through the living-room window at the battered
old fire escape. 'Whoever he was, he's a brave bastard.'

'Oh, he was really creepy. He just looked at us and nodded,

as though seeing us confirmed what he already knew. Then he
asked us where you were.'

'What did you say?'

'Nothing. David picked up the phone and said he was going
to call the police. And then the guy was gone.'

'Do you remember what he looked like?'

'I don't think I'll ever forget. Just seeing him there, in the
window, it's going to be imprinted on my mind for ever.'

'Darkish hair,' said David, getting tired of the melodra-
matics. 'Old-fashioned glasses. About five eleven, maybe six
foot. Slim. Clean-shaven. In his mid-fifties, I'd say.'

'I know him. I think he's in charge.'

'Yeah, but of who?' Samantha asked.

'Of whom,' David corrected her, earning himself a dig in the
ribs.

'That's what I'm going to find out.'

They wanted to know what I'd discovered in Sicily, and I
told them about the doctored autopsy report, leaving out the
method by which I'd come by this information and what had
subsequently happened to the person who'd given it to me.

'And where's Luke?' asked a puzzled Samantha.

'I don't know,' I said. 'I think he might be involved.'

'What?' she exploded.

'I don't know for certain. He was just acting very suspiciously.'

'You're kidding,' said David. 'Luke and Charlie – they were
friends since they were little, right? I can't see him having anything to do with this.'

'Well, I think you'd be surprised. Just be careful if he comes
to see you – don't tell him that I'm back, just say that your
cover got blown and you didn't see the point in staying.'

'What are you going to do now?' asked Samantha in a faint
voice.

'It's probably best if I don't tell you,' I said. 'I'm sorry that I got you mixed up in this. The less you know now, the better.'

'But—' began Samantha, but David stopped her.

'I think you're right,' he said. 'C'mon, Sam, let's get our stuff together and leave Kate to it.'

I handed over the clothes Samantha had lent me, and they packed up their bags. At the door, Samantha gave me one of her patented puppy dog looks.

'Please, Kate,' she said. 'Go to the police. If you've got evidence that Charlie was murdered, I'm sure they'd look into it.'

'I'll think about it,' I said, only half-meaning it.

David gave me a baleful look, and I could tell he'd realized I'd put them in danger.

'I'm sorry, David,' I said, but he pulled the door shut without replying, closing me in.

Although time was of the essence, I had to get clean. As I removed my shirt, I noticed a few spots of what looked like dried ketchup on the sleeve. When I realized it was Bianchi's blood I just sat there, seconds tick-tocking into minutes as I stared at the dark red specks. I didn't know what to do with the shirt. Washing it seemed disrespectful somehow, like assuming a washing machine could remove guilt as it removed food stains. Should I wear it for the rest of my life, like a hair shirt, a punishment for my crime?

'Get a grip,' I told myself, scrunching up the shirt so the stains were hidden from view, and shoving it at the bottom of my chest of drawers. I knew I'd need to dispose of it at some point in the near future.

I placed the rest of my clothes in the laundry basket and had a shower, the hot water burning the grazed skin on my knuckles. Even after using half my shower gel I didn't feel clean. The warm, metallic smell of Bianchi's blood was like a phantom odour that the soap couldn't eradicate.

Was it Luke who had murdered her? Had he found out the truth about Charlie, and wanted revenge? Or was she killed by the people who had hired her in the first place?

Part of me wanted to follow Samantha's advice and go to the police, to ask for help. But what could I tell them? I couldn't pass on evidence that a coroner in Sicily had faked an important detail of my husband's autopsy report without making myself a prime suspect in her murder. And there was no way I could be honest with them and admit that I'd broken into her house and hurt her. Even if they believed me when I said I'd left her alive, I'd still be spending the next few years in an Italian prison.

And what would it all be for? What would their reaction be to my big revelation that Bianchi had swapped the word 'spaghetti' for the word 'pasta'? Something told me it wasn't going to lead to the set-up of a massive Interpol taskforce.

No. I couldn't take the risk. I couldn't trust them to push it as far as I would. I wasn't prepared to sit in some cell in Sicily while my husband's killers covered their tracks. No leads would be left when I came out.

I got out of the shower and rubbed at my skin with a towel till it went pink. When I was dry I tugged on a clean pair of jeans and a white short-sleeved T-shirt that Samantha must have uncovered at the back of a drawer. Then I sat myself down at the desk and pulled my laptop towards me.

The keywords *Graziani* and *Bianchi* pulled up nothing recent on Google, so I went onto the BBC News site and searched for recent news stories on Sicily. Finding nothing, I tried *The Times*, then finally got lucky with the *Guardian*.

It was only a brief article, obviously written without much to go on, and said just that two bodies had been found, that the police were treating the deaths as related and suspicious, and that the journalist had gathered that both of the deceased were government officials. So Luke wasn't one of the corpses. I wasn't sure whether to feel relieved.

Until later in the day the news wasn't going to tell me anything useful. I needed to know how Graziani and Bianchi had died, and whether the police had released any descriptions of people they wanted to question.

Even if I wasn't wanted by the Sicilian police, I had a horrible feeling that the men in suits would still be after me – perhaps more so, now that they knew I'd been in Sicily, turning over rocks.

Where to start, though? I stood in the centre of the living room, hands on hips, and rotated slowly, looking at all the furniture and furnishings in the flat.

Having seen too many films where safes are hidden behind pictures, I turned over all our picture-frames, just to find bare wall beneath them. I took the backs off all the framed photos and checked that there weren't any notes hidden between the photos and the backing sheet. I shook out each sofa cushion covering, even though I remembered taking them off to be washed just a few months ago. I looked inside each DVD and CD case, and flipped through the pages of every book. One, John Irving's *A Prayer for Owen Meany*, still had a bookmark in it. Charlie had been reading it that summer, but had forgotten to pack it. Now he'd never finish it. I threw the book across the room, and kept searching.

I emptied the kitchen cupboards, but found nothing but a few stray grains of rice and lots of spilt salt. I bent over to look under the coffee-table, the desk and the kitchen table, but there was nothing taped beneath them.

I didn't bother with the bathroom, since unless Charlie had concealed something in a half-empty bottle of talc, I was pretty sure I'd used up all the toiletries that had been sitting on our shelves a year ago.

That left the bedroom. I lay on the carpet and checked under the bed, and went through every single pocket of Charlie's clothes. All I found was some lint and a ticket stub from our visit to last year's Anthony Gormley exhibition at the Hayward Gallery. I remembered walking along the South Bank with Charlie, and swallowed hard. Certain memories of him were like desiccated trees, sucked dry by my attempts to bring him to life in my head. And yet sometimes I'd remember a particular moment for the first time, and suddenly my husband was beside me again, an abundance of green in the desert of my memories. I could see him now, laughing at some witty comment a busker was making as we walked by, the sun on his face, his eyes shining. 'I love you, I love you, I love you,' I said silently to my memory of him.

I sat on the bed and went through our files of important papers. All present and correct; no surprises there. The box of memorabilia – love notes, birthday cards, drawings we'd done for each other – well, that had to be approached with a certain steely detachment. The photo albums were likewise flipped through with a refusal to look at the photos themselves. Then I remembered how I'd come to be sitting on my bed looking for whatever incriminating evidence had prompted someone to kill my husband, and thought it worthwhile to go through the pictures again, this time looking for someone in the background that I wasn't expecting to find there – Cesare perhaps, or the suited man in the old-fashioned glasses. But the people in the background were the same bunch of familiar friends and complete strangers they'd always been.

I put the photo albums back on the shelf, and took down Charlie's work folders, which he kept on the top of his wardrobe. There wasn't much there, since most of his designs were stored on the computer as electronic files, but I found a few old blueprints from his college days, and some of the little sketches he'd make whenever he came across a building or detail he liked.

I opened one folder, and a USB pen dropped into my lap. The folder had some odd bits and pieces in it, such as a photocopy of a Gary Larson cartoon, a postcard of the now demolished Carnival Hotel in Las Vegas – *that* made me smile – and a couple of pay slips. Then I remembered where the folder had come from: a work colleague of Charlie's had handed it to Luke at the wake, explaining that it was things from the clear-out of his desk that they thought I might want to have.

Running out of other options, I picked up the USB pen and went back to my laptop, taking the sketches with me.

The memory stick seemed to be a back-up of the hard drive of Charlie's work PC. I browsed through the files, but couldn't see anything that stood out. There was a folder called *Personal*, but it only held some info about Charlie's pension and the wedding list of some friends of ours who had got married six months after us. I ran a search for all the files that had been created or modified in the three weeks leading up to Charlie's death, and went through them one by one.

When I reached the cached HTML files of the websites Charlie had been visiting, I hit paydirt.

Body of unidentified man found in Hudson, I read. *Death being investigated as homicide.* The first lot of headlines were dated over two years previously, before I'd even met Charlie. Turned out the body was missing most of its face, thanks to a blast from a shotgun, with the teeth too shattered to help in ID-ing the corpse. Then I double-clicked on a cached webpage from a true-crime blog, dated a month later.

Shotgun victim identified as Federico Calabresi, I read, and the name was like a knock on my heart. I thought it might be a name I knew.

Federico Calabresi was a well-known figure in the world of organized crime. When his associates were asked why they hadn't reported him missing, they apparently told investigators that they believed Mr Calabresi was taking an extended sailing vacation in the Bahamas. Speculation is of course rife that this was a Mob hit by either a rival family, or – considering the apparent lack of concern on the part of Mr Calabresi's associates – an inside job. The investigators in this case have a difficult job; not only is it impossible to perform a ballistics match between a shotgun and the pellets it fired, but the state of the body when it was discovered, along with the number of possible suspects who would profit from Federico Calabresi's death, means that the New York branch of the FBI will have a hard time even finding someone to charge.

I sat staring at the screen, elbows propped up on the desk in front of me, hands cupped over my nose and mouth. Federico Calabresi looked back at me from his photograph – taken, mercifully, before rather than after his death. He was a heavy-set guy in his forties, with receding, sandy-coloured hair and a moustache. If you didn't know he was a mobster, you would have taken him for a nice guy. He was smiling almost bashfully, as if he didn't enjoy having his photo taken. He didn't look like someone who knew he was about to have his face ripped off by shotgun pellets.

'No, Rico, no!' That's what Charlie used to cry out in his sleep, his voice hoarse. I'd shake him out of his nightmare. The first time he said that name, I asked him what it meant.

He told me that a guy called Rico had been driving the car that his parents had died in. They were at a birthday party for

some old friends, and his dad had had a little too much sangria. Rico had offered to give them a lift home, not bothering
to tell them that he'd had a little too much sangria too. He'd
run a red light, swerved to avoid the pedestrian crossing the
road, and wrapped the car round the traffic-lights. Charlie's
dad, in the front passenger seat, had died instantly. Charlie's
mum, in the back, didn't like to wear seat belts because they
gave her indigestion. She flew forward, and cracked her skull
on the back of Rico's head. Rico didn't even feel it; he'd been
cut in half at the waist and was already dead. Charlie's mum
died of brain compression in the ambulance on the way to the
local hospital.

In Charlie's dream he was in the car, sitting next to his
mother in the back, seeing the red light, shouting at Rico,
trying to stop what was about to happen.

Or at least, that's what he'd told me.

Chapter Seventeen

The doorbell rang, and I jumped in my seat like a frog on a barbecue. Closing the webpage and lowering the laptop screen, I went to the window and peeped through the gap in the curtains. Kytell's head snapped round at the tiny movement, and when he saw me he raised his eyebrows. I buzzed him in, biting my thumbnail as I closed the door behind him.

'You okay?' he asked. 'You seem a bit edgy. You find what you were looking for?'

'I'm not sure,' I said, indicating the laptop. 'Take a look.'

He sat down, his massive frame making my normal-sized chair look like it belonged in a doll's house. His hand was twice the size of the computer mouse.

'I don't get it,' he said after a while. 'What's this got to do with Charlie?'

'He had nightmares about a man called Rico,' I explained. 'You remember Charlie's parents died in a car crash? Well he told me that this guy Rico was the one driving the car.'

'Who, him?' Kytell asked, pointing at the photo of Federico Calabresi on the laptop screen.

'I don't know if that's the same one. I s'pose not, judging by the fact that Federico Calabresi was shot and the Rico in Charlie's dream died in the car crash.'

'So what are you thinking?'

'That maybe Charlie was having nightmares about this

man's murder, and tried to cover it up by telling me he was dreaming about his parents' death.'

Kytell leaned back in the chair, which creaked. 'When did he first mention this Federico guy's name? When he rang to tell you that his folks had died?'

'No, he didn't tell me there was anyone with them in the car. He said it was someone else's fault, and that they'd died in the accident too – but I just assumed he meant the person who was driving the car that they collided with.'

'So when did the Rico guy's name first come up?'

'Not until he mumbled it during a nightmare, and I asked him about it,' I said.

Kytell regarded me with a, 'Well, that's that,' look.

'Oh Kytell, you don't think Charlie killed him, do you?' I whispered.

All the frustration and adrenaline of the last few days suddenly became too much for me to take. I'd thought I could handle whatever I found, but I hadn't expected to find that Charlie had lied to me. Did I even really know him? How could he have hidden something like this from me? I wanted to scream at him, to demand answers, but he wasn't there to give them, was he?

'Argh, Charlie!' I yelled, fists clenched.

My brother stood up and pulled me to him. He wrapped his chunky, warm arms around me, and it was like being encased in armour. 'Shhh, shhh,' he soothed.

'But what if I never find out what happened to him?' I said in anguish. 'What if all I find out is that he was wanted for murder? Jesus, Ky, do you think that's the only reason he came here?'

Kytell pushed me away, his hands on my shoulders. He had to lean down in order to look me in the eye.

'Search your heart,' he said. 'You knew Charlie. I think you knew him better than he knew himself, to be honest. You think he was capable of blasting someone in the face and dumping them in the river?'

I laughed then, tearfully. 'No,' I admitted.

'No, neither do I. And he came here for you, not for any other reason. So there'll be some other explanation for why he was looking up this Calabresi guy that you just ain't found yet. Right?'

'Right,' I said, stepping forward and hugging him again. 'Thank you. Thank you for all of it.'

The doorbell rang again, and we moved apart.

'You expecting someone?'

I shook my head. Kytell nodded at the laptop and I pulled out the memory stick and wedged it into my pocket.

My brother went to the window and eyed our new visitor through the chink in the curtains. When he saw who it was, he went running to the door. I followed him, saw him wrenching the front door open, and there was Luke. Remembering that my T-shirt only had short sleeves I automatically crossed my arms, folding them over my chest.

'What are you doing here?' Kytell snapped at Luke. 'Stay the fuck away from my sister!'

Luke looked at the bull-sized Kytell warily, but stood his ground. 'Kate?' he said to me, looking past Kytell. 'Kate, it wasn't me, I swear. Please, I need to speak to you.'

'Didn't you hear me?' said Kytell, planting a huge hand in the centre of Luke's chest and pushing him back two steps. '*I said*, stay the fuck away from my sister.'

'Don't you want to know why I was there?' said Luke. 'Why I was with Cesare?'

Kytell raised his fist and Luke dropped back.

'Kytell, don't,' I said. 'Let him in.'

My brother glanced back at me over his shoulder. 'You sure?'

'He can't hurt me while you're here.'

Kytell reluctantly stepped back and let Luke past. Luke looked at me, hurt in his pale blue eyes. 'I wouldn't ever harm you, Kate.'

'Whatever,' I said, arms still crossed. 'Go in, then – you know the way.'

We walked with him through the door to the flat, then closed it and locked him in.

'Like that, is it?' he drawled as Kytell took the mortice-lock key and put it in his pocket.

'Yeah, it's like that,' rumbled Kytell, folding his massive arms and leaning back against the locked door.

I didn't have time for the testosterone display. 'Luke, did you kill Graziani?'

'No,' he said. 'Did you?'

'Oh fuck off,' I jeered. 'You saw us leaving.'

'Yeah, and then *we* left. For all I know, you came back to finish off the job.'

'How about you tell me what the hell you were doing there in the first place?'

Luke took a deep breath, rubbing his forehead, and sat himself down at the kitchen table. 'You don't have any painkillers, do you? The Rock here did a real number on me – my ribcage looks like someone's been painting-by-numbers in green and yellow.'

'Sorry,' I said with a fake smile. 'I used them all up.'

He sighed. 'Fine. Look, we were there for your own good. I knew you were suspicious of Graziani, even after Cesare told you he was a straight arrow, and we were worried you were going to get yourself in trouble. And we were right! Christ, Kate, you were there with a knife.'

'Cesare was there with a bloody gun!' I pointed out. 'And since when were you two such good mates?'

'He was there for you, for Charlie – not for me.'

'Bollocks. The two of you were protecting Graziani.'

'No. We were protecting you from yourself. I mean, Jesus, Kate, what the hell did the two of you do to that poor doctor?'

'We did enough to find out she helped to cover up Charlie's murder,' I said.

'Is that why you killed her?' Luke asked. He stood up then, wincing, holding his ribs. 'Jesus, I thought Lunkhead here got carried away, but it was you, wasn't it?'

'We didn't kill her,' I said through gritted teeth.

'Who are you trying to kid?' Luke said wearily. 'I know how mad you are about Charlie, and I know what kind of shitty impulse control you have. You're telling me that woman confessed to being involved in Charlie's death, and you just said "Grazie signora" and walked away?'

'Think what you want,' I said, arms still folded tight across my chest. 'I really don't care any more.'

'So tell me then,' said Luke. 'What's the great mystery of Charlie's death?'

'She said she changed the autopsy report.'

'And how did she change it?'

I tilted my chin at him defiantly. 'She revised what she'd entered as the stomach contents, so they matched the meal we knew he'd eaten.'

'What did it say before, then?' asked Luke.

'Spaghetti,' I said.

'And she'd changed it to . . .?'

'Pasta.'

'For fuck's sake, Kate!' Luke roared. 'That's hardly evidence of murder!'

'Don't you fucking pretend it doesn't mean anything,' I swore back at him. 'Don't you dare! It *has* to mean something.'

'Kate, you've got to stop,' said Luke. He took my hands in his. 'Look what's happened since you started searching for Charlie. Two people are dead. You've hurt someone – killed her, for all I know. For the past three years you've been like my baby sister, and now we can't even trust each other. Katie, I know you're hurting, I know you are. God knows I miss him too, but I'm just so worried about you.' Tears welled up in his eyes, making them even bluer. His voice was starting to crack. 'That wasn't Charlie in the photo. You know that, right?'

I just looked at him. He tugged at my hands, which were curling into fists in his palms.

'All you found out – if it means anything at all – is that the meal Charlie ate with you wasn't the last one he had before he died. Who knows, maybe they changed the report because they had a nice, cut-and-dried case that they couldn't be bothered investigating any further. Maybe Graziani just thought it would be better to be vague about the stomach contents, knowing that you'd be picking over every detail. Christ, maybe Bianchi just made a mistake. Maybe she was a lush, and in her drunken haze she identified the wrong shape of fucking pasta. It's no big deal, Kate! It certainly doesn't warrant a bullet in the back of her brain!'

'I didn't kill her!' I yelled in his face. In my frustration I made the mistake of twisting my hands out of his grasp, and revealing my bare forearms.

Luke caught sight of them and stared down in shock. He grabbed my wrists again, this time turning them so he could look properly at the large pink welts that transversed both my arms at just under the elbows.

I let him look. Kytell watched from a few feet away, remaining silent. It was no revelation for him; he'd sat by my side at the hospital for as long as they'd let him stay, and visited every day at the mental health unit where I'd been sectioned.

Finally Luke met my eyes again. 'When?' was all he could say.

'Months ago,' I told him. 'You were away. One of your business trips.'

'Why didn't you tell me?'

'What was there to tell? I tried to go, to be with him. It didn't work.'

'Kate,' he said, his face close to mine. He could tell I was prevaricating. He whispered in my ear: '*Why didn't you tell me?*'

'Honestly?' I said. 'Because I didn't want you watching me. I knew you'd want to move in, or have me move in with you. I wanted to have the freedom to try again, if I needed to.'

He shook his head in disbelief at what I was saying. 'How did you do it?'

'The usual. Twenty painkillers, a bottle of JD or something, and a razorblade in the bathtub.'

Unfortunately, because of the state I was in, I'd forgotten to turn off the taps. The bath overflowed, and Agnetha came up to tell me their ceiling was leaking. When I hadn't answered the door she let herself in with the spare key we'd given them in case we ever mislaid our own.

She found me in a bath full of cold water and blood, and dragged me out. We waited on the sofa for the ambulance, with her pressing towels onto the cuts to try and stop the bleeding, me drifting in and out of consciousness, and poor Hannah trapped downstairs in the wheelchair, calling up to know what was happening.

'My poor child,' Aggie had said to me, wrapping my shivering, naked body in the throw from the sofa. Through heavy eyelids I had watched my blood seep into the thick, colourful beach towel she'd wedged in the crooks of my elbows. 'My poor, poor child.'

Luke took a step back from me, turning away towards the kitchen.

'I can't believe you did this,' he said. I couldn't see his face, just the line of his slumped shoulders. He sounded strangely distracted. 'You should have talked to me. You should have spoken to me first.'

'Why?' I said, not unkindly. 'What could you have said that could have possibly made a difference?'

He sighed and turned back in my direction, though he still wasn't looking me in the eye. 'I'm so sorry,' he said.

'Luke?' I had to raise my voice to get him to look at me. 'Don't be weird with me. *I'm* sorry – I know how hard it would have been for you if it had worked. But there's nothing you could have done differently, nothing that would have stopped me trying to be with him. Don't take any of this on yourself. I just couldn't bear being without Charlie one more second.'

Luke held my face in his hands, his eyes beaming like search-lights into mine, reading me. 'Promise me,' he whispered. 'Promise me you won't ever try anything like that ever again.'

I smiled at him sadly. 'I can't promise that. I can promise that I've got greater priorities though.' Luke's hands slipped from my face, and I could feel my expression hardening. 'Finding *them* comes first.'

The doorbell rang and we all froze.

'Luke?'

'I didn't bring anyone,' he said.

Kytell went to look out of the window, but I put out a hand to stop him. 'Let me look.'

I edged my way to the end of the curtain and peeked through a small gap in the fabric.

'Oh shit,' I said.

'Who is it?' whispered Luke.

There were three uniformed police officers and two in suits on the steps outside. The shorter detective, the one in the long mac, banged on the front door. 'Police! Can you come to the door, Miss Grey!'

'Fuck,' rumbled Kytell.

I hurriedly pulled on my jacket, covering up my arms, and ran to the other side of the flat, to the window that overlooked the garden. The fire escape was basically a death trap held together with rust, but it would have to do. Then I saw the two cops in their smart black and white uniforms, hovering in the garden to cover my escape route.

'Go down to Aggie and Hannah's,' ordered Luke. 'Quickly, before they bust their way in here.'

'I can't,' I said. 'I can't involve them. You two go there though – there's no need for them to find you too.' I could see them hesitating, so opened the door to the flat and herded them out. As they reluctantly went to the downstairs apartment, the police rang the doorbell again, rapping on the front door for good measure. Hannah, curious as to what was making such a racket, opened her door and nearly jumped out of her chair when she saw Luke there, poised to knock.

'Sorry!' I mouthed at her. 'Can they?' I indicated Luke and Kytell.

She rolled her eyes. 'It's okay,' she mouthed back, and beckoned the two of them in. With one last look back at me, Ky – who would have waded past all five cops to clear a path for me if I'd asked – closed the door behind them, and I was in the hallway on my own.

I swung open the front door, stepped out, and shut it behind me. Only then did I meet the gaze of the detective who'd been calling my name.

'I'm Kate Grey,' I said. 'What do you want?'

The detective had one of those faces that good police officers develop when they've spent a number of years playing their cards close to their chest. He looked me over in a couple of seconds, assessing me almost subconsciously on a number of levels; was my body poised to make a run for it? Was I carrying a concealed weapon? Was I injured, or did I have any blood on my clothes?

'Miss Grey, I'm DI Collins.' He showed me his warrant card. 'We'd like you to come down the station for a chat.'

'Sorry,' I said. 'I'm a bit busy today. Can we make it later in the week?'

'It won't take long,' he said, placing a hand on my elbow and trying to steer me down the steps to the pavement. I lifted my elbow out of his grasp.

'No,' I said. 'Sorry. Maybe some other time.'

'Miss Grey, trust me, it'll be easier on you if you just come with us now.'

'Easier on me?' I laughed. 'Nah, easier on *you*, I think. Easier for you if I don't have a lawyer, and you don't have to play to a time limit. You want to talk to me, you'll have to arrest me.'

DI Collins reached out again, for my arm this time. I batted his hand away, hard, and with a lightning reaction time he went under my swing and grabbed my right elbow, spinning me round and slamming me against the front door.

'Kate Grey, I'm arresting you for assaulting a police officer, under section 89 of the 1996 Police Act. You do not have to say anything, but it may harm your defence if you do not mention now something that you later rely on in court. Anything you do say may be given in evidence. Do you understand these rights as I have explained them to you?'

'Yeah,' I said, face squashed against the painted wood of the heavy door, arm twisted behind my back.

'I'm going to release your arm. Do not turn around. Raise your hands and lay them on the door. Feet apart.'

I did as he said. The female uniformed officer stepped forward and frisked me.

'She's clean,' she said.

'Come on then, let's go and have this chat,' said Collins, escorting me down the stairs and into the back of a Panda car. He even did that thing of putting a hand on my head so I didn't bang it on the car and try to sue him for police brutality. I'd been arrested before, at the tender age of fifteen, and it was all starting to come back to me.

Collins sat in the front passenger seat on the short drive to the police station, but he looked straight ahead, almost ignoring me. I wondered what I could say that might make them believe I was innocent of Bianchi's murder. It was tough without knowing how they'd become aware of me.

The thing was, I'd had rules about arrest drummed into me, and number one was 'Don't open your mouth'. So when DI Collins observed that I hadn't seemed too surprised to see them, I said nothing.

'I expect you want to know what we'd like to speak to you about,' he tried next. He looked in the rearview mirror for my reaction. I stared out of the window, focusing on the cars passing by in the other direction. 'That's fine, just keep going right ahead pretending this whole experience is incredibly boring for you,' he said, tapping his fingers on the dashboard. 'But I can tell you this for nothing, Miss Grey: the British police are a lot nicer than the Sicilians when it comes to interview technique. I know who I'd rather speak to.'

I was never very good at keeping my gob shut. 'Good to know,' I said, nodding at him, and smiled without showing my teeth. He turned away, and we spent the rest of the brief journey in silence.

*

The cell I was in was chilly and smelt of piss. A stainless-steel toilet sat in the corner, only affording a little privacy from the watch-hole in the cell door. There was a small window in the wall, but it was too high up to look out of.

I sat crosslegged on the concrete ledge that jutted out from the wall. A thin, canvas-covered mattress provided some padding. I was shitting myself, driven crazy by not knowing how much information the police had. Who'd told them about me? Was it someone who'd known I'd harassed Bianchi in her offices, or worse, someone who'd seen me at her house? Was it Graziani, which would mean that someone else had died at his farm, not him? Without knowing how they knew about me, talking meant I risked being caught in a lie.

I stood up, pacing the cell, remembering reading somewhere that guilty people tended to relax after they were arrested, even going to sleep, whereas innocent people freaked out. I couldn't imagine why you'd relax at the prospect of being charged, but maybe waiting for the axe to fall is worse than the chop. Personally, I couldn't imagine not trying up until the last possible moment to escape my fate.

I forced myself to sit back down, and focus. What evidence could they have already? What evidence might they get?

They could have evidence that I'd been in Bianchi's house. My gloves were off when I'd hit her, and I could have inadvertently left prints. If so, I was fucked. My fingerprints were already on file, which could explain why they'd arrested me. And now they'd identified me, there would probably be other trace evidence, such as stray hairs, that could fuck me over too.

A search of my flat would uncover the shirt with its drops of Bianchi's blood. Still, a few drops couldn't be evidence that I'd killed her, could it? Well, that would depend on how she died. Luke had told us Bianchi was shot – and come to think of it, how did he know? Or was 'a bullet to the back of the head' just an expression rather than the literal execution method? Either way, if he was right, at least they weren't about to find the murder weapon with my prints on it in the apartment.

Unless Fifties Specs Guy and his mates are more devious than even you give them credit for, I thought. That would be perfect – making me a patsy for Bianchi's murder would keep the truth about Charlie's death safe for good.

I had just two goals. One was keeping my brother safe. The pay-as-you-go mobile I'd used to ring Kytell from Sicily was back at the flat, and if the police found it, with his criminal record they'd know he was involved.

The other goal was to find out who'd killed Charlie.

Everything else was secondary. Luke's freedom, my freedom; everything could be sacrificed to achieve those two goals. If it became clear that the police had enough evidence to get me extradited to Italy, I would confess to what I'd done to Bianchi – if it meant I could tell them what I'd learnt and convince them to carry on my search for the truth.

I heard footsteps in the corridor outside and steeled myself. My cell door was unlocked, and there stood DI Collins in his pale grey suit. There had been a change since our little car journey just an hour ago. Not even his poker face could hide the fact that something had unsettled him.

'We've got someone who wants a word with you,' he said.

If it wasn't CID that were going to be questioning me, that meant the Italian police were already involved. This wasn't a fishing expedition – they had something good on me.

'Where's my lawyer?' I said.

Collins looked at his watch. 'He's on his way. Look, you don't have to say anything if you don't want to. Just hear these guys out.'

'Do I have a choice?'

He looked at me, and his head was tilted slightly as though he was trying to work something out about me. What was he wondering? 'No, I don't think so,' he told me.

I couldn't read anything else from his face. I straightened my shoulders and followed him out of the cell.

He led me past the custody desk and up the stairwell to the second floor, where we stopped in front of a door marked *Interview Room 5*. Collins knocked, then opened the door without waiting for a response.

The room was largely in shadow thanks to the half-closed blinds blocking out most of the afternoon light. There was a large desk, its shorter side against one wall, but no one sat at it. Instead there were four empty chairs, one of which was pushed away from the desk at an angle, as though inviting me to sit there.

A man stood at the opposite end of the room, his back to us, regarding his own reflection in the large mirror that covered most of one wall. I looked him over, trying to work out if it was Graziani, but this man was taller, leaner, although he had short dark hair also. It was too gloomy in the room to make out his features in the mirror, despite my squinting. I stepped forward, waiting for him to face me. I wanted to see my next adversary.

'Hello, Kate,' I heard a familiar, American-accented voice say. 'I'm sorry you had to get pulled in like this.'

The man finally turned round and looked at me, arms out in apology.

'What the hell?' I said, taking a step back in shock. I made for the door, but it had already closed behind me, and wouldn't open from the inside without a code.

DI Collins had abandoned me; I was alone with the man who had accosted me in the bar of the Moonlite Hotel in Miami.

I turned round again, not wanting my back to this guy. He smiled at me reassuringly, and took off his distinctive glasses to rub the lenses clean on his tie.

'You don't have to worry about the cops,' he said. 'They think you're working for us. A couple of my men are in the room on the other side of the mirror, making sure they're not eavesdropping on this conversation, so you can be free with what you say.'

I eyed him warily, keeping my distance.

'I don't blame you for being suspicious. We haven't exactly been straight with you. I hope you'll understand why, when I tell you the background to this case.' He slid the fifties-style spectacles back on, and pulled a leather card-holder from his breast-pocket. He held it out to me, and after a moment I snatched it from him.

It was an ID card. The photo of him was a few years old; his hair was shorter now, and he'd lost weight. He still had the same hard eyes though.

'How do I know this is real?' I asked him, handing the ID back.

'You think we get to interrupt a murder investigation without proper authorization?' pointed out Special Agent Stanley Daultrey of the FBI.

'Bit outside your jurisdiction, isn't it?'

'Somewhat,' he admitted. 'Luckily our countries have a lot of enemies in common, so we're used to a bit of cooperation.'

'Am I a murder suspect?' I asked him bluntly.

'No. We managed to intervene before an EAW was issued.'

'An EAW?'

'A European Arrest Warrant. We've told both the Italians and the Brits that you've been working undercover in Sicily, and that you came into contact with both Graziani and Bianchi, but were categorically not involved in their deaths.'

I laughed. 'Why would you do that?'

'For the same reason I tried to warn you off in Miami – in an apparently vain attempt to keep you safe.'

'And what possible interest could you have in keeping me safe?'

Daultrey was suddenly solemn. 'Well, Kate, it's what Antoni would have wanted.'

I was baffled. 'And who the hell is Antoni?'

The FBI agent reached out and gripped my shoulder, as though preparing me for something.

'Your husband, Kate. Antoni was your husband.'

Chapter Eighteen

I was trying to speak, but no words were coming out.

'I realize this is something of a shock to you,' said Daultrey. 'Believe me, Antoni wouldn't have wanted you to find out this way. In fact, he didn't want you to *ever* find out. But needs must. Keeping you in the dark is just putting you in danger.'

A knocking sound came from the two-way mirror, and Daultrey came closer.

'That's my guys telling me your detectives aren't giving us as much privacy as we'd been promised,' he said, keeping his voice low. 'I can't tell you any more here. You'll have to trust me. Come with us.'

I stared at him, at his eyes, the colour of frozen mud. They were the eyes of someone who had seen too much.

'I don't know,' I said.

He nodded, as though he'd expected nothing less. 'We'll arrange for you to be released without charge. You'll get your belongings back, and Detective Collins will offer to get you a ride back to your apartment. Take him up on his offer if you like. I'll understand. But if you decide you want to know how your husband ended up dead in Sicily, turn him down. Walk out the door of this precinct, and take a left turn. We'll be waiting for you two streets down.'

Daultrey offered me his hand. Surprised, I shook it.

'I can see why Antoni fell for you,' he said with a rueful smile. 'Over the past week you have demonstrated that you share his stubborn streak. With a vengeance.' He turned for the door and punched in the code that released the lock. Then he swung back to me, his face dead serious once more.

'Kate, if you decide not to pursue this, just one word of warning. Luke Broussard is not what he appears.'

And with a decisive nod of his head, he left the interview room. The door swung shut behind him.

I sat down hard on the nearest chair.

What now?

Just as Daultrey said, Collins took me down to the custody desk and they returned the keys, wallet and belt they'd confiscated from me. I could feel the detective's eyes on me, trying to work me out. I hoped he wouldn't ask me any awkward questions, like why an English girl was working for the FBI, and I think Daultrey must have warned him off, as all he eventually said was, 'I'll see if one of my officers is free to take you back to your flat.'

'Thanks, but that's not necessary,' I told him. I hadn't made any decision yet about Daultrey, but I certainly didn't want to spend any more time in the company of the Met.

Collins escorted me to the police station's reception area. I breathed a sigh of relief as I stepped out onto neutral ground.

The sun was in my eyes. I looked from left to right down the road. Light bounced off car windscreens. Some teenage boys walked past me, laughing at something one of them was saying into his mobile. They checked out a girl who was walking in the opposite direction, her short skirt showing off lean, tanned legs. Windows down, a car radio sent out breezy R'n'B to the street. The buzz of London in the summer had never failed to catch me before that moment.

Was it true that my husband's real name was Antoni, not
Charlie? Why would he have lied to me? And why would the
FBI be interested in protecting me, to the extent of following
me to the UK, and tracking me down in Sicily? It seemed like
a lot of manpower to look after someone who wasn't even a
US citizen. And if they were so adamant that I was in danger,
why did they seem prepared to leave me alone if I took a right
turn, and headed home?

I'd been running from Daultrey and his agents for the last
week. It was too much of a paradigm shift to trust them now,
to put myself in their hands. If I got into that car, no one
would know; not Kytell, not even the police. My instincts told
me to walk away, and to do it quickly.

I took an uncertain step to the right, and began to walk
back home. Back to my poor brother, who I'd got caught up
in God knew what. Back to a man I'd thought was my best
friend, but who I could no longer trust. Back to the empty flat,
where nothing was waiting for me but a laptop with cached
webpages about a murder; a mystery that I'd probably never
get to the bottom of now. The scars on my arms began to
burn, as they sometimes did when I had pain I needed to
externalize. They wanted me to cut them open again, so they
could fulfil their purpose.

I wasn't meant to be here any more. A flesh and blood
person had gone, leaving just her shadow smeared behind on
the pavement. What was the point of going home? What was
I trying to protect, to prolong?

Flashes in my head of the life before me: the weddings I
would go to on my own, the toys I'd buy for other people's
children, the single occupancy discounts on hotel rooms, the
Valentine's Days without cards or flowers, the Christmases at
other people's houses, the painfulness of a beautiful sky with
no one to point it out to.

I saw myself as an old woman, sitting in a garden, watching an autumn leaf dance across the lawn. My hair was white, my hands gnarled and wrinkled. I was still wearing the wedding ring Charlie had put on my finger forty years before.

'Watch it!' said a man I nearly walked into as I spun on my heel and headed in the opposite direction. Paving stones blurred under my feet as I began to run. Two turnings after the police station, a dark car with tinted windows pulled away from the kerb and braked in front of me. The back door yawned and Daultrey was the one sitting there, holding it open.

I slid into the back seat and pulled the door shut. We sped away.

They took me to the Docklands, to an office building twenty storeys high. We went up in the lift to the eighteenth floor, sharing it with some stockbroker types who seemed to be heading up to the roof for a fag break.

'Yeah, you guys should come along next time,' one was saying to the other, getting out his pack of cigs and his Zippo lighter as though he needed to be ready to spark up the second he was outdoors. 'The place is *in*sane. Seriously.'

'Absolutely, we're there,' said City type number two, who was running his eyes over the heels of my boots like someone with a major shoe fetish.

'Eighteenth floor,' said the posh recorded voice of the lift. 'Doors opening.'

An odd threesome – the FBI agents in their suits, with me in between them in my blue jeans – we walked down the corridor together past the other offices with their company names etched into the glass walls that separated them from each other. The office space the FBI were using was right at the end. *Brompton Holdings*, said the sign. A young woman in a smart blouse was sitting at the reception desk. She nodded at Daultrey, but didn't even look at me. We went past her, into the part of the space hidden from view of the corridor.

The room was empty apart from a large desk and four chairs, like the set-up in the interview room back at the police station, even to the extent that blinds kept out the late-afternoon sun. Daultrey switched on a lamp whose yellow light pooled in a circle over the desk. He pulled out a seat for me, and took one opposite.

A blonde woman walked in, wearing a dark suit and high heels. I recognized her as the agent I'd spotted on the shuttle bus at the airport, when Luke and I had got back from Miami.

'This is Special Agent Angela Taylor,' said Daultrey as she handed him a file.

She nodded at me, sitting down next to Daultrey and crossing her legs. I nodded back.

Daultrey started to open the file, then paused.

'This isn't something that can be easily sugar-coated, and some of it is going to be hard for you to hear,' he said. 'Are you sure this is what you want?'

'Yes,' I said, my mouth dry. 'I need to know it all.'

He looked down at the table. 'For various legal and . . . other reasons, I can't tell you *everything* we know,' he went on. 'Some things must be dealt with via the proper channels. But I'll tell you everything we're sanctioned to impart, and perhaps a couple of things that Washington would rap my knuckles over.' He looked at Agent Taylor then, and she nodded, but with an 'it's your funeral' expression in her eyes.

I felt bolted to the chair as he reopened the file and handed me a photo of Charlie in a dark blue suit, smiling, the Stars and Stripes behind him. He was holding up a badge. His hair was short, and he was clean-shaven. He looked about twenty-five.

'He came top in his class at the Academy,' said Daultrey.

'He was an agent?' I said in surprise.

Daultrey nodded. 'Straight out of the Academy he was placed in the New York field office, working Missing Persons initially, but he soon showed a talent for undercover work. He was under for two years before he was offered a couple of jobs by the Mob. He gradually earned their trust, especially that of Federico Calabresi, a pretty low-level hood who was mainly involved with soft drugs and prostitution. With Calabresi vouching for him, he took the oath within another couple of years and became a made man.'

Daultrey leaned across the table, raising his eyes from the file to my face. 'You have to understand, Kate, this was a major accomplishment. It's notoriously hard to infiltrate the Mob. They tend to only trust those within their pre-existing community. Antoni was already something of a legend to those in the Bureau who were aware of his work.'

'I don't understand,' I said. 'I thought you had to kill two people or something before you could get made.'

'You know about the Mob?' said Daultrey, as though it would make things easier for him if I did.

'Not really,' I said, wanting to keep things simple. 'I've seen *The Sopranos*.'

'I see,' he said. 'Well, you're right, he had to "prove" himself to earn a place. When the target of the planned hit became known to us, we set it up so that this guy was told of his imminent murder and whisked off to a new life in Bermuda with a new name and new passport. We gave Antoni something he could use as proof he'd killed him – a posed photo of the so-called corpse, a piece of jewellery, a finger cut off some poor bastard about to be buried in Potters Field.

'During those three years he was in deep cover, I could only see him perhaps once a month. I know it was incredibly hard for him – he was spending almost his entire life in the company of men he was betraying on a regular basis, in constant fear of discovery. He had nerve, your husband. In fact, I'd say he was the bravest man I've ever met.'

Daultrey had to clear his throat. I stared down at the photograph of Charlie in his uniform. Why hadn't he felt able to tell me this? As far as Daultrey was concerned, my husband had been a hero.

'What went wrong?' I asked.

'He himself was betrayed. That was what went wrong.' Daultrey suddenly seemed very, very angry. 'Someone within the FBI – we don't know who – must have opened their mouth, because the truth about Antoni became known. An attempt was made on his life. He managed to escape, but Federico Calabresi was not so fortunate.'

'They killed him,' I said.

Daultrey nodded. 'As a punishment for his lack of judgement.'

Maybe this was why Charlie had hidden his past from me. If he had felt any genuine affection for Calabresi, he must have also felt guilt about his fate.

'Antoni wanted to remain an agent after testifying, but it just wasn't possible. He was given a new identity – Charles Benson – and relocated. He refused surgery to alter his appearance, telling me he'd given the bastards enough satisfaction in losing his identity. I think he wanted people to call him Antoni again after living so long as Giuseppe Carlo; it was very hard for him to be free of the Mob but still forced to use a name that wasn't his own.'

'Giuseppe Carlo?' I whispered. It sounded so strange on my tongue.

'The name's familiar to you?' asked Daultrey.

'No. It's just something makes sense now. In Sicily, last year, someone called him Carlo rather than Charlie, and he reacted badly. Now I know why.'

Daultrey nodded and carried on. 'Antoni had minored in architectural design at college, and with a few false references he soon found a job in the San Francisco area with a small architectural firm. He'd been living there nearly eleven months when he decided – against my advice – to vacation in Las Vegas with an old childhood friend. And there he met you.'

'And there he met me,' I echoed. 'And I suppose it didn't go against your advice to marry me?'

To give him his due, the agent did look slightly abashed. 'He didn't ask my advice, Kate, but no, you're right, I would have strongly recommended that he take the opportunity to relocate to Britain.'

'So I was just a new identity to him?' I said, my words feeling sour in my mouth. 'A way of hiding from the Mob?'

'No,' Daultrey said, looking at me sternly. 'Don't even think like that. I can't believe Antoni's feelings were anything other than a hundred per cent genuine.'

'Is that why he was so happy to come over to England?' I said. 'Was the whole story about his parents just a lie?'

'Antoni's parents passed away a long time ago,' admitted Daultrey. 'But look, can you blame him for being happy to come over here? He'd already left all his friends, his brother, behind him when he changed his identity. He had nothing to lose.'

And there it was. Two words that grew in the room, an invisible behemoth that it seemed only I was aware of.

'His brother?' I repeated.

Daultrey and Special Agent Taylor exchanged glances. Daultrey shuffled through the file, and then passed over a second photo.

'You may recognize him. Joe Cantelli. Antoni's twin brother.'

It was Charlie, but it wasn't. The man in the photograph looked like a 95 per cent copy. He had the same colour hair, but it was shorter and without a parting. The greatest difference was in the man's posture, the way he held himself; his shoulders were more hunched, and his smile was different. It was like looking at a photograph of a very skilled impersonator pretending to be Charlie.

'It must have been a huge shock to you, seeing Joe in that photograph your friends the Carvers took,' said Daultrey. 'It was a million to one that you'd ever learn about Joe, and to be honest I really wish you hadn't. You wouldn't be in the danger you're in if the Carvers had just picked another damn restaurant that night.'

My voice was shaking as I said: 'I'm not sorry they found him for me. Charlie had a brother, he had family. How could you have kept that from me?'

'How?' laughed Daultrey without humour. 'You think these people would give a second's thought about taking you out if they believed you were a threat? The only reason they didn't kill you too was because a double drowning would look that much more suspicious.'

'So they killed him. They're responsible.'

'I'm sorry, Kate. We tried to keep him safe, but he trusted the wrong people.'

'What do you mean?' I asked.

'How do you think they found you? And how do you think they knew you'd believe it was an accident? Who do you know who could say for sure if you were in on your husband's secret, or completely oblivious to his past?'

I knew immediately who Daultrey was talking about. 'No. He wouldn't.'

'Who set up your meeting with the Crestenzas in Sicily?' Daultrey pushed.

'No,' I said. 'He told me when he flew over that he didn't know them.'

'Try and remember, Kate. Who arranged that meeting? Did Antoni tell you about it before you left for Sicily?'

I frowned. 'We heard from them when we were already there.' And then I remembered. 'He told me Luke had let them know we were in the area.' Yet I could distinctly remember asking Luke if he knew the Crestenzas too, that night when we were drinking Jack Daniel's by the ocean, and that he had shaken his head. 'But are you saying the Crestenzas were involved in Charlie's death? They can't have been! Anyone could see how much they loved him.'

Daultrey shrugged. 'They did, you're right. They practically raised him after his folks died. The mistake they made – Antoni too – was in trusting Luke to find a safe place for their meeting.'

'They were followed?' I asked.

'No. The supposedly safe house they were sent to belongs to Cesare Amato, a capo in la Cosa Nostra. The old country still has ties to the new. After he verified that Antoni was the same man who had infiltrated their New York family under the name Giuseppe Carlo, they got in place and waited for the right time to present itself. They didn't have to wait long.'

'That doesn't make sense,' I protested. 'If Luke was going to betray Charlie, he could have done it at any time over those two years. Why wait that long to sell him out? And why make it look like an accident? Surely their normal technique is to empty a clip into someone.'

'You've certainly been paying attention during those *Sopranos* episodes,' Daultrey said, eyes narrowing. 'Well, you're right, that is generally their preferred method of execution. But the man who had your husband murdered didn't *want* anyone to know that he'd been executed. That was the whole point. Some guy in the Mob kills an agent, and every law enforcement officer in the country comes baying for Italian blood. For this reason, the families in the east have a rule – whack an agent, and get whacked yourself. They don't want the heat. Same reason why they couldn't do it here in Britain – you don't take someone out without getting the nod first from your London counterpart. No, they had to keep it under the radar. Taking care of Antoni in Sicily was so much easier: the Sicilians don't share their American brothers' reluctance to murder members of the judiciary system, and he knew he could buy people off if his plan turned out to have holes in it.'

'Bianchi,' I said. 'And Graziani.'

Daultrey nodded. 'Graziani turns out to have been on the payroll for a long time. Bianchi we're not so sure about, but from the looks of her house and her car, she was certainly getting paid overtime for something.'

'But why didn't you protect them?' I asked him.

'Protect them?' he said. 'We had no idea they were involved until they turned up dead.'

'But weren't you tailing us?'

Daultrey shook his head. 'Your clever little switcheroo with the Carvers worked, Kate. By the time we realized where you'd gone it was too late.'

'You told CID I was in the clear.' I stared at him. 'How do you know I didn't kill them both?'

'Because they were executed Mob-style,' said Daultrey, his eyes darkening, 'and quite frankly, Kate, you don't seem the type.'

There was a picture in my head of Bianchi as I'd left her in the house, hands bound, feet still tied to those metal sofa legs. A sitting duck for the men who came for her after me.

Daultrey saw my expression and pushed a bottle of water over to me.

I took one gulp, then another, feeling a bead of sweat run down my forehead. 'Graziani's kids,' I said. 'His wife.'

'No,' Daultrey reassured me. 'Just him.'

'At his house?'

'They took him into the woods at the back of his property.'

'Was it Luke?' I asked. 'Luke and Cesare?'

'We don't know. The wife's description fits them though.'

'They were there,' I told him. 'We came for Graziani, and they were already there. They wanted to stop me talking to him. Cesare had a revolver.'

'What happened?'

'Graziani came out of the house with a shotgun. Wanted to know what the hell we were all doing on his property. I accused him of covering up Charlie's murder, and – well, let's just say they made me leave. We went back to the hotel . . .' I didn't want to refer to Kytell by name; if they hadn't identified my brother by now, I wasn't going to help them '. . . and you know what happened after that.'

'They must have done Graziani then headed over to Bianchi's,' mused Daultrey. 'If they knew you were onto those two, they couldn't run the risk that Graziani and Bianchi might turn state's evidence and testify.'

I thought about Luke's behaviour over the past week; his attempts to convince me that I was crazy, just creating a mystery out of thin air, and the way he only came with me to Miami when he knew he couldn't stop me.

'Luke didn't want me to go to Miami,' I said. 'He didn't want me to find Joe Cantelli.'

'No,' said Daultrey. 'Because finding Joe would mean discovering Charlie wasn't who he said he was.'

'So that guy we went to see in Miami – Bruno Luna,' I said,

my brain beginning to build a mosaic with all the little pieces, 'did he know Charlie, after all? If Joe was staying at his place, I mean.'

'It's possible,' conceded Daultrey. 'Antoni didn't mention him, but he could have met him at some point. We are pretty sure that Luna and your friend Luke know each other.'

I remembered drinking coffee in that Cuban café, and coming back from the washroom to catch Luke talking on his mobile. Had he been ringing Bruno Luna, to warn him we were coming?

If I'd been Luke, wanting to keep me away from the truth, I'd have headed out on my own earlier that morning and paid the maître d' of El Cangrejo Dorado to keep his mouth shut. Then when the waiter put in a surprise appearance and ruined things by giving us Alejandro, I'd have suggested we take a break from the hunt – lunch at a local café perhaps – and created an opportunity to call Bruno Luna and come up with a back-up plan.

'Shit!' I swore. 'Claudette – Bruno Luna's maid. She took me to one side, told me she had information about Joe. I went to her *botánica*, and it turned out she knew sod all, but still, that's not something I think Luna would be happy about.' Had Luke passed on the fact of our meeting to her employer?

Apparently so. The next photo Daultrey handed me was of Claudette, a hospital curtain forming a backdrop behind her, her eye swollen shut and her lip split. 'She won't press charges,' he told me. 'All she'll say is that she had an accident at work, fell down some stairs.'

I had to look away from the photo.

'At least she's not dead,' said Daultrey. 'She'll heal.'

'Charlie's brother hangs around with a nice bunch of mates,' I said.

Daultrey took the photo from me, putting it back in the file.

'They grew up in a rough neighbourhood,' he said. 'Antoni took exception to it, and went one route. Joe took a shine to it, and went another route.'

'But I thought he was a contractor, a builder,' I said. 'Are you saying he's a hood?'

'No, not at all,' said Daultrey. 'If he'd been in the life, there's no way his brother could have gone undercover. Joe's got a couple of priors, but they're minor. He had what you might call a misspent youth, that's all. His business is doing well, and apart from a few suspicious tax returns, it's legitimate. But he is still friendly with a lot of the guys from his old neighbour-hood, and some of them make their money from far less legitimate means.'

'Like Luke,' I said bluntly.

'Luca De Santis served three years in Nevada State Penitentiary for intent to supply. Hence my decided reluctance for Antoni to hook up with him for a vacation. He had seemed to go straight when he got out though, to give him his due, and he and Antoni had grown up together. I trusted Antoni's judgement. It was a mistake.'

'De Santis?' I said, almost laughing now. 'He told me his name was Broussard. *Charlie* told me his name was Broussard.'

'When he moved to the UK, he changed it. He was De Santis when you first met him in Las Vegas, though.'

I thought back and realized I hadn't even known Luke's sur-name till Charlie had come to live with me in London.

'Jesus Christ,' I said. I put down the bottle of water, wish-ing it was whiskey. Everything I thought I knew about my life was falling down around me. It was like finding out your brick house was really just a film set made of cardboard and cellophane windows.

'I know this is a hell of a lot to take in,' said Daultrey, 'but—'

'Do you know who gave the order?' I asked.

He sat back in his seat. 'I said earlier that there were some things we couldn't tell you.'

'But is that because you don't know, or because you're not authorized to tell me?'

Special Agent Angela Taylor was looking down at the table, uncomfortable. Daultrey was watching me though, not feeling at all awkward at denying me information that he would have gone crazy for, had he been in my position.

'For Christ's sake, I'm entitled to know who killed my husband!' I yelled. Swearing under my breath, I twisted out of my seat and stalked the room.

'You'll just have to trust us, Kate. We're putting this all together, but it takes time. But you have my word, the man responsible will be caught, charged and convicted. I'm going to see to it he spends the rest of his days in prison.'

'That's not good enough,' I said. 'Don't you have the death penalty in New York State?'

Agent Taylor glanced up at her boss. He didn't return her gaze. 'We do,' he said.

'Look, I'm not stupid,' I told him. 'The order can have only come from the head of the family, and I could probably find out his name from fucking Wikipedia.'

Daultrey shrugged. 'Well, maybe you should use that method then. That way, if you decide to do something stupid, I won't get canned and lose my pension.'

He had me pegged, and he knew it. To get what I wanted, I was going to have to try the softly softly approach.

I sat back down. 'So what now?'

He pushed the file to one side. 'Well, I'm afraid you're in serious danger. Worst case scenario, you're now on a hitlist. I believe De Santis has a soft spot for you, but he had some serious gambling debts, and when faced with the choice between

giving you up and losing his own life, he'll make the same
decision he made with Antoni. He knows where you live, he
knows your friends, he knows your habits. You can't go anywhere that he might know about.'

'Are my friends and family in danger?'

Daultrey's head tilted a little to one side. 'We've got a watch
on the Carvers, but I imagine your other friends don't know
anything that might put them at risk. As for family, I wasn't
aware you had any.' His dark eyes locked onto mine. 'In fact,
you're a bit of an enigma, Kate Grey.'

'I fell out with my parents a long time ago,' I admitted,
glancing down at the label on my water bottle, picking away
at its edges. 'Luke's never met them. But my brother – Luke
knows about him. I need to call him.'

'We can protect him,' Daultrey assured me, his eyes switching from high beam to low. 'Just tell me where he is.'

'He can protect himself,' I said. 'And he already doesn't
trust Luke. But I would still appreciate being able to warn
him.'

Daultrey nodded. 'Of course.'

Kytell, Samantha, David – all at risk because of me.
Claudette – hurt because of me. Bianchi and Graziani – dead
because of me.

'I need some fresh air,' I said, pushing back my chair as I
stood up. 'I assume I'm safe in this building?'

Daultrey waved a hand, rising to his feet as though it was
ungentlemanly to remain seated when a lady was standing. I
let myself out of the room, and walked past the receptionist
without a word. The corridor was empty, but there were office
workers waiting by the lifts, apparently finally calling it a day
and heading for home, or maybe to the local bars. I couldn't
even remember what day it was.

All the lifts were going down. I gave up, pushing through

the emergency exit doors that led to the stairwell. The fluorescent strip lighting on the cold concrete steps seemed
unnecessarily harsh to my tired eyes, but it was only two
flights up, and I had the joy of emerging into a pink evening
sky.

A summer breeze stroked my face, lifted my hair. I wanted
to feel the warm air on my bare skin, so I took off my jacket
and stood with my scarred arms turned to the orange sun.

The city stretched out around me, buildings jutting up into
the stratosphere, some silhouetted by the gold-streaked clouds,
others reflecting the setting sun in thousands of glinting windows. In the distance I could see the massive wheel of the
London Eye, slowly, slowly revolving. Even this high up you
could hear cars tooting, and the faint whine of an ambulance
siren.

I crunched through the gravel and fag butts to the edge of
the building, where a four-foot-high barrier of steel and rein-
forced glass bordered the roof. Looking over it to the ground
far below made my stomach lurch, just as it had at the top of
that bungee platform in Vegas. Well, you've done it before, I
reminded myself. The only difference is, this time there would-
n't be a harness strapped to your ankles. I wondered if I'd find
Charlie waiting for me at the end of this jump too.

I had my hands on the barrier, thinking how easy it would
be to swing my right leg over and pull myself up, when I heard
Daultrey speak.

'You look like you need a cigarette,' he said. I hesitated, my
back to him, knowing I could still get up and over before he
could reach me. My elbows and arms remained tensed, ready
to raise me up.

'I can help you kill him.'

Slowly, the muscles in my arms and legs relaxed and my
hands let go their grip on the top of the barrier. I turned to

face him. He'd taken off his suit jacket and had rolled up his shirt-sleeves, and was smoking a cigarette. His white shirt and tanned face were bathed in the sunset light, the sun winking in the glass lenses of his spectacles.

He held out an open fag packet to me, and after a moment I stepped forward and took one. He snapped a flame from his lighter. I leant towards him, cupping the flame with my hand as it danced in the evening breeze, and sucked at the cigarette till the tobacco at the other end glowed the same colour as the sun.

I stepped back and we looked at each other, exhaling smoke in silence. No one had followed him up here; it was just the two of us.

'His name is Luigi Sorrentino,' Daultrey said. 'He's fifty-two years old, lives in Manhattan, drives a BMW and a Ferrari. He has one ex-wife, no kids. We have his schedule for the next four days. On Monday he's leaving New York for a short vacation. I'm sure you'll appreciate the irony when I tell you his destination is Las Vegas. On Wednesday he has tickets for a show. He has requested an escort for the evening. I can swap her for you. You could get close enough to kill him.'

I just looked at him, trying to work him out. 'Why? Why would you do that?'

His eyes were dark, deadly serious. 'I'd kill him myself, but I have a family. A wife, two girls. If it was just me I'd drop him in a heartbeat, but I'm not risking my family.'

'Charlie meant that much to you?'

'He was the best agent I ever had. When you work that closely with someone – when they're trusting you with their lives – well, there's a bond there. And I let him down, Kate.' He sucked at his cigarette, and when he spoke his words came out low and grey, and dissipated into the air: 'I let him down.'

'Do they know you're having this conversation with me?' I asked him, nodding towards the roof door, meaning the other agents.

'No. I'll tell them you're coming to the US so we can better protect you. When the time's right, you'll take off. We'll find you in some seedy joint at the end of the night, drunk out of your mind. The barkeep and two regulars will swear you kept them company all night.'

'What, your team wouldn't be suspicious when they find Sorrentino dead a couple of days later?'

Daultrey shrugged. 'Not of me, no. Of you? Probably. The thing is, not one single person in the FBI would try and make a case against Antoni Cantelli's widow for the murder of his killer.'

'Even if the FBI gave me a free pass, I'm guessing Sorrentino's friends wouldn't be so understanding.'

'You're heading for the Witness Protection Programme already, Kate. I'm just giving you an opportunity to settle the score before you disappear.'

'The Witness Protection Programme?'

'Come on, honey, you're not stupid. We can't protect you for ever. You're going to need a new identity, to go someplace where De Santis would never think of looking for you.'

Disquieted, I glanced down. Far below us, on the murky Thames, a clipper boat traversed the river, white froth churning up in its wake.

Did I trust Daultrey? At this moment in time, the only person I trusted was Kytell. But the FBI agent was giving me options I just wouldn't have on my own. I wasn't going to take out Sorrentino without first making sure he was Charlie's killer, but there was no reason Daultrey had to know that – just like he didn't need to know that I had no intention of going into Witness Protection. He could get me alone in a room with Sorrentino and a loaded gun in my hand; I'd never manage that alone. And there was something else he could get me too.

I brought the cigarette to my lips and felt a buzz that wasn't just nicotine starting to zing through my body, waking me up, making me alert, making me strong.

'I need to see Joe Cantelli,' I said, smoke streaming out of my mouth.

Daultrey looked taken aback. 'That's not going to be straightforward.'

'I realize that. But I'm not coming with you unless you promise me you'll arrange a meeting. Las Vegas is only a few hours from where he lives; it's not as if I'm asking him to come all the way to London. I just need to see him. Just once. Because as soon as I'm in Witness Protection, that's it, I'll never be able to. And he's Charlie brother, Stanley. Come on, you can't deny me that.'

'Okay,' he said. 'We'll contact him, I promise.'

'That's not good enough.' I shook my head. 'If you want Charlie's killer dead as badly as I do, then you'll have to sort this out. I'm not going after Sorrentino until Joe's agreed to meet me.'

'Fine,' he said, dropping his cigarette and grinding it into the ground. 'But Kate, you're going to have to stop calling him "Charlie".' And as he had in that bar in Miami what seemed like an age ago, his mouth twisted as he said the name. He looked at me then, and he was angry. 'His name was Antoni. I'd appreciate it if you at least gave him the courtesy of using his actual name.'

I threw down my cigarette, still lit, onto the gravel. 'Screw you, Daultrey,' I said. 'I married him under that name, and buried him under it too.' I walked past him to the door, putting my jacket on, pulling the sleeves over the scars he must have seen but had not commented on. Just before I went through it, I turned back to him.

'Thank you for giving me Sorrentino,' I said. 'But don't think because you knew Charlie longer, you knew him better. I've spent the last twelve months without the other half of my *soul*, Daultrey. And you're not volunteering yourself to cut the throat of that motherfucker who took him away from me, so pardon me, but I'll call him whatever the hell I fucking please.'

He grabbed my arm, and I had to resist the urge to punch him in the face.

'You're a fighter, Kate,' he said, 'and that's good. You're going to need that anger. But in front of the other agents, you need to play nice. As far as the FBI is concerned, you're a loving wife who had no idea what the hell kind of mess she was getting herself into. Now she knows, she's terrified, and wants nothing more than a new identity in a nice little town far away from the nasty men who hurt her husband. *Understand?*'

I wrenched my arm free. 'Yeah. I understand.'

I pushed through the door, careering down the concrete stairs.

'Kate,' he said, then again, when I was at the top of the second flight of stairs: '*Kate.*'

I stopped and looked up at him, framed in the doorway, the strip lighting flattening his features, and the great, deep clouds of the dusky London sky stretching out behind him.

'I am on your side,' he said.

'Yeah, Stanley,' I lied. 'I know.'

Chapter Nineteen

Daultrey and I sat in the back seat of the black car on the street where I lived. We were waiting for the other agents to finish their security sweep.

'As I said, worst case scenario is that a hit's out on you,' Daultrey had said when we returned to the meeting room, pretending in front of the other agents that everything was okay, and we hadn't just been plotting murder. His transformation back into straight-laced suit had been worryingly impressive. 'Best case scenario is that they're going to try and frame you for the Graziani and Bianchi murders. Which means the British police need to search your flat as soon as possible, before the Mob have a chance to plant something there. Is there anything you want to pick up first?'

'Yes,' I'd said, thinking not just of the shirt with the specks of Bianchi's blood, but also of the phone with my brother's mobile number on it. There was no way I was going to risk leading anyone to Kytell. 'And I need to pack some clothes.'

We'd headed back down to the car, where Daultrey had introduced me to a bald black guy with a neat moustache. 'Special Agent Walter Wilson,' he'd said. Wilson had shot up the corners of his mouth in an approximation of a smile. 'And the gentleman driving is Special Agent Marshall Jerkins.' Jerkins had a blond crewcut and a square head. We'd glanced at each other in the rearview mirror. He was the guy from the airport, the one I'd forced to tell me the time.

Special Agent Taylor knocked on the car window.

'The area's clear,' she said.

I slipped into the house, not wanting my downstairs neighbours to realize I was back. Lord knew what Kytell and Luke had told them. I remembered Kytell trying to warn me about Luke, and felt immense relief that I didn't have to worry about my brother misplacing his trust.

The flat appeared just as I'd left it. I threw some clothes in my holdall, beginning to feel sick of the sight of it. Remembering Daultrey's plans for getting me up close and personal to Sorrentino, I tucked my sexiest dress on top. The bloodstained shirt and the pay-as-you-go mobile I'd taken to Sicily went in a plastic bag that I zipped into a side pocket.

I took one last look around the place, wondering if I'd ever see it again. It was full of memories of the man I loved, but his absence was more palpable here than anywhere else I could be. On the wall was a calendar of days he'd never see. A TV guide on the coffee-table for programmes he'd never watch. I looked around and saw a ghost of him cooking in the kitchen, playing cards with Luke at the table, cuddling up with me on the sofa with the lights out as we watched some cheesy horror film. Leaving this place felt like leaving him.

Taking a framed picture of us from the shelf, I flipped up the catches on the back and removed the photo from the glass. We were in wetsuits, sitting on the edge of a boat with our hair dripping, laughing. We'd just come up from swimming with tiger sharks, and were laughing because sometimes that's what you do when you've been terrified but survived. The sharks had been interested in us, but not in a carnivorous kind of way. However, I'd been glad I wasn't a fish.

Charlie's eyes were the same colour as the ocean water that sparkled behind us.

I tucked the photo into my back pocket, said a silent good-bye to our home together, and closed the door behind me.

I made them take me to the centre of London, back to the Thames. I wasn't about to take the risk of dumping the evidence in a canal and having them come and look for it after I'd left. The shirt was wrapped around a half-brick I found lying around on the shore near the Oxo Tower, then tied into the plastic carrier bag. I squeezed all the air out of the bag, then threw it with all my strength out into the jade-coloured river.

'Litter bug,' said a passer-by, scowling at me from the walk-way above.

I ran back up the steps and headed for Gabriel's Wharf, get-ting out the mobile and calling Kytell's number. As it rang, I kept a watch on Daultrey and the other agents, waiting for me twenty feet away in their sleek black cars.

'Kate?' Kytell answered. 'You okay? What happened?'

'Christ, Ky, I've got a lot to tell you, but now's not the best time. Look, I've got a lead on who might have killed Charlie. If anything happens to me, you've got to promise me you'll make sure you find the fucker and take care of him.'

Kytell freaked out. The phone actually rattled in my hand, and I had to hold it away from me before my eardrum burst.

'Ky! KY! Stop cursing.'

'Kate, you're crazy. Let's get together and talk about this. If you want this guy killed I swear I'll arrange it, but you should-n't be going after him yourself! What the hell are you thinking? Seriously, Kate, don't rush into this. Get your bear-ings, I'll call in some favours, we can do this properly.'

'No. There's only a small window of opportunity. Just

promise me that if you don't hear from me by Friday you'll make sure you find out the truth about Charlie and get justice for him.'

'I promise,' said my brother. 'Just tell me the name of this guy you reckon's responsible.'

'No,' I said. ''Cos I know if I do, I'll get to the States and he'll be dead already. I need to look him in the eye and know for sure he killed Charlie before I let anything happen to him. I'll send you his name just before I go after him, in case . . . well, in case anything happens to me.' I took a breath. 'I'm going to have to dump this phone now. I can't take the risk they'll use it to prove you were there in Sicily.'

'No, wait, don't—'

'I love you, Ky,' I said, and broke off the call. Then I took out the SIM card, threw it on the pavement and ground it under the heel of my boot. Agent Jerkins and Agent Taylor got out of the sedan and scanned the surrounding area with their blank gazes. Taylor looked at me and pointed to her watch. I nodded, picked up the crushed SIM card and dropped it into one of the drains in the gutter by my feet.

PART III

Las Vegas

Chapter Twenty

Vegas took the best parts of the world and recreated them with a sheen of luxury. Here was the Statue of Liberty, the red track of a roller coaster looping around her as she stood watch over a scaled-down version of the Brooklyn Bridge. Here was the Eiffel Tower, glowing gold, beside a sparkling air balloon of dark blue and crimson. Here was the Doge's Palace in Piazza San Marco, complete with gondoliers in stripey shirts who serenaded their passengers as they steered them along the turquoise canals inside the Venetian Hotel. Here was the gleaming black pyramid of the Luxor, guarded by a perfect Sphinx who would never be worn down or chiselled away.

Here was Kate Grey, with revenge in her heart.

The other agents never said anything in front of me, but sometimes I caught them exchanging glances behind Stanley Daultrey's back. He relayed to me what he'd told them: that since we had a few days before the Witness Protection Programme was ready for me, he had acquiesced to my request to go back, for one final time, to the place where I'd met my husband, their brother-in-arms. I had the feeling Daultrey had played the guilt trip card. The final wish of a woman whose husband had died for his country and so on. I didn't really care if they believed him or not, as long as they weren't going to get in the way of me finding Sorrentino.

Daultrey had booked us into the Regal Hotel and casino, which was themed along the lines of Tudor England. I think he thought it would make me feel at home. We were checked in by a woman in a factory-made version of Anne Boleyn's favourite dress, and shown to our room by some poor guy in a jester's outfit.

Our rooms, like the rest of the hotel, were panelled in oak. The sofas and chairs were made of studded dark red and green leather, and the beds were, of course, fourposters. Oil paintings in ornate frames were bolted to the walls. In addition to the chandelier in the centre of each suite, lamps of coloured glass radiated light.

'Nice,' I said quietly to Daultrey. 'Didn't know the FBI had such a good budget for overnight accommodation.'

'Oh, the hotels in this town like to show their appreciation for our work by giving us a substantial discount,' he told me with no hint of irony.

Each suite had two bedrooms and one living room. As the only woman in the team, Agent Taylor had the other bedroom in my suite. Daultrey and Wilson were in the suite on our right, with Jerkins and another agent on our left.

We spent Tuesday night at the gambling tables. Rather, I spent it at the gambling tables, accruing and losing chips stamped with the Regal's trademark golden crown, while the agents stood guard around me. Back in my bedroom at the end of the night, I sat at the anachronistic computer with free internet access and Googled Luigi Sorrentino. There were a couple of newspaper stories on him, one with a photo. I looked at the man who had apparently ordered Charlie's death. He was a big guy, balding, with little dark piggy eyes and a mean face. Later, lying in bed, I stared up at the dark canopy above me, and saw that face superimposed on the brocade material. I dreamt about him, about chasing him up stairs, around corners, through doorways. In the end, he was chasing me.

I spent the next day tense with anticipation. I couldn't eat, already full up with butterflies, so just drank endless cups of coffee. For one precious moment during the day it was just Daultrey and me.

'Is it on?' I asked, and he nodded.

'Go to your room at half-eight,' he said. 'I'll come by with the intel.'

'First things first,' I said. 'When am I seeing Joe?'

Daultrey's gaze skittered away along the walls. 'Kate, I'm not sure that's really such a good idea.'

'You promised me,' I said, feeling myself flushing. 'Stanley, I need to see him.'

Daultrey was shaking his head. 'I've made overtures, but I think his wife, Marisa, is very apprehensive about you meeting with him. She heard about you tracking him down to Miami, and she feels threatened.'

'What, she thinks I'm going to try and steal her husband?' I laughed.

'Well, you were in love with someone who looked just like him,' Daultrey pointed out.

'No,' I said. 'Trust me, her marriage is safe. I just want to meet my brother-in-law.'

'Look, I'll see what I can do.'

'No, Stanley,' I said, my words hard as diamonds. 'You'll arrange it. I'm not going after Sorrentino until you've set this up.'

Then Jerkins came back in the room, and I had to return to pretending to read the paper.

I had hours and hours to kill. Back in my room I lay on the bed and stared at the wall, trying so hard not to think about

Charlie and all the lies he'd told me. I knew that my Charlie and Daultrey's Antoni were the same person, that the man Daultrey had known was different only in name and occupation from the man I knew. It was still Charlie. And I even knew why he'd never told me the truth; I understood that strange emotional mix of guilt and protectiveness. And yet I felt sadder than I had since Charlie's death. I felt as if I'd lost him all over again.

I wondered what I'd feel when I saw Sorrentino. Despite what I'd told Daultrey, I wasn't about to kill him without asking any questions. If I'd been unwise to trust my own husband, I certainly wasn't about to take anything Daultrey said at face value.

And if after speaking to him I *was* convinced he was responsible for Charlie's death – what then? I remembered the fury I'd felt with Bianchi, the rage that had made me run at Graziani despite the shotgun in his hands. Would it really be that hard to take his life? Would the act haunt me for the rest of my days . . . or would his death be the only thing that would let me sleep at night?

We had an early dinner in the room. 'You feel like hitting the tables again this evening?' asked Jerkins.

'No, I'm knackered,' I told him. 'I think I might have an early night.'

Taylor looked at her watch. 'You sure?'

'Yeah. I'll have a bath, maybe read for a bit.' Neither of them looked exactly disappointed; they had full control over the remote with me out of the room, and could talk shop without worrying about me listening in.

In my room I got out of my clothes, changed into the complimentary bathrobe and scrubbed my face clean with one of the carved soaps. Then I sat on the bed, feet jiggling nervously, and waited for Daultrey.

At a quarter to nine, I heard him come into the suite and say something to his agents.

'She's turned in already,' Taylor's voice said, but Daultrey ignored her and rapped on my door.

'Come in,' I called out, trying to sound sleepy.

Daultrey stepped into the room, a large envelope under his arm, and closed the door quickly behind him. He looked as tense as I felt.

'Run a bath,' he whispered. We went into the bathroom, by the tub with its huge gold taps, which I turned till water thundered into the bath. The noise covered up our voices.

Daultrey was jacketless, his shirt-sleeves rolled up to his elbows. His forearms were tanned and strong. He ran a hand through his hair, and then put his hands on his hips.

'You still up for this?' he said.

'*I* am,' I said, though in all honesty I was terrified at the thought of making myself so vulnerable. 'Are you?'

He ignored the question. 'Sorrentino's staying at the Babylonian. He'll meet you at a bar there called the Sultan's Elephant, at half-nine. He's been told your name's Alexandra.

'Sorrentino's got tickets for one of those Cirque du Soleil knock-offs. Afterwards, if things go according to plan, he'll bring you back to his suite at the Babylonian. The guys he's with know his routine, so they'll give you some privacy. Make sure you ask him to take a shower; all the girls in the service insist on it, so he'll get suspicious if you don't. Anyway, it could give you a chance to get yourself together. After you've taken care of him, leave as quickly as possible by one of the back exits. Find some alleyway out of sight of security cameras and change into a spare set of clothes; something practical and dark. Take a cab to Monterey's Bar – if the cab driver doesn't know it, tell him it's on the road out to Reno. When you get there, don't go straight in the bar. Walk a mile into the desert, dig a hole, and get rid of the clothes you were wearing when you took care of Sorrentino. Burn them if you can. Then go back to the bar and get busy drinking until we come to get you.'

'Simple as that,' I said.

'Let's hope so,' he grimaced. 'You got appropriate attire?'

'Yeah, I brought a dress with me.'

'Good.' He shook open the envelope and pulled out a long, blonde wig.

'You're kidding.' Two blonde wigs in one week?

'I most certainly am not. Do you know how many people are going to see you with Sorrentino over the course of the evening, not to mention the security cameras in the hallways of the Babylonian? When you get to the hotel, go in the casino, find some facilities, put on the wig and take off your jacket before you go to the bar. Understood?'

'Understood. But what are you proposing I kill him with, my sparkling wit?'

Daultrey just looked at me, and then pulled a pair of surgical gloves and a revolver out of the envelope. I took the gun off him, swinging open the cylinder and making sure there were bullets in every chamber before snapping it back in place. I immediately felt less vulnerable.

'It's a .38 special,' Daultrey said, a curious expression on his face. 'But maybe I don't need to tell you that. For someone who lives in a country with a handgun ban, you sure seem to know your way around a weapon.'

I shrugged. 'Blame all the American cop shows on the telly.'

'Well, it's a very reliable weapon. Just bear in mind, you don't have an unlimited number of bullets. Use them wisely.'

I looked at my watch. 'So how do I get out of here without Angela spotting me?'

'Leave that to me,' he said. 'Any more questions, or are you good to go?'

'Just one,' I said. 'When's my meeting with Joe?'

Daultrey's glasses were getting steamed up in the vapour from the hot bathwater. He took them off. He looked very different without them – more human, softer.

'Joe will be here the day after tomorrow,' he said. 'He wants to see you, but he's bringing Marisa and the kids. Marisa's idea, I think, but Joe says it's safer for him, and probably for you too, if he tells everyone they are taking a family vacation in Vegas for a few days.'

I closed my eyes briefly. 'Thank you, Stanley.' My last connection to Charlie, and I'd be seeing him in a matter of hours.

When Daultrey left the room I changed into my low-cut scarlet dress, the sleeves of which only just covered my scars, put on the ruby and diamond earrings Charlie had bought me for our first anniversary, and made up my face. I went heavy on the eye-liner and mascara, and slicked on a couple of layers of red lipstick. With the stiletto heels and blonde wig I looked as if I was going for a job as a Lana Turner lookalike, which seemed rather appropriate given her predilection for made guys like Johnny Stompanato.

I carefully tucked the wig into my bag, along with a pair of jeans, a black shirt, some flipflops and a packet of make-up removal wipes. And the Smith & Wesson revolver.

Through the door I could hear Daultrey talking to Taylor. I put my ear to the wood, and overheard him telling her, 'Go on, you've been on duty all day – go and have some fun.'

'You're sure, sir?' she asked him, and he told her, 'Yeah, go, go.' Five minutes later, he knocked on my door. I came out wearing a long black summer jacket that covered my dress.

'The Babylonian's down the other end of the Strip,' he said. 'You've got time to walk it. Don't get a cab, just in case. And look – just make sure you're not alone with him until you're ready, and that gun is in your hand. Understand?'

'Okay,' I said. 'Look, Stanley . . . thank you for this.'

Daultrey smiled awkwardly. 'No, thank *you*, kid. Good luck, okay? And be careful.' Then he dipped forward and clumsily kissed me on the top of my head.

Chapter Twenty-one

Being in Las Vegas was like looking at the world through a kaleidoscope: a constantly shifting pattern of shimmering light and colour. The whole city burned in blue, red and gold. It electrified the air, igniting the eyes of the tourists who walked the Strip.

I stepped out from the chilled air of the hotel into the Nevada night, and it was like walking into a block of heat. Jostled by a gang of hen-night party girls in fluffy pink Stetsons and hotpants, I stood aside and let them pass, taking the opportunity to scan around me. A few feet away a woman with dyed red hair and too much eyeliner checked out the window of a shop selling liquor and souvenirs. Across the road, a guy in a sharp black suit shook a cigarette out of a pack of Craven A's, clicking his lighter with a flick of the wrist. He caught my eye and smiled at me, which ruled him out as a tail as far as I was concerned. Other than these two loiterers the crowd was moving steadily along, a current of men and women intoxicated by the noise, the glitz, the promise of doubling their dollars by dawn.

A couple of laughing college boys stumbled past, one hugging the other's head in the crook of his arm. He was wearing a T-shirt with the slogan *what happens in Vegas stays in Vegas*.

As I walked on to my rendezvous with Sorrentino, I tried to become a different person. My usual stride became a sashay, hips swinging with each step. The stiletto heels made me taller, the push-up bra made my breasts bigger.

The exterior of the Babylonian was like a desert palace – white-walled, with palm trees and hanging brass lamps. A ten-feet-tall elephant carved from dove-coloured marble stood by a decorative pool filled with rose petals and gurgling water. I walked past the doormen in their Arabian robes and found the washroom.

And there in the toilet stall in the Babylonian casino, tying my real hair back tight on my scalp and pulling on the blonde wig, the transformation was complete. Goodbye London girl Kate Grey. Hello Vegas escort Alexandra. I swallowed hard and left the restroom.

The Sultan's Elephant Bar was decked out in gold-painted carved tables and brightly coloured sofas with silk cushions. I glanced around for Sorrentino in the low-level lighting, trying to recognize him in the rosy glow cast by the lamps.

There. In the corner of the bar, where he had a view of the whole place, where his back was unexposed. He was with another man, a lanky guy in a dark suit who saw me coming before Sorrentino did, and leant in to whisper of my arrival in his boss's ear.

I walked over to them, incredibly self-conscious in my tight red dress, and Sorrentino stood up to meet me. He was tall, at least six three, and built like an ox. He wore a cream-coloured suit and navy tie, and his receding hair was gelled back along his skull.

His small black eyes looked me up and down, lingering at my cleavage and my legs.

'You must be Alexandra,' he said, taking my hand and kissing it. 'Very pleased to meet you. Call me Luigi.'

'Luigi,' I repeated, hoping my voice didn't betray my nerves. 'How are you?'

He turned to his associate, who remained seated, sucking on a cigarette and watching me carefully through the smoke. 'This is a friend of mine, Aldo. He's just leaving.'

Aldo had thick eyebrows, pockmarked skin and a mouth with an in-built twist to it. He looked like any other gangster until you met his gaze and saw the intelligence there, assessing you as if he was shining a spotlight into your brain. My skin goosepimpled, my instincts telling me this man had immediately seen me for who I really was.

My instincts must have been wrong: rather than denouncing me, Aldo crushed his cigarette and got to his feet. 'I'll see you later, Lu,' he said, shaking Sorrentino's hand. Without a word to me, he left.

'Please, have a seat,' Sorrentino said, indicating the empty spot on the sofa next to him. 'What can I get you to drink?'

A waitress appeared like magic at his side, wearing harem trousers and a little silk top that exposed her perfect stomach. A large imitation emerald nestled in her navel.

Absinthe would have been nice, or failing that, a triple whisky. I tried to think what a high-class hooker might order. 'Do you have any white burgundies?' I asked.

'Mâcon, Saint-Véran, Jobard, Louis Jadot,' she reeled off.

'Jobard would be perfect, thank you.'

'Of course, madam,' said the waitress. 'And for you, sir?'

'Jim Beam,' he told her. 'Double, no ice.'

Left on our own, he moved closer to me. I had to resist the urge to flinch when his thigh brushed against mine. I hated being so close to him. He smelt of over-strong aftershave and breath mints.

Sorrentino turned towards me, resting one arm across the sofa back. 'So, Alexandra,' he said. 'That's a beautiful name. Beautiful accent too. Where you from – Great Britain?'

'England,' I said, nodding.

'London?' Luke observed once that non-Europeans thought all English people lived in London. I suppose it's a good bet.

'No, I'm from a small town in Norfolk,' I lied.

'"*No fuck*"?' he repeated, laughing. 'That doesn't sound like somewhere a girl like you would come from, if you know what I mean.'

I forced a smile. 'And where do you call home?'

'I'm from New York,' he said. 'Brooklyn originally, in case you couldn't tell from my accent, but I live in Manhattan now. Got a lovely apartment looking out over Central Park.'

'It sounds charming,' I said. 'So what are you doing in Las Vegas? Are you here for business or pleasure?'

'A little of both, I hope,' he said, smirking, and squeezed my knee with his paw-like hand. Thankfully, just then the waitress brought our drinks.

'A glass of Jobard for the lady,' she said, setting down drinks mats and placing the chilled glass of white wine in front of me. I reached for it with a slightly trembling left hand, and as she said, 'And a Jim Beam, no rocks, for the gentleman,' my wedding band caught the light.

Glancing sideways at Sorrentino, I quickly picked up the glass so it covered the ring. He didn't appear to have noticed, too focused on signing the bill to his room. I put my other hand around the glass too, and slipped the platinum band onto one of the fingers of my right hand.

Plenty of escorts were married women, of which I'm sure he was aware, but I was also pretty sure that Sorrentino was something of an expert in high-class call girls, and he might become suspicious of one sloppy enough to forget to remove her wedding ring before meeting a client.

I sipped the wine.

'Is it good?' he asked.

'Yes,' I said. 'Thank you.'

'Are you hungry? Would you like something to eat before the show? We've got a little time.'

'Thank you, but I ate earlier. If you're hungry though, please go ahead.'

'That's okay,' Sorrentino said, waving a hand. He had a ring of his own, a big diamond in a gold setting on his pinky finger. 'Although I might have something for you to eat later, if you know what I mean.' He waggled an eyebrow, and I tried not to gag. He had a strange smile, his upper lip curling up to show little white teeth.

'You know, when they told me Donna wasn't available, I've got to be honest, I was a little disappointed,' he continued. 'But you're a knockout. How come I haven't had the pleasure before?'

'Well,' I said, thinking fast, 'I'm not on the agency's books. If a girl becomes unwell and the agency doesn't have anyone they can call in, it's the girl's responsibility to find a replacement.'

'Really?' Sorrentino said, eyes trailing down the curve of my neck and flicking across each breast. 'So are you telling me you're new to this?'

What to respond? He was obviously quite turned on by the idea of breaking me in, but it wasn't safe for him to think me too naïve.

'I've been on a date or two,' I said.

He reached out the hand that was resting on the sofa back, and stroked my ear, before lifting up my earring so it glinted in the light. 'And who bought you these beautiful earrings?' he asked, his voice soft. 'One of your "dates"?'

'Actually, they were a present from my mother and father,' I said. 'For my twenty-first birthday. Family heirloom.'

'Your family has great taste,' he said, taking his hand away from my ear and resting it once again on the sofa back.

'Thank you.' I sipped at my wine, nervous. 'What about you?'

'What about me?'

'Do you have family?' To my ears, it sounded like I'd asked about 'Family' with a capital F.

'My ma's still alive,' he said, 'but if you're after a family member with taste, you're not talking about Ma. She likes to collect those figurines – you know, the ones that look like babies? Creepy stuff. I got a sister too, younger than me. No kids though, least not that I know about.'

'Would you like children?' I asked him, taking a rather large gulp of wine.

He shrugged, raising his glass. 'Sure. Was my ex that didn't want them – was worried they'd ruin her figure. But I think my current girl is pretty keen, so if things work out I might have a few little Luigis running around the place before I get too old to enjoy them.' He sank a big slug of whiskey. I could tell discussing children with me was making him uncomfort-able – hard to think of a woman as purely an object for sex when you've talked about motherhood with her – and to be honest I didn't want to hear the hopes and aspirations of a man who I knew might never realize them.

'Personally, I don't have a maternal bone in my body,' I reassured him. The wine was thankfully starting to relax me somewhat, and I could feel myself getting more into character. 'Just couldn't do it. You can't decide on a Friday afternoon to spend the weekend in Paris, or have spontaneous sex on the dining-room carpet for fear they'll walk in on you.'

'Last time I had sex on the floor,' Sorrentino told me, the grin back, 'I got carpet burns on my knees. Seriously, Alex-andra, they were bright red, one was even grazed on the bone there. I spent a week trying to keep them covered up in front of my girlfriend, but she comes in on me when I'm showering, and I just hear this shrieking: "Luigi, you dirty sonofabitch, you been fucking around on me?" on and on.'

'So I take it she wasn't the one with carpet burns on her back?' I said, winking at him.

'No,' he said. 'No, she was not. I told her, one of the guys dropped a contact, we were just looking for it, that's all it was. "What, did you take off your pants before you instigated this search operation?" she says. She's not dumb, I'll give her that.'

'Did she forgive you?' I asked.

He waved a hand. 'She knows which side her bread is buttered on. Certain things have to be overlooked, to keep the peace.' Luigi stopped then, meeting my eye and smiling at me. 'You know, I like you,' he said. 'You're very easy to talk to. Kinda non-judgmental.'

'You're rather lovely company yourself,' I said, trying not to choke on the words.

He shot out his wrist, checking the time on his large gold watch. 'Finish your drink and we'll hit the road, sweetheart.'

We took a cab down the Strip to the theatre. On the way there Sorrentino slipped an envelope into the front pocket of my handbag, and I realized then that I'd forgotten to prompt him for my payment. Thank God he'd given it to me off his own bat – it surely would have raised his suspicions if we'd got much further into the evening without me bringing it up. Any call girl with more than two brain cells always gets her money upfront.

It was one of those shows where the floor audience are sat around tables rather than in rows of seats. Sorrentino and I were in a box to the right of the stage. We ordered more drinks from our waiter and watched the rest of the audience filter in. Families, couples of retirement age, newlyweds, groups of women on hen nights, smaller groups of men hoping to get lucky with the groups of women. Everyone seemed happy, laughing at each other's jokes. A woman with very short dark hair sat nestling into the side of a bearded man, who stroked her cheek and whispered to her. Five women, glittering in their nightlife finery, tried one another's drinks, threw back their heads laughing at a joke, caught the eye of a couple of handsome guys at a nearby table. And I sat high above it all, next to a man who might have murdered my husband.

The lights went down and the show started; incredible acrobats threw themselves around the stage, hung in the air like luminous moths. Some philosopher once said we only found things beautiful because we found them sad. I didn't quite agree with him, since being happy had never stopped me being able to appreciate beauty, but it was only since losing Charlie that it became painful to see something beautiful. It actually hurt.

I sat back. Sorrentino was bent forward, forearms resting on the balcony wall, totally engrossed in the performance. I stared at the back of his head, at the roll of neck fat just above his collar. If only I'd had a knife, it would have been so much easier to slide it in from behind than to have to look him in the face as I did it. He wouldn't even see it coming.

But I needed answers first. I knew I'd have to wait. I downed my wine and signalled to the waiter for a refill. In the interval I told Sorrentino I was going to the powder room, but instead I stopped at a payphone and called Kytell's mobile. It was in the early hours of the morning back in the UK, but I knew he'd be up and I was right. He answered on the second ring.

'Kate?' he said. 'That you?'

'The name of the person I mentioned before is Luigi Sorrentino,' I said. 'Head of one of the New York families. If I don't call you back later, be careful. I love you.' I hung up before he could say anything.

*

The performers took their final bow, and my stomach clenched. The beginning of the end. Soon there would be no turning back.

In the cab on the way back to the Babylonian, Sorrentino's hand slipped under my dress and I felt his meaty fingers gliding up my leg. He found the lace tops of my hold-ups and I could feel his fingers digging into the soft flesh of my inner thigh.

Please, please, just get to the damn hotel, I willed the driver. And yet when I saw the white walls of the hotel appear in the windscreen, the feeling of panic just got worse.

Sorrentino escorted me through the entrance, a hand at the small of my back. In the elevator it travelled further south, cupping my buttock. I smiled at him thinly, watching the numbers change on the display as we ascended.

The ping the lift made as it reached the twenty-eighth floor made me jump. My heart punched against the inside of my chest as Sorrentino found his room and opened it with his key card.

The second the door was shut behind us he was on me, pressing me against the wall, slipping his tongue into my mouth. He ground his crotch into mine, and I could feel his erection.

He licked my neck, squeezing my breasts and rolling his palms over them as if he was making bread rolls. 'Suck me, baby,' he moaned in my ear.

Jesus Christ. 'Patience, darling,' I whispered seductively, struggling hard against the urge to shove him off me. 'I'll give you the best damn blow job of your life, but first I'd love it if you'd take a nice hot shower.'

He kind of flopped against me, then pushed away from the wall. He walked around the room, scratching the back of his head.

'You are some pricktease,' he said. 'Look at my fucking hard-on.' But he grudgingly kicked off his shoes and started undoing his shirt. As he undressed he picked up some car keys that were lying on the side and went over to the wardrobe. I heard beeping as he opened the room safe. The keys went inside, followed in short order by his watch, a wallet and a roll of cash. Then more beeping as he relocked the safe.

'No offence, sweetheart,' he said.

'None taken,' I told him.

He went into the bathroom in just his underpants, and I said a silent prayer of thanks when I heard the shower start. I was angry at Daultrey for coming up with a plan that involved Sorrentino thinking I was his for the taking – couldn't he have sneaked me in as a maid or something, for Christ's sake? If Sorrentino had refused to stop when I'd asked ... but I snapped my mind away from that particular horror movie and tucked my coat and bag in the closet, knowing I was in trouble if I got blood on them. I snapped on the gloves and pulled my .38 out of the bag, then went looking for Sorrentino's gun.

It wasn't in his wardrobe, bedside table or coat, so I had to assume it was in his safe, along with his other valuables. It made me nervous not having it in my hands, but I'd just have to stay between him and the safe.

Cocking the revolver I waited, blood and adrenaline thundering through my body. I could literally hear my own heartbeat thumping in my eardrums.

The shower stopped, and I tensed, holding my breath. A few moments later Sorrentino came out of the bathroom in a robe, and stopped dead when he saw me.

His eyes narrowed. 'What the *fuck*?' he said, when he saw the gun trained on him.

'Face down, on the floor,' I said. 'Hands together behind your head.'

'Oh, for Christ's sake, I'll give you the combination,' he said. 'It's 0514. Although I doubt you'll find anyone dumb enough to fence the stuff for you once I put the word out.'

'I'm not after the contents of your safe.'

'Then what *do* you want?'

'I want you to lie face down, on the floor, with your hands clasped together behind your head.'

He was trying to size up the situation, in the same way a predator that's cornered will assess the best chance of escape. There were therefore bound to be some raised hackles and teeth baring as he tried to look intimidating in the hope that I'd just let him be. Playing dead was not in his repertoire.

'I'm not lying down,' he said. 'Sorry, but it's a hell of a lot harder to shoot someone if you've got to look them in the face when you're doing it.'

'I'm not here to kill you,' I said, though I maybe should have added the caveat 'unless you tell me something I don't want to hear'. 'I just want some answers.'

'Answers to what?' he scowled.

'Let's start with the question of who killed my husband.'

'Lady, I don't know who you are or what you're talking about,' said Sorrentino.

'No. No, of course you don't. You probably think I'm wearing a wire.'

'No, in fact I don't. Confessions aren't generally admissible in court when the guy being recorded had a gun pointed at him at the time.'

I nodded. 'Good point. So you can tell me the truth. Like you say, inadmissible as evidence even if I was wearing a wire.'

He shook shower water out of his eyes. 'You are some crazy fucking bitch, you know that?'

'Don't antagonize a woman with a .38, you fat fuck,' I said, my own anger rising. Nostrils flaring, he looked like a bull facing a matador, eyes like little cannonballs. 'I want to hear about the last hours of my husband's life. I want to know who else was involved; who actually physically killed him.'

His upper lip twitched. 'You're gonna have to help me out here. Narrow down my field of options.'

'I'm the widow of Charlie Benson,' I said. My voice was shaking, but my hands were steady.

'Never heard of the guy.' I found myself moving closer to Sorrentino, found myself wanting to crack my gun against the side of his skull till he was bleeding out of his ears.

'You knew him as Giuseppe Carlo.'

He laughed. 'Don't tell me. Oh, this is so sweet. That motherfucker's dead?'

I watched him carefully. 'Don't fuck around with me. You know he's dead.'

'Alexandra, sweetheart, or whatever your fucking name is, I swear on all that is holy that I did not kill Giuseppe Carlo. Despite the fact he whacked a very good friend of mine, and therefore I would have dearly loved to put a bullet in the son of a bitch myself, I did not have that privilege.'

'He killed someone?' My mouth was dry. I swallowed and tried again. 'Who? Who did he kill?'

'Oh, your darling husband didn't happen to mention that, then? He killed Federico Calabresi. He blew his face off with a shotgun and dumped him in the Hudson. So what happened to Carlo? He end up in some alleyway with his tongue cut out, what?'

'He drowned,' I said, my head starting to hurt.

'Doesn't sound like one of our guys,' said Sorrentino with a frown. 'Maybe it was karma. Or maybe it was just an accident – did you ever think of that?'

'It wasn't karma,' I said. 'It was murder. And from what I hear, it was someone in your organization.'

Sorrentino raised his hands up, huffing in exasperation. 'Look, I haven't even seen that piece of shit in God knows how long, let alone put a hit out on him. And my guys don't do nothing without my say-so. I think you'd better take a good hard look at whoever put you onto me, because I'd say they've got something of a hidden agenda.'

The awful thing was, I knew he was telling me the truth. He hadn't killed Charlie; it was obvious he hadn't even known he was dead. I was sure enough of this that I didn't even want to put a bullet in him just to be on the safe side.

I closed my eyes, just for a second, feeling so tired. I'd thought tonight might be the beginning of the end. I'd thought tonight I'd finally find out what had really happened to Charlie, and that I might find the strength to exact some kind of vengeance. On Sorrentino first, with whoever he implicated in Charlie's murder next on my list. Now I didn't even seem to have a list.

I backed away to the closet, keeping the .38 trained on Sorrentino. I punched 0514 into the safe, searching for Sorrentino's gun. I found it – a blue-black Beretta 92 with a spare clip – and took his car keys too for good measure. Grabbing my coat and bag, I stepped backwards to the door and scrabbled behind me at the handle till it opened.

'You should probably kill me, you know,' Sorrentino said as I stood in the doorway. His eyes had gone stone cold. 'Because if I find you, you're dead.'

Chapter Twenty-two

I flew down the emergency exit staircase and out into the night.

'Taxi!' Safe inside the cab, I asked the driver to go to a hotel at the other end of the neighbourhood. When the cab dropped me off I found one of those side alleys Daultrey was talking about that weren't monitored by CCTV. Looking around to make sure no one was in the vicinity, I stuck my wig in my bag over the two handguns, put my jeans on under my dress, then whipped off the dress over my head and pulled on my shirt. There was just enough room for my heels in the bag when I swapped them for a pair of flipflops.

I knew I didn't have to worry about the cops. No way Sorrentino was calling them. No, what I was worried about was him tracking me down himself.

I wiped my face clean with a couple of make-up remover wipes and, transformed back into Kate Grey, I went looking for a payphone.

'Kate?' My brother sounded scared.

'It's me, Ky. I'm okay. It wasn't him. Don't do anything.'

'What the fuck is going on?'

'I don't know. I'm not sure who I can trust.'

'So come home.'

'I will, I promise. There's just someone I need to see first.'

'It doesn't sound safe. Kate, just leave it.'

'I can't. I'm sorry, Ky. I love you.'

Hanging up on him, I returned to the main street and hailed another taxi to take me back to the Regal.

It may have been a mistake to let Luigi Sorrentino live, having held a gun on him and humiliated him, but I couldn't help feeling relieved that I hadn't had to kill him.

To say the agents looked surprised to see me when I burst into our suite was something of an understatement. Angela Taylor looked from my furious face to Daultrey's grave one, and then down at the floor.

'What the fuck, Stanley?' I said.

'Why aren't you in your room?' snapped Jerkins. 'How are we meant to protect you if you sneak out to go God knows where?'

'Oh, Stanley knows where I was,' I said. 'What was your plan, Daultrey? You wanted him taken care of, and thought you'd use me to do it?'

Daultrey grabbed me by my elbow and propelled me into my hotel room, slamming the door in the faces of the other agents.

He turned on me. 'What the hell are you doing back here? The plan was for you to go to Monterey's and wait for us to find you!'

'Well, there was a change of plan,' I said, throwing my bag on the bed and grabbing a miniature bottle of whiskey from the minibar. I swallowed its contents in one, wanting the taste of Sorrentino out of my mouth.

'Is he dead? Did you manage it?'

'No, Stanley,' I said, glaring at him. 'He's not dead. You know why? Because he didn't kill Charlie. Now do you want to tell me why you lied to me?'

Daultrey sat down hard in the chair by the bedside table. He looked stunned.

'How do you know it wasn't him?' he asked.

'I just do. It was obvious Sorrentino didn't have a fucking clue that Charlie was dead. Christ, you don't even have the facts straight on Rico Calabresi – you told me Sorrentino had him killed, but Sorrentino thinks Charlie was responsible! So why don't you tell me where you're getting your shitty information from?'

Daultrey took off his glasses and sat with them in his lap. 'A friend of mine at the Bureau. Told me they had a wire tap in which Sorrentino said that their vacationing mutual friend had been taken care of.'

'Yeah? Did you hear this recording yourself?'

'No,' he admitted. 'No, I'm sorry.'

'What's his name?'

'Whose name?'

'The name of your so-called "friend" at the Bureau who lied to you.'

Daultrey jammed his glasses back on his face. 'Now hold on a goddamn minute. I'm not saying he lied. We could just have misinterpreted which vacationing friend Sorrentino was referring to.'

'Could he be the mole?' Daultrey wouldn't look me in the eye. '*Well*?' I raised my voice. 'Could he?'

Daultrey stood up. 'No,' he said, but I knew he was lying. 'Look, this is my problem. Let me deal with it my way. I'll dig around. I don't want you going to Washington on some crazy vendetta when you don't have all your facts straight.'

'Yeah, God forbid I should be stalking innocent men with a .38,' I said sarcastically.

'Speaking of which,' said Daultrey, and held out his hand for the gun.

'I don't know,' I said. 'Maybe I should hang onto it. I'm not sure I trust you any more.'

'Kate,' he said, looking hurt. 'Don't be like this. I wouldn't do anything to harm you.'

I regarded him for a moment or two, then handed him back the gun. I still had Sorrentino's tucked at the bottom of my bag – a fact I wasn't going to share with him. Let him think that I was unarmed; see if that would bring an attack worming its way out of the woodwork.

'Thank you,' he said.

'Good night, Stanley,' I said, and waited for him to leave before getting in the shower and scrubbing away any traces of Luigi Sorrentino's sweaty hands.

The next day the agents all regarded me with suspicion, aware that something – although what, exactly, they couldn't know for sure – was going on between me and their boss. Daultrey himself kept a low profile, appearing only to tell me that Sorrentino had returned to New York, and there were now thousands of miles between us.

I took the precaution of finding a safe hiding-place for Sorrentino's gun and bullets, and the blonde wig, stashing them behind the bath panel. I couldn't trust the agents not to search my things, and knew if I put them in the safe the hotel management would happily give Daultrey the master code to open it.

When I was six or seven my brothers and I used to love a game called 'Murder in the Dark'. One player was the murderer, but no one knew his identity. The lights went out, and when they came back up, someone would be 'dead'. And you'd look round the room at the other players, trying to work out which of them was responsible. Now it felt like I was playing that game for real. Could I trust Daultrey? Did I believe him when he said he'd been lied to? I should have taken off when I realized Sorrentino wasn't responsible for

Charlie's death, but that would have meant giving up on seeing Joe. I knew I was taking a risk – that if Daultrey had really been trying to set me up, there was a very good chance that this meeting with Joe was another fabrication – but all the paths I'd taken so far had led to dead ends. This was the only path left for me to take.

There was a rap on the door and Daultrey came in without waiting for a response.

'They're arriving tomorrow morning,' he said. 'We'll be heading down to their room at eleven o'clock sharp.'

Apparently he realized he needed to regain some trust, because he held out a familiar manila folder to me. I got out of bed and reached for it. Charlie's file.

'Don't leave it lying around,' he said. 'Now Taylor's gonna come in and talk to you about the Witness Protection Programme. Can I trust you to stick to the subject?'

It seemed he was worried I'd let his team find out about the Sorrentino incident. 'You can,' I assured him. I tucked the file under one of the four-poster's pillows, and showed him the palms of my hands in a 'see, no evidence of subterfuge here' kind of gesture. He nodded curtly and left the room.

I didn't have to wait long for Special Agent Angela Taylor. Not bothering to knock, she strode into the room in a smart grey suit and heels, her blonde hair tucked up in a chignon, all businesslike efficiency.

'So Agent Daultrey has asked me to talk you through the process of joining the Witness Protection Programme,' she said, and proceeded to tell me about how my new name would be allocated, how they'd provide me with a place to live and a job, and a back story I could give my new friends and neighbours.

'What people on the Programme tend to find most difficult,' she said, 'is not being able to make contact with their loved ones from their previous lives. Not ever. No phone calls on your mom's birthday. No Christmas cards. No emails.' If I was seriously considering letting them give me a new identity, I might have been getting upset at the thought of never seeing Kytell again, but I knew it wouldn't come to that. Not that I was going to share this with the FBI just yet.

'At least you won't have to go through the trauma of plastic surgery,' she commented. I raised an eyebrow. 'Well, you have the advantage that these men have never met you; they can only recognize you from photos,' she explained. 'It tends to be the witnesses who have lived or worked with the people they testified against who are in the most danger of being recognized. Sometimes we have to completely alter their appearance. Make them look like another person entirely.'

One of the other agents brought up some pizza and I half-heartedly ate a slice. It tasted like cardboard in my mouth. I left them to it, snuggled up in bed with Charlie's file.

It contained his application form for the FBI, and I stroked a fingertip over his signature. It wasn't my husband's – obviously the name was different – but it was his handwriting. I'd decided against changing my name to Mrs Kate Benson when Charlie and I married; my own name meant something special to me, and Charlie had never minded. Now I wondered if he might have been more old-fashioned, more traditional about me taking his name if I'd have been changing it to Mrs Kate Cantelli.

There were supervisor reports, all glowing, and many letters of recommendation. He'd received a citation for bravery after intervening in a grocery store robbery on a day off. Then there were notes from Daultrey, his contact when he was undercover, detailing the information he was providing about the Family he worked for. As time went on the information became more damning, more specific. Sorrentino's name came up often.

The best thing in the file was the stack of photos. It was a treasure trove for me – picture after picture of my beloved Charlie, showing him from every possible angle. That one of him in his uniform for starters. Another where he was in a suit, hair combed back, trying to look serious although I could see a smile hiding at the corners of his mouth. Lots of sur- veillance photos where his hair was longer, brushing his collar, and he was in casual clothes, playing the part of a mafioso. In one he was stripped to the waist, playing a game of basketball. You could clearly see the jagged sun of his Celtic tattoo, and I flashed back to the autopsy room in Sicily, the blackness of the tattoo against his fish-white skin. I closed my eyes, willing myself not to be sick. After a couple of slow breaths, I opened my eyes again and found a picture of him knelt down on the pavement next to a boxer dog. He was scratching under its chin, and it had an expression of unadulterated bliss. The dog actually seemed to be smiling. That was my Charlie: the man who could make even dogs smile.

'The fact you're so good at poker worries me,' I'd said once.

'Why?' he'd asked, smiling.

'Because if you can bluff that well, you can probably lie that well too.'

His smile had vanished, and I'd stroked his face, wanting to bring it back. He'd pulled me close, wrapping me up in his warmth.

'Trust me,' he'd whispered in my ear. 'I love you. Just trust me, and I promise everything will be okay.'

He hadn't told me that he'd never lie to me. I should have seen right then that his promise was in some way an evasion, but then I had my own reasons not to push for complete honesty.

I put the photos back in the folder and slid it under the pillow. When I slept, I dreamt of Charlie in a fairground, walking through a hall of mirrors. I ran to him, reaching out for him, but instead of finding a living, breathing person, my hands just bounced off the glass that held his reflection. When I turned to find the real him, no one was there, and then all his images were gone.

I woke up with anxiety gnawing away in my stomach, and wondered if I'd made a dreadful mistake. How on earth would I cope with seeing my husband's twin? Surely I would shatter into pieces seeing his face. Could I bear to see Charlie, knowing it wasn't really him? Despite my assurances to Daultrey, I wondered if all those longings would surface at the sight of his identical twin.

I changed my outfit at least three times, unsure if I wanted to make myself look attractive for Joe or not. In the end I settled on my blue jeans and a plain white shirt.

Pacing the suite, I tried to distract myself by watching the TV channel that one of the newly arrived agents – extra protection with Joe and his family in the hotel – had switched on. CNN's anchors told us about unrest in the Middle East, conflict in Western Africa, and earthquakes in California. The Fed – an Agent called Oxford Johnson – looked familiar, but with my brain spinning I couldn't remember at what point in their surveillance of us Luke and I had come across him.

'You okay, Miz Cantelli?' he asked as I wore out the carpet next to him.

'Yes, I'm fine. Just a bit nervous. It's not every day you meet your dead husband's twin brother.'

'No, I guess not,' he said. 'You might want to lay off the coffee though. I'm not sure it's helping.'

I looked in my hand, surprised to find a coffee cup there.

'How many have I had?' I asked him.

'Well, let's see. There are about two sachets left, and I've had two, and Wilson had one, so I'd estimate you've had five.'

'Oh shit,' I said, putting the cup down.

'There's camomile tea if you'd prefer,' said Agent Johnson.

'Not my cup of tea,' I said. 'Sorry, no pun intended.' Johnson laughed politely. 'So, Agent Johnson,' I said, 'why "Oxford"? That's an unusual name.'

He shrugged. 'My ancestors were from England. My parents are very proud of their British heritage.'

'Really?' I said. 'What's your brother called – Cambridge?'

'No,' he said. 'Stratford.'

I started laughing, then realized he wasn't joking, and snapped my jaw shut.

Daultrey came into the suite and I spun around to face him. 'They're here,' he said. 'Taylor's babysitting their kids, taking them to some movie down the street. Let's give them a quarter hour to settle in, and then you can go say hi.'

The twenty minutes seemed to take only twenty seconds to go by, and then we were heading down two floors in the lift and walking along the plushly carpeted hallway to Room 624. A voice in my head kept repeating: 'It's not Charlie. *Remember*, it's not Charlie.'

It felt as if we were paying a visit to a ghost.

We stopped in front of 624, and I swallowed hard. Daultrey knocked on the door and I held my breath, trying to prepare myself for seeing Joe. Agent Wilson let us in, leading us along a dark green corridor into a suite of polished wood and a colour scheme like jousting flags, so similar to our own. And then we were in the living room, light streaming through the windows, and there in front of me was Joe Cantelli.

Chapter Twenty-three

He was sitting on a sofa next to a pretty brunette in an elegant maternity dress, and it was suddenly as if Charlie was back from the dead. I couldn't get any air. Then he rose to his feet, a nervous smile bobbing on the surface of his face, and the illusion disappeared like rain on sand. The smile was too goofy, the motion too staccato. When Charlie moved it was fluid, natural, like an animal that takes its skin and muscle for granted. Joe moved more like an action figure.

'Hey, Kate,' he said, and gave me a big hug. I was grateful for it; it gave me a chance to blink away my tears. I could smell a woody aftershave, and the gel that was making his hair spike up. He felt bulky, as if he spent half his life in the gym, although I suppose it was due to all the manual labour of his construction work.

We stepped apart, and I couldn't help staring at his face. Although all the elements were there – Charlie's nose, his cheekbones, his jawline – it somehow looked wrong, like a bad photocopy. And yet I felt a deep and immediate affection for him, this stranger with my husband's face.

He cleared his throat. 'This is my wife, Marisa.' His voice was deep, and the Italian-American accent was strong. I wondered if Charlie had lost his original accent, or if he deliberately suppressed it to go along with the Benson identity.

I tore my eyes away from Joe and nodded hello to Marisa.

She watched me with arctic blue eyes, not even attempting a smile, and stayed put on the sofa.

'So can I get you something?' he asked. 'Some coffee, or tea maybe? Or you wanna raid the minibar for something stronger?'

'Just some water, please,' I said, my voice so quiet it sounded as if it must be coming from another room.

'A water for Kate,' Joe said, heading over to the minibar. 'And for you gents?'

'Nothing for us,' said Daultrey. All the agents remained standing, as if they were waiting for something to happen that would require them to be on their feet.

Joe handed me a bottle of mineral water and indicated the seat opposite the sofa. I sat down, and he followed suit.

'I understand you saw me in some photos from Miami,' he said, leaning forward in his seat, elbows resting on his knees. He was wearing jeans, and a sleeveless black T-shirt that showed off his impressively muscled arms and shoulders. Marisa saw my eyes skimming over him and her mouth shrivelled up.

'I thought,' I started, then had to take a sip of water as my throat was so dry. 'I thought it was Charlie.' I shook my head. '*Antoni*. I mean, at first I thought it was Antoni. That's why I came over. I'm sorry if I caused any embarrassment for you.'

'No, no,' he said, waving a tanned hand. 'Don't be silly. If you hadn't, I never woulda known that Antoni had a wife. You know, it's great to meet you. I'm just sorry it had to be under such unpleasant circumstances.'

I nodded. 'I suppose it was too risky for him to tell me about you. He couldn't come back here, so why bring it all up?'

'I'm sure he wanted to tell you,' said Joe, although to be honest he didn't seem that sure. 'He just got so used to compartmentalizing things, till in the end I guess it was just easier to keep all the different parts of his life separate.'

It was very odd, watching him. So much like Charlie, but off by ten degrees. It was sort of like he was wearing Charlie's skin.

'So tell me,' he said, with a return of the goofy grin. 'How did you meet my brother?'

And so I told him about the lift breaking down in the Carnival Hotel, about falling in love at first sight. About the bungee jump, and the visit to Gino's, and our wedding just a few days later. He seemed enchanted, but from the corner of my eye I could see Marisa looking completely unimpressed.

I told them about our flat in Islington, and Charlie's job at the architectural firm. It almost seemed as if I was talking about him in the present tense, as if he was still alive.

'No kids?' asked Joe, and something bit at my heart.

'No,' I said, glancing at Marisa's distended belly. 'When's your latest due?'

Joe patted his wife's stomach with his left hand. 'About a month,' he said. 'Another girl.' Marisa put her hand over his, playing with the gold wedding band on his ring finger as though she wanted to draw my attention to it.

'Congratulations. And you have two other children?'

'That's right, Joe Junior and Gabriela. Hey, you wanna see a picture?'

He was already digging around in his wallet, and handed me a folded-over photo of their two children. Joe Junior was obviously the oldest, with a mop of dark hair and two front teeth missing. Gabriela was fairer than her brother, with long curly blonde hair, but she shared his conker-brown eyes. They were cute kids.

'They're beautiful,' I said, feeling a sudden longing to hold them both in my arms. Charlie's kin, his flesh and blood. Oh, why hadn't I got pregnant with his child when I had the chance?

I think Joe could see I was getting upset. He cupped my hands in his, stroking them. 'It's okay,' he said. 'Maybe we can arrange for you to meet them some day soon.'

'I'm afraid not,' interrupted Daultrey. 'Kate will be entering Witness Protection imminently. This is it, guys.'

Both Joe and I looked down at the floor, then back up at each other.

'So tell me about Antoni growing up,' I asked, trying to smile. 'What was he like as a kid?'

Joe related funny stories about their childhood; how they'd run rings round their parents, and about the pranks they played on their cousins. He started on an anecdote about their dog Gruffer, a St Bernard/Great Dane cross that they used to ride like a horse when they were little kids, but halfway through his story Marisa finally piped up.

'Listen, all this reminiscing is very nice, but I'm afraid our kids will be out of their movie soon, and we've got lunch reservations. Kate, it was lovely to meet you.' She was rising to her feet with something of an effort.

I glanced at Joe, who was staring down at the floor in barely disguised anger. I guessed this was Marisa's insecurity surfacing. Who knew, maybe she had good reason to want to keep other women away from her husband. He didn't seem to appreciate her possessiveness though.

And I still had questions that needed answers.

'It's lovely to meet you too, Marisa,' I said politely. 'But you might want to sit down again. I'll just be a little bit longer.'

She looked round at Daultrey with eyebrows raised, but he just looked back at her, expressionless. Glaring at me, she perched back down on the edge of the sofa.

'Joe, sorry for bringing this up,' I said. 'I just need to know: do you have any idea who murdered your brother?'

He looked up at me, searching my gaze from left eye to right and back again. 'Why are you asking me this, Kate?'

'Do you know Luigi Sorrentino? Could it have been someone in his organization, someone after payback for Federico Calabresi?'

Joe went rigid, and he shot a glance over to Daultrey. Daultrey shook his head at me, but I ignored him.

'How do you know about Luigi Sorrentino?' Joe asked me, his voice tight.

'Someone told me he was the one who killed your brother. He says he wasn't, and I believe him. But he also said anyone else in his organization that wanted Antoni dead would need his permission to kill him, and I need to know if that's true.'

'He says he wasn't? You've seen him?' He looked absolutely furious. 'Well, I don't know who's been filling your head with crap, but you don't need to find the man who killed Antoni, okay? He's already been dealt with.' He raised a hand in Daultrey's direction. 'And no, Agent Daultrey, I'm not going to go into details. I just want Kate here to know that my brother's already been avenged.' He grabbed my wrist, pulling me closer. 'Stay away from Sorrentino,' he said forcefully. 'Okay?'

'Okay,' I whispered.

He released my arm, leaving white fingermarks on my skin. There was an awkward silence, then Daultrey cleared his throat.

'Wilson, Johnson, will you please take Kate back up to the suite?'

It hadn't been enough time. Despite all the differences between the twins, I thought I could happily spend the afternoon on the other side of the room from Joe, gazing at him in my peripheral vision, pretending he was Charlie. I wanted to hear more stories, to gather every little colourful thread of detail about my husband to weave into my tapestry of memories. I didn't want to leave.

Joe stood up, and I embraced him. I closed my eyes and tried to make believe it was Charlie I was holding, but the smell and feel of him was just wrong. Finally, in more ways than one, I let him go.

'Bye, Joe,' I said, kissing him on the cheek.

'Goodbye, Kate,' he said back, dipping his head towards me.

And I walked out of Charlie's brother's life.

Chapter Twenty-four

Special Agent Wilson and I went up in the lift. 'How did you know about Luigi Sorrentino?' he said in his Droopy Dog voice.

'Luke mentioned him,' I lied.

'You said you'd met him,' pointed out Wilson.

'I just wanted to see what reaction I got. When would I have had the chance to meet Sorrentino? I haven't been to New York for years.'

Daultrey was furious when he got back to the suite. He pushed me into my room, and keeping his voice low so the other agents couldn't hear him, he laid into me.

'What the fuck do you think you were doing, bringing up Sorrentino?' Christ, I put my career on the line for you giving you that intel, and you don't give a shit about the fact I could lose my badge, my pension, maybe even go to jail?'

'I'm sorry, Stanley,' I said. 'The fact is, your "intel" turned out to be a load of shit. You said Joe had dodgy friends, and I thought maybe he'd know more than the FBI seem to. Turns out I was right.'

'Well, now we know,' Daultrey said. 'Whoever killed Antoni has obviously been taken care of.'

'If we can believe him,' I said.

'What? Why would his own brother lie?'

'To protect me,' I told him. 'Maybe he thinks if I believe Charlie's killer is dead I won't place myself in any more danger by going after the bastard myself.'

Daultrey gripped me by my upper arms. 'No – that's not the way it looked to me. Kate, you've got to let it go now. We both have. It's time to move on with our lives. Tomorrow you'll meet with our guys from the Witness Protection Programme, and before long, this will all be far behind you.'

Room service brought us up some lunch, but my appetite was still absent. I ate just a few mouthfuls of my eggs Benedict, then pushed the plate away. I kept thinking about Joe Cantelli. He wasn't Charlie, but he was as close as I was going to get. Was I really never going to see him again?

Agent Jerkins was wolfing down his bacon cheeseburger as if he hadn't eaten in years. He'd covered his fries in so much ketchup it looked like a crime scene, each chip a dismembered body part. Or maybe that was just my ghoulish mood.

Agent Taylor came in talking on her mobile. 'Sure, sure,' she was saying. 'Fifteen hundred hours tomorrow. We'll be there.' She hung up.

'Your appointment with the guys at Witness Protection is scheduled for tomorrow afternoon,' she told me. 'I'll check the flight times, but we'll probably need to leave about noon-ish.'

'Do we know what I'm going to be yet?' I asked, thinking I should feign some curiosity. 'Shop assistant? PR agent? Surgeon? What's my name going to be?'

'We don't know that stuff,' said Jerkins, swallowing an extra large bite of burger. 'Only the US Marshals do. It's so we can't be intimidated, tortured or bribed into giving the infor- mation to the bad guys.'

'That makes sense,' I said, nodding.

'The major downside to the Programme,' said Taylor, pick- ing up one of Jerkins' chips and scraping off some of the ketchup on the side of his plate before sticking it in her mouth, 'other than the lack of contact with your family, of course, is that you tend to end up at the lower end of the career ladder. It's often too risky to have you doing the same job you were doing before, so you have to start off in something relatively unskilled and either work your way up or take night classes to requalify.'

'So not a surgeon then,' I said. For a brief moment I pictured what life might be like if I took them up on their offer of a new identity. Alone in a new place, with no one knowing my past.

Taylor looked at her watch. 'Jerkins, shouldn't you be making that call?' she said.

He checked out the clock in the room, then reluctantly set down the burger. 'Back soon,' he said, leaving us alone in the room.

I was intrigued by the timepiece I'd seen on her wrist. 'That's a nice watch, Angela.'

'Thank you,' she said. And rather than regarding it again, the way most people would following a compliment, she pulled her sleeve down to cover it up.

'A Patek Philippe, isn't it?' I asked her, with a crocodile smile.

She wafted her other hand at me – a 'don't be silly' gesture. 'It's a knock-off. I got it in Hong Kong for fifty bucks.'

'Really?' I said. 'I thought the FBI might have frowned on their agents buying counterfeit goods.'

She stood up then, rubbing her arms as though she was cold. It's a great 'tell' if you're into reading people; it's one of the ways in which someone might soothe themselves when they're feeling nervous or uncomfortable. 'What they don't know won't hurt them, you know?' She spent the five minutes till Jerkins returned fiddling with the TV, trying to avoid me without being able to leave the room, while I wondered how a junior FBI agent could afford an eight-thousand-dollar watch.

The agents swapped shifts at 8 p.m.; I could hear Taylor and Jerkins saying good night. There was a knock at my door. It was Agent Oxford Johnson, dressed down for once in a T-shirt and chinos.

'Hey there,' he said. 'If you're all packed, I was wondering if you were in the mood for eating out tonight. Well, I say "eating out", but I just mean heading to one of the hotel restaurants for a change. I'm going a little stir crazy stuck in these suites all day, so Lord knows how you must be feeling.'

Fifteen minutes later he was escorting me to the Ocean Grill, a restaurant at the Regal that served what the Americans called 'surf'n'turf' – seafood and steak. The place was all bronze and blue neon, and the waitress taking our order wore a sharp black waistcoat and killer-heeled boots.

'I guess the Olde England theme doesn't really translate to fish,' said Johnson with an ironic smile.

'It's hard to find antique Day-Glo lighting,' I agreed.

Johnson ordered a bottle of Sauvignon Blanc for us to share, and by the time our starter arrived we'd already drunk half of it.

'I hope you don't mind me saying this,' he said, spearing a forkful of salad, 'but it seemed pretty rough on you this morning. Seeing the Cantellis, I mean.'

My heart was suddenly heavy. 'It was strange,' I said quietly, 'being in a room with someone who looks just like my husband, when a few days ago I didn't even know he existed. Christ, a few *weeks* ago I had no idea about any of this. Not just that my husband had a twin brother, but that Charles Benson wasn't his real name, that he was an FBI agent, that his death wasn't an accident.'

'Was Joe what you were expecting?' asked Johnson.

'I don't know. When I walked in, I was terrified he'd be just like Charlie.'

'And he wasn't?'

'No. Not really. He looked like him, but he sounded different, smelt different, moved differently.'

'You still looked like someone had punched you in the gut,' he said.

I looked up at Agent Johnson. He looked back as though he was expecting candour, aware he was exploring a painful subject.

'I thought I'd hidden it better than that,' I admitted. 'The thing is, it still *felt* like it was Charlie I was looking at.'

'What do you mean?'

'Sometimes, when I woke up before Charlie, I'd lie there just watching him sleep. Watching him breathing, his eyelashes on his cheek, the way his chest would rise and fall. I'd drink him in. I loved that face so much. Joe isn't Charlie, but he looked so much like him that I couldn't help feeling some love for him.'

'Here's a difficult question for you,' said Johnson. 'If he didn't have a wife and kids, could you ever see the two of you getting together?'

'No,' I said immediately. 'The more time I'd spend with him, the more I'd see the differences between him and Charlie. Even if he smelt right and moved right and sounded right, it would have been a cheat. He's not Charlie, and he never could be.'

We finished the bottle of wine and ordered another to go with our main course. I was starting to feel the effect, along with Johnson, who'd dropped his fork twice. Johnson was telling me about his wife. Apparently they'd met in college, and he'd only had a couple of girlfriends before her. He seemed to regret missing out on playing the field.

'Let me ask you something,' he said. 'When did you know Charlie was "the one"?'

I flushed. 'Um, sort of the minute I saw him,' I said, remembering that feeling of being home. 'What about you and Deb?'

He pulled a face. 'Sort of never happened. It was just the longer we were together, the less it seemed possible we'd ever split up.'

'That doesn't necessarily mean you shouldn't be together. That whole thunderbolt thing – it's just pheromones, isn't it?'

'You think?'

Nope, I didn't think that. Well, the rational part of my brain did think relationships were built on initial attraction based on the body's assessment of the chances of reproductive success, followed by a period in which compatible likes, dislikes, hopes and dreams either strengthened or weakened the physical bond. It was just that the less logical part of me knew I'd never be happy again without Charlie, and it was nothing to do with missing his pheromones. Once you've found your soulmate it's hard to believe it just boils down to hormones and DNA.

Two pieces of the same jigsaw. Two halves of the same soul. You can't even talk about it without sounding like a cliché, and yet there's no other way to describe it. You're a series of ridges and contours; an interesting shape in its own right. And it's not until you find that person with those opposite gaps and peaks that slot so perfectly into your own that you even realize you weren't whole to begin with.

'My grandma used to say that just after God created the earth He sat straddling the land, a whole heap of pebbles in His lap,' Johnson told me. 'And He cracked each pebble in half and threw one half into the Pacific and the other half into the Atlantic, to drift away to opposite ends of the world. And you know what those pebbles were?'

I shook my head.

'The pebbles were souls, but when He split them they became people.'

'I'm far too drunk to talk sensibly about such an important issue,' I told him. 'Let's change the subject.'

'You know, you're very bossy,' he said, slurring his words slightly as he pointed at me with his fork. 'Very bossy, and very annoying.'

'I'm sorry,' I said, laughing at him.

'I thought we were gonna have to chase you all over Europe,' he said, laughing too. 'You were pretty good at giving us the slip.'

'Thank you – I think.'

'Poor Dr Bianchi though. That wasn't nice.'

'No,' I agreed, thinking Johnson was going to need some coffee soon.

'Not a good way to go.'

I didn't want to think about it. 'Is there a good way to go?'

'Me? I'd like a bullet in the back of the head. Bam bam, lights out, no warning. Not having my throat cut like some goddamn farmyard animal.'

I stood up, somewhat unsteady on my feet. 'I'm going to the loo,' I told him. 'When I come back, we'll have some pudding and some coffee, and then we'd better sober up a bit.'

The toilets seemed very brightly lit after the subtle lighting in the restaurant. I locked myself in a cubicle, trying to get my head straight.

When Daultrey had told me that Bianchi had been killed 'Mob style', I thought he'd meant she'd been shot. I was no expert on the Mafia, but I did know they preferred guns to knives. Had he lied to me about how she'd died? And if so, why?

Maybe coffee wasn't such a great idea. Maybe what I

needed to do was to loosen up Agent Johnson even more. Washing my hands, I headed back into the restaurant.

Earlier that morning, I'd thought Oxford Johnson looked familiar, but assumed it was because I'd clocked him at some point during the Feds' surveillance. Now, as I walked back to our table, I saw a waiter grinding black pepper onto the steak of the man at the table next to ours and everything suddenly made sense.

Because the pepper made Johnson's nose twitch, and he let out three short sneezes, like laser beams.

He'd been wearing sunglasses and a baseball cap the first time I'd seen him, but still I was sure: Agent Johnson was the man at the restaurant in Sicily who had noted down what Charlie ate for our last meal together.

Chapter Twenty-five

I stopped dead in my tracks, my feet refusing to work. I didn't have time to figure out what this meant – I knew I just had to *move*.

Edging backwards till I was out of Johnson's line of sight, I kept a careful eye on him as I slipped past the other tables, praying I could make it to the door before he saw me.

Just four feet to go. Three, two, one. The maître d' held the door open for me, and I was gone.

I ran for the lifts, my heart-rate doubling in seconds. It seemed to take forever for the elevator doors to open. I jumped in and jabbed my thumb repeatedly on the button marked 6. The doors closed again and the lift travelled upwards. I watched the display over the doors, each number lighting up in turn until 6 shone red and the doors opened.

My footfalls made no sound on the carpeted floor as I ran along the brightly lit hallway to Room 624. I hammered on the door, desperate to see him, praying he was still there.

The door flew open and there was Joe. He was wearing a clean white T-shirt and had obviously just showered; he had a towel in his hand that he must have been using to dry his hair.

'Christ, Kate, you okay?' he said, seeing my panic. And as I burst into tears: 'Are you on your own?'

Not wanting him to think we were safe, but unable to speak

and explain myself, I shook my head hard. 'Come on in,' he said, looking up and down the hotel corridor before ushering me into the room and closing the door behind us. He brought me down the hall and into the soft darkness of the living room, where just a couple of lamps cast out yellow light.

'Where are the agents?' he asked.

I took a breath and finally managed to speak. 'Probably right behind me,' I said, my voice too loud.

Joe's expression changed, becoming more closed off. Putting a finger to his lips, he pointed in the direction of the kids' bedroom.

'Oh God, the kids,' I said, trying to calm down. I felt like I was hyperventilating. 'I'm sorry, I shouldn't have come here.' I forced myself to keep my voice down. 'Where's Marisa?'

'She's playing the slots,' he said, grimacing as though he knew it looked odd, her out gambling while he stayed in by himself and looked after the kids. 'Kate, what the hell's wrong? Is it Sorrentino? Is he here?' His large arm muscles flexed as though he'd happily take a shot at Sorrentino if he got the chance.

'No, it's not that. Joe, I can't believe it. I've been so stupid. It was them all along, Daultrey and the Feds. If that's even what they are. Christ, I can't believe it.' My voice was getting high again.

Joe took me by the elbow and steered me to the sofa. He got a vodka miniature out of the minibar and handed it over as he sat down next to me. The shock of recognizing Johnson had sobered me up in double-quick time, and I was quite happy to down the bottle in one.

'Take a deep breath,' Joe said. 'And another.' He rubbed my back with firm strokes. 'Okay, tell me again. Whaddya think the Feds have done?'

I'd got my breath back, and the rest of me was slowly

coming under control too. The room seemed so quiet, a haven.

'I don't know how much you know about the way your brother died,' I started, keeping my voice low so I didn't disturb the children. My hands were shaking, and I put the empty miniature bottle on the coffee-table. 'It sounds like something out of a *Columbo* episode, but basically whoever killed him used his stomach contents to fool everyone into thinking he died the day he disappeared.'

'Who told you this?' asked Joe, frowning. 'Daultrey?'

'No. I found it out for myself. Daultrey would never have told me in a million years. Jesus, I've been such an idiot.' I banged my forehead with the heel of my hand. Joe grabbed the hand and pulled it down by my side, clasping it between his own.

'Go on,' he said.

'They made a note of what he ate for lunch the day he went missing. Then they mimicked it on the day they actually killed him. He was in the water for so long that it was only the stomach contents that pinned down a time of death.'

Joe was nodding. 'Okay,' he said. 'So what's all this gotta do with Daultrey?'

I stood up, the adrenaline making it unbearable to keep still. I paced the room. 'He told me it was Sorrentino who killed your brother. But it was *them*. The agent I just had dinner with, *the one that's currently meant to be protecting me*, is the same motherfucker I saw that day writing down "spaghetti, tomato sauce, red wine".'

Joe was looking at me with a strange expression on his face.

'What, Joe?' I asked him. 'What do we do? Do you think they're really federal agents?'

'I don't know,' he said, standing up and patting my arm. 'I'm pretty sure they are. Look – you a hundred per cent sure this guy is the same guy you saw back in Sicily? I mean, you say you just ate an entire meal with him before you recognized him. You can't have got a good look if it took you that long.'

I twisted away from him. 'I'm sure. I knew I'd seen him before, it just took him sneezing a stupid sneeze for me to remember where.'

'But why would they bring in the one guy you might recognize as being involved?' he pointed out.

'Because they don't know I saw him,' I insisted. 'I never told them I noticed someone writing down what Charlie ate.'

Joe nodded. 'Okay, it's okay. Kate, you gotta calm down.'

'But what do we do now? Who can we tell? Who would believe *me* over a federal agent?'

I was on the verge of tears again. The puzzle I'd slowly been sorting into a clear picture was a blur again. Exhausted, I wondered if I'd ever find out the truth about what had happened to Charlie.

'I'm sorry,' I said again to Joe, and all my nervous energy seemed to drop away. 'Really, I shouldn't have come here. I think I'm putting you in danger.'

'It's okay,' he said softly, putting a hand on my shoulder.

'No, it's not. Your kids, Marisa . . . It's just you're the only person I know I can trust.'

His eyes looked almost black in the low light, his pupils were so dilated. Just a narrow ring of iris glowed blue.

'You're my last link to him,' I said, so quietly I could hardly even hear myself. 'I'm so scared now I've found you that I'm going to lose you too.'

'Don't say that,' he said. 'We're family.'

I laughed shakily, tears in my eyes. 'I can't believe he has a little niece and nephew.'

'Hey, they're your niece and nephew too,' Joe said, and that made me start to cry again.

'Can I see their photo one more time?' I asked.

'Sure.' He picked up his wallet from the side-table and handed me the picture of Joe Junior and Gabriela. I looked at their happy faces, their shining brown eyes, the edge of the photograph feeling light as air on my fingertips. *My niece and nephew.*

Wait. Something . . . something was wrong with the picture.

My heart began to thud again.

'Your kids, Joe,' I said, trying to sound casual. 'Are they adopted, or Marisa's kids by a previous husband?'

'No,' he said. 'Why?'

I said nothing.

The blue-eyed gene is recessive – you pair it with a brown-eyed gene, and brown wins every time. So if you're a man with blue eyes, and your wife, like Marisa, also has blue eyes, you can only pass on that same colour to your children.

Which basically means it's nearly impossible for a man and a woman who both have blue eyes to have brown-eyed children.

I pushed past him and threw open the door to the kids' room. Maybe Marisa had some secret lover who'd fathered the children without Joe realizing they weren't his, in which case I'd find them tucked up fast asleep, dreaming the easy dreams of the innocent.

The room was empty, the beds neat, undisturbed. There were no signs of occupancy, no children's suitcases or books or toys.

I stood with my back to Joe, unable to work out why he would want to deceive me. And my subconscious, that had been ticking away constantly in the background over the last insane couple of weeks, started doing its job again, flicking images in front of my mind's eye like playing cards.

Photo after photo of Charlie, from every angle. Photos of his eyes, his nose, his jawline, his smile. And an echo of

Taylor's voice, telling me that their plastic surgeons could give you a completely new face, make you look like another person entirely.

The man behind me wasn't Joe Cantelli. God knows what his real name was. All I knew was that he was someone they'd cut and sculpted till he could play the role of my dead husband.

And if he wasn't Joe Cantelli, he would have no loyalty to me. He was one of them.

I slowly turned round. The man I'd thought of as Joe stood silhouetted in the doorway. With the light behind him, his face was in shadow.

I had no weapon. The gun I'd stolen from Sorrentino was in its hiding-place back in my room. My only chance was to pretend I still believed this man was my brother-in-law.

I thought quickly. 'It was Marisa, wasn't it?' I said to him. 'She was worried I was going to try and steal you from her, and that not even her pregnancy would put me off. So she manufactured two kids just to make sure that only a woman with no morals at all would go after you.'

He said nothing. I took a step closer, trying to smile, trying to read his face in the darkness.

'She needn't have worried,' I said. 'I haven't even looked at another man since Charlie died. Not even someone who looks just like him would work for me. I may as well just join a nunnery.'

His hand twitched and I stopped, just a couple of feet from him. The movement had made the light behind him reflect off his wedding ring.

I frowned. The band hadn't looked gold in the light. It had looked silver.

My feet moved of their own accord, taking me closer. My hands reached out and pulled his left hand towards me.

It wasn't the same ring I'd seen before. It was platinum now, like mine.

I dropped his hand like it was on fire.

His white T-shirt seemed almost luminous in the blackness. I reached out a shaking hand to the sleeve on his right arm and pushed it up to his shoulder. There was a Celtic sun tattoo there, still covered in places by smears of faint, skin-coloured stage make-up.

I fell backwards, legs stumbling behind me, and landed on the edge of the nearest bed. I scrabbled back until I felt solid wall behind me.

The man in the doorway stayed where he was.

'Kate,' he said.

The word, 'No!' burst out of my lungs. 'You're not him. You can't be him.'

'Kate, I'm so sorry.' The deep 'Joe' voice was gone. The voice that replaced it was achingly familiar.

'He wouldn't do this to me. It's another trick.'

The man stepped into the room and closed the door behind him. It was just the two of us, in the now completely dark room.

He came towards me, but when I shrank away from him he sat instead on the bed opposite.

For a moment he sat there silently and all I could hear was my panicked, raspy breathing. Then he started to speak.

'I'm going to tell you what happened,' he said. 'Right from the start, the complete truth. Please hear me out. You can decide then . . . what you want to do.'

I just stared at him, a blank shape in the darkness.

'Daultrey lied to you,' he said. 'Your husband wasn't really called Antoni Cantelli. He wasn't an FBI agent either. He was the son of a Mafia boss, and his real name was Giuseppe Carlo – Joe. Joe Carlo.'

'No,' I said, but the man kept speaking.

'He wasn't interested in following in his father's footsteps. He went to college, became an architect. He loved his family, but he found it easier to live in a different city. He didn't lead a completely separate life – a lot of his friends made their money from crime. He didn't really like it, but at the same time, to him it was normal.

'Then one day he witnessed a murder. A contact in the DA's office got warning to him that there was physical evidence that placed him at the scene. The FBI came after him. They knew he hadn't committed the murder, but they threatened to prosecute him anyway if he didn't turn in the real killer. His father had the resources to create a new identity for him, and he left his job, his home, and moved to another city.

'And then he met you.' I had to swallow hard to get past the lump in my throat. 'Everything changed. Life suddenly meant something again. The only thing he found hard was being away from his family, from his mother and father. He had to lie to you, to tell you that they were dead, because he knew you'd find it suspicious that he never saw them, that they never wanted to meet you. But after two years of being away from them, he thought the people who were after him would have given up; that finally they could all meet somewhere and it would be safe.

'It wasn't. The Feds found him there. They waited until he was on his own, swimming in the ocean, and tricked him: he came across a boat, and a blonde woman in the water, panicking, looking like she was drowning. He swam over and helped her back on the boat, then a guy came out of nowhere with a Taser gun.

When he came to, he was handcuffed to a guardrail. He thought they were just capturing him, not thinking too much at that point about why they didn't just get him extradited if they knew where he was. It wasn't until he saw. . .' The man seemed to be struggling to speak. 'It wasn't until he saw a man called Ben Gerber that he started to understand. When he saw the tattoo they'd given him. And he noticed that they were the same height, the same weight, had the same colour hair and eyes. Gerber was like a kid. He didn't have a clue what was happening to him. He didn't even know how to swim.'

I sat on the bed, hardly breathing, hardly moving. My hands were clutching on tight to fistfuls of the bedsheets. I couldn't even think straight, though I was taking in everything he told me.

The man was quiet for a long time, and when he spoke again his voice was ragged, and I could tell he'd been crying.

'Joe Carlo realized then how far these people were willing to go for what they wanted. And what they wanted was a puppet on the inside. They took him back to Chicago, told him to tell his family that things had gone badly wrong in London, that he was in trouble, and that when a dead body matching his description had washed up on the beach he'd taken the opportunity to fake his death and return home. The Feds instructed him to become a proper part of his family's business, to learn as much as possible and feed it back to them.

'But he couldn't do that to his father. He couldn't run either, since the only reason the Feds had left his wife alive was so the threat of them hurting or killing her was always hanging over him. So he told his father the truth, and between them they arranged to only pass on half-truths and exaggerations; nothing that would ever lead to one of their own being brought down. It was only meant to be temporary. He was trying to find out what Daultrey's endgame was – where the weak points were in his plan, in his team; how he could be brought down. His father was making contacts in London, trying to find someone who could be trusted to snatch his daughter-in-law from under the noses of the people watching her, get her to a safe location, and not give her up if they were threatened or bribed. They had to be sure they wouldn't be double-crossed. Joe just couldn't risk losing her. But he was terrified he was running out of time.

'You see, for a long while Daultrey was happy with the intel he got, but it was getting to the point where he was insisting on more when Joe took a trip to Miami to meet up with a Cuban contact, and saw some friends he knew from back in England in a restaurant there. He thought he'd left the restaurant in time, that they hadn't seen him. And then an old friend of his called him up and said: "Your wife knows." And he should have been scared then, he should have been worried, and he was, but he was also absolutely fucking ecstatic. Because even though Daultrey had told him she was dead if she ever found out the truth, that's all he'd wanted to do for the past year – get back to her, tell her the truth, tell her everything, and set them both free.

'Daultrey caught up with her, warned her off, but she was stubborn and wouldn't give up. They were going to kill her, but Joe made sure the Feds knew that if they did, *nothing* would make him go back to work for them. In fact the consequences for them would have been much, much worse, but he knew Daultrey worried more about his grand plan than he did about his team's personal security.

'Joe told them he had a way to fool his wife into thinking she was wrong, after all, and eventually they agreed to go along with it. He knew that, if it worked, there was a good chance that afterwards the Feds would take her somewhere he'd never find her, but he was out of options. He was so desperate he could only see one move at a time.'

His voice seemed to get lower, more raw. 'He knew it

would be hard to see her walk in through that door, but he had no idea how hard it would be to see her leave through it. It wasn't until he believed he was never going to see her again that he finally understood how much she must have hurt all this time.'

The man's shape became clearer as he came towards me in the grey darkness. He knelt down in front of me, hands grasping my legs, and lowered his head into my lap. I could hear how hard he was breathing. My hands flexed, wanting to feel his hair between my fingers, wanting to pull him towards me, but self-preservation held them back. He raised his head and took my right hand, kissing my palm, his breath at my wrist, cupping my hand around his mouth.

'No,' I gasped, suddenly panicking and pulling my hand from him. I pushed away from him with my feet, and my boot caught him on his shoulder. He fell backwards, having to put out a hand to steady himself.

We were both silent for a moment. In the stillness I forced the words out of my closed-up throat.

'You don't understand,' I said, and I was shaking. 'If you're not him, I don't think I'll be able to take it.'

He reached sideways and the lamp lit up the room. I snapped my eyes shut, unable to look at him.

'Kate,' he said, and I felt his gentle fingertips stroke my face. 'Katie, it's me. I promise. I promise. Just trust me.'

He came closer, the mattress shifting beneath me as he sat to the side of me, and this time he didn't smell of Joe's aftershave or hair gel. He just smelled like himself. I leaned into him, close enough to feel the warmth coming off him. I slowly, slowly, opened my eyes.

Whatever had turned him into Joe Cantelli – the posture, the attitude, the voice – it was all gone. In its place was my husband's beautiful, familiar face. I reached up in wonder and held his face between my hands, examining the curve of his mouth, the line of his nose, and every other contour of his features that had been mapped onto my heart, finally looking into blue eyes full of love. He smiled, and there was nothing goofy about it.

This time, when I kissed him, it was like coming home after long years of exile.

Charlie.

Chapter Twenty-six

We lay under the white sheets, hidden inside a cave of bed-clothes from head to toe. We were entwined, legs curled around each other, arms enclosing. I listened to him breathe, feeling his ribcage expand and contract against my breast, and couldn't imagine ever feeling happier than I did at that moment.

'We should end it now,' I murmured, stroking the short, diagonally growing hairs at the back of his neck.

'A suicide pact?' he said, kissing the little mole on my shoulder. I could feel his smile in the kiss.

'If we end it now, we'll never have to risk being apart again. We know we'll be together for the rest of time.'

The bedside lamps on either side of the four-poster made the sheet stretched above us glow white, as if we were enveloped in clouds.

'Let's just stay here for ever,' he said. 'I'm sure Daultrey would be happy to keep paying the room bill. We'll do a John and Yoko, and sustain ourselves on packs of nuts from the minibar.'

'Hell, if Daultrey's paying, let's go crazy and order room service.'

When he breathed out, I breathed in the air that had just come from his lungs. Then I breathed it back into him. We were cocooned together.

'We'd better not order any garlic bread,' he said, and I burst out laughing. He hugged me tight. 'God, you don't know how much I've missed that. Listening to the sound of your laugh. *Making* you laugh.'

I kissed his mouth, feeling amazed that he was real, flesh and blood, alive beside me. I was terrified that at any moment I might wake up and find this was just a dream. I thought of all the moments over the nightmare of the past 377 days when I'd just longed to be with him again, and marvelled that my wish had come true. I wanted to disappear into him, to merge into one person so we could never be separated again.

'I'm so scared I'm going to lose you again,' I whispered. I could see he was staring at the white scars on the inside of my elbows.

'Just promise me,' he said, his voice hoarse. 'If anything happens to me, that you won't hurt yourself again.'

I stroked his dark hair. 'I can't, Charlie, I'm sorry. I need to be with you.' I grinned. 'God, I even used to think ahead and worry about you dying of old age before me. And now I *pray* I'll get to wake up one day next to your wrinkled, elderly corpse.'

He shook his head, only half-smiling. 'But what if there's no afterlife? What if you kill yourself to be with me, and there's nothing there?'

'Then I'll be nothing,' I said softly. 'But I'd rather be nothing than be without you.'

He kissed me long and deep. I felt as if we were floating through sunlit clouds. We knew it couldn't last for ever, this suspension of questions and consequences, but I wanted nothing more than to keep the world paused for just a few more hours.

It wasn't so dreamlike and unreal for him; he knew he hadn't lost me for good. But for me, my lover had come back from the dead. I just wanted to hold on, scared that if I let go of him I'd suddenly wake up back in my bed at home, alone again. Charlie, however, knew he had to focus on the future if we were going to enjoy one together.

He kissed me again, but it had a finality about it. He threw the sheet off our heads, and we were back in stone-cold reality.

'I need to work out what Daultrey's playing at,' he said, sitting up. 'You said you talked to Luigi Sorrentino?'

Reluctantly, I pulled myself up into a seated position. 'Daultrey told me about him when he spun me the story about you being an FBI agent. He said Sorrentino had Federico Calabresi killed for vouching for you, and then ordered your murder in Sicily.'

'Fuck,' said Charlie. 'Why would he do that? I can see why he needed to blame someone, but why use a real name?'

'It's more than that,' I admitted. 'He offered to help me kill Sorrentino.'

Charlie went rigid. 'He did *what*?'

'He made it sound as though it was the only way he could get justice for a fellow agent. That's why we came here, because Sorrentino was staying at the Babylonian. Daultrey gave me a gun, and arranged for me to get him alone. He wanted me to kill him.'

'Jesus Christ,' said Charlie, visibly paler. 'You tried to kill Luigi Sorrentino?'

'I didn't get as far as actually firing the gun, no. I wanted to get some answers out of him first, and it was obvious he didn't know what the hell I was talking about, so I left.'

Charlie took a breath. 'What did you tell Daultrey? How did he react?'

'I told him his information was wrong, and that whoever had given it to him was probably this mole that he blamed for your cover being blown. He wasn't happy, but at the time I thought it was just because he didn't want the other agents to know what he was up to.'

'They knew,' said Charlie. 'They're all involved up to their necks. Taylor was the woman who pretended to be having difficulty swimming that day they took me. Johnson was the guy who rang Daultrey on his cellphone and told him I'd eaten spaghetti and red wine. Wilson was the bastard holed away in the yacht's little kitchen area, cooking up Ben's last meal. Jerkins told Ben he was going to teach him to swim, told him how brave he was getting his new tattoo, told him how happy they all were to have him as their friend. And that fucker Daultrey was the one who took away the ladder so Ben couldn't climb out of the sea. And all of them – *all of them* – just stood there and watched him splash about in panic and beg them for help before he went under.'

There was nothing I could say. I waited for him to calm down.

'Tell me how you found out about the stomach contents,' he eventually said.

I told him about the mismatched dates on the autopsy report, how it had convinced me that something had been covered up, and how a small part of me had hoped it was related to the DNA match between the samples taken from our room and the corpse.

'I still don't understand how they managed it,' I said. 'Not unless they managed to bribe the testing lab like they obviously bribed Bianchi and Graziani.'

'I do,' said Charlie. 'When I was locked up on the yacht, I heard Ben ask what they'd done with his toothbrush and comb.'

'Shit,' I said, his words prompting a distinct memory of watching as a forensics guy in white overalls put what I'd thought was Charlie's toothbrush in an evidence bag. 'Sofia told me a master key had gone missing that day. They must've broken in while I was still on the beach and swapped them, the bastards.'

'How'd you find out about Bianchi and Graziani?' Charlie wanted to know.

So I told him it all; about breaking into Sabrina Bianchi's house to interrogate her, and about going after Eduardo Graziani. Although Charlie was bothered by the lengths I'd gone to to find the truth, he didn't react at all when I told him about being warned off Graziani by Luke and Cesare.

'Daultrey told me it was Luke who betrayed you, who said you were in Sicily.'

Charlie shook his head. 'No, it wasn't. Daultrey found out I was meeting my parents there. He followed them.'

My mouth twitched. 'The Crestenzas are your parents?'

He touched my knee. 'Yes. Obviously their surname is Carlo, not Crestenza, but they *are* called Francesca and Angelo. They were very happy to finally meet you.'

I decided to let that particular deception go. 'So you trust Luke?' I asked.

'Of course,' Charlie said. 'I'd trust him with my life, and with yours. All he's been doing, all this time, is trying to protect you.'

'By helping Daultrey and the rest of those fuckers to give me the runaround?'

Charlie laughed, and pulled me close for a kiss. 'Don't you think you'd have been safer staying at home and not playing crazy vigilante across the globe?'

'Well obviously, but if he'd just been honest with me from the start, maybe I wouldn't have had to come running here trying to find you.' I rubbed my face. 'Jesus, when it happened, back in Sicily, how could he have watched me wait for them to find your body, and not say a word?'

'He didn't know then. It was a month before I was able to get word to him. Look Kate, he wanted to tell you, we argued about it all the time. It was me that insisted he kept you in the dark. They were watching you, and I knew if you found out I was still alive you wouldn't be able to hide it. We had a plan to get out from all this, and I thought if you could just stay safe in London for a few more months . . .'

'Yeah, but I *wasn't* safe, was I?' I said, twisting up the underside of my arms to confront him with my scars. His face went dark, and after a moment he bent his head and kissed each scar. I could feel his black hair brushing against my skin, his warm lips on the scar tissue. 'You can't just kiss it better,' I said.

'I know,' he said, his voice thick. 'But I can't go back and change the past either. God knows, I wish I could.'

'Why?' I said, wanting to hear him say it. 'What would you do differently?'

'I'd tell you the truth, right from the start. Before we even got married. I'd tell you about my family, about Luke, about being on the run from the Feds. When they'd taken me, and you were grieving, I would have found some way of letting you know I was still here.'

'Even if you knew it would put me in danger?'

He nodded, and I could see he was trying not to cry. 'Because I'd know, if it was me, that there was nothing they could do to me that would be worse than thinking you were gone.'

I held him as tight as I could. It was all I needed to hear.

'It's okay,' I whispered in his ear. 'I forgive you.' He hugged me even harder.

Then the moment passed, and it was time to go.

I pulled on my jeans, smiling at him across the rumpled sheets as he did the same.

'Have you spent the last twelve months in the gym, Charlie?' I teased him, watching the six-pack of his stomach muscles contract as he buttoned his fly.

'I've spent the last twelve months thinking I'd better be god-damn ready to fight or run. Don't be thinking I'll be keeping this up once we're drinking mojitos on a yacht in the Indian Ocean.' Tugging his white T-shirt over his head, he cleared his throat. 'Look, can I ask you something?'

'Fire away.'

'If I'd told you the truth about my family on the day we met, would it have scared you off?'

'Actually,' I said, pausing in the middle of doing up my shirt, 'I have a bit of a confession to make. My—'

Someone hammered on the door, and we both froze, holding our breath. A pause, and then they hammered again.

'It's Johnson,' the agent yelled through the suite door. 'Let me in.'

'Shit,' I whispered. 'He must be looking for me.'

'Hide in the closet,' Charlie said under his breath. 'I'll pretend you're not here.'

'No,' I hissed back. 'What if they search the rooms for me? The best thing is to pretend I still think you're Joe.'

'But then you'll have to leave with him!'

'If they think I'm still going along with the Witness Protection Programme plan, they won't be as careful with me as they will if they find me hiding under your bloody bed!'

'No, it's too dangerous. If we stay quiet, maybe he'll think we've gone.'

We both heard the click of a door lock, and then the sound of Agent Johnson entering the suite.

'Fuck!' I mouthed at him, then took a split-second decision and ran into the living room before Johnson could get to the end of the corridor and see that the room was empty. I just had time to run my fingers through my mussed-up hair before he appeared in the living-room doorway.

'Sssh!' I said in a low voice, a finger to my lips. 'Are you trying to wake up the kids?'

He blinked at me, not sure whether he should play along or not. 'Sorry,' he said finally. 'I forgot. Why didn't you answer the door?'

'Don't take it personally,' I said, pretending I was still quite drunk. 'I just didn't want to be interrupted.'

'Where's Joe?' J ohnson said, peering round the corridor to the master bedroom. A toilet flushed, and Charlie came back in the room.

'Hey there, Johnson,' he said, back in his 'Joe' voice. 'Thought I heard someone. If you've woken up those kids there'll be hell to pay, my friend.'

'Sorry,' Johnson said again. 'I was just looking for Miss Grey here.' He turned back to me. 'Where the hell did you go? I've been looking all over this goddamn hotel for you.'

Charlie put his arm around me. 'Chill out, Johnson. She's been with me. I don't know what the two of you were talking about over dinner, but she got upset and wanted a little chat. If you were so worried, why didn't you call the other agents in?' He was trying to make me see that Johnson had been more worried about Daultrey's reaction to my loss than he was about recovering me.

'Yes, well, I'm glad you're okay, Miss Grey, but it's time to leave. I think you've had enough excitement for one night.'

'Jesus, you sound like my dad,' I complained. 'Let's hit the tables. It's too early to go to bed.' We had an advantage over Johnson – we outnumbered him. If it looked like we couldn't persuade him to let me loose in the casino again, I was going to try and take him out.

'I didn't say you had to go to bed,' sighed Johnson. 'But I do think you should sober up a bit before you do any more gambling. Unless you want to blow your life-savings all in one night.'

'Good advice,' said Charlie, slapping Johnson on the back. 'Keep an eye on her, will ya? Don't let her play anything that requires any skill or the casino will be laughing.'

'Roulette it is,' Johnson assured him. 'Come on now, Miss Grey.'

I turned to Charlie. 'Good night, Joe,' I said, holding onto him and going onto tiptoes so I could kiss him on the cheek. 'Bellagio,' I whispered in his ear so quietly that only he could hear me. Then, more audibly: 'Thank you for everything.'

Charlie squeezed my arms, staring at me as though if he wished it hard enough, we would both be spirited away to the South Sea Islands. 'Goodbye, Kate. And good luck in your new life.'

As Johnson marched me down the hallway to the lifts, I could feel a metaphysical cord tying me and Charlie together, a glowing golden line stretching down the corridor and up the elevator shaft as we travelled up to my room. We were connected again, and I couldn't help smiling to myself, as if I was harbouring some secret treasure within me.

Wilson looked up from the TV as we let ourselves into the suite. 'The aftershocks in California are pretty bad,' he said, and the tone of his voice made him sound as though he was accusing us of being responsible.

'They're used to it,' said Johnson unsympathetically.

'I'm gonna get changed, then we can hit the roulette tables,' I said, winking at Johnson.

'Think again,' he said. 'You've given me the runaround enough tonight.'

Wilson looked up at that. 'What did she do?'

Johnson looked away, hands in pockets. 'Oh nothing, she's just been breaking my balls.'

'Agent Johnson,' I said in a sing-song voice, still pretending to be tipsy, 'can I have a little word with you in private?'

Wilson raised his eyebrows as Johnson looked to him for approval. Then he shrugged, as if to say 'on your head be it'.

Alone in my room with Johnson, I played with the hem of his T-shirt. 'I'm sorry I was a bad girl,' I said. 'I promise I'll play nicely this time.'

'Kate, I just can't trust you. I'm meant to be protecting you – what would Daultrey say if you went running off round the hotel again on your own?'

'I won't, I promise,' I said. 'Let me go and explain to Stanley, I'm sure he'll be happy for you to take me out again.' I made for the door, and he grabbed my arm.

'He's probably in bed asleep,' he said. 'Don't disturb him.'

'Really?' I said. 'It's still quite early.'

Johnson looked at me, face set, trying to work out whether or not I was threatening him.

'Please,' I said again. 'It's just been a really shitty day, and I could do with some fun. I'm sorry I ran off – just all that talk about soulmates upset me and I wanted to talk to Joe. But I'm okay now. I'm fine. I just don't want to spend my last night of freedom – well, of relative freedom – eating room-service food with Wilson, watching the bloody news. Come on, let's go out, let's have a few drinks and keep each other company.'

I can't say what made Johnson relent. Was it the threat of me grassing him up to Daultrey, the flirting, or some genuine sympathy for me? Did they have plans for me that made him think this would be more than my last night of freedom – it would be my last night on this earth?

'Fine,' he said. 'Be quick.' And he left me alone in the bed-room.

I closed my door behind him and quickly threw a clean pair of jeans, a black top and my flipflops into the same bag I'd taken to meet Sorrentino. Then I stripped down to my undies and locked myself in the bathroom, getting the wig, gun and clip out of their hiding place behind the bath panel and shoving them at the bottom of the bag.

As I slid the scarlet dress down over my body I could sud-denly smell Charlie on my skin and it was hard not to start crying. At home I had his clothes, his pillow, the duvet cover, and I'd been painfully aware that the familiar scent of him had become so faded that soon it would have lost the potency to bring him to life in my mind.

I'd been walking a dark path without him, unable to see a future ahead of me. And in the space of an hour, suddenly that path had been lit by a thousand lamps, stretching miles into the distance, lighting the way.

I stepped into my stilettos and put on my ruby and diamond earrings that Charlie had given me two years before. I didn't want to leave without them. Everything else could stay.

'Wow,' said Johnson when I reappeared in the doorway.

'Hmm, babysitting duty don't seem so much of a chore any more, huh?' grizzled Wilson.

Johnson's checking out of my cleavage in the lift as we made our way down to the casino floor, then his hand at the small of my back as he guided me through to the roulette tables, made me think that maybe the flirting had helped to swing it, even if his main motivation was avoiding pissing off Daultrey.

My patience lasted only half an hour, by which time I was so desperate to see Charlie again that I couldn't wait any longer to move on to the next stage of my plan.

I slid off my seat, pushing my chips along to Johnson. 'You look after them for a while,' I said. 'I'm gonna visit the little girls' room.'

He picked up both our chips, and hopped off his seat. 'Not on your own you're not.'

'I'll be okay,' I tried to tell him.

'Well, better safe than sorry. Come on.' And there was the hand on the small of my back again, steering me towards the ladies' toilets. 'I'll wait here,' he said at the entrance to the loos, then turned round, his back to the wall, right hand clasping his left wrist just like a Secret Service man. I could see him scanning the room for threats – as if I had anyone to worry about other than him and his friends!

I found a stall at the end of the row of cubicles and quickly changed into my jeans, black top and flipflops. The top, which was tight at the bust but flared out around the waist, meant I could tuck the Beretta, safety on, into the back of my jeans without it showing through the fabric. The spare clip went in my pocket, where it could have passed for a pen or a lighter. Tying back my hair, I dipped my head and pulled on the blonde wig. Re-emerging like Superman from his phone box, I twisted round to check out my back view, making sure the gun wasn't visible under the top.

I'd left the red dress and stilettos inside my bag, in the stall. Having been pawed by Sorrentino in it, I was happy to leave it for some Vegas vulture to pick over.

Hovering by the door, I waited for a batch of women around my age to finish blowdrying their hands and reapplying their lippy. When they left, I followed them out, trying to make it look as though I was one of their party. My face was turned away from where Johnson should have been standing. He was waiting for a girl with a black bob in a bright red dress and heels. If he was still in the same position, his back to the wall, he would only see the rear of a woman with long blonde hair, in jeans and flipflops.

I couldn't check. I could only carry on following my new friends, praying my deception had worked.

'Keep walking, keep walking,' I said under my breath, willing the women to take me out of Johnson's sight. If they stopped at the nearest table and I carried on, I'd be exposed.

'I think JT said he'd see us at the bar,' I heard one of them say, and said a silent prayer of thanks.

Not daring to look behind me, I could hear my own pulse as I got further and further away. Then we rounded a corner, in theory out of his line of sight. Breaking away from the girls, I looked over my shoulder. No one.

I started to hurry then, not wanting to run in case it drew too much attention, but desperate to get away. The fleur de lys pattern on the carpeted floors charted my progress – twelve fleur de lys from the exit, then five, then one, then I was gone.

Outside, I was assaulted by neon and traffic and the dry heat of the desert. In the distance I could see the Paris Hotel, a blur of blue lightbulbs in the shape of a hot-air balloon. I knew the Bellagio was opposite. I began to run then, side-stepping other pedestrians, zipping in between them, toes gripping my flipflops. Someone swore at me as I pushed past them, and I knocked the drink of some girl coming out of a fast-food joint clean out of her hand. Dark brown liquid and cubes of ice scattered over the pavement. I kept running, ignoring her cries of indignation, concerned only with reaching my goal.

He was there. Still wearing his white T-shirt, waiting by the fountains, the only one of the hordes surrounding him who wasn't interested in the dancing jets of water. He was looking nervously around him, watching for me.

I darted across the road, cars blaring, and he heard the

horns and turned to me. I was only a few hundred yards away. He broke into a smile of relief, and I grinned back at him, pulling the wig off my head, starting to laugh. We'd made it.

Then a black SUV with tinted windows screeched to a halt beside him. A door opened, and I saw a man reach out and pull him towards the car. I rocked to a standstill, my mouth dropping open in shock. His eyes widened as he lost his balance, and he looked at me in fear. He held a hand out to me. It wasn't a call for help, but raised as a barrier, a stop sign. Even a few seconds into an ambush, his instinct was to protect me.

I started to run again, but already his feet were disappearing into the back of the SUV and the door was slammed shut. The people around him barely noticed, too enraptured by the Bellagio's water ballet. The SUV peeled away from the pavement, speeding past me too quickly for me to do anything other than spin 180 degrees and chase after it. It immediately veered down a side street, and by the time I reached the turning all I could see were two red tail-lights disappearing off round another corner.

Chapter Twenty-seven

I was rooted there for a moment in panic, my brain unable to function. Charlie was in danger, and I couldn't cope with knowing that. What should I do?

I had only one advantage. I knew who had taken him. The man who had opened the door and dragged Charlie into the back of the SUV was Luigi Sorrentino's right-hand man, Aldo.

I dropped to a crouch on the street, trying to focus, earning strange looks from the people around me. Sorrentino obviously hadn't left Vegas at all – or at least if he had, he hadn't taken Aldo with him. They had kidnapped Charlie because they knew it was his wife – me – who had threatened Sorrentino. They were either going to hurt him to find me, or hurt him to hurt me. I could only pray for the former, knowing it increased Charlie's life expectancy.

'Fuck!' I yelled out, making one girl jump away from me in fright. A guy with a bushy beard and sunglasses shook his head at me in disgust.

The ridiculous thing was, I knew I had an ally against Sorrentino. Someone who wanted him dead. It was crazy, but maybe it was Charlie's only hope.

I knocked on the door, not sure if anyone would be there. It was just a moment before the lock mechanism clicked and the door swung open. He was on his mobile, looking harassed, his shirt-sleeves rolled up.

Daultrey's jaw literally dropped when he saw it was me. Angela Taylor, also on her cellphone, was pacing behind him. When she looked over his shoulder and saw me, her eyes widened as though life was just too crazy for her to cope with any more.

'She's here,' she said into her phone.

'Come back to the room,' Daultrey told the person at the other end of his own phone, and snapped it shut. 'You'd better come in,' he said. I stepped into the dragon's den, and Daultrey closed the door behind me.

'I need your help,' I said. Daultrey gazed at me in disbelief. 'They've taken Charlie.'

He turned away then in exasperation, now knowing for sure that I'd discovered the truth. 'What happened?' he asked eventually.

'I was meeting him on the Strip. A black SUV pulled up. Sorrentino's lieutenant dragged Charlie into the car. They drove off too fast for me to follow them. Please, you've got to help me.'

'I'm not sure it's wise for us to get involved,' Daultrey said.

'Oh fuck you!' I yelled at him. 'You're involved up to your necks. How can Charlie keep giving you information if Sorrentino's got him chopped into little pieces and thrown off the Hoover Dam? Look, you use your contact to help me find him, and I promise you, I'll finish Sorrentino off this time.'

Taylor looked at Daultrey, but he wasn't interested in swapping glances with her. His cold, muddy eyes just appraised me. I stared back at him, trying to make him see how determined I was to protect Charlie.

He thumbed his phone open again, speed-dialling a number, gazing at me as the connection was made and his call was answered.

'What gives?' he asked. I couldn't hear the response, and Daultrey's lack of reaction made it hard to guess what it might have been.

'Mata Hari here saw it happen,' he said. 'He still alive?'

I swallowed hard.

'Good,' Daultrey said. 'Can you keep him that way? What's Sorrentino after?' Then, after a pause, 'I think she'd be willing. How do you see this playing out?'

He turned away from me then, but I could hear the smile in his voice as he said: 'No, I think that's our only option now. Call me back when it's set.'

Daultrey faced me again, closing his phone. 'My contact says Charlie's still alive. Sorrentino's only interested in finding you. So far Charlie's not given you up, but trust me, he won't be able to hold out for long. No one does.'

'So your contact can negotiate a swap?'

Daultrey shrugged. 'He says Sorrentino's only interested in you. He doesn't want to start a war with the Carlos, which is what will happen if he executes one of them.'

'So what are we waiting for?'

Sorrentino hadn't even bothered to change hotels, perhaps hoping I'd try and track him down here.

'You sure you can trust your contact?' I asked Daultrey as we walked through the lobby of the Babylonian. 'After all, he told you Sorrentino went back to New York.'

'Sorrentino *did* go back to New York,' said Daultrey curtly. 'But then he went looking for Joe.'

'You can stop calling him that,' I said, jabbing at the button that called the lift. 'I know who he is now.'

Daultrey smirked at me. 'Yeah. And his real name's Joe. Not that you'll ever have a chance to get used to using it.'

'Why do you hate me so much?' I said. 'Christ, there's only one of us with any good reason to hate the other, and it's not you, mate.'

The lift arrived, and Daultrey waited till we were in it before he replied. 'It's all the time and goddamn energy I wasted trying to get you off our backs,' he said, pressing the button for the thirty-first and thirty-second floors. 'You just couldn't let it fucking lie.'

'Well, I'm sorry if I got in the way of your little blackmail technique,' I said as the lift doors shut and we began to move.

'Oh, not just that, Kate, not just that. You've got to take some responsibility for Graziani – and Bianchi – too. Graziani helped us out because he hated the Mob so much – he didn't take a cent. But then you go poking your nose in, he starts to wonder if our motives were quite as pure as his, and then suddenly there's another loose end that needs dealing with.'

I stared up at him. '*You* killed Graziani?'

'It was your fault. You got him asking questions that frankly we didn't have the answers to. And of course once we'd dealt with him there was the issue of Dr Bianchi – we couldn't just leave her to tell the Sicilian cops about you and what she'd done for Graziani. So now you've got those deaths on your conscience: if you hadn't meddled, they'd still be alive. Joe wouldn't be getting the shit kicked out of him right now. You wouldn't be five minutes away from having to put a bullet in someone.' He sighed with what seemed almost like satisfaction, as I tried to stop my head from swimming. 'I hope you're happy.'

The lift pinged as it settled on the thirty-first floor, and Daultrey stepped out.

'And Sorrentino?' I said, reaching almost blindly through

the door and grabbing his arm. 'What about him? Why do you want him dead?'

He pulled his arm out of my grasp. 'I'll be waiting for you down here,' he said as the doors began to close. 'Try not to lose your nerve this time.'

I just had time to give him the finger before the lift doors cut us off and I ascended to the next floor. My breathing and heart-rate were increasing with every step along the hallway to Sorrentino's room. It was on the other side of the hotel from the room he'd been in before, and I could see the gold-plated sheen of the Mandalay Bay's exterior through the window at the end of the corridor. Blinking back tears, I took a deep breath and knocked on his door.

Although Daultrey's anonymous contact was expecting me, Sorrentino wasn't. To him, I'd be arriving like a birthday present wrapped in a big red bow. Well, beware Greeks bearing gifts.

The fish-eye lens in the door went dark and I heard loud, excited talking.

'Let me pat her down first, boss,' I heard through the door, and just had time to realize there was no way I was getting into that room with Sorrentino's gun in my possession before his lieutenant was in front of me. There was blood on his shirt.

'If you've hurt him, I'll fucking kill you,' I said. Aldo just laughed, closing the door behind him, then held a finger up to his thin lips.

'I've got a present for you,' he whispered, and handed me a Glock semi-automatic. I looked up at him in surprise.

'*You're* Daultrey's contact?'

'Take it,' he said. 'You got your own?' I nodded. 'Hand it over.'

His rat-like face broke into a yellow-toothed grin when he saw it. 'You were going to take out Lu with his own gun?'

I didn't bother to reply, just put the gun in the back of my jeans, where the Beretta had been.

'Okay,' he said. 'Let the games begin.' And he unlocked the door and pushed me through it.

Sorrentino was in a larger room than before, a suite. Moroccan-style lamps cast hatched black shadows along the floor. He sat, arms stretched out, on a dark leather sofa. Two goons were with him – one standing guard beside him, the other by the large TV, which was playing a black and white James Cagney film. He was rubbing his bruised knuckles.

Charlie was slumped in a chair, his head down so I couldn't see his face. His wrists were tied to the arm rests with what looked like the belts from a pair of bathrobes. His ankles were tied to the chair legs with gold silk ropes that could only have come from the long white drapes at the windows. They'd ripped the shower curtain from its hooks and spread it out under him to stop any of his blood from staining the carpet.

Red blood covered his white T-shirt. It dripped from his nose and pattered quietly on his jeans.

'Well, this is a nice surprise,' said Sorrentino, sipping from a glass of Scotch.

'Is he dead?' I said.

'Nah – he's still bleeding, isn't he?' pointed out Sorrentino, putting down his glass and rising from the couch. 'He's just passed out.' He turned to Aldo. 'She carrying?'

Aldo nodded, handing over the pistol.

Sorrentino huffed out a laugh as he examined the gun. 'You are some crazy fucking cunt.'

'I'm here now,' I said. 'You can let him go.'

'Oh I can, can I?'

The sarcasm in his boss's voice made Aldo chuckle, and

Sorrentino smiled his small-toothed smile at him. I was off-guard, not expecting him to be able to move so fast: without looking at me, Sorrentino swung the back of his left hand and cracked me across the jaw.

I fell to my knees, stunned. My whole face felt like it was vibrating. I tasted blood in my mouth and then felt something hard on my tongue. With some pain, I opened my mouth and spat out whatever it was. A tooth rolled across the carpet.

A moan came from the other side of the room. I looked up, squinting through my left eye where my vision was blurred. Charlie had raised his head and was trying to speak but there was something stuffed in his mouth that was gagging him. His lip was split and there was a cut on the bridge of his nose. Blood was pouring from a gash on his scalp. Our eyes met. His were full of despair.

'Hey, Lover Boy's awake,' said Sorrentino. 'You know he's been very brave, Alexandra, or whatever the fuck your name is. Very noble. Bobby over there's been beating the shit out of him for a while now, but he just wouldn't give you up, even when he was sucking on the business end of a .38.'

'Please,' I said. The left side of my face was numb, and my voice sounded slurred. 'Please, just let him go. Killing him will start a war. You don't want that.'

'You started the war, you stupid bitch. Coming after me, you started it.'

'No. I'm not a Carlo, they don't even know who I am.'

He ignored me. 'You know, Joe, I gotta admit it, you have taste. Your girl here looked pretty hot with blonde hair, but it was, you know, sorta cheap. The brunette look is a lot more classy. And I just love that sexy accent. I can see why you fell for her, I really can.'

Charlie struggled against his bindings, trying to shout, and that just entertained Sorrentino even more. He stalked over to me, and I scrabbled away. Should I go for the gun? What chance would I have with the two goons there?

'Come on, baby, up you get,' he said, grabbing me under the armpits and yanking me to my feet. 'Let's finish what we started the other night.' His fingers digging into my arm, he propelled me into the bedroom, kicking the door shut. I could hear Charlie going crazy in the other room, and one of Sorrentino's guys telling him I'd brought it on myself.

Sorrentino shoved me onto the bed, his small black eyes alight. 'Now are you gonna play nice? Maybe if you're *really* nice, I'll think about letting him go.'

I closed my eyes and knew the truth. I met his gaze.

'I don't believe you,' I said quietly.

And then the light went out of his eyes, the playful smile disappeared, and there was nothing left but a predator going in for the kill.

He lunged at me, and I went for the gun, but he pinned me to the bed and I couldn't move my arm. The heavy weight of him trapped me against the mattress. I tried to lift my hips to push him off me, but my feet couldn't get a purchase on the slippery silk sheets. He fought against my flailing limbs, his nostrils flaring, and punched me hard on the side of the head. The whole room went black, my ears ringing, and for a moment my struggling weakened. He shifted his right arm so it pinioned my shoulders to the bed. With his left he unbuttoned my jeans and yanked down the zip. My right hand was finally loose. He raised my hips off the bed so he could pull down my jeans, and I wrenched the gun free. Pushing it in the narrow space between us, I pulled the trigger.

It sounded like a firework exploding. He staggered away from me, and though I kept pulling the trigger, all I heard were empty clicks. Sorrentino collapsed against the wall, sinking to the floor, legs splayed. There was a black hole in the centre of his shirt, just above his paunch. It was smoking. As I watched, the wound gasped red blood, a line of it travelling down the material and pooling in his crotch.

'Shit, did he shoot her?' I heard Aldo say from the other room, his voice getting closer. 'Boss?'

Sorrentino's eyes seemed blank, but he was still breathing. I pulled the spare clip from my pocket and with fumbling fingers took out each bullet and loaded them into the empty magazine of the Glock, slotting it back into place with a click. I flicked off the safety, cocking the gun so there was a bullet in the chamber.

'What if it was her?' I heard one of Sorrentino's guys ask him.

'Can't be, I frisked her.'

'Then why isn't the boss answering? Maybe she shot him with his own gun.' Someone pounded on the door. 'Lu, you okay?'

The door opened and I raised the Glock. The guy who'd been beating up my husband, Bobby, saw me aiming a gun at him and, eyes widened to the size of dinner plates, hastily pulled the door shut again.

'She kill him?' said his friend.

'I don't know, Nicky. All I know is she's got a fucking gun!'

I got to my feet and zipped up my jeans. My hands were shaking. I looked at Sorrentino, but he was too far gone to look back. I couldn't tell if he was still breathing or not.

Holding the gun in front of me, I came out of the bedroom. Aldo, Bobby and Nicky were all pointing their own guns at me.

'Is he dead?' asked Bobby.

'I have no quarrel with you. Just untie my husband and let us go.'

'Are you kidding?' said Nicky. 'You shoot the head of one of the New York Families, and you think we're just gonna let you walk out of here?'

'So if he's dead, who's the new boss?' I asked, swallowing the blood from my still-bleeding tooth socket. I knew it would be Aldo – what other motive could he have for wanting Sorrentino dead?

Bobby and Nicky exchanged glances.

'It's me,' said Aldo. 'As Lu's cousin, I'm next in line.' I just looked at him. His cousin? Nice family.

'So what do you say? Seems like it's your decision now.'

Our guns still raised, we waited for Aldo's verdict. His eyes were on me, but he turned his head to address his men.

'Get going,' he said. 'I'll deal with this.'

'You sure, Al?' asked Nicky.

'Someone will have heard that gunshot and called down to Security. You'd better get out of here before they show up.'

They didn't need telling a third time, holstering their guns and leaving us alone.

With them gone, there was just Jimmy Cagney's voice on the TV and the sound of Charlie's ragged breathing. Aldo and I both lowered our guns.

As he went into the bedroom to check on Sorrentino, I put the safety on the Glock and laid it down on Charlie's lap, gently pulling the gag out of his mouth.

'Oh Jesus, Kate, thank God,' he said, and rested his forehead against my stomach. 'I thought he was going to rape you. Did you kill him?'

'Yes, she did,' said Aldo, coming back in the room. 'Nice shot, Kate. Right in the heart.'

I closed my eyes for a moment, but knew if I was going to feel any guilt about it, it would have to wait until we were both safe. I untied Charlie's hands and he started to untie his own ankles, watching Aldo warily the whole time.

'You gave Kate the gun?' he said, more of a statement than a question. 'You organized this?'

Aldo shrugged. 'More like I put the pieces in place then sat back and let it happen.'

'You didn't have the balls to take him out yourself?'

Aldo's already thin eyes narrowed. 'It's not about balls, Joe, it's about brains. You of all people should understand that. You were earning pretty decent money without being in the life, and look what you've got now you're made – a bloody nose and a wife with a contract out on her.'

'So what now?' I asked, retrieving the semi-automatic and going to the table to pick up a napkin with which to wipe down the gun.

'Don't do that,' said Aldo, and I glanced up to see he was once again training his pistol on me. Charlie immediately rose to his feet, shielding me with his body.

'You want me to leave my prints on the gun?' I said.

'Well, how else are the cops going to know what happened?' he said with a smile.

I stared at him. 'And what did happen?'

'You came in, found Joe here dead, killed by Lu. You shot Lu. Then you killed yourself. Your prints will be on the gun. The gun will be in your hand. There'll be gunshot residue all over you. Case closed.'

'I don't think so,' I said, thumbing off the safety switch and aiming the Glock at his head.

He just smirked at me. 'I don't know if you noticed, but it's empty now. You think I'd give you a fully loaded gun?'

I shot him in the centre of the forehead.

For a moment he just stood there, that stupid sneer still on his face even though the contents of his skull were spread out on the wall behind him. Then his knees buckled and he fell backwards.

'Top of the world, Ma!' Jimmy Cagney was yelling from the TV.

I dropped the gun.

Charlie pulled me to him, hugging me to his chest. His T-shirt was wet with his blood, but for a moment at least I was just happy to have his arms around me. 'Katie,' he said into my hair, sounding shellshocked. 'Jesus, I'm sorry.'

I untangled myself from him, squatting down on the carpet and picking up the gun again. I used the hem of my black top to wipe my prints off it, then dropped it back down onto the floor.

The bathroom was the only pristine room left in the suite. I walked in and scrubbed my hands up to the elbows in the gleaming white sink, wiping blood from my mouth with one of the hotel's flannels. The curtain rings in the shower hung empty from their stainless-steel rail.

'There's no point you washing away the gunshot residue if you're gonna leave your DNA everywhere,' said Charlie, coming in behind me and putting the wet flannel in his pocket.

'In that case I hope you picked up my molar off the carpet too.'

We looked at each other's reflections in the large mirror above the sink. We both looked like ghosts in the harsh electric light. He put a hand on either side of me, his forearms pinning me in.

'I should have got here sooner,' I said to his bruised and bloodied reflection.

'You shouldn't have come at all.'

'Don't say that.'

'After what I've put you through, you should've run and never looked back.'

There was so much pain in his eyes that I couldn't look away from them. I'd forgiven him, but I didn't think he would ever forgive himself.

I leaned back against him, rubbed my head against his.

Making contact, letting him see I still needed him. The bene-
diction made his eyes well up.

'I'm so sorry,' he whispered.

'You need stitches,' I said, unable to bear seeing his anguish.
I turned around in his arms, taking the flannel from his pocket
and pressing it against the still-bleeding cut just behind his
hairline. He watched my face as I tried to stop the flow of
blood.

'They didn't give you a choice,' he said gently. 'You know
that, right? Aldo Malfi was going to kill us both. So was
Sorrentino, he just would have raped you first.'

'I know,' I said. It didn't seem to matter.

He made me look at him, taking my face in his hands and
tilting it up towards him. His eyes were blue as an August
summer sky.

'We'll get through this,' he told me. 'I promise.'

A sharp rap at the door made both our heads snap in the
direction of the living room.

'Security! Please come to the door!' demanded a voice from
the corridor.

Charlie grabbed me and pulled me into the bedroom, only
recoiling slightly from the sight of Sorrentino's body slumped
like a washed-up whale carcass on the floor. He locked the
door behind us, then went over to the drapes. I heard a sliding noise and realized he wasn't opening a window but a
balcony door.

We stepped outside, sliding the door shut behind us, and
immediately heard sirens.

'You bring a couple of parachutes?' I asked, aware that we
were on the thirty-second floor. Little red and blue lights were
dancing down the Strip towards the hotel.

Charlie pulled himself up onto the ledge, his black hair ruf-
fled by the wind.

'You've got to be kidding me,' I told him.

'Look,' he said, nodding downwards. I peered over the edge of the balcony. About eight floors below us, one of the Babylonian's raised pools glowed blue, illuminated by under-water lights.

'It's too high,' I said. 'The pool won't be deep enough.'

'What choice do we have? Death penalty or potential paraly-sis, take your pick.'

I grabbed his face in my hands and kissed him hard, then swung myself over too so we were side by side in the midnight air. We could hear the security guys letting themselves into the room, and their shouts as they found Aldo's body.

'You remember what to do?' said Charlie.

'Yeah. Let's go.'

He put his hand on mine. 'On three. One – two – three!'

We stepped backwards into nothingness, and plummeted towards the empty pool. I resisted the instinct to hold my nose, knowing the force of the water hitting my elbow could mean I ended up breaking my own nose. The moment I felt the warm water I scissored my legs, my limbs providing resist-ance against my body's velocity. Still under the water, I opened my eyes as my descent reached its limit, and saw Charlie a couple of feet below me. Had he hit the bottom of the pool? I pushed myself down, watching him. Then I saw his legs kick, and I shot up to the air.

He broke the surface, flicking the wet hair out of his eyes. 'You okay?' he gasped.

'Yeah, you?' He nodded, and we both swam to the edge of the pool, hauling ourselves out of the water. My limbs were tingling with adrenaline. As we ran to the fire door that led back into the hotel, I looked up at Sorrentino's balcony, just in time to see a face appear over the edge. We vanished through the fire door before he had a chance to look our way.

'Can we get out on the street without going through the casino?' I asked Charlie as we ran, drenched, along the corridor.

'Maybe if we use the fire exits,' he said. 'But it will probably set off the alarm.'

'You think we've already set it off by using that door from the pool?'

'Maybe. I guess we'll find out soon enough.'

We bounded down the stairs.

'Fucking flip-flops!' I yelled as they came off for the fourth time, picked them up and carried on running barefoot.

By the time we reached the ground floor I was dizzy from the combination of adrenaline, two punches to the head, and the effect of spinning round the corner at the end of each flight of stairs. I didn't know how Charlie was managing to stay on his feet.

We left the stairwell and found ourselves at the end of another identikit corridor. More cautiously now, we padded to the end of the hallway and Charlie poked his head around the corner. He took my hand and pulled me to the left. At the end of this new corridor was a fire exit; the sight of a little green running man had never before filled me with so much relief. We jogged towards it.

A security guard appeared from a turning halfway down the corridor. He had a walkie-talkie in one hand and a Snickers bar in the other. Charlie and I both froze; we couldn't help it. The security guard looked at us suspiciously, his eyes travelling over our sodden clothes and dripping wet hair.

'First floor!' he cried into his radio. '911!'

We turned on our heels and ran for our lives in the other direction. This end of the corridor was signposted *casino floor*, but we had no choice. The guard behind us was fumbling for his gun, apparently unwilling to let go of either his walkie-talkie or his chocolate bar.

We burst through the doors, Charlie's hand tightly gripping mine. The casino was packed, each table bursting with gamblers, gurgling slot machines coughing up catchphrases and showers of coins. Some of the punters were too intent on their bets to pay us much attention, but those just watching the games turned to observe us as we ran past, and a croupier at a blackjack game signalled to his pit boss.

Then the security guard slammed through the door behind us, gun drawn, and all hell broke loose. A waitress carrying a tray of drinks screamed and dropped them on the floor. A large guy in a Budweiser T-shirt saw us running towards him, an armed man in hot pursuit, yelped loudly and stayed rooted in place. We dropped each other's hands in order to run around him, sprinting past the poker tables. Another security guard, his gun in his hand, was running from the direction of the bar to try and cut us off. We ducked left, heading towards the slot machines, people pushing each other to get out of our way. I could only pray that the guards wouldn't dare to use their weapons with so many bystanders to get caught in the crossfire.

We raced down between the roulette tables, Charlie in one aisle and me in another. The second security guard was gaining on us. I glanced over my shoulder to see how close he was, and the next thing I knew, I was flying across the floor. Winded, I pushed myself up and saw Charlie realize I wasn't next to him and look back in horror. As the guard landed on me, his knee in the small of my back, I just had time to see Luke appear out of nowhere and drag Charlie into the maze of slot machines before my face was pushed into the sticky carpet and my hands were cuffed behind my back.

Chapter Twenty-eight

It was one o'clock in the morning. I sat on my own in a box-like interrogation room in LVPD headquarters, handcuffed to a steel chair that was bolted to the floor. A fan buzzed out lukewarm air from the corner of the room.

The security guards had passed me over to the cops. They'd turned the hotel inside out searching for Charlie, but as I was still here on my own I could only assume he'd managed to get away.

The homicide detectives had tried to question me but I'd refused to say anything other than that I wanted a lawyer. I was waiting for the public defender to turn up. I wondered if I was still entitled to legal counsel, not being a citizen, or if I needed to call the British Consulate. It didn't really matter – either way, I was screwed. The cops might have believed I'd killed one man in self-defence, but not two. Especially not with a bullet in one man's heart and a bullet in the brain of the other, but no stray bullets in the wall, no superficial wounds to either victim. I would look like someone who knew what she was doing.

One of the detectives – a black guy in a yellow shirt who reminded me of Kytell and therefore made me homesick – came into the room with a set of keys and uncuffed me.

'You're letting me go?' I said, rubbing the sore ridges where the cuffs had dug into my skin.

'Not exactly,' he replied in a deep baritone. 'We're turning you over to the Feds. If you're such an important witness I don't know why their protection detail on you is so shitty, but at least you managed to survive tonight. Good luck with the rest of your life. I get the feeling you're gonna need it.'

'No,' I said immediately. 'No, don't let them take me. Please. You don't understand – they're involved in this!'

'I know. It's their case.'

'No, they set it up!'

'It was a sting, huh?'

'No,' I said. 'It was murder.'

He just laughed at me. 'Uh-huh. And it was the CIA that assassinated JFK, right?'

'Look, I'll admit to killing those men at the Babylonian,' I said. 'I'll sign whatever you want, just don't turn me over to them, *please.*'

He pushed me out into the Homicide Department's open-plan office where Daultrey, looking composed and relaxed in a lightweight trenchcoat and dark grey suit, was shaking the hand of one of the police officers.

I tried to run away from him, but the detective grabbed me by the neck. 'You want me to cuff you again?' he rumbled in my ear.

'No,' I said, my airway half-choked by his large fingers.

'Then calm the fuck down.'

'They'll kill me,' I gasped.

'Thank you, Captain,' Daultrey was saying. 'We appreciate your help with this.'

'Always happy to pick up your slack,' said the officer with a shit-eating grin. Daultrey pretended to chuckle, but his smile dropped away the second his back was to the man. He came towards me through the desks.

'How are you, Kate?' he asked, feigning concern.

'Fuck you, Daultrey,' I spat at him.

'There's no call for that,' he said. 'I know you've had a rough night, but we're here now. Come on, let's get going.'

'You've signed the transfer of custody papers?' asked the detective.

Daultrey fixed his high-intensity beam on him. 'Of course, Detective.' He looked me over. The police had taken my clothes as evidence, and had given me blue plastic overalls to wear. You could see my black underwear through the fabric. 'Where are her clothes?'

'At the lab.'

Daultrey's lips thinned. 'We'll head down there and pick them up.'

'Okay,' said the detective. 'But why bother? They'll be done in a couple of days. Save your own lab boys the trouble.'

'It's no trouble,' Daultrey assured him. 'Thanks for all your help, Detective.'

He took me by the elbow and manoeuvred me out of the department and along the corridor. As we reached the top of the staircase that led out of the building, I turned back to look at the detective, praying he'd have smelt that something was hinky, that he'd be watching me go with unease in his eyes. But he was laughing about something with his captain, not even looking in my direction, and I knew he'd dismissed me the minute I'd walked out of his door.

Agents Jerkins and Taylor were parked outside. Daultrey pushed me against the side of the car and used a plastic tie to bind my hands before shoving me into the back seat and getting in beside me.

No one spoke as we drove, other than Daultrey using his cellphone to call Johnson and get him to have the evidence transferred from LVPD custody to the FBI.

'If I'd known you were going to help us cover it up, I

wouldn't have taken the risk of jumping off the balcony,' I said. He ignored me.

'Where's Joe Carlo?' he asked.

'Fuck you,' I replied.

They drove past the Regal and out into the suburbs. We ended up in a dark neighbourhood full of late-night shops with grilles in the window and dodgy men and half-naked women on every street corner. We turned left at a batch of wasteland that was nothing but grit and litter, and parked up next to a derelict, boarded-up house.

'Go check it hasn't turned into a crack den in the last six weeks,' Daultrey ordered Jerkins. He jumped out and came back a few minutes later with the all-clear.

Inside it smelt of damp and rat droppings. Daultrey pushed me into the back room, all cracked linoleum and huge water stains on the walls.

'Let me guess,' I said. 'My turn to get tied to a chair.'

'What goes around comes around,' he said, arms raised in an amused shrug.

'I don't know where Charlie is,' I said. In a way, it was true. Still, I knew if I told Daultrey that my husband was with Luke then there was a good chance it would help the agent find him.

'We'll see,' he said. 'Even if you don't, I might still find this kinda fun.'

Hours later, I swam out of unconsciousness. Still woozy, I tried to recall where I was and how I'd got here, and why my hands felt as if they were on fire. Then I remembered, and jerked fully awake.

Daultrey was sitting across from me, elbows on his knees. He'd put his glasses back on, but his hair was still dishevelled.

He tilted his head when he saw my eyes open. 'Had enough yet?' he asked.

I looked down at my left hand. Every finger was now crooked and swollen. My right hand was better. Only two fingers on that hand were broken.

'After your fingers, we'll get to work on your nails,' he said. 'Or maybe I'll send Wilson down to the all-night hardware store and he can pick up some pliers to finish off your dentistry work.'

'I don't know where Charlie is,' I mumbled through a split lip.

Taylor sighed in exasperation. 'I'm going outside for a smoke.'

'No,' said Daultrey. 'Go upstairs. We don't want anyone to see us.'

'There's no one around here *to* see us,' she said. He glared at her. 'Fine,' she shrugged, and I heard her high heels on the bare wood of the staircase. Daultrey and I were on our own.

'I don't mind if you smoke in here you know,' I said to him, trying to pull the corners of my mouth up in a smile, but not quite having the energy for it.

His jaw was knotting. 'You're some piece of work,' he said. 'What's your story? Where did you come from? Kate Grey's not your real name, I know that.'

I blinked slowly, too exhausted to keep my eyes open for more than a couple of seconds at a time. 'It might not be the name on my birth certificate,' I mumbled. 'But it is my name.'

'Why did you change it?' he asked, leaning forward, curious.

'None of your fucking business.'

He jumped to his feet and grabbed one of my few remaining straight fingers.

'No no no no no,' I said through clenched teeth, but he

snapped the finger as though he was breaking firewood. Agony flared in the joint and for a few seconds I couldn't speak, couldn't breathe.

Daultrey fell back into his seat. 'I was going to buy a boat,' he said. 'A fifty-five-footer. Even had the name picked out – *Celestine*. Summers would be spent sailing Cape Cod, Martha's Vineyard, the Hamptons. In the winter, when it was too cold, I'd head south for the Bahamas, the Caribbean. With the amount of money Aldo Malfi was going to earn as head of the Sorrentino family, my unofficial retirement fund would be full in just a couple more years.'

One thing I'd learned early on when Charlie and I were skydiving, or caving, or deep-sea diving, was that your biggest enemy was panic. You have to shut down your imagination, so you're not thinking about how narrow the tunnels are back up to the surface, or how dark the sea is beneath your feet. As soon as you start to panic, you're done for.

But I was thinking about how much longer I could hold out before I gave up Charlie. I was thinking about having my teeth pulled out one by one. I was thinking about what came at the end, when they'd got what they wanted. Would it be quick? Would it hurt more than this? Would I have to watch it happen to Charlie before it happened to me?

I needed to switch off my brain, to put up a wall between me and all those dark imaginings. I had to distract myself. I had to distract Daultrey too.

'The Carlos,' I said.

'What?'

'Why don't you do for them what you were going to do for Malfi? They run Chicago. Sorrentino ran just one of the five boroughs.'

'You have no idea what you're talking about,' he said. 'The Carlos are finished. Why do you think Malfi got me to drag you and Joe into his beef with Sorrentino? Angelo Carlo is an old man. Joe was never going to take over as head of the family, and his brother Paolo is too young and hotheaded to be made *capo di tutti capi*. His sister's pretty level-headed, but these guys can only cope with two kinds of women: relatives and girlfriends. They'd never work for a woman. That's where Aldo Malfi was going to come in – he's got a nephew who's a capo in the Carlo organization. With Malfi's backing, there was a good chance of getting him promoted to the top spot.'

Daultrey looked as if someone had shot his puppy. 'It was perfect symbiosis. Him feeding me just enough intel on his rivals to get them pinched. Me letting him know what angle we were working, so he was always two steps ahead and knew which of his men might be susceptible to being turned. Even with him just the underboss, even with me taking care of my own team, I was pulling in five times my salary every month. Do you have any idea how much more I could have made with Malfi running both the Sorrentino and Carlo families?'

If he was talking, he was less likely to be breaking my fingers. I had to maintain the conversation.

'You can't kill me,' I said.

'No?' He pulled a face. 'Why the hell not?'

'I'm officially in your custody. My name's on file at the Las Vegas Police Department. Someone will notice if I go missing.'

'Who says you're going to go missing?' he said, just as Angela Taylor clattered down the stairs and reappeared in the dingy back room.

'Angie,' he said. 'Let's do some role play. Show Kate here how we can make her disappear.'

Taylor smiled. 'Well, I'd need some hair-dye. Or a wig. Stan here knows where to get some good ones. Maybe some colour contacts too. Anyways, I turn up for the meet with the US Marshals at Witness Protection. "Hey there! I'm Kate Grey from the UK".' Her accent was worryingly good. '"Portland? Yes, that sounds like my cup of tea. A grocery clerk at Wal-Mart? Perfect." We keep it up for a little while, then Kate appears to "do a runner", as you Brits call it. Wouldn't be the first time a witness has decided their new life isn't for them. We'll make sure your credit cards get used in a couple of places, just so they don't suspect foul play.'

'That's just one of our options,' said Daultrey. 'One of the more complicated ones. My personal preference is a little more simple: put six bullets in you, plant a gun in your hand, and claim you were about to fire on a federal officer.'

'Bullshit,' I said. 'You think they'd believe you when my hands look like this?'

He shrugged. 'So we'll say you skipped out on us, and then some poor Cajun can find your bloated corpse two months later in a Louisiana swamp. How's that sound?'

He stood up then. I tried to back the chair away from him, my bare feet sliding on the dirty lino, but he pushed down hard on the arms of the chair, locking me in place.

'Don't,' I pleaded as he took hold of my thumb.

His phone rang.

Giving me a 'you're a lucky girl' look, he let go of me and walked over to the other side of the room, checking the display to see who was calling.

'I wasn't expecting to hear from *you*,' he said to whoever was on the other end. When he heard what they had to say, he turned back to me, and his eyes were granite. He gave them an address and hung up.

Crouching in front of me, he got close enough that I could smell the whiskey he'd been drinking, smell the fag smoke on his breath.

'Looks like we might not need you after all,' he said. 'Still, if our mutual friend is wrong, we'd better not lose you *quite* yet.'

I closed my eyes. They'd found Charlie. We were both dead.

There was silence. Daultrey murmured to someone in the kitchen. I heard the strike of a match as he lit up a cigarette. Outside, something howled. I couldn't tell if it was an animal or a human being.

When I opened my eyes, Taylor was sitting cross-legged in Daultrey's chair, not a hair out of place, her nylons perfectly even and ladder-free. She was studying me.

'How did you get this way?' I whispered to her.

'What do you mean?' she asked, as though it was a strange question.

'You can't have joined the Bureau to do this. How did it start? Was it something small? Did he ask you to do something you weren't quite happy with, but once you'd done it, you just rationalized it away?' I was so thirsty, but knew if I asked for water they'd probably use it against me. 'And then the next thing he asked of you was bigger, but he managed to talk you into it, or maybe you talked yourself into it. And then a few years down the line you look back at it all and realize there's no way out of it now. You can never leave it behind, never start again. You have to just embrace it. Christ, you're the FBI equivalent of Enron.'

Amazingly, she seemed to take exception to that. 'No, we're not Enron,' she said, as if she had a sour taste in her mouth. 'They got rich while the little people suffered, people who'd invested in them for their retirement or their kids' college fund.'

I coughed out a laugh. 'Oh, you tell yourself only bad people get hurt – is that right? So it's okay because it's only criminals that are suffering as a result of what you're doing. What about Ben Gerber, the man you drowned? Wasn't he innocent?'

A line appeared in the centre of her forehead. 'He was a petty crook. How do you think Stan found him? Caught him in the act, told him he had a choice: either a couple of years in the pen, or turn informer. For a while he was quite useful to us, but then he started hanging out with a better crowd, smartened up his act, and stopped serving his purpose.'

'So you found another purpose for him,' I croaked. 'Jesus, Angela, that's cold.'

She turned away then, looking for Daultrey. 'He was no loss to society; he had the IQ of a doormat,' she said distractedly. 'Anyway, recidivism rates being what they are, I'm sure he would have reoffended at some point.'

'Are you?' I asked her.

Daultrey reappeared in the doorway, pointing at me with the lit cigarette in his hand. 'Don't talk to her,' he said. I wasn't sure who he was warning, Taylor or me.

Taylor stood up and did her powersuit shimmy into the kitchen. Light from the streetlamps outside reflected off Daultrey's glasses, making his gaze two blank squares. He turned back into the kitchen too, and I was left alone.

I tried to dredge up some resourcefulness, but there was nothing left. I was in my underwear, tied to a chair, in the middle of a deserted street in a rundown neighbourhood. Most of my fingers were broken, which meant not only could I not untie myself, I'd also find it impossible to unlock a door or a window-latch. The three people guarding me were all armed, uninjured, and carrying FBI badges. Adrenaline was the only thing keeping me conscious. I dropped my head – too full of despair even to cry – and waited.

Twenty minutes later, there was a knock at the door. Seven raps in the 'shave and a haircut – two bits' rhythm. Daultrey checked through a gap in the boards that covered the front windows, then opened the front door. He shook hands with someone, then stood aside to let him in.

The man walked into the back room and looked at me coolly, scanning down over my half-naked body, broken fingers and bloodied face.

'Hello, Kate,' he drawled. 'Looking good.'

Chapter Twenty-nine

Now I started to cry. 'What are you doing here?'

'So you got a location for me, De Santis?' asked Daultrey.

'No, Luke,' I said, tears running down my dirty face. 'No, don't tell him, please don't tell him.'

Luke got a pack of Marlboros out of his jacket pocket and lit up. 'He's at 1508 Elsmere Drive.'

'On his own?'

'Yeah, from the sounds of it. His guys are on their way from Chicago though, so I wouldn't dawdle.'

'What's the location like?'

Luke sucked at his cigarette. 'I've only been there a coupla times. From what I remember, it's big, detached, in its own grounds, with high hedges surrounding the property. Private. Oh, and there's a security gate.'

'Sounds like we're gonna need you there to get us in.'

He shrugged. 'I was planning on coming along. I wanna keep an eye on the little lady over there. Joe told me she's managed to give you the slip twice already. I don't wanna take the risk she'll do it again. The Carlos find out I was behind this, I'm a dead man.'

Daultrey looked down at me. 'Kate? You're being awfully quiet. Don't you want to give De Santis here a piece of your mind for betraying you?'

Luke shook his head. 'You're wasting time.'

I knew the best thing was to keep my mouth shut. The only reason I was still alive was in case Luke's information didn't check out.

Daultrey gathered the agents together in the kitchen, leaving me and Luke alone with just Taylor watching over us. He brushed down the chair opposite me, not wanting to get dirt on his immaculately pressed black trousers, and took a seat.

'You fucking snake,' I said, hot tears coursing down my face. 'I swear, if I ever get the opportunity, I'm going to kill you.'

'Now, children . . .' said Taylor. 'Play nicely.'

Luke just smiled at me, but it was a smile that didn't come close to reaching his glacial eyes.

'Charlie trusts you,' I said. 'How can you do this to him?'

'I need the money.'

'What's *wrong* with you?'

'Maybe I didn't get enough love as a child.'

'Christ, Luke.'

He just watched me, hardly blinking. 'He does love you, you know.'

'Yes,' I said, teeth clenched. 'I know.'

'In case you thought it was just an act, an escape route. He didn't know how bad you were. He called every day to find out what you'd been up to. Wanted to know everything – what we'd talked about, who you were seeing, what books you were reading, what music you were listening to. He'd buy the books, the albums, so he could be reading and listening to the same things. But I didn't tell him the whole truth. He couldn't have handled it. He thought you were doing okay.'

'Why are you telling me this?' I asked him, fighting back the tears, not wanting him to see me cry.

'Because you'll both be dead soon, and I thought you'd want to know.'

Daultrey came back in. 'Untie her, Taylor. And find her some clothes. Those overalls are shredded, and driving her round in her underwear is gonna attract attention.'

'Stick her in the trunk,' suggested Luke.

'It's a hatchback, De Santis. It doesn't have a trunk.'

'My car does,' Luke said. 'I'll take her.'

'I don't think so,' Daultrey replied. 'I'm not a hundred per cent sure I can trust you yet.' He leaned closer. 'Just remember, we can indict you on the Calabresi murder anytime we like. Put one foot wrong, De Santis, just one foot . . .'

'*You* killed Federico Calabresi?' I said. 'You're the reason Charlie had to go on the run?'

'Ironic, isn't it?' observed Daultrey. 'Your husband gave up his family, his career, all to protect De Santis here. And look how he's being repaid.'

Luke got to his feet, dropping his cigarette onto the lino and crushing it under his shoe.

'Can we please leave?' he said to Daultrey.

Taylor had refused to cover me in her jacket – 'it's Hugo Boss!' – so I was wearing Jerkins'. He was so tall that it came halfway down my thighs. I sat in the back row of the car, flanked by Daultrey on one side and Johnson on the other. Taylor was driving.

My swollen, mangled hands were bound in front of me. Johnson stared out of the window, apparently unable to look at me. Taylor was humming along to the song on the radio – 'Don't Worry, Be Happy'.

We followed Wilson and Jerkins, who were being driven by Luke in his cherry-red Maserati. He was all I could think about, feeling like I'd taken a bite of a sweet and juicy apple only to find maggots at its core. Remembering his friendship with Charlie, the way he'd be there at a moment's notice if we ever needed him, always just a phone call away. Remembering how quickly he'd followed us to the UK, and how happy Charlie had been to see him, even meeting him at the airport and taking time off work to help him find a flat. Remembering how many times during the last fortnight Luke had put obstacles in my path to finding Charlie.

'He was helping you then, all along?' I said, trying to swallow down the taste of betrayal.

Daultrey leaned forward in his seat. 'Angie, slow the hell down. I don't wanna get pulled over.'

'I'm trying to keep up with De Santis,' Taylor pointed out.

'Trust me, he'll slow down too when he notices you're not on his tail.' He reclined back again. 'All along,' he confirmed to me.

'So how come he didn't tell you we were heading to Sicily?' I said.

'He did.'

'And you just stood back and let me question Bianchi?'

'Let's not prettify things, Kate. You didn't "question" Bianchi, you beat answers out of her.'

I looked down at my twisted fingers. Maybe karma existed after all.

We were now in one of the more affluent Vegas suburbs. The houses were tucked away at the end of long driveways, protected by gates, and shielded from view by hedges and trees. Luke's car turned left then right, slowing as he drove down Elsmere Drive. His tail-lights flared red as he braked halfway between one house and another, hidden from the occupants' sight by fencing and bushes.

Daultrey made to get out of the car. I put my hands on his arm.

'Please,' I said, my voice shaking. 'Don't do this.'

'I have to,' he said. 'You, Carlo and De Santis are the only ones who know about my relationship with Malfi. I have to take you out of the picture. I'm sorry.'

He was going to kill Luke too.

'Luke!' I cried out of the open passenger door. 'Don't trust—'

Daultrey's hand spidered over my face, pushing my head back against the car seat, crushing my nose under his palm.

'Shut the fuck up,' he said, getting out of the car door and then leaning back in to thump me. I managed to deflect the full force of the blow with my elbow, holding it up to protect my face.

Johnson was taking off his tie. I tried to fight him off, but couldn't use my hands, and he put a knee over my lap to stop me kicking him as he forced it into my mouth, yanking the ends behind my head and making a knot that only seemed to get tighter the more I struggled.

In the low beams of the car's headlights, Daultrey leant into Luke's car and agreed some plan. He returned to the car and murmured something to Taylor through the driver's side window, and Taylor killed her headlights. Daultrey got in next to me, nodding his approval at the improvised gag. He slammed the door shut and unholstered his gun, screwing on a silencer. The other agents followed his lead, then we waited while Luke revved up his Maserati and drove up to the next gate.

I watched him stick out a finger and press the buzzer. I couldn't hear what he said, but a moment later the gate opened with a low whine. Luke drove through it. Taylor took off the handbrake, went into first and followed him through the open gate.

It clanged shut behind us.

'Taylor, get out here and scout out the perimeter. Johnson, go round the back to cut off his escape route.'

The agents slid out of the car, each going in different directions. Luke's car continued smoothly up the paved driveway to the house where Charlie waited, alone and in danger.

I can't explain how it felt, knowing my husband was about to die and there was nothing I could do. Knowing that no matter how much I protested, no matter how much I fought, by the end of the night we would both be dead.

Daultrey's gun was nestled by my side, but with the gag in my mouth I couldn't have raised the alarm anyway. Luke's car braked, but he didn't switch off the engine. After a few minutes Taylor reappeared, climbing into the driver's seat and turning round to talk to Daultrey.

'It all looks quiet,' she said. 'All the rooms I can see into are empty. The only one with the drapes shut is the room over there.' It was the room to the left of the front door. 'No lights seem to be on. Either he's not there, or he's keeping a really low profile.'

Daultrey got out his cellphone. 'Make your move,' he instructed.

We both watched from the bottom of the driveway as Luke got out of the car, Wilson and Jerkins dropping out from the far side into crouching positions. One hid behind the car as the other crept up alongside the wall that bordered the front door, concealed from whoever might open it.

Luke rang the front doorbell. Seconds passed, but there was no answer. I prayed that Luke was wrong, that the house was empty. After trying the bell again, and waiting a few moments more, Luke stepped forward and pushed at the door. It swung open. Had Charlie seen them coming, and bolted for the back door? Would the next sound we heard be the pop of Johnson's gun as Charlie tried to escape out the back?

Tentatively, Luke went inside and we heard, very faint: 'Joey?'

Wilson and Jerkins followed, guns drawn.

There was silence. Then, in the darkened windows of the front room, we saw a series of muzzle flashes, as if someone had let off a soundless firecracker.

I held my breath.

Someone lurched out of the house. I could tell from the pale blond hair that it was Luke. He staggered down the driveway to our car. Daultrey wound down his window, and when Luke was closer we could see that his shirt and jacket were soaked with blood on his left side. He was clutching his stomach.

'The fucker shot me,' he said.

'Is Joe Carlo dead?' snapped Daultrey.

'I think so – Wilson clipped him pretty good.' My skin felt suddenly drenched in ice water, sweat like beads of frost breaking out on my flesh. 'Jerkins is dead. Wilson got shot too, he's gonna need medical attention.' Luke looked down at himself, at all the blood. 'Though probably not as badly as me.'

Daultrey opened the car door and got out, dragging me with him. My legs nearly collapsed under me as I tried to stand on the solid brick of the driveway. He half-pushed, half-hauled me up to the open doorway, his gun still jabbed into my side. Taylor opened her car door and followed us.

The black entrance loomed in front of us. I dreaded going in, terrified I'd find Charlie's dead body there, staring sightlessly up at the ceiling. Daultrey shoved me through.

A pair of muffled thuds came from behind us. We both turned round, in time to see Angela Taylor drop to the ground like a marionette whose strings have been cut. Luke stood beside her, the gun in his outstretched hand still aimed at the place where her head had been just a split-second before.

Daultrey jumped through the doorway, slamming the door behind him to shut out Luke. He crouched down, looking around him, trying to get his bearings. We were in a large hall with a marble floor. There were three doors off each side, and another two at the back of the room. A curved staircase led up to the first floor. All was quiet in the gloom.

Daultrey didn't want to let me out of his sight. He pulled me down to his level and made me stumble to the back of the hallway, probably hoping I'd catch any hasty bullets. The door on the left led into the spacious kitchen. The back door was open, and we could see the path into the garden. In the faint moonlight I could make out Johnson, laid out on his back, dark flowers of blood in three places on his shirt.

'Shit,' Daultrey swore. He took a breath, then closed the back door and locked it shut before Luke could use it to get to us, then dropped back into a squat.

A creak came from upstairs. It distracted Daultrey, and as he raised his face to the ceiling I ran at him, using my body weight to knock him off his feet. We rolled on the tiled floor. He twisted me over, pinning me beneath him. My hands were crushed under my body, and I screamed. Stifled by the gag, it was nothing more than the bleat of an animal caught in a trap.

Daultrey rolled off me and I lay there, holding my reverberating hands as still as I could, tears of agony gliding down each side of my face.

'Get up,' he hissed, holding the gun on me. 'Get the fuck up or I'll shoot you dead right here, I swear it.'

Almost hyperventilating, I pushed myself backwards on the terracotta tiles, till I felt the kitchen island behind me. I was able to use my legs and the resistance from it to push myself onto my feet.

Using me as a shield, he stole back into the hallway, his eyes accustomed now to the lack of light. Unable to spot anyone on the upper floor, he took me to the staircase and we climbed it one step at a time. He stopped to listen again for the creaking sound we'd heard, but all I could hear was my ragged breathing.

We were nearly at the top of the sweeping staircase when all the lights came on. The whole house was suddenly lit up, the night turning from grey to black in each bare window. And we could see everyone.

Angelo Carlo was standing at the top of the staircase. He was wearing a waistcoat, and his shirt-sleeves were rolled up. There was a gun in his hand, and flecks of blood in his white beard. A few feet from him on the landing was a young guy who looked like a skinnier version of Charlie, but with brown eyes instead of blue. He too was armed. On Carlo's other side, a curly-haired woman, about Charlie's age, stood feet spread, a shotgun in her hands that was aimed at Daultrey's head.

Daultrey didn't know who to aim at, so he aimed at me.

'Back off!' he barked at the three people above us. I wanted to know where Charlie was, to cry for Angelo to tell me that his son was okay, but all I could do was make unintelligible moans.

'Daultrey!' said a voice behind us. Gripping me to him, his .45 by my ear, Daultrey rotated us round.

Charlie stood at the foot of the staircase. His face was cut and bruised, but he was standing tall and straight. The relief almost made me laugh.

He had a gun in his right hand.

'It's finished, Daultrey,' he said.

There were two men down there with him, both armed. Six guns were trained on Daultrey. I could sense him weighing up his options.

'Fuck you,' he said, and raised his .45 towards Charlie.

There was a crack, and Daultrey seemed to hover on the

steps for a few seconds before plummeting down the staircase. He landed with a crunch on the bottom step, face down, his fractured glasses flying across the floor. Half of the back of his skull was missing.

Angelo Carlo flicked the safety catch of his gun back on. I sank down into a sitting position on the cold marble step, and Charlie came leaping up the stairs three at a time to get to me.

Chapter Thirty

Charlie found a pair of scissors in the kitchen and cut off the plastic cuffs that bound my wrists. There was a sleeveless dress in one of the wardrobes upstairs that buttoned up the front, meaning I could put it on without risking my fingers getting knocked. Charlie helped me into it, then buttoned it up for me.

We walked through the hallway. Daultrey's body was gone, and one of the Carlo lieutenants was using bleach to clean the blood off the floor.

The French windows in the back room were open. A guy whom Charlie had addressed by the nickname Foxtrot was squirting lighter fluid over the contents of a barbecue oven, using his cigarette to set the pile of evidence alight. Charlie threw the plastic tie and Jerkins's jacket into the flames and we watched them burn. I could feel the Vicodin Charlie had found me starting to take effect.

Luke was sprawled on one of the sofas, pressing a towel to the wound in his side. I went over to him; sat down beside him. He tried to smile at me, but was in so much pain it came out as a grimace.

'I'm sorry I doubted you,' I said.

'I don't blame you,' he said and met my eyes. 'I didn't tell them Charlie was in Sicily,' he told me, 'but the bit about Rico Calabresi's true.'

'You killed him?'

He nodded. 'He owed me money, and I owed someone else. Rico wouldn't pay up. I got desperate.'

'Jesus, Luke.'

He lifted a hand and stroked my hair back from my face. 'I've had to hide myself from you,' he said with a sad smile. 'Charlie can take me because he grew up with me. He knows how far I'd go for him because he'd go as far for me. We're brothers. Can you live with it, though?'

It was just what I'd been running away from. 'I don't know,' I told him honestly. 'I suppose we'll have to find out.'

The first few notes of 'Nessun Dorma' started to play, and I looked around in confusion. Angelo Carlo patted down his pockets and then pulled out a mobile phone. Pavarotti stopped singing when Angelo flipped the phone open.

'*Buena sera*,' he said. 'How are you, my friend?' I couldn't hear the person on the other end, but whatever he said made Angelo frown. 'Unfortunately, now is not a good time. We're in the middle of a . . . spring clean.' I assumed that was code for 'getting rid of the bodies of five FBI agents'.

'What kind of problem?' Angelo was asking. He listened, and then his eyes swivelled to me. 'Really?' he said. 'How interesting.'

I shifted in my seat, feeling suddenly uncomfortable.

'I think you're a bit late,' Angelo told whoever was on the other end of the line. 'This person you're after – is she in her early thirties, black hair, grey eyes?'

Charlie's head snapped round, and he stared at his father. Angelo didn't return his gaze. 'She's right here,' he said. 'I shall see you in a few minutes, my friend.' He snapped the phone shut.

'Pop?' said Charlie. 'What's going on?'

The other lieutenant appeared in the doorway carrying a

bag. 'All cleaned up,' he told Angelo. 'They're in the Ford. You want I should take them now?'

'Not yet, Sal,' said Angelo. 'Can you drive it around to the back? Our friends from London are just a few minutes away, and they don't need to see a car full of dead federal agents in the driveway.'

'Sure thing,' said Sal. He brought the bag over to where Charlie was stood by the fire. 'Found it in the back of the Ford, Joe. Got some blue overalls in it, plus some evidence bags with clothes in 'em.'

Charlie ignored him, still frowning at his father.

'Everything goes in the fire, Sal,' instructed Angelo, not taking his eyes off me. Sal nodded, doing as he was told, then heading out to move the car.

'Pop?' Charlie said again. 'What do the Harpers want with Kate?'

'That's a good question,' Angelo nodded. 'Kate, would you like to answer it?'

I walked over to Charlie. 'We should leave,' I told him. 'I mean right now, before anyone even realizes the Feds are missing, before Sorrentino's guys have time to regroup and come after us.'

There was the buzz of an intercom, and Foxtrot went into the hallway to answer it. 'Hey there, Grant,' he said. 'Drive right in.' Moments later we heard a car pull up outside the house. Foxtrot stuck his head round the door. 'They're here,' he told his boss.

'Is she in danger?' Charlie demanded, stepping in between me and his father.

'Let them in,' Angelo said.

We heard the front door open, and Foxtrot greeting the Carlos' guests. 'Come right in,' he said. 'You gotta excuse the mess, we had a little trouble tonight.'

'Foxy, mate, not a problem,' said a familiar, Cockney-accented voice. 'Now where's my little girl?'

Charlie turned to stare at me.

'Your girl?' repeated Foxtrot as he came back into the room accompanied by a beefy bloke with salt-and-pepper hair and a sunbed tan.

The new arrival grinned when he saw me, grey eyes crinkling at the corners.

'Katrina!' he said. 'Long time no see.'

I managed a rueful smile back. 'Hi, Dad.'

Chapter Thirty-one

'Harper's your *dad*?' asked my incredulous husband.

'Charlie, I'm so, so sorry,' I said. 'I was trying to tell you in the hotel room, but Johnson arrived and—'

Kytell had to duck his head to fit through the doorway. He pushed past my father and came straight for me, only stopping at the last minute when he saw my hands. His beaming face fell when he took in my broken fingers.

'Who did this to you?' he rumbled. 'I'll fucking kill them.'

'We already did, Big Man,' said Luke laconically from the sofa.

Kytell looked at me for confirmation and I nodded. Relaxing a bit, he kissed my forehead. I saw his eyes widen as he saw Charlie.

'Fuck me, mate. You're not dead then?'

'It's a long story,' Charlie said, staring at me.

'What the hell are you doing here?' I asked Kytell.

'You think I was just going to sit at home waiting for you?' he said. 'I know you didn't want Dad involved, but fuck it, Kate, he seemed like the best person to go to. Turns out he knows Sorrentino; had dealings with him in the past.'

'He's a nasty piece of work,' said my father, scowling.

'Even by your standards?'

'I admired your balls for going after him, love, but we wasn't gonna let you do it all by yourself. Was he the one did this to you?'

'No,' I said. 'It's a long story. How did you know I was in Las Vegas?'

Kytell chuckled. '1471, dumbass. You think I can't look up an area code on the Internet?' I'd been so wrapped up in getting revenge for Charlie that I hadn't even covered my tracks properly. 'And when we realized the Carlos were in town too we twigged they were probably in on the party.'

'So you and the Carlos are big mates all of a sudden?' I said.

'These are the guys I told you about. The ones Luke hooked us up with. I haven't actually met 'em myself – keeping out of things, like I said I was.'

Luke waved a hand around. 'Kytell, may I introduce Angelo Carlo, Paulie Carlo, Fran Carlo the Younger, and Foxtrot. Joe I believe you already know. Carlos, this is Kytell Davis, Kate's brother, and, apparently, a member of the Harper clan.'

'Kate, can you please tell me what the fuck is going on?' Charlie said angrily.

'I told Ky about Sorrentino, so if I didn't make it, he would still be taken care of,' I tried to explain.

'To be honest, that's not what I'm confused about,' said my husband tightly. 'What I'd like to know is why you didn't tell me that the guy who runs things in London is your fucking father!'

'He doesn't run the whole of London,' I said. 'Just south of the river.'

'Oh, that explains why you didn't bother to mention it!' he yelled sarcastically.

'Don't you lecture me about honesty,' I shouted back. 'You of all bloody people should understand why I didn't want to tell you my dad is a crook.'

'Oy, less of the crook,' said my father. 'I'll have you know I'm a respectable businessman these days.'

'Oh, so you don't kneecap people any more then?' I said, exasperated.

'Nah,' he said, shrugging. 'Got guys to do that for me now.'

'Wait a minute.' I suddenly remembered something Charlie had told me back at the hotel. 'Charlie, you said your father was making contacts in London, trying to find someone who could snatch me – is this who you were talking about?'

It took a moment, but slowly all the anger and tension escaped from Charlie's face, and all that was left was the joyously familiar sight of my husband laughing.

It was something of an awkward reunion, what with Angelo and my dad having been forging Anglo-American relations for the past few months now without any idea that they were in-laws. But once Sal had driven off with the bodies of the five dead federal agents, with instructions to 'stick them in the same place we stuck Hoffa', Angelo brought out his best single-malt Scotch and the mood lightened. By the time the Mob doctor arrived to patch up Luke, bandage my fingers and dose us both up with generous amounts of morphine, the two crime lords were entertaining each other with stories of their offsprings' reluctance to join the family firm.

'She could take a shooter apart and put it back together again by the time she was five,' my dad was telling Angelo. 'She was a great little shot. We could really have used her in the business, but her mum wanted her to go to a posh school and learn how to be a lady.'

Angelo nodded, sipping his whisky. 'The same with Giuseppe. The women can cope with their husbands, their brothers being in the life, but it's a different story when it's their own babies. Joe's grades were so good, Francesca said it would be a waste not to send him to college.'

Dad snorted. 'Katrina's grades were bloody rubbish. She

was a lazy kid. Got expelled from not one boarding school but two. In the end we gave up on her and stuck her in the local comp with the boys. Her accent was a bit too posh though, what with all the stuck-up girls she'd been hanging out with, so she got bullied a bit. The boys were gonna sort it out, but she always insisted on fighting her own battles, so they taught her some of the moves I'd shown them. She was a right little scrapper, a tough thing. Thought she'd make a good villain one day. You Italians don't let women in your line of work, do you, Angelo?'

Fran refilled her glass of Scotch.

'No, no,' Angelo said. 'They can be useful, but they don't take the oath, they don't have the same code. You can't trust them to act the way a man would.'

'My girl, though,' said Dad, tipping his head and emphasizing his point with his glass, 'my girl would've been great. Bit of a temper, but sometimes that's a good thing. Nah, her real problem was she was just too bloody moralistic, especially with the prossies.'

'With Joe, it was the drugs,' said Angelo. '"*Papa, why do you have to make money out of hurting other people?*" Very naïve.'

'Naïve?' echoed Charlie, who, like me, had been listening in silence, not drinking. 'You saw what it did to Luke's mom.'

I looked over at Luke, who was lying with his eyes shut on the sofa. I couldn't tell if he was awake or not.

'A bad drugs problem,' said Angelo to my father, his voice low. 'Coke to start with, then heroin. Overdosed when Luca was just a kid. No father to speak of – my wife and I raised him.'

'You haven't met my other son Kytell before,' started Dad, and I knew he was going to launch into the story of Ky's mum, and the fact that she'd been a hooker on his books. I didn't want Kytell to have to sit there while a bunch of strangers heard about his past. The doctor had just finished bandaging my last broken finger, and I thanked him and got to my feet.

'Dad, I'm grateful to you for coming out here,' I said. My father looked surprised, a whisky glass hovering at his lips. 'I know you're probably thinking this is the start of something – maybe me coming back to the family, accepting my roots—'

'You'd be bloody good,' he told me. 'Face it, Kate, it's in your blood. Look at your fella! You can't tell me you're not meant to be in the life.'

'—but it's not. What I've learnt is that I'm prepared to kill for those I love. But that's true of so many people, Dad. I'm just better at it, thanks to you. And since me and Charlie are still alive, maybe I should be grateful to you for that too.'

I walked over to Angelo Carlo then, and kissed him on both cheeks.

'Thank you, Angelo. For everything. But now, if I can, I'd like to take your son away with me. We'll have to go a long way, and you won't be able to see us for a long time. Please tell me that's okay.' I swallowed hard. 'I promise, I can make him happy.'

For a moment I thought I saw a film of tears in Angelo Carlo's eyes, but then he gave a slow nod and they were gone.

'I know you can, Katerina. You have my blessing.'

Kytell smiled at me as I walked past him to Charlie. My husband's eyes were dark as he looked up at me. I stroked his face with my ridiculous bandaged hand.

'No more secrets?' I whispered.

He stared back at me, and I could see behind his eyes that he was finally beginning to understand, as was I, why we had been so drawn to each other right from the start. He broke into a smile just as the first ray of red dawn light cracked on the edge of the sky.

'No more secrets,' he whispered back.

PART IV

Some months later

Chapter Thirty-two

There's not a cloud in the vast blue sky.

A speck of white appears on the horizon, shimmering in the heat haze. It grows larger as it nears; triangles of white sails billowing, snapping tight on the breeze.

A woman in a bikini and baseball cap, all salty hair and tanned limbs, stands at the back of the boat, steering it through the water. On the front deck a man in khaki shorts, skin stained brown by the brilliant sun, leans against the rails and watches the edge of the sky.

'Here,' he says. 'This is perfect.'

Within minutes the anchor is dropped, the sails strapped back against the rigging. The two have become old hands at this, working in unison, every movement well-practised and precise. Now they rest on the deck, stretched out on a large white towel. The only sound is that made by the ocean as it slaps against the side of the boat.

The woman's long black hair fans out around her head like raven wings. She smiles up at her husband, two dimples appearing in the middle of her cheeks. He leans down and kisses her, feeling the heat of the sun on his back. They were drinking virgin Mojitos earlier, and she tastes of mint and brown sugar.

'Happy Birthday, Joe,' she says. Turning over, she reaches for a bag that's tucked hidden under a deckchair, handing it to him with a grin.

Curious, he digs around in it and pulls out a book. An old paperback with the pages bent and the cover torn. He laughs when he sees the title.

'I can't believe you remembered,' he says.

'You didn't read it while . . .' She doesn't finish her sentence, not liking to refer to the year they spent apart.

'No,' he says, inclining his head to push another soft kiss against her lips. 'But we're in the middle of nowhere. Where the hell did you find it?' It's been many miles since they were anywhere near a bookshop.

'That old place we stayed at last month. They had a shelf of books for sharing.'

He lies back, opening up the book, reading the first few familiar pages. He's been wondering what the characters have been up to for nearly two years now. It strikes him suddenly how lucky he is that he's got a second chance to read it, to finish it. How often do people get to go back, to recover what they'd lost? He holds the book to his chest, closing his eyes for a moment.

She doesn't miss this. She doesn't miss anything. She strokes his hair, while behind him each wave reflects the late-afternoon sun like a thousand tiny mirrors.

He turns to her, resting his head on her shoulder. She holds him, and he strokes her slightly distended stomach. The skin there is taut, beginning to stretch. His other hand takes hers, fingers intertwined. They lie like this for a long time, until the sun starts to disappear from the sky and the Indian Ocean turns a deeper blue.